The Singularity

The Ruach Saga
Volume One – Second Edition

Mark A. Cornelius

THE SINGULARITY

THE RUACH SAGA
Volume One – Second Edition

With Illustrations by
Shay Cavender

Dedication

To my God and Savior, and His Spirit who allows me to serve to His glory.

To Patti and Shay—you are God's salt and light in my life. This work of his would not have happened without you.

Thanks to Chris Slonecker for your theological assistance, Jeanine Hinkle for your heritage information, and Joe Schrott for keeping my POV honest. Thanks to Erik and Nathan, your technical prowess shines almost as brightly as your love, my sons. You continue to amaze your father. I am deeply honored by each of you for helping make The Singularity a reality.

Thanks to my readership, whom I pray will be blessed as I have by this work.

The Unexplainable is happening

V4641, a mini-quasar at the center of our galaxy has begun to affect the Planet Earth and the rest of our solar system in inexplicable ways. In trying to determine how such a thing could happen, Danny Adamson, a physicist turned science editor for N.H.Q. Broadcast Services has discovered not only an inconceivable connection between Earth and V4641, but also a critical miscalculation in the understanding of the creation of the universe. This error when corrected, suggests that our planet's stability and the longevity of the human race may be grossly over-estimated.

Why "The Singularity"?

The proportion of things we do not know grows rather than diminishes with each discovery we uncover. We create theories and laws for things unexplainable; adjusting and redefining the phenomena to meet our explanations, thus attempting to alter the phenomena to prove our theories and laws.

Must...

...a Singularity obey finite physical laws if it is infinite?

What if...

...there is only one Singularity manifesting itself in different forms?

...we are creating laws to explain a mystery that cannot be explained?

...the Singularity is the one and only constant in the universe?

...we are altered by the actions and definition of The Singularity, not the other way around?

Those who believe all things can be answered with man-made formulas and theories—are confronted with a dilemma—there is no scientific explanation as to how and why V4641 is affecting Earth. Enter the protagonist, Physicist expert Danny Adamson, his team, and his mentors. They conclude that something much greater than anyone has proposed is indeed happening. Danny's walk to a stronger faith in the face of certain catastrophe and his observations about science and intelligent design make this a compelling read for both the unbelieving and doubtful.

As worldwide turmoil increases there is an ever-increasing population of readers who are curious about Biblical Prophecy and who are hungry to know how to watch for the signs leading up to End Times. This work will attract those who are seeking explanations about how—even if—God is working in the universe today. The story is designed to attract both believer and non-believer toward a compelling look at the evidence of a God who is moving His plan forward toward an ultimate purpose. I hope you are as convicted in the reading as I was in the writing.

Mark A Cornelius

Main Characters

Danny Adamson – main character, narrator, works for N.H.Q. Broadcast Services as Science Editor and Research Analyst.

George Adamson – father of Danny Adamson

Mary Adamson – mother of Danny Adamson

Misty Adamson – wife of Danny Adamson

Jake & Sylvia Adamson – son & daughter of Danny & Misty Adamson

Brenda Anders – President and CEO of the Green Order Coalition

Steve Billings – Submersible and Bathysphere pilot

Pastor Fale – Former minister to Danny Adamson

Reb. Moses Folzman, Ph.D. – *The Rabbi*: Professor Emeritus of Physics and Rabbinical Studies at the Technion. Taught Hindeland and considered the most brilliant physiotheologist alive.

Professor Fitzgerald E. Hindeland, Ph.D. – *Fiz*: Department Chairman – College of Physics, University of Texas in Austin. Brilliant Physicist and mentor to Danny and Brandon. Characteristic – debunker of assumed theories.

Brandon Lader, Ph.D. – *Quartermaster*. He is a research analyst for OutReach Corporation, close friend of Danny Adamson and a former student of Fiz Hindeland.

Spencer L. Lynd, Ph.D. – Director of The Hive – Hubble Telescope Monitoring System at R.I.T.

Gregory Blueroad – First United States President of Native American heritage.

Darius Mede – World Trade Organization Chairman

Winston Torin, Ph.D. – Director of M.I.T. Astrophysics Department

Jonathan Trimble – President and CEO of Network Headquarters Broadcast Corporation

Travis Chang – University of Texas: Ecology, Evolution and Behavior Center Teaching Associate

Tonda Peterson – University of Texas: Humanities Professor

Roxanne Temure – University of Texas: Drama and Media Production Student

Mustif – Austin Texas Resident

Primary Locations

Atlanta, Georgia – Network Headquarters Broadcast Corporation

Austin, Texas – University of Texas Complex, Quantum Systems Department

Baltimore, Maryland – The Green Order Coalition Headquarters

Challenger Deep in the Mariana Trench

Franklin, Tennessee

Geneva, Switzerland – World Trade Organization

Mammoth Cave, Kentucky

Naveh Shaanan, Israel – the Technion-Israel Institute of Technology

Rapid City, South Dakota – Homestake Mine Deep Underground Science and Engineering Laboratory (DUSEL)

Rochester, New York – The Chester F. Carlson Center for Imaging Science at the Rochester Institute of Technology

V4641 Sagittarii – region of Sagittarius A in the Constellation Sagittarius – 1,600 light-years from Earth near the center of the Milky Way

V4641 Sol plus One-C – 7 light-years / 2.14 parsecs from Earth

SIN·GU·LAR·I·TY — NOUN,

1. –the state, fact, or quality of being singular.
2. –a singular, unusual or unique quality; peculiarity.
3. –Mathematics. SINGULAR POINT.
4. –Astronomy. (in general relativity) the mathematical representation of a black hole.

Out beyond right and wrong is a field...I will meet you there.

—Rumi – 13th century Persian poet and mystic

He determines the number of the stars; he gives to all of them their names.

—Psalm 147:4, The Bible

Entry One

"I haven't seen it or touched the place physically, yet I know it exists. Most any child could determine it if they can just be pointed in the right direction. After all, you don't have to know how a clock works to figure out what it's designed to do."

—Reb. Moses Folzman, Ph.D.
regarding the Challenger Deep
section of the Mariana Trench

SOMEWHERE INSIDE DANNY

There is no time, it is the end…
…Or so it seems. Flesh and bone gone away, burned…frozen…neither. I was. Now I am not. And then…

"Danny…what are you doing? We've got to go right now…"

ATLANTIC OCEAN

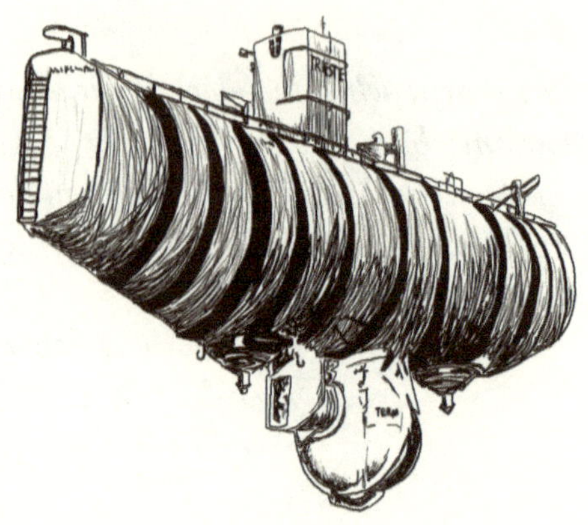

Three A.M., Greenwich Mean Time, and I'm one of two people currently occupying the cockpit of the Alvin III, a highly advanced manned submersible. Watch me nervously adjusting unfamiliar controls—I'm a certified diver, not a submersible pilot—trying to get the ship's trim angle right as we descend. Where are we descending? Approximate longitude 30 degrees West, latitude 45 degrees North – 200 miles Southeast of Greenland: Over a section of the Atlantic Ocean, containing the longest of the world's submerged mountain ranges.

I've been in this cockpit on several other occasions, but never as command pilot. My first experience in this craft had been less than inspirational. The Woods Hole Oceanographic Institution gang, my current funding source, has given all of us 'non-staffers' several *baptisms* in Alvin III, even allowing me to take the controls for a brief period as we ran trial tests to a meager 6,000 feet, a walk in the park for this baby.

But this trip, I'm the one in charge during the entire dive and we're descending to 12,000 feet—twice the depth I have ever explored. I'm <u>so</u> not ready.

While we pop, creak, and groan our way into the darkness, Steve Billings, the designated copilot for this jaunt, feels compelled to act as tour guide.

"Danny, you of course remember Alvin I's exploits including locating a lost hydrogen bomb in the Mediterranean Sea in 1966, exploring the first known hydrothermal vent sites in the 1970s and surveying the wreck of RMS Titanic in 1986."

I'm not remembering—as we pass 3200 feet, there's a high-pitched squeal below the deck plating that is keeping me from doing so. The loud *crack* and *twang* announce additional pressure on the outside hull. "Whatever happened to Alvin II?" I nervously joke. The dead-silence reaction I receive along with a solemn shake of the head from Steve says all I need to know. There is an increasing snapping sound too close by and I'm just beginning to realize my interest in abyssal studies doesn't include actual field trips.

So what am I doing in Alvin III? Fishing—what I call fishing anyway. The DEEP COSMOS Project group—Woods Hole's somewhat bipolar title for our exploration team—had spent hour upon hour prepping an HROV (Hybrid Remotely Operated Vehicle) for its excursion into the Challenger Deep, the deepest underwater canyon known to exist on Earth.

The data gathered by the HROV along the watery ridges of the Mid-Atlantic Range, would be invaluable in determining the accuracy of our instruments for an ultimate manned mission to the Challenger Deep in the Pacific Ocean…

"…But that's not enough," I had argued with the project leader. "We can't adequately validate what we trust the equipment to show us unless we also supervise the results first hand." Was I out of my mind, arguing such an obvious point with the Woods Hole staff?

"I assume you are volunteering for the duty?" The project leader was already writing my name on the assignment roster.

I assaulted him with my thoughts. *I most certainly am not volunteering!* But my actual spoken response was more cowardly. "There are other people far more familiar with submersible capabilities and who know how the sensors react under real-time conditions…"

"—But none who have as good a grasp of the terrain and oceanic conditions; I'll have Steve Billings go down with you." *Had I just been ordered into the breach?* "Besides, you'll need the piloting experience for later missions." The project leader had just nicely justified my demise.

And so we sink—our high-tech coffin is performing exactly to specifications. Steve is a good guy and tries his best to encourage me. "That's a good decent rate—your horizon needs adjusting though."

So does my blood pressure.

"Ambient External Temperature: Four degrees Celsius. Saline content: 7,000 parts per million."

…Perfect conditions to die in.

"…Depth 4,200 meters and leveling off."

Out the side portal—a pair of eyes reflect off the lights. More. schools of eyes. Thousands of swimming eyes—are we the ones under observation by the locals? Concentrating on the readings helps me ignore the surreal external images as well as the unwelcomed noises attacking the shell of our fragile egg and which shout impending doom.

Ask her.

What? Where did that thought come from? I'm submerged in a dark cold world with an audience of alien creatures and my mind wanders there?

You want to. She's beautiful, intelligent and she wants to be asked. You know it deep inside. Deeper than this place you explore now.

I can't think about that now. I'm in over my head, literally, with other developments; like monitoring the rapidly increasing pressure impacting the eggshell skin of this ship. One unforeseen flaw in its fragile surface and we will be 'no more'. It is only a thin thread that keeps this ship and its crew alive.

This Atlantic spot we occupy has been selected to test our communications and telemetry equipment because of its depth and because it's not so far from Woods Hole's comfortable home waters off the Massachusetts coastline, that if trouble were to arise, we could load up our gear and zip back to safe harbors. Trouble is about to arise.

Maybe if I pretend I know what I'm doing…"Set course 18 degrees east northeast."

"…Toward that outcropping? Why do you want to go there?"

Oh no, Steve has just realized I may not know what I'm doing. "Let's see how sensitive the new Ultrasound microphone is. We can test it by bouncing a sonar signal off the adjoining canyon wall."

"Great idea," Steve responds, inspired by my stupidity.

I'm such a poser.

Steve actually seems to believe I'm not making this stuff up as we descend and he settles back into Co-pilot mode: "Depth 4,482 meters and holding; distance to target, point-five kilometers."

When I'm in uncomfortable situations—and this certainly qualifies as one of the most of those—I start talking to myself. *Your target is Misty, marry her. Stop daydreaming, Danny boy, you've got to get your mind off of your life and onto your job. Wait, I didn't mean it that way…I need a distraction, something in the real world. I know—I'll try humor*

"…Fire forward torpedoes!"

"What?" Steve is confused again.

I have always wanted to say that—Steve is not amused. As we near the rock wall, the outside lights reveal an eerie landscape of juts and crags, any one of which could skewer us if a sudden random current in the right direction catches us by surprise. I open my mouth and suggest a seemingly innocent activity. "Let's *bounce* a sonar signal and see what we pick up on the speakers."

Co-pilot Steve complies and the audible *ping* predictably rings through the cabin. A totally random idea comes to me. "I want to run an acoustic wave test to see what kind of effect we can create at this depth. Send another ping and feed the response to the external speakers."

"What will that prove?"

"Give me a ping. One ping only, please." Steve doesn't get that joke, either—obviously, he isn't a Sean Connery fan—but he does as he's requested. The result is attention getting. The ping turns to a rippling buzz which reverberates from seemingly nowhere and everywhere around us. I can feel it in my seat and in my teeth and in the very atmosphere of the cockpit. Steve tentatively touches the front viewport and I can tell by his immediate pullback reflex action that the pane is vibrating as well.

"Sweet!" is his response, but there is as much tension as curiosity in his voice. "Why did it do that?"

"Resonant harmonics—the 'astro-boys' and 'rockhounds' play with it all the time—bouncing different frequency signals off objects to get them to vibrate. We…they…want the objects they're studying to sing back to them."

"…Astro-boys and rockhounds?"

"…Astrophysicists and Geophysicists."

"Yeah, I got that. It just sounded funny coming from you—you're a little bit of both, aren't you?" Steve has read my background. I'm beginning to like him. "I've never seen that done with underwater gear—we only want to know a depth, bearing, distance and shape."

"Pretty boring—is there a way to increase the signal intensity?"

"…What for?" Steve is just full of questions.

"The reaction we got last time suggests we're in the…right harmonic key—a lucky happenstance. Maybe we can create a cyclical reverberation, you know, like a tuning fork that is touched to a piano string which is tuned to the same pitch."

Steve shrugs his shoulders, "I never played the piano." Still, he obediently increases the sonar intensity by a factor of one and presses the button again. This time, the ping-turned-buzz begins to settle into a persistent throb. We both hear something else that doesn't sound good at all. Toward the bow and starboard side of the Alvin III, a rumble; it ebbs and flows with the deep harmonic cascade we have created. The music I've conjured up soon turns from a pleasant lullaby into a heavy metal rock concert. The thousand eyes outside realize this too, and wisely scatter.

"Steve, take the controls."

"Why?"

"Because you know this ship better than I do—get us the hell away from that rock wall, fast!"

As Steve reacts, reversing the propellers with precise, but painfully slow results, we begin inching to our stern. The crumbling pile of rock and mud before us gives chase and the rumble of the chaos reaches into the heart of my fears—we're going to be simultaneously shaken and crushed to our doom.

You should have listened, Danny. You should have asked her. I'm listening now, and I swear that, if Steve gets us out of here with our lives, I'll spend the rest of mine with Misty!

Yes, we escaped the rockslide with micrometers to spare and no, I wasn't kicked off the project. I'm sure I would have been, but something happened which took precedence—the project funding was cut off completely.

An attempt was made to raise more funding, but things quickly bogged down into a quagmire of politics, misunderstanding and financially induced turf battling. We were informed that the DEEP COSMOS Project was to be placed into "permanent reconsideration and review status", meaning it would not see the light of day again until ice was discovered in a well known satanic hangout. I was sent packing, back to my origins at the University of Texas with a friendly pat on the head for my aggressive approach, which signaled to anyone curious enough to scan my background that I was *Persona non grata* to all of academia.

Interestingly, Steve Billings volunteered to drive me to the airport to catch my flight. As he helped me get my luggage out of the car he paused and offered his hand to me. "I'll deny this if anyone asks," he said, his eyes first focused on our grip, then coming up to meet my gaze, "but I think you would have led this project to some amazing discoveries. Everyone else here thinks you have a death wish, but if you ever need a pilot to go the extra mile with you…I'm your driver."

I almost killed the guy and he wants more—what is it about me which attracts masochistic devotees?

"Woods Hole let me know you were on your way back," Fiz, my mentor and collegiate father figure at the University of Texas in Austin says without looking up from his laptop. I've walked into Fiz's lab without advanced warning, wanting to surprise him. It is I who am blindsided.

"All your books and materials are boxed up and are waiting for you in the next room to be cleared out. I've arranged for your grant and stipend to be paid out through the end of this quarter and I've provided you an extraordinary reference letter. If there's anything else you think we need to cover, just email."

It's the kindest way I've ever heard him permanently say goodbye to an outgoing protégé. I now think that the opportunity to join the Woods Hole project—even though the invitation would not have come without his influence—was some sort of evil trial devised by Fiz to test my loyalty. I believe I've failed his final exam.

Who is this Fiz guy and why does he carry so much weight in my life? Great question: After wrapping up my undergraduate studies, it was Fiz who lured me into the realm of quantum physical mysteries. He convinced me that this little blue ball we exist on is actually only able to function by the grace of forces much larger and greater than anyone except he had contemplated. During my junior year of undergraduate studies, my notorious curiosity and the attraction of his eccentric style got the better of me and I joined up with the Physics team—I was quickly assimilated into Deep-Space and Astrophysical studies, with a charge from Fiz to become an expert in the contradictions between quantum and molecular physics. I blame him to this day for the schizophrenic nature of my scientific approach.

As for my current upheaval, being fired is not exactly the right term for what's happening. It is Fiz's double edged sword—his parting gift to me. He knows I'm not cut out for academic studies or the politics therein, but he sees the greater *me* in my insatiable curiosity. So, he has made a phone call—only one call—that's enough. And then I receive a phone call, only one call—that's enough.

The Science Room of a rather large news organization in Atlanta, Georgia just so happens to be looking for an expert—not just any expert— they need someone who has a broad range of scientific knowledge, highly placed connections in the scientific community, a bent for writing and skills in broadcast communications. Did I mention that they want someone with an insatiable curiosity?

Other than the broadcasting skills, I fit the bill to a tee—in our one and only telephonic interview, the owner and his managing editor say they can teach me media presence as long as I'm not a complete social nerd and they have it by good authority that I'm not one. The actual position and responsibilities aren't ever explained to me and the compensation is described as competitive. Oddly, none of that matters. The fact that someone wants me, just as I am, is enough. I accept over the phone and arrangements are made for me to fly to Atlanta. Thank you, Fiz.

Only one last thing to do before leaving Austin, I need a cup of coffee desperately. Coffee…that reminds me; here I am this far into my story and I haven't even explained how I met Misty!

It was an accident really, I had pulled an 'all-nighter' in my first year as a research assistant, I can't ever remember what formulaic overlay was giving me fits at the time, but I had to get my head straight and I actually recall thinking that the air in the lab felt like I had used up all the oxygen. Coffee breeds oxygen in the brain—it's a well known law of physiology—I had to have the 'good stuff'. The 'good stuff' was readily available 24/7 at a place just off campus called the *JavA*…

"—Last cup. We need to save some for an experiment they're running on the psychology lab rats at the University to see if they run mazes better if injected with Hazelnut Cream or Sumatra Bold."

This statement had come in the form of a voice above and to the right of my table at this comfortable café—my favorite hangout because of the 50's style chrome legged tables with matching chairs and the fact that it was a Wi-Fi hotspot. The server's comment was intended as a joke of course, but I wasn't paying attention and held my cup up without even acknowledging her presence. As I keyed in an equation one-handed on my laptop, I mumbled, "Hazelnut."

I could hear the cup being filled and another attempt at banter, "Your hair is on fire."

So focused was I, that I didn't remember until afterwards, my retort, "Sure, put it out, please." And she did, with the untouched glass of water that had been sitting on the table next to me. It was my own fault really, as were most of the mistakes I made in courting her—correction—her courting me. But at that moment I became aware, as never before, that someone actually desired my complete and full attention. I had thought I knew what it was like to be a commodity when Fiz, and then Woods Hole, had thrown the lures out, but it was Misty who fought to yank me from my introverted ways.

While science had excited me to chase and challenge all the questions in life, Misty awakened in me a new conviction—take NOTHING at face value—to unashamedly challenge all the supposed answers others had told me <u>must be true</u>…

—And at this moment only one thing is true, I want Misty to marry me and move with me to Atlanta. I enter the *JavA* once more, but now with a quest—coffee is only the excuse. She's at the counter working on a customer's ticket and looks up curiously from her scribbling as I walk resolutely and unhesitant towards her.

Misty's expression turns to one of puzzlement as I bend down on one knee before her and proclaim before her and to the minimal crowd of patrons who have witnessed my approach, "I've just been given a second chance at life and I realize I would be wasting it without you. Please share yours with me."

As I hand her the engagement ring, her look changes a final time, eyes closed and exhaling in obvious relief. Misty agrees to the truth of this moment, accepting the ring as she responds through smiling tears, "What took you so long?"

Entry Two

"In God's dwelling place, there is no If, there is no Then, there is only Now."

—Reb. Moses Folzman, Ph.D.
acceptance speech to the Nobel Committee, 2014

SOMEWHERE INSIDE DANNY

This is no mere solar system, galaxy or cluster—it is greater. There is noise here, humming, hissing; rhythmic beauty. There is motion in things moving and things trying not to move and things just being things, things larger than possible, things smaller than understandable—spinning, visibly and invisibly. Where am I? A dream, but everything is too bright. I can see silhouettes against the blinding pulse—it appears that I'm flying, there is no ground, no sky; no limits.

Nothing else is 'here' and 'here' is ALL. There is no explanation, but here, there is no need for explanation. There are other creatures here! One approaches. It's long, sleek, very large and reflects many colors…iridescent, yet brilliantly white with a silver sheen—ever changing, ever the same. Pure—beautiful. A word comes to my mind…Dragon…<u>yes</u>, it's a dragon—wings, tail and…sad. It has a broken horn and from somewhere I hear singing—mournful, tragic. It stares at me and smiles—my heart breaks at the sight. The dragon opens its mouth and everything trembles, shakes, roars around me. It is thunder; it is the world reborn. It is raw power and I'm consumed by it.

ATLANTA, GEORGIA

I'm about to have lunch with my boss, Jonathan Trimble—sole owner and Head Ego of Network Headquarters Broadcast Corporation. N.H.Q. as it's known in the media. Trimble has brought me into his organization with two directives: *Make us the Junk Science Experts* and *Make all science, Junk Science.* After three highly ineffective months of producing grade-school quality pieces on solar flares and penguin cohabitation in the Antarctic, the reckoning time has come.

Lunch with Jonathan Trimble is known in N.H.Q. land as an opportunity for one of two events to take place—I'm looking forward to either a very unpleasant reprimand or termination. I just can't seem to find my rhythm nor capture the vision of my benefactor's dream or the imagination of my audience.

"Danny, what motivated you to go into physics?" Trimble asks me in the form of a greeting as we are being seated at his table at his favorite bistro by two dedicated servers who busy themselves to ensure our every need and their expected high-end tips are catered to.

The question seems innocuous so I jump right in. "I really wasn't driven to get the higher degree or honestly, even the first degree—the process just sort of happened as I followed my interests."

Are those gardenias I smell? Immediately a bouquet appears on the serving table beside us. The floral fragrance makes love with the orange sauce decorating the breast of duck appetizers being prepared by our personal chef.

"I wasn't sure what I wanted to do in life—after all, I was still a kid and I was disillusioned—it was the popsicle-sticks that moved things forward."

"What?" Trimble chuckles before a bite of spinach dip on a club cracker enters his mouth.

"Well, there was a lot of encouragement in the seventh grade to explore the world of mechanics—in particular, a project where we were given popsicle-sticks and asked to build a working machine. My classmates dutifully charged ahead, producing fulcrums, levers, wedges and inclined planes ad nauseam."

Trimble motions with his eyes for me to sample the gazpacho in the bowl that has magically appeared before me. After politely obliging, I continue my explanation.

"There was nothing interactive put forth by the rest of the kids with sticks—all the ideas required an outside force to function. I wanted to see if there was…another way, an unthought-of function. I just wasn't…"

"…Satisfied?"

Satisfied—good word, I think to myself. "I've always had, I guess even at that age, a sense that there's many more than one angle—things no one else is looking at. Like with the popsicle-sticks. I took five of them and started playing with the idea of creating a combination *machine-puzzle*. Could the five sticks be somehow placed in a pattern that would hold itself together—operating as a spring and a wedge at the same time?"

"Why five?"

"Totally random, no…that's inaccurate. I came up with the idea after having been to a church service. I remembered the homily which was about David choosing five smooth stones for his slingshot…"

"…To slay the giant."

"Right: Seemed like as good a number as any at the time. I came up with the pattern formed by using two sticks connected at the bottom with a V shape. Then I set another stick underneath, vertically in the center of the V. The tricky part came next—I placed two more opposing sticks at the top of the V horizontally, the first overlapping the outside V sticks, but woven under the vertical stick—this stick was pushed down about midway in the center of the V. The fifth stick was then placed above the other in a parallel, except overlapping the vertical stick and woven under the V sticks, connecting the first and locking everything together."

As I speak, Jonathan Trimble actually takes one of the linen napkins from the table and begins to sketch out my description with his pen. Not one of our servers or the Bistro manager hovering nearby even flinches. So as my boss fumbles with a few of the finer points, I help out by reaching over and correcting his drawing. In the end, a reasonable facsimile prevails.

Trimble examines his rendering and then asks, "How did your instructor like your approach?"

An odd question to ask! "I got a D on the project. My teacher wanted motion, action…something to 'Wow' him. My machine worked without working. I was stubbornly proud of the concept though, and actually won a scholarship to The University of Texas based on a paper I wrote later in high school expanding on the idea."

"How did that sensation of being a maverick, charting new territory make you feel?" The veal had arrived so Trimble reapplies to his lap, the serviette we had just desecrated and begins cutting his meat into precise bite-size portions, arranging each piece he has cut into neat rows that he appears to be shaping into some sort of mosaic.

"Honestly? Lonely—a little—don't get me wrong, I love the way I'm wired and it…drives me to strange discoveries. But, I suppose I'm sad that the rest of the world doesn't seem to give a…"

"…You're wrong you know."

"What?"

"People do give a damn," Trimble continued. "They just don't give it in the same way you do. And to get them to share a little more about what their *giving a damn* is, you have to shock them out of their past diet—feed them a tiny delicacy for the present and then offer them a feast beyond what they could ever have expected for the future."

Suddenly this mealtime adventure has taken on new proportions. Obviously, this five-foot six-inch pencil of a man has more to him than meets the eye. He's a master at finding ways to entertain people into a response which he might then utilize to fill his empire's insatiable monetary appetite. In this place, I'm both student and lesson.

"By the way, I am firing you," Trimble says next.

I suspected as much would be the case, but his homily on my behalf had given me false hope. Oh well, it's just another of those inevitable failure-milestones with which I'm becoming all too familiar.

"Now let's get busy!"

"Excuse me?" I only thought I was confused before. "You just fired…"

"I terminated the old boring scared adult-you who was trying to please, rather than challenge. Don't you get it? There's something inside you—a switch that somehow got flipped to the ON position. It causes you to desire one thing and one thing only."

This One-Thing, I have to hear. I keep my mouth shut as Jonathan Trimble elaborates. "You want to know the unknown. It's the beacon in your head and in your heart that refuses to be switched off. I can see that, but you're not taking advantage of the light it's providing. I want that kid who intuitively knew there was something else out there. I want his excitement for discovery in full gear without brakes to stop its motion."

I look down at Trimble's plate which he has continued to fiddle with this whole time. After savoring the meat, he resumes his dissertation. "You can't possibly know how this meal tastes to me—how the flavors translate from taste buds to cerebellum—but you can see very clearly that the meal does please me. You can then discern that I'll want to pursue the pleasure again, maybe even wanting to try it under different circumstances, with different side items or in combination with sauces. If you were a chef, you'd want to repeatedly prepare and serve me exactly the same meal again because you'd think that's what I wanted.

"That would be a mistake! I'd eventually tire of the experience, so you'd have to add to or manipulate the ingredients to tantalize me—even further playing off, but not wanting to lose the original delight. The more you're able to expand the recipe without jeopardizing the original experience or over-feeding the appetite, the better chef you will become."

All charged up and ready to take on the world again, I'm suddenly ravenous. The veal calls out my name and I get ready to devour it when I notice my host's eyes fixed on me. He's not through bestowing his wisdom, so I set my own utensils down again and wait for him to continue. "You're wrong about yourself as well, Danny. The world doesn't seem to care for the same reason that you didn't care until suddenly, you did: A new way of viewing the same old stuff appeared one day and the old became new, even…fun."

A new thought hits me. I never again have to worry about staying inside the box because I've now been given permission to blow the stupid thing to smithereens. And that's exactly what I intend to do.

After blossoming into the *real* investigative Junk Scientist I was born to be, I boldly suggest a transfer out of N.H.Q. corporate offices to their Nashville, Tennessee location. My reasoning seems sound to me—if I stay too close to the amalgamated animal, I'll be tempted to play with the beast and it might tempt me into its den to swallow me whole. N.H.Q. is the penultimate *box* after all.

Jonathan Trimble agrees to the transfer on one condition—I have two years to find a major *Theme*. A Theme, as N.H.Q. (aka Jonathan Trimble) defined it, is a story or subject focus that will simply not go away for at least a six-month duration. It won't go away because of its sheer fascination-factor. A great example of a Theme in the past was former President, Bill Clinton. Like him or not, the guy had nine lives and each one took the follower on a trail to dozens of new stories, every one seemingly more provocative than its predecessor. No small task being asked to come up with a scientific equivalent of William Jefferson Clinton, but I've rediscovered my confidence and feel up to the challenge.

V4641 SAGITTARII – REGION OF SAGITTARIUS A IN THE CONSTELLATION SAGITTARIUS

Peer into the Before. Look in awe at the formation: Exquisite destiny in the making—a roiling point of perfection—immovable object meeting unstoppable force—beginning and end meeting in concert. I sing with it. We join, we dance—our symphony nears its zenith. Sing with me, a new song…

Soon after the move to Nashville, Misty and I become newly proud parents to our daughter Sylvia and two years later, Jake. They are the focus of our personal life as we settle into the community of Franklin, Tennessee, just outside Nashville. The irony is that Brandon, who had become my best friend when we were fellow Doctoral Research assistants at The University of Texas, has taken a position with a unique bio-tech engineering firm located in the very same town. OutReach Corporation is tied in with Vanderbilt University and Medical Center and works exclusively with NASA to determine how organic substances might behave in non-Earth environments.

Word has it that Fiz had taken Brandon Lader's departing very hard (much more so than his dismissal of me, I'm sure), but my old professor's loss is my gain. Brandon and I quickly reestablish our bond and he becomes the touchstone to my former roots in the scientific arena.

I identify an area of interest and then use it as an excuse to do a boy's-night-out. But in our case, we're both still such test tube nerds at heart that we actually do spend our evenings investigating scientific anomalies instead of sampling the entertainment venues of Music City USA.

A self analytical word, which I've never used to describe my life prior to this point, creeps into my consciousness. I'm *content*.

Entry Three

Now let it be known to thee and all around thee that Newton's laws of motion have slight flaws.

They are false laws, for they are not always true.

Beware of flawed laws for they, like false prophets, may lead one astray.

Now the true laws shall be Einstein's laws of special relativity.

And they shall be true laws because they are always true.

And thou and all others shall obey these laws, for it has been commanded.

—From The Bible According to Einstein
©2004 by Jupiter Scientific Publishing Company

V4641 SAGITTARII – REGION OF SAGITTARIUS A IN THE CONSTELLATION SAGITTARIUS

You have called me to come to you quickly. I have heard your cry, will you hear mine?

FRANKLIN, TENNESSEE

"So, tell me again why you're leaving?"

Her answer is a stinging slap across my face—the force enough to slice the inside of my cheek as it collides with my teeth. The blood feels good, reminding me that I'm not losing my mind. This is very much, reality.

Her second response is a deeper strike—the verbal kind. "You spend hours in your study, absorbed in this project of yours—long nights, early mornings and everything in between. Even when you're not in there, you're in there. The children don't know you, I…know you too well. This isn't going to change. You're destroying us. I have to save us. This is the only way, thanks to you—I hate you for it."

"But you know why I've been doing this, you know what had to take place, it's Wait, I'm not destroying us, this is for us. You know I have to. You agreed!"

"…I went along. Danny, I love you, what else was I supposed to do? You convinced me that this thing was happening. I believe…I believed you—but now? You're out of control."

She's right, of course—she always has been—she always will be. I need her. "I think I have it worked out. Just stay, if we get separated…I can't promise it will be safe."

"You can't promise safety at all, that's the problem. We have nothing left. <u>Nothing</u>! No relationship, no security, nothing. I'm taking Jake and Sylvia to your mom's place…just…just get this thing done and then call me. We'll figure it out from there."

And they are no longer here. Frightened, tearful, clinging hugs from my two little 'pop stars'—sweet Sylvia, the dancer and singer extraordinaire; Jake, the future rock legend—suddenly on a mystery tour they do not and cannot understand. Misty, soul mate Misty, doing what she does so well: Protecting passionately what is hers; even her love for me—she packed it with her other 'essential' belongings buried deep, safe harbored from the storm of her breaking heart and drove off into the darkness.

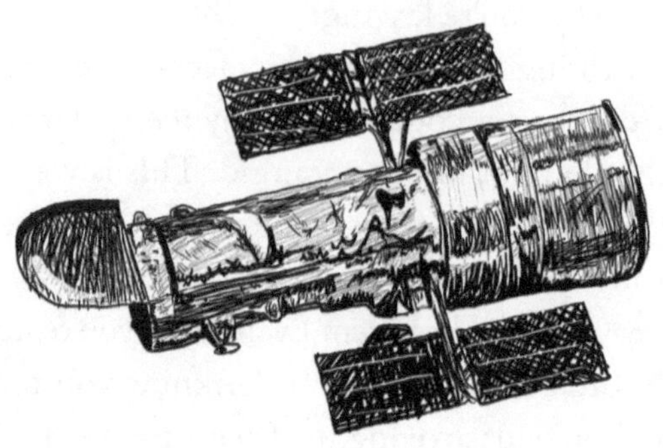

ROCHESTER, NEW YORK – THE CHESTER F. CARLSON CENTER FOR IMAGING SCIENCE AT THE ROCHESTER INSTITUTE OF TECHNOLOGY

I seem to be in a lot of places at once, don't I? You're probably already asking yourselves, "How can this character talk about what's going on somewhere in deep space while simultaneously playing out a domestic crisis in Franklin, Tennessee?" How can I know all these things at once? I can't. But I do. This is a developing ability for me which I'll explain in the near future. Right now, there are more important things to explain, like what the fine folks at the R.I.T. Color Imaging Center are up to at this very moment.

The C.I.C. of R.I.T. is where the Hubble Telescope was born and where the Hubble Telescope's Space Eye reports to. It's from C.I.C. that all the news agencies and all the pop science junkies grab nifty pictures to feed to us—the brain numbed public. They paint the pictures and add dimension to the radio telescope signals and translate the x-ray/ultra-wavelength data so that us little people can understand them.

The C.I.C. is the current dream child of Spencer L. Lynd, Ph.D., Director of The Hubble Telescope Monitoring System. To Spencer L., in his dreams, the C.I.C. is a bastion of ultra-tech equipment housed in a futuristically designed chrome and concrete fortress with the interior feel of a starship. However the reality, along with his inherited title of 'Director', came with an inherited budget of…not much. The 'not much' amount is so embarrassingly not much that Spencer hides it even from his staff. In truth, everyone knows it's pitiful because of how the true C.I.C. looks and operates.

Let's take a peek at the real C.I.C. Walk with me down a narrow linoleum floored hallway with walls of cinderblock and metal doors with little wire-laced square windows inserted near the top of each entry. The corridor ceilings assault pedestrian traffic with florescent lighting in such poor repair that there is a flickering effect no epileptic in their right mind would care to encounter. It's an eerie place, made eerier by the monochrome hallway—doors, floor, ceiling, all having been assigned a very not much budget color scheme of eggshell off-white, creamy grey nothingness. At the end of the hall, there is a door marked simply, **The Hive**.

The Hive is actually the Hubble Hive, where all telescopic data from the great lens-in-the-sky arrives. Unlike Spencer's dream center, this room is about the size of two standard 20 by 15 foot classrooms combined. That would seem adequate, but for the numerous computer terminal stations crammed into the space—separation of each unit is in the form of cheap carpeted dividers.

There is a distinctive smell to this place too—imagine 30 not-so-hygienically-minded computer geeks who think deodorant is for job interviews only. Each hoards their own personal stash of not-so-hygienically preserved foodstuffs purchased from a nutritionally insensitive, but convenient corner market.

Of course, Hubble is not the only telescope out there—it was The Scope for a long time, but because of governmental oversight, economic conditions and lots of other factors, the budget to expand and "boldly go out" was lost or gravitated to other academic galaxies. So that now, much is expected from little.

On Spencer's desk, which is also somehow wedged into The Hive, can be found The Trinity—Three 48-inch monitors that face toward

Spencer who has scanning access to the other's monitors. Spencer has desire—Spencer the hunter, prowls for the One Thing that will mean All Things.

The stuff they now find matters little to the commercial realm which supplies all important capital for maintenance and expansion of the program—hence Spencer's budget woes. He tracks the activity of his Hive in hopes of discovering that which will illuminate the universe at new levels—grabbing the attention of politicians, academic board, and alumni alike, drawing accolades, applause, a guest lecture series and most important: creating a funding magnet.

I have brought you along with me today to observe this great swarm of quantum activity because of what is happening…right now. Look at Spencer's face lit in reflection by The Trinity—totally at peace with his universe, alpha brainwaves just oozing out of his cerebral cortex. Now notice the appearance of curiosity, a raised eyebrow, head tilting over more toward his left shoulder, the movement of his chair closer to the screens and the change in hues of his facial landscape as he toys with his joystick. If we were to do a biochemical test right now on Spencer, we would detect a seldom produced agent in his physical makeup—a slowly but ever-increasing buildup of adrenalin.

If we come over behind him and glance at The Trinity, we will see something else unusual in Spencer's behavior—typically not capable of being entertained with the image of a single event—he has now imposed one glimpse of one anomaly on all three screens. As we continue to watch, he overlays the identical date-time sequence of the observed event, only not coming from the eye of Hubble, but from the Chandra X-Ray Observatory also in high Earth orbit. Look, Spencer has gone completely antiestablishment and feeds in a final overlay of said anomaly—registering the exact same date-time sequence from the National Radio Astronomy Observatory in Chile, South America. See him pressing several keys on his console, glancing down; then up at the screens again?

It seems that Spencer is doing the unthinkable. He has put one item on all three screens of The Trinity, thereby breaking his long-established practice of keeping multiple exploration options open. Spencer has done this for good reason—his dream has come alive—The Hive has discovered unlimited funding.

FRANKLIN, TENNESSEE

I'm standing in the middle of my living room…how long…minutes, hours…replaying my life as a virtual real time movie, trying to figure out with my very limited brain, how I came to be in this place—no wife, no family, no life. I must have missed something, some special clue or code or formula that would have helped me avoid…avoid what? Being me?

Is that the sun coming up in the window? No. Car lights, a shadow blocks the streetlight through the window as it moves across the front lawn, now a face in the picture window peering in—how strange—it's Brandon. I don't want to see him right now, but the incessant beating of his fist on the door and his pleading voice, implore me to respond. Even so, my body refuses to move from the center of the room toward the threshold to open the door. It will have to be up to him. "Come on in."

"It's locked, you idiot!"

Misty must have used the key on the way out to lock me in, protecting others from my wicked presence. My legs reluctantly respond to my mental urging. I cross to the entry way, turn the deadbolt and Brandon doesn't hesitate, he charges into the unlit room almost knocking down the beast that I've become.

"Danny, what are you doing?" Brandon sounds almost panicked. "We've got to go right now. I just found out that…"

"…Misty and the kids are gone."

"What? How?…When?"

His question seems so foreign. I need a point of reference. "What time is it?"

"It's 4AM. I tried calling your cell, but…you mean gone, gone?"

"…To my mom's place."

Brandon finally grows tired of talking to me in the predawn shadows, reaches to turn on the lamp by the sofa, surveys the room and gives me a curious look. "What's that on the floor? What's that on your face?"

"…Blood."

"You hit her? Wait…you bit her?"

"Not exactly"

"Dude, if you hurt her in any way, I'll…"

"It's my blood."

"Oh. Sorry. Look, I really am sorry—that's all going to get worked out—you've got to trust me. We've got to go, NOW!"

I don't ask why; I don't ask where. I let him lead me to the car as the birds start stirring in the trees. What a beautiful spring day it's going to be for everyone else. I guess it was good I hadn't changed into my night clothes. As the world around me awakens, I climb into the passenger seat of Brandon's car and it invites a strange reaction—as a nest, comfortable and warm—in its embrace, I fall immediately to sleep.

SOMEWHERE INSIDE DANNY

Infinitesimally vast: Yes, a paradox—a speck within a Speck. That Speck, The consuming Speck means business: Serious Business. Everything surrounding 'Serious Business Speck' ceases to exist, including me, the consumed speck—sucked in to be part of a great light.

But something else is happening—a battle of some sort. Within Serious Business Speck—beauty and terror. Dark things try to enter the great light. It is really no battle at all—over before it starts.

I have completely misunderstood space—never really took the time to study it—space was fiction more than science to me. Now I am space. I am a fact of the fiction.

SOMEWHERE ON INTERSTATE 40 IN ARKANSAS

I wake from my bizarre dream to see a blurry image of Brandon's face focused on the road. My eyes slowly adjust to reality and I rub them to help wipe away the cake of sleep that has accumulated during my nap. The sun is behind us on its morning ascent. *He's not wearing his sunglasses yet. That makes our direction west.* Silly me, of course we're headed west; the signs all point to it—literally—another green I-40 W sign informs us from the side of the road. I try reading his mood and it proves difficult.

Dr. Brandon Lader is all business, all preparation, all anal. His absolute silence says this cannot be a good day for him. His frustration is a result of my quest and makes us strange bedfellows—victims of circumstance and our own poor choices. For Brandon, it's all an unsettling inconvenience; for me…

I stare out at the lights on the side of the road—some ice out of a fountain drink from Brandon's last fast-food stop, now in a paper napkin pressed against the left side of my face. The swelling from Misty's right hook to my jaw is starting to subside and my friend begins to query me as we speed down a nearly empty Sunday morning interstate route. "Tell me more about the Challenger Deep?"

Oh, oh, why is Brandon pressing this button? "10,924 meters deep, almost seven miles below the ocean surface." I drone.

"Yeah, I know all that. Death Valley of the Pacific Rim—a small slot-shaped valley at the southern extreme of the Mariana Trench—I mean tell me what you know about what's happening there now?"

I plead ignorance, "You mean besides the normal venting and routine tectonic teeth gnashing?"

"Danny, the whole area is showing signs of Harmonic Resonance—geophysical vibrations that are nearly identical in the crust and down into the planet's core. The readings indicate the harmonics have been increasing for some time."

What Brandon is suggesting is just not possible. A simplistic description would be driving a car that was always moving the same speed, never slowing down for curves, or never speeding back up once through the curve. Add to that, the road itself and the Earth under the road all perfectly synchronized, spinning in space—all at the same exact speed. Pretty picture, but every grade school science student learns that the gravitational attraction of the moon, other planets, the sun and who knows what other forces, pull, and push our little home all over the place on its ride through the Milky-Way without any hope of a constant or comfortable ride. The illusion—like a trip in a limousine with just the occasional jostle, is just that—a romantic fantasy ride.

Translation…The fact is that no one has ever proven Harmonic Resonance to have happened. What my best friend is suggesting is that the facts, as we know them, are changing.

V4641 SAGITTARII – REGION OF SAGITTARIUS A IN THE CONSTELLATION SAGITTARIUS

The past, the present, the future, have no meaning outside of the One. It is time for motion. All things must come together.

Entry Four

"Just because we define a thing does not mean we comprehend a thing."

—*Darius Mede – Chairman,*
World Trade Organization

SOMEWHERE ON INTERSTATE 30 IN TEXAS

So how did the current situation develop—why did my wife slap me silly and then walk out on me? How did Brandon Lader, Ph.D. end up conveniently at my front door the morning after and is now driving me to some undisclosed location? Sounds awfully melodramatic, doesn't it? Maybe I should write a book.

If I did, it would speak of *Content Danny Adamson* who existed for about six years. *Content Danny* would make time to spend with his children. And as busy as he was, *Content Danny* would find opportunities with Misty to escape parenthood thanks to Brandon, the consummate Dutch Uncle and physicist.

I would write about a particular getaway to the Smokey Mountains when Misty would ask *Content Danny* one of her notoriously frank questions. "Why does all this beauty exist?"

Content Danny wouldn't be able to help her with an answer. His past differed radically from hers—outside of his formulaic cocoon, he wasn't quite sure what beauty was. His dad had died early—*Content Danny* was not content then. He was thirteen years old. Remember that church service I was describing to Jonathan Trimble? Actually, it was at a funeral—*Malcontent Danny's* father's funeral. Why didn't I share that before? It still hurts. Why am I sharing it now? It's important enough to work through the hurt.

Sorry; too deep, too fast. Getting back to the highlights of my significant childhood experiences—*Malcontent Danny's* dad had been a salesman…a smoking, social drinking salesman…who worked hard and meant well, but who typically traveled more than he domiciled. His absence caused *Malcontent Danny's* mom to question her reason to continue life.

Interestingly, when the family found out about *Malcontent Danny's* dad's cancer and its terminal course, *Malcontent Danny's* mom found her reason to live. Amazing as it seemed then and now, all she needed to do was decide there was a better way. She found that way in the Church and never looked back over her shoulder in fear of her demons pursuing her again. *Malcontent Danny*, on the other hand…

—Have you now picked up on the fact that I was playing with popsicle-sticks for a project the day after my father's funeral? Boy-Howdy, that was *Malcontent Danny the schoolboy* alright—burying the pain down in the darkness—drowning it deep enough in the ocean so it could never reach back up to touch him again. Ironic isn't it, that in burying the pain, he became the perfect scientific student, coldly and methodically searching out the hidden recesses of his life's laboratory?

I'm OK now though—<u>really</u>. All that stuff is in the past. I'm still trying to figure out the answer to that 'what is beauty?' question though.

"Danny, did you hear me? The Challenger Deep is resonating into the core."

Oh yeah, that's where all this backtracking started, wasn't it—Brandon stating some ridiculous claim of an implausible phenomena at the bottom of the ocean? I have that problem—letting a string of thoughts carry me away to reopen old baggage—and I can rummage around in my trappings for hours at a time without some rude interruption from the present to bring me back. Just such a disturbance is occurring this very moment—my cell phone is also resonating and I look at the screen to see who might be calling. **Unknown Number** is the only message the device is willing to reveal.

"Brandon, this call may be Misty, so hold on a second."

"Tell her I'm glad she decked you—you need a good jolt."

"Hello?"

"Danny, I found you. Thank…"

"DUDE! You just threw your phone out the window!" Brandon exclaims, dumbfounded at what I've just done.

"Stop the car Brandon." I'm becoming frantic because he's increasing speed instead of slowing our momentum—his foot pressure on the accelerator seems to be a reaction to my equally weird phone-tossing action.

"Danny, are you listening? You just threw your flipping phone…" This is more of Brandon being stupefied and I'm tired of it.

"STOP THE CAR NOW. NOW! NOW!"

Brandon has to be as shocked as I am at the sound of my screaming voice. The screeching tires are my backup chorus—struggling with the road to end our forward momentum. I leap out the passenger side door before we've ended our shrieking sonnet and immediately lose my footing. After six rolls—thank God we're by a grassy section next to the road—I somehow catch my balance and start running back the direction we had come from. "Please still work, please still work, please still work, please, please, please…there!"

In a bush, suspended like a Christmas tree ornament, hangs my phone—brightly shining—waiting for me to pluck it out. "Hello? Who is this? Who are you?"

"Danny, I'm OK, it's me.

"No, you're not. You're dead! My father is dead. Who _is_ this _really_?"

"I couldn't reach you. You weren't listening. I'm sorry, there is no time."

"I threw you away, you were in a bush. I had to find you…you're dead. <u>Who is this?</u>"

"Danny, there is no time, you must listen. Ask me a question only I would know."

"I…your voice…" *How are they doing this?* <u>*Who is doing this?*</u>

"Please, something only I would know."

"I…when I was twelve, you and mom had a fight…"

"You're crying. It's very hard to understand you…"

"OF COURSE I'M CRYING. WHY SHOULDN'T I CRY? YOU'RE DEAD. I LOVED YOU. I DIDN'T GET TO TELL YOU!"

"You did tell me but tell me again now. What happened when your mother and I argued?"

"She had been drinking or was on pills, I don't know. You were trying to stop her. She called you names…awful…she said you were never there for her…for us, and you yelled back. You'd been drinking too. You…she told you that she hated you…she went back to the bedroom. You went out the door to the back yard and…"

"…We had a swimming pool and I walked out and stood on the diving board. But…"

"…the pool was empty. It was winter. And you just stood there. I watched from the window."

"Just for a little, then you came out…"

"I walked over to be near you. I knew how you were hurting. I wanted to say something, but I couldn't. I didn't know what would help."

"But you did say something. Not out loud. You said it though—in your heart—and I heard it. You said it over and over. Do you remember what it was?"

"I love you."

"Yes."

"I love you, Dad. I hated you two for fighting and for mom's problems and for your job that took you away and I couldn't fix it. But I loved you and I didn't say it then."

"You're saying it now and I can hear you. Can you hear me?"

"Yes. Yes! I hear you."

"Do you believe this is me?"

"I…it is you. Yes." I'm still having problems convincing myself this is reality.

"I love you too, son."

"I know." *Breathe slowly, Danny boy.*

"Now you must trust me. Hang up the phone."

"What? No! I…where are you? We need to…I can't do that…"

"…There is no time, Danny. Can you hear me?"

"Yes, but I…"

"…I had to find a way to reach you. Now that I have, it's all right."

"Please don't go. I want to tell you more; I want you to…"

"…There is no time. Trust me. Hang up the phone and before you do anything else—listen. Really listen. Don't stop listening until you hear."

"I don't understand."

"Danny, how do you know this is really me?"

"I just…do. You…no one else knows these things."

"Then trust me now. Be silent, listen with all your heart and hang up."

And I do—knowing I might also die at that moment.

I can hear it. I can hear everything: The rush of a passing car, radios within their cabins lulling drivers along; a bird rustling on a branch of a nearby tree; my heartbeat hammering within; fast footsteps approaching, louder with each fall—sandals, I know those sandals.

"Danny, great—you found your phone. What was that all about? Who was…"

Brandon isn't used to running. I know this because I can hear the way he's breathing. His raspiness competes with the whooshing of the unconcerned traffic rushing by…I hadn't known he's a closet smoker, but I know it now.

"Brandon, be quiet."

I guess he's hearing something too—a threat or maybe the strange out-of-world sound of my voice. He joins my silence. It's a hard silence—more difficult because everything around me invades—the outside chatter, sneaking in—the rustling of the grass and the turning of pebbles under our feet; oppressively loud. The thoughts inside me want—<u>demand</u>—attention. So many things to ponder, distractions to my attention—so much has changed. Things within me nag—I want none of it. Even my inner pleadings for silence are unwanted noise.

Slowly, slightly at first, the breeze picks up. But I can't feel its touch on my arms and my face. It's in my ears or—no it's somewhere else—from another place. Its pitch doesn't increase, but all other things seem to diminish…gradually until only the one thing, the very good thing, is all that greets me.

I've missed you son.

"Danny, I'll call a…do you need a doctor?"

Brandon thinks I've lost it, I'm sure. I know my friend can't hear the spirit's voice. All he can hear are my replies. "Dad, where are you now?"

"Danny, your dad is…" My friend in the driver's seat is trying to be delicate in reminding me of what he believes to be true.

"Yeah, <u>I know</u>. I'll explain soon, hang on Brandon." I feel like an old-style receptionist trying to handle two incoming calls at once—both demanding immediate attention. "Dad, can…can we do this more? Will this be the last…"

Don't worry, Doc (He always used to call me that! He gave me that nickname!), *I'm here now. Not always, but when you need me.*

"That's good because I have so many questions. Is there a reason we're…connected now? Are there others like…you? Can I see you?"

Right now you just need to realize there's no time.

"Right, you said that."

Remember it.

"Right, okay, I'll remember. What's the urgency?"

There is just no time. You need to explain that to your friend. I'm going away for a bit. Listen for me.

"But…"

Just explain it to your friend. I love you.

And he's not there. I can feel the absence—lonely, bitter—an emptiness which immediately floods my consciousness full with the events of the last two days: Misty and the kids leaving; this weird para-parental encounter; all my memories sequestered away for protection; now rising up as tears over the dam. Brandon tries to help hold back the overwhelming current.

"Danny, can I…" He wants so badly to calm his lunatic passenger.

"…Brandon, there's no time."

"I'm taking you to Fiz." Brandon reveals this piece of information as if it's some sort of great revelation. But of course he's taking me to Fiz, where else would he be taking me?

I say nothing as we speed through the Lone Star State. I ponder the passing pine forests, reflecting back on why this direction is so necessary—why there is no time.

Several months back, I found my Theme—four years later than Jonathan Trimble's deadline for me to do so. To their credit, N.H.Q. had been very patient, allowing me the time and resources to explore and create television programming far beyond even my expectations. To my credit, I increased their ratings 300% with my fresh approach to scientific study. As for the Theme; I didn't recognize its significance at first (It was one of those things that start off simple). The real Theme credit should go to my pal, Professor Brandon Lader, who was with me through the process of writing a script on for N.H.Q.'s Cable Network Science Program.

Most quantum guys hypothesize that the mass of the universe is primarily made up of a light-refracting *goo* popularly called Dark Matter. No, people don't call it *goo*—that's my term actually. *Dark Matter* is a favorite trolling ground of junk scientists because there's so much speculation and so little fact about it; therefore, anyone can come up with a theory and not meet much resistance. I think the idea of Dark Matter is silly because it's based on an effect, not a cause, and so I was more interested in disproving the Dark Matter theory as opposed to substantiating it.

I had done a little preliminary work, attempting to find any research done on Dark Matter existing within or near the darkest of all places— black holes. After all, if a black hole sucks in everything around it and the stuff surrounding a black hole becomes more highly compressed as it is sucked nearer, there should be lots more Dark Matter *goo* there.

I had recruited Brandon's help because of his access to OutReach's high power telescopic tools and collaborative resources. I asked him to focus on one particular and very challenging black hole example right in our own backyard—V4641 Sagittarii, smack dab in the center of the Milky Way in the massive star cluster known as Sagittarius A.

Since V4641 is the closest black hole in the neighborhood—a scant 1600 light-years away—and because it is unique in its structure, V4641 should be the perfect observation ground for Dark Matter.

The advantage of V4641 is that its binary star is shooting material straight into the companion dark hole—perfect because someone looking in the right place with the right equipment should be able to measure the volume of the material flung into the black hole.

The plan was to compare data from this unique binary star system before, during and after its rather nasty little temper tantrum observed in September 1999 when V4641 shot out immense quantities of X-ray radiation and then quite unexpectedly dimmed before settling into its normal routine again—that historic phenomena still has astrophysicists scratching their heads.

V4641 was the perfect empirical field study. If the volume of sub-atomic particles called neutrinos could be measured using OutReach's equipment, it would be simple to then search for *clumps* of those signatures further away from the black hole. If they could be found in any great quantity, then it would potentially point toward the existence of Dark Matter.

Interesting fantasy and good media material, especially considering I had been doing all this to actually quash the concept of Dark Matter—my speculation was that; much like us, neutrinos primarily hang around big things like stars and planets and aren't really interested in dark empty places. If I could prove that neutrinos don't exist near black holes, it would go a long way in debunking Dark Matter. I would have the perfect Theme material and would make Jonathan Trimble a very happy man.

"Look, I don't pretend to understand what's in your head right now, but before we get to the University, I've got to know—why did you have me going on a wild goose chase?"

Brandon's tone suggests he's not happy with me right now. I try the innocent puppy dog approach. "What wild…?"

"Come off it man!" Obviously, he's not a puppy dog fan. "I'm your best friend and my grade point average says I might even be smarter than you, so why am I sneaking around the galaxy trying to find neutrino signatures that don't likely exist, while you're off doing harmonic resonance studies on the Mariana Trench?"

Brandon deserves the truth. "I'll answer your question, but it requires your answering two questions first: One—are you telling me there are no neutrino particles streaming into V4641?"

"Inconclusive." He says. "The readings were too faint, but if I were a betting man, the fact that the readings are so faint leans toward proving your supposition."

No Dark Matter, yes! "Second question—what would lead you to believe I'm doing resonance studies in the Pacific Ocean?" I give him my most innocent look, hoping my cover is not blown.

"OutReach's equipment I borrowed was having a problem correlating some findings. I uplinked to your laptop to cross check the data and typed in the word *resonance*. I was patched immediately to a new site full of Earth Harmonic Core telemetries." Brandon's stare back at me suggests he knows far more than he's letting on. This is becoming uncomfortable.

"And where did you say these core readings came from?" I ask, hoping beyond hope that he's just speculating based on sketchy research.

"That's a third question but I'll answer it anyway. It came from the highly secured total data dump you stealthily acquired before leaving the DEEP COSMOS Project."

Busted.

Confession time—probably now would be a good time to explain something I had done which some may consider to be inappropriate. Others may use a stronger word—*illegal*. Long story short—when the Woods Hole project ended, all of the research data was dutifully collected and downloaded into their archives. I know because I was part of the team assigned to the final collection. We were given specific instructions to make sure <u>all</u> information was correctly categorized, stored and security protected. It was then to be buried in the mainframe archives of the Oceanographic Studies Institute.

As an additional precaution—supposedly because of my demonstrated intimidating manner—I was given the onerous task of getting sworn statements with signatures from all members of all teams, binding them to silence. No sideline thesis or extracurricular projects would be allowed— no access to the material for at least 20 years. The project had been born in secrecy and it would die there—short-lived and long forgotten. They had relegated me to this task as a perceived punishment. I received it as an opportunity…

…Because there had been a small glitch. Being the gatherer of autographs, I was never asked for mine—one of those bureaucratic *misfires* that happen from time to time. Feeling an intense sense of duty and obligation to my task, I rationalized that a backup copy of all the research material should be kept offsite in case the original data somehow became corrupted. The mega-flash-drive—tucked safely in my backpack—would do the trick. I also felt compelled to tell no one of my precautions to insure the security of the content.

There was no holding back now. I had been reviewing the results from the DEEP COSMOS Project for some time. The correlation between the eruption of V4641 and the beginning stages of Harmonic Resonance at the Challenger Deep source was irrefutable—these strange oscillations began precisely at the same time in September 1999 when V4641 hiccupped. There were two mysteries at work here: The first being that our planet's core is molten and isn't thought to be a very capable vibration conductor. The second mystery lay in the fact that the two were not time related—the event in Sagittarius A, having occurred centuries ago even though it was just recently observed. Would the observation of an X-ray burst near a black hole and the beginnings of an Earth-bound anomaly be coincidence or some queer collaboration? That's what I had wanted to investigate. I now tell Brandon all of this, admitting also that my behavior was smoke and mirrors. It had to be—otherwise the wrong people might have found out and my jig would be up.

"You should have told me," so much disappointment in my friend's voice.

"Yes, I should have."

AUSTIN, TEXAS

Home of great barbeque—the correct kind, made with beef, simmered for…ever, over a mesquite fire—and wonderfully succulent TexMex cuisine. Funny isn't it, how some of us define the places we've lived by the food we ate there? Okay, if that doesn't 'do it' for you, how about the Frio River on a hot August afternoon, floating in an inner tube: Ambient temperature below the inner tube—58 degrees Fahrenheit; above the inner tube—98 degrees Fahrenheit. The ice-cold drink held firmly in hand as you lazily drift down river with not a care on your mind—39 degrees Fahrenheit: This too is Austin.

Neither of those Austins are where Brandon is transporting me. We're on our way to the School of Physics at the University of Texas main campus—another universe all together.

Entry Five

"If I didn't know better, I'd think that Rocket Technology and Astrophysics were created for no greater purpose than to give us the microwave oven, the copy machine, duct tape and sticky notes. Come to think of it, maybe I don't know better."

—*Spencer L. Lynd, Ph.D. – Rochester Institute of Technology Hubble Project Director*

AUSTIN, TEXAS – UNIVERSITY OF TEXAS COMPLEX, QUANTUM SYSTEMS DEPARTMENT

Fitzgerald E. Hindeland is his real name—no one had the story right about how he had gotten his nickname. Some reasoned that it came from childhood—just a shortened version of the 'proper'.

It wasn't until I was working at U.T. as one of Professor H's assistants, that I was given the duty of Historical Protector. As I was huddling in front of my computer terminal, Fiz had come quietly up behind me and asked—almost accused…

"…Why do you think?"

He timed the query perfectly with my biting off a mouthful of two-day old pizza which immediately launched back out of my mouth and somehow managed to maintain enough moisture content to stick to the terminal screen.

"…Sir?" I had stammered as I reached for a towel to repair my snack's crash site.

"Why do you think I am called Fiz?"

I suspected he had heard all the myths and the tone of his voice somehow didn't suggest he was looking for rote information. "I don't have a clue."

"I'm not asking for authentication, I'm seeking speculation—so get with it, Child!"

He called everyone 'Child'. I had even heard him address the Dean of the UT College of Science as 'Child'. No one refused the title when he administered it and when he wanted an answer, he tenaciously insisted on a response.

"I…suspect that a name like that started accidentally, like…a theory—kind of a 'what if'?"

That got his attention—mine too, the words seemed to be coming from someone else's mouth.

"Continue."

"A name like Fiz could come from an action or a reaction. Maybe something happened that you first accomplished and which locked in your reputation or…"

"…Or?"

There was no backing out now, "…Or something happened that shouldn't have…maybe even something that was supposed to have happened…didn't. It…fizzled?"

I discovered from him then, what a powerful weapon silence can be. In the right hands, a minute of empty air could melt the indestructible, move the immovable or completely cripple the confidence of a first year research associate. I was about to blurt out an apology, or anything to end the void, when he responded.

"…The latter."

"I…"

"You are wondering why I'm asking you. You are trying to figure out what purpose there could be? So, I'll tell you. You are now the *Keeper*.

"The…" I wasn't doing too well with completing sentences under the circumstances.

"…Keeper, Keeper! You are the only one that will know. But you must KEEP it! Never let it go—as in eternally. Do you understand?"

"I…"

"…'Yes' or 'no', Child—simple as that—no promises or swearing or blood oaths—'yes' or 'no'!"

"Y…Yes."

"Fine, here's the story…"

…Simple as that, he confided to me his version, the real version… which I still keep hidden, even though I'm no longer associated with UT. Fiz had defined the duration of my duties plainly—*Eternal.* I've gotten pretty good at 'keeping' over the years—especially keeping the reality of my own problems hidden from myself. Fiz never explained why he entrusted me with his personal treasure. Was I just a convenient well to whisper into? I still don't know. Why am I even confiding this part of my history, now sharing this morsel of my secret identity? Because there is no time!

Brandon and I enter the lab that I had abandoned six years before and there, at the desk, sits the man who had shaped my opinions of the world more than any other. An older Fiz? He seems ageless—his shaved head takes care of that. He's just as lively, just as urgent, but there is something changed in his look—a different step to his gate?

"My God, the prodigal has returned. Quartermaster, go fetch the fatted calf—better yet, three; you know how I take mine. Child, do you still only take pickles and cheese on your burger?" He remembers my fast-food preferences—it seems a haunting honor of some sort. As is the reminder of Brandon's bestowed moniker—*Quartermaster*.

Brandon seems anxious to get to work, "Fiz, I brought Danny here because…"

"I know why you're both here! Don't argue, just go—I'll take care of this one."

Brandon and I share a quizzical glance before he quickly departs, understanding full well the danger of questioning our mutual mentor. Fiz and I walk to his office, where he points me to one of his leather reading chairs. Fiz takes his position in the other, his favorite, by the window looking out toward Eastwoods Park. Never one for pleasantries, the Department Chairman of the University of Texas College of Physics begins exploring in my direction, head tilted down resting on hands clasped below his fuzzy chin, eyes peering over the top of his reading glasses.

"What do you know about the Harmonic Resonance that appears to be taking place?"

"How do you…?"

"Stop inquiring and start producing!" Fiz snaps. "What do you know?" His Israeli-accented English never fails to command. For some reason, even a casual request comes out as an order from Fiz's mouth.

"Since 1999, there has been a steady increase in resonance centered on, but not limited to the tectonic subduction zone of the Mariana Trench. The resonance is permeating from the crust into the mantle and possibly affecting the Earth's core, harmonically."

He just stares for…at least two hours it feels like…then nods and states, "There's no need for any more details now. We need to be absolutely prepared for the Web Conference. There is not a moment to waste."

Web Conference, what Web Conference? "Whatever you need me to share before you start, let me know, I have all the data…"

"Before I start?" Fiz chuckles whimsically. He turns his head to peer out the window as if he has already dismissed me and is exploring another world. "Child, you are leading the conference."

Quartermaster…Brandon has returned. We're wolfing down our respective burgers, but mine seems absolutely tasteless. I've been asked to lead a conference I didn't even know was going to take place on a subject I'm not…I'm not even sure what the subject is!

"You'll need to address their questions of how an *on*-Earth Harmonic Resonance event such as this, correlates with the aspects you encountered when researching Sagittarius A." Fiz is in hyper mode and I'm suddenly exasperated.

"I'm sorry Fiz, but we've got to stop for a minute. I really think it's important you understand…"

"I already told you I know why you're here! Do you need me to vocalize it? Fine. Your world's falling apart! You're here to have it fixed! Now, can we move forward?"

I find myself asking him a strange question. "…Which world?"

Now he smiles as his eyes scan a page of a book he is holding in his lap. "They are connected, Child: The world that you see; the world that should be. We have only a little time now to determine from those two, if the world that will be, is going to exist at all."

"So what do we know <u>is</u> happening?" Brandon is warming up to the challenge of the assignment.

My brain screams at me to stay quiet—I have no business being here— my mouth ignores the command. "Look at the evidence: We have readings that indicate the Earth's core is in the beginning stages of some sort of change, causing it to resonate—we don't know how or why this is possible."

Brandon adds his two cents. "These readings appear to be concurrent with the unusual activity emanating from Sagittarius A, but that has to be coincidental because, even though it was first recorded in 1999, the activity there began 1400 years ago."

Fiz stops reading his book, takes off his glasses and stares through us both. "Why are you so concerned with impossibilities and improbabilities?"

"Isn't it important to understand the limitations of what we do know?" *Duck, Brandon!* I plead telepathically.

The book hits my friend squarely in the chest. I watch alertly for any other objects possibly coming my way, but Fiz only had one weapon. He's up and out of his chair. "Never mind," he exclaims while retrieving the tome from Brandon's grasp and then leafing to a specific page. "Listen, observe, don't tell me what can't be done—show me what can be done!"

Fiz remains standing, head down, looking at several pieces of paper taped into the book. From my position in the room, I'm having difficulty seeing what he's examining. The leaves appear filled with penned writing and hand scribbled equations randomly on the side bars. He looks back up directly at me, removing the paper from its safe harbor. "I apologize," he offers. "There is just so much to do and you need to open your faculties in order to be able to understand. Child, do you remember this?"

Fiz hands me the folded sheets and the very transfer engulfs me: The smell—aroma residue of an old coffee stain…hazelnut? The texture—it came from my favorite and now completely used up scientific journal; the script is my notorious left-handed block print. The title—an almost aggressively italicized flourish—reads, **Evolutional Echo Tracing…**

…I'm whirled back to another moment, when I first handed him the document. It was so precious to me then and I had forgotten it even existed because of his reception at the time…*Can you prove any of this?* I told him I could not because there was nothing to prove it with. *Then waste your time on more important abilities!* That was that—he was telling me after a casual glance at my mini-masterpiece how unimportant both the work and the worker were. That part I had not forgotten—it's why I had sought out the opportunity at Woods Hole and it's why I am who I am today. But until this moment, I hadn't considered those two actions as reactions to his brusque brush-off.

"It wasn't ready then. You weren't ready then," Fiz speaks softly into me. Now you and your world are changed. And I need you to become who you were always meant to be."

"Here's what needs to be done." *Thankfully—a game plan!* Fiz hands out marching orders and I take my long-lost treasure over to my laptop to start the *review and polish* process. Brandon plops down at a terminal and starts organizing as much related material as he can ferret. "I want all your ideas and findings, no matter how absurd or extraordinary they may seem to you. Every associate and undergrad is on call, so if you need help, ask for it."

The energy level has just ramped up. I suddenly realize it is Monday afternoon and I've not touched base with anyone at N.H.Q., but it seems insignificant for the moment. If we can determine what is happening inside the planet and outside the solar system and somehow tie them together…N.H.Q. will also be the benefactor. *Focus.* But then there's Misty and the kids. Where are they and shouldn't I be pursuing them? *Focus.* The real question is: What is causing Earth's harmonic issues and is V4641 somehow connected to the activity? *Focus!*

Fiz was also born of a tumultuous moment. Part of his story I had heard well before meeting him. To me it had originally been a well-known tale without real faces or names; just a title—*Jews in Nazi Germany.* Fitzgerald E. Hindeland's embellishment put flesh to the bone.

Migrating from Saint Petersburg, Russia to Munich, Germany during the depression era, his soon-to-be parents had somehow managed to hide from the Germans the fact that they were both Ph.D. level physicists and ethnically challenged. They had quickly realized that living conditions under the Third Reich presented no better prospects than did the promise of Stalin's Five-Year Plan. "Mama and Papa Holocaust," as Fiz lovingly referred to them, calculated they would be the victims, not the benefactors in this environment, so it was time to move once more, and quickly.

Fortunately, the Hindelands had other marketable talents—Mama H. possessing a soaring soprano voice and Papa H. being something of a piano prodigy. They were able to blend into a troupe of traveling actors who entertained the German army along the occupied front and escaped the grasp of Hitler's plan in a most elegant of ways. They toured their way out, one evening in Southern France, discreetly making an exit—stage left and onto a Palestine bound freighter. My mentor, their one and only little bundle of hope, was conceived sometime thereafter as a legitimate citizen of the newly formed State of Israel.

Raised in struggle mixed with determination and hope, Fiz inherited his parent's academic acumen and developed something else very unique—an attitude of confrontation toward assumed authority. "Little one," his papa would chide, "you wake up with a chip on your shoulder and go to bed with a two-by-four." It was an American euphemism Fiz's father had picked up from some newly acquired university friends. All three of the Hindelands became prestigious components of the quickly expanding Israeli *Intelligentsia*, but it was Fiz who ultimately made a significant name for himself in astrophysics.

Why? He refused to think inside the box. More than that, he was adept at proving that the box didn't even exist and demonstrated the ability to formulate accurate calculations for extended space travel (something that Albert Einstein would actually compliment him for at a conference later in Geneva). Fiz was eventually courted into the Goddard Space Flight Center in Greenbelt Maryland. From there, he was moved to NASA research in Houston, TX where much of the Apollo and Voyager projects were influenced through his scrutiny.

But NASA was just not big enough for Fiz. Again, the Box-breaker escaped and made the boldest move of all. He walked unannounced into a Board of Regents meeting at the University of Texas in Austin and proclaimed, "I have come to take you on a journey into the unknown."

So compelling was his proposal to create an independent free thinking physics research lab, that he was awarded a budget twice that of any other lab in the country and complete autonomy regarding staff and direction. From that day forward, Fiz and his gang, never disappointed; identifying and defining anomaly after anomaly of the universe. Nothing proved too incredible or unsolvable for this physics giant and his charges…nothing that is, until I came along.

While I'm working with Fiz and Brandon in the U.T. lab, another conversation is taking place. This one is in French and is occurring thousands of miles away—yet I'm picking up the dialogue in my head, as if the participants are in the room with us. I speak only a couple of words of French so, to translate, we're going to have to get creative. The conversation is between two technicians monitoring the output of the Antares Neutrino Telescope which resides off the coast of Toulon, two-point-four kilometers under the Mediterranean Sea.

Antares is one of only a few sites on the planet specifically designed to peer at Neutrino Masses emitted from our sun and other fission sources. Neutrinos pass easily through the Earth's crust, but for whatever reason, become trapped by the pressures of the ocean. Water is Kryptonite to neutrinos and it allows us to observe and measure solar neutrino output to some degree.

I don't know the guys at Antares, but with my "out of body ears" I'm listening carefully and hear them call each other by their names, Jacques, and Claude. J. & C. are very focused on something. It's easy to tell because when the French become excited about something, they talk more rapidly…kind of like the rest of us…only in French. You can see that their interest is centered on the readings on one of their monitors.

Voila, our two Frenchmen seem to be having a disagreement—Jacques pounds his fist on the table and points at the equipment, Claude shakes his head back and forth and utters one of the few French words I understand. *Impossible*! Our boys are silent for a moment and just stare at the screens before them. Now they simultaneously nod their heads in agreement and both repeat the word out loud in unison. "*Impossible*."

It's Claude who is inspired to pick up the phone; making a call to a professor he studied under in the United States for a summer internship. He had apparently made enough of an impression on this professor because he was given a cell phone number to call should he ever run into unexplained issues such as this. The line takes a moment to connect and an actual live person answers by identifying himself. "This is Fitzgerald Hindeland."

Entry Six

AUSTIN, TEXAS – UNIVERSITY OF TEXAS COMPLEX, QUANTUM SYSTEMS DEPARTMENT

"I made a few calls telling the heads of physics at Duke and Massachusetts Institute of Technology and also the head of the Hubble Project at Rochester Institute of Technology about your supposition," Fiz explains. "They're interested enough to sit in on this by video conference." The two LED screens on either side of the stage flash alive and the bearded faces of several obvious academicians stare out at us. *Interested enough to sit in*, I muse to myself. Knowing Fiz, these specialists in Quantum Theory were instructed by the master himself.

But then again, an invitation from Fiz to any gathering is tantamount to an audience with the Pope. Even if not a Catholic—for curiosity sake alone—who would refuse? Fiz gives me a reassuring nod—obviously, he senses my anxiety—and simply states with a whimsical smile, "You're up, Child."

I'm standing near a podium, center stage, and my first inclination is to search for an escape hatch under said pedestal. I ignore my animalistic instincts howling inside for me to head for safe harbor and instead plunge, headfirst, into the frothy depths.

"We are going to present you with some rather unsettling material. The purpose for telling you this up front is because it may initially appear that we are presenting theory, not fact. Please be patient as the initial information is shared and it should become clear as we go along that all of this information has not only been cross-checked but corroborated by other credible sources. With the help…"

"…Excuse me," a voice from all the audio speakers in the room booms out with way too much volume and of course, a piercing feedback squeal that Fiz quickly adjusts down from the sound board he's conveniently standing beside. I glance up and one of the *Bearded Wonders* on screen—a guy with wire-rimmed glasses (there's another with black horn-rimmed ones) is tapping on the microphone, not sure if he is being heard. "Excuse me," again loud, but controlled to tolerant levels this time thanks to Fiz, "Exactly who are you?"

Of course these people wouldn't know or recognize me, just as I don't recognize them. What do I tell them? How do I explain my presence here?

"Shut up, Winston," Fiz commands. "I have given Professor Adamson the floor and that will be enough reason for you to respect and listen to what he has to say."

I look over at my one-time life-instructor and mouth words no one else can see, "*I'm not a professor!*" Fiz merely brushes both hands in a whisking motion in my direction, signaling me to continue.

I dare not refute him and so move forward. "According to our readings, the behavior of the well-known binary phenomenon known as V4641 which formed 1600 light-years from Earth seems to be reacting in… sympathy with local geological events. I…we see at least a coincidental effect in the data. The timing of both the distant and the local anomalies suggest an even stronger correlation implying V4641 is actually causing the Earth-based changes…"

Hands go up everywhere in the room, There's another "Excuse me" from both *Winston Wire-rim* and *Whoever Horn-rim*. Fiz simply turns off their audio, turns on his own and directs, "Children, hold your questions. Professor Adamson has much more to explain." Hands go down and I'm given another "*proceed*" nod from Fiz.

"I need you to bear with me for several reasons. Because of the strength of the signal we are receiving, we have concluded that all previous measurements of the V4641 phenomena are possibly in error. What's more, we have had to find new measurement methods because of readings shared with us by the Antares Neutrino Observatory. It appears that the neutrino count has significantly diminished. We have verified the data and…"

The room rivals any volcanic eruption I've ever monitored for noise level. People are shouting and trying to get other's attention. Everyone clamors to be heard, not the least of which being Drs. *Wire-rim* and *Horn-rim*, the two mimes on screen who Fiz continues to keep in mute prison. Even Fiz is having difficulty getting everyone to be silent after my absurd comments and he finally walks to the podium beside me, taking the microphone out of its holder. The room, thinking he is about to set me straight, immediately calms. He scans the audience for would-be up-stagers and seems satisfied that no one will interrupt again so he simply hands me the microphone and walks back to the sound board. I plunge ahead.

I'd better talk about the elephant in the room. "Uh, the Antares Observatory information is most definitely accurate. It means that, either neutrino generation has been reduced somehow or that these particles are being attracted…somewhere else. We are at the beginning of the exploration process, to determine which supposition is correct by using a technique known as Evolutional Echo Tracing. E.E.T. has proven successful in the laboratory and is now ready for application.

"The application is the question. The trick is; where do we start our trace? Is there a neutron echo, outside our own solar system, strong enough to trace?"

"Fiz, may I have a word without being ejected from the meeting?" Now a convenient subheading on the screen announces that the friendly face seeking permission is none other than Spencer Lynd, Ph.D., head of the R.I.T. Hubble project whom we've already met in theory, but not in practice—that's about to change. "Go ahead Spence" encourages Fiz.

"I'm uploading some material to you that I think you'll find interesting. Regarding some recent activity we noticed concerning V4641. Before I send this though, I have a question for Dr. Adamson." *Good grief, now I'm a professor and a doctor!* "Have you run any recent Doppler scans on the region?"

I look over to Brandon who shakes his head back and forth and then I answer, "No sir, we didn't think a light spectral analysis would expand our findings in any way."

"Quite understandable—but because of some strange readings on our systems, the Hubble Center ran a spectral analysis of V4641 in the Sagittarius A sector just yesterday."

"What did you find, Spence?" Fiz isn't the most patient of hosts—I could hear the *GET ON WITH IT* tone in his voice.

"Well actually, instead of trying to explain it—which frankly, I can't— let me show you." With that Spencer's face was replaced on screen with a Doppler spectral image. There is a time-stamp and location heading at the bottom of the picture that reads *March 15, 13:42 pm EST- Sagittarius A*. The image shows the familiar Sagittarius A field signature, but with a subtle difference. The spectrograph indicates a full Red-Shift reading— very normal and comforting, confirming that our little blue ball, Earth in our cozy little solar system, is still whizzing <u>away</u> from the center of the galaxy as it should be doing. But there is also another spectrographic signature marked with the identical time-stamp heading and it indicates a full Blue-Shift reading. That should be making everyone involved with this conference scratch their heads because it suggests Earth is speeding <u>toward</u> Sagittarius A.

Spencer continues, "We had been scanning the area for 15 minutes prior to this time stamp. The pictures taken during the first 15 minutes do not reveal this abnormality, so it seems we have captured the precise moment of the changed conditions. *March 15, 13:42 pm EST, GMT minus 5.*" Of course, considering V4641 is 1600 light-years away; that means, this change in direction originated somewhere back in the 17th century, C.E.

"It gets better," Spencer is whimsically smirking now. I'm sure this is mad-scientist stuff to him and the fact that he is the presenter must reek of irony to him. "When we filtered out the activity influence from V4641 and reexamined the first spectrograph, everything went back to normal. This means…"

"We get it Spence the problem reading is coming directly from V4641." Fiz again, trying to move things along.

"You're missing the point. The fact that V4641 is the only event in the area that is showing a Blue-Shift means that <u>it</u> is coming to <u>us</u> and it's coming quickly."

"By quickly…you mean?" Fiz asks.

"Well, that's another puzzle. We've had a constant eye focused in the direction of V4641 ever since…things changed. The blue-shift signature of the black hole disappears at various points in space between us and its original position…and then reappears, seemingly in closer proximity to Earth. Without a fixed point of reference and consistent readings, we have no way of knowing exactly where it is and *when, how, or* even *if* it will begin to affect us."

Fiz is running his hand over his finely shaved dome—I've learned from experience that he only does this when he is truly intrigued. "Spence, please, what readings are you seeing from V4641 right now—in real time please?"

"That's the final mystery and really what I wanted to speak to you about." Spencer sounds relieved to finally be able to share his discovery. "As of approximately one hour ago, V4641 has vanished completely as if it never existed."

No one else speaks—the stillness of the room as complete as the vacuum of space. Another thought hits me—an instant replay actually of *Yesterday Me. Yesterday Me* is standing by the side of the road picking his phone gingerly off the branch of a bush and is about to converse with my father the ghost. *Yesterday Me* glances at the time on the cell phone readout before bringing the device to his ear. It proclaims *12:42 pm CST* which is *13:42 pm EST military time, 8:42 am Greenwich Mean Time*, the same as on the timestamp Spencer has just shown us.

SOMEWHERE OVER THE ATLANTIC OCEAN

We are now traveling at subsonic speed in the private jet of an unnamed regent with the University of Texas. I'm told that Fiz has never requested this kind of excess before, but that the regent has allowed use of the transport for as long as the good Doctor needed. I'm also told that I'm not to ask where we are now jetting. I probably shouldn't even pretend to know that, by my calculations (through the cabin windows I see there's a big body of water beneath us. It's Five am, Central Standard Time and the sun is at the nose of the plane), we're headed east over the Atlantic Ocean. *Should I set my watch to another time-zone? Which one?* I hope I won't be shot for my reasoning powers.

As we cruise at altitude, we are engaged in a private web conference with several people I've not met before. One in particular, whom I'm told to refer to as 'Sir', is fairly well known by his other title, 'Mr. President'. The other gentleman is Darius Mede, current head of the World Trade Organization. This is the big leagues and I'm sure there are fifty secret service, FBI and CIA types reading my dossier at this moment deciding if I'm expendable. Up until now, I hadn't even considered the idea that there was a dossier on me. If there wasn't one, there certainly will be.

Pancakes, that's what I smell. Sure enough, I can see a flight attendant scurrying back and forth behind the curtained galley, preparing breakfast for us. Now my attention is successfully divided between the yearnings of my stomach and an international web-conference—I feel a painful jab to my shin and come quickly back to the matter at hand. My mentor is giving me his best "*pay attention*" look.

"Fiz, as my Chief Science Advisor (*I didn't know that!*), I depend on you to forewarn me about this kind of thing. How did this get past you?" The President of the United States has just nicely dressed down my hero. Fiz is scribbling on a table as he formulates a response. The words he has written are double underlined and boldly state, DON'T CALL HIM CHILD!

"Ch…Sir, I have given you as much warning and information as I have received. I'm sure you understand that this new condition has taken us all by surprise."

"I understand, I didn't mean to put you on the defensive." *The leader of the free world apologizing to my hero—Okay, that's better, and amazing.* "How much time do we have?"

"Well, that, Mr. President, is the million-dollar question. To know that; we have to understand how this event is moving, it's projected velocity and how far out its effects reach. We're simply not sure yet and we don't even know if there are methods or equipment capable of measuring such things. We'd be guessing at best."

"Your best guess then." *It is a command.*

I examine the President's features via the web monitor—the wavy black hair, the stocky, but athletic shoulders, the bronze complexion and deep crevices in his facial features not only betray the pride of his Native American heritage, but also a determination to make good on his promises. So far—in my book; and now I realize, in Fiz's book too—he's done so.

Fiz replies simply, "…Soon."

"Come on Fiz! You know I need more than that! Are we talking soon in weeks?…Months? Years? What?"

"Greg." *Did Fiz just call the President of the United States by his first name?* "The answer could be "yes" to any of those. This may be difficult to comprehend, but we are not talking about a time event here. Neither motion nor location define it: It is…different from anything we've ever observed."

"What about this Adamson fellow? What does he say? Is he reliable?" *This is Mede speaking. I don't like him immediately.*

"Daniel Adamson is the most brilliant mind I've ever encountered." *What? Who is Fiz talking about?* "Not because of <u>what</u> he thinks, but because of <u>how</u> he thinks. He is by far the expert on this subject and I have placed my complete trust in him." *I didn't know that!*

"Well then, Professor Adamson, please enlighten us," *Mede again. Is that a wart on the end of his nose?*

"I'm not a professor. I'm the National Science Editor for N.H.Q. Broadcast Services."

Dead silence on the other end of the line, then Mede persists. "There seems to be some confusion then because your dossier (*There is one!*) suggests a rather impressive list of academic accomplishments including a foundational grant and current tenure listed at the University of Texas…"

"Yes!" Fiz breaks in. "That's all valid information. What Danny… Daniel meant to explain is that he maintains his faculty chair as an adjunct professor with special privileges. I made the arrangements to allow him to serve on staff at N.H.Q. because of his broad and capable perspective. As you know, N.H.Q. funds a significant portion of our Physics Department. That's also why he is on this trip instead of in the research lab with his assistant Dr. Brandon Lader.

…Brandon—my assistant? This is all so far out of the realm of reality that V4641's vanishing act is starting to appear tame in comparison.

"Dr Lader is this man's assistant? The Dr. Lader of the NASA/ OutReach Project?" asks the President of the United States of America. *Oh no, it's about to rain fire.*

"Yes, Ch…sir, he and Professor Adamson both have special security clearance—you'll see it in their files. They remain under my purview-and-call when investigating circumstances such as we have right now. You were the one who signed the approval back when I agreed to be on your team. How could this kind of thing have surprised us so? If it were not for you and me, Mr. President—setting this system up in the first place—we may never have known about this impending event."

"Okay Fiz, you've taken me to the woodshed and I'm duly reprimanded, let's all get on the same page for a moment. Because of the nature of the information, maybe we shouldn't be trying to identify whose problem this is, but rather what <u>we</u> should do about it." *Didn't he say that in one of his campaign speeches? It still sounds good.* "Back to basics—what is it we need to accomplish? Who needs to know about this and who is in charge?"

Fiz hesitates what seems an eternity before responding to the question. "Mr. President, we can have no game plan until we gather more facts. We have assembled and informed a team of people from a number of prominent research facilities and universities and Professor Adamson will be the one to determine strategy and implementation…with my over-site, of course." As he finishes speaking, Fiz puts a firm hand grip on my arm to stop me from jumping out of my chair to object.

"We defer to your good judgment," replies the President. I hope you don't mind Darius joining you at Naveh Shaanan (*Where?*) as an extra pair of eyes. He'll be very helpful in getting support and cooperation from the world community, should that become necessary."

Fiz continues to restrain me. "That is very thoughtful, sir. Darius, I look forward to seeing you again."

"Likewise, Dr. Hindeland. Likewise."

"Please tell me what that conversation was really about?" Incredibly, it is Fiz asking me this question. I've learned from past experience that it's a method he uses to teach—asking of the student, the question he knows to be on the student's mind. I respond in kind.

"First, please explain to me how I became an adjunct professor without ever knowing and for that matter, how I'm supposed to develop strategies and actions for a project I just now found out I'm heading up?"

Fiz proves better at this than I am. He simply dismisses my question. "All in due course—we have more pressing matters."

Right now, my pressing matter has to do with what I'm expected to do with the little information we've gathered. "Listen Fiz, I need more to go on here. We have no way of measuring this phenomenon and for Evolutional Echo Tracing to work; we need a fixed point to start with."

"Which," Fiz cuts in, "is why we are speeding to another source who I believe will have those answers. But what I want to do right now is call Jonathan Trimble to explain your mysterious disappearance. We don't want any odd stories appearing that suggest you've been abducted by aliens."

"That would probably make more sense than what is really happening."

"I don't disagree, Child."

Fiz is on the SAT Phone at the back of the plane placating my boss while I sit at a desk attached to the bulkhead of the cabin. I look down and somehow my phone has found its way to my hand. I press Misty's speed dial number and then the hang-up button; dial again, hang-up again… asking myself, *what will I say? How will I explain?* There are no answers and no time to find them. This is nuts. I'm nuts!

Suddenly very depressed, I glance to my left at the exit door and I actually contemplate the experience of pulling the big red EMERGENCY lever that would expose us to the atmosphere. Would I feel the depressurization? How long would I stay conscious as I plummeted toward the ocean's surface? What would be the duration of my broken body's decent to the sea bottom or would my corpse only become a tasty shark meal? Meanwhile, my thumb continues its physical mantra—dial, hang-up, dial…

"Ever wonder why the word innumerable exists? If the numbers don't exist to explain something, why even bother trying?" Fiz has come up stealthfully behind me and I'm jerked from my thoughts by his incalculable question.

"I didn't hear you come up. Do I still have a job?"

"Your boss is both concerned and intrigued. I assured him that he has first stab at anything we come up with that isn't classified top secret by my boss. He wishes you well."

"Fiz, there's no one else to talk to and…I need someone to hear…This is going to sound crazy to you, but…"

"Oh you mean about talking with your father? Yes, Quartermaster told me about your unusual antics and no, I'm not going to have you locked away. Danny (*He never calls me Danny!*), there has been a common theme beginning with the ancient civilizations of Earth to the present which science has poorly researched and even more pathetically addressed. It is the concept of a spirit within and the continuation of that spirit beyond physical boundaries."

"Fiz, I don't know how to rationalize…how to <u>believe</u> what I've come to know as <u>unbelievable</u>. The easiest way to explain it has to be either by sleight-of-hand or by insanity."

"Child, maybe the true crazy people are the ones who refuse to acknowledge or tap into that spiritual essence. Maybe the only sanity we know originates, not from what we see so clearly, but from what dwells in the invisible. Maybe for the first time, things are becoming real for you?"

Now Fiz is starting to sound like a fringe case himself. Maybe it's part of what's happening with the planet and out in Sagittarius. Or possibly I'm imagining all of this. I don't know and suddenly, I don't care. "I don't mean to sound unappreciative—you're always here when I need you and that means a lot. I asked you to listen and you did, but with everything going on, I'm…suddenly really tired."

"Then sleep, Child. I need you at your best when we land."

"Where are we going? What is Naveh Shaanan?"

"You will see. Now rest."

Wings everywhere, huge—obscuring my vision—a flight of frenzy. There are bodies too—I can't make them out. Beasts? Men? Monsters? I'm surrounded and there's a battle going on. Two armies of horrific size and shape—half animal, half human, with multiple heads, beautifully frightening. I've got to hide, but there's no place they can't find me. Terrible thunder—no…voices, no…singing, but…also a chorus of anger—vicious jealousy! There's something both opposing forces want. They won't stop until the prize is taken by one side or the other. Who's winning? Blood is a river to my waist, trying to flood me in its current—I want to vomit. A hand from nowhere reaches out to lift me above the torrent. The touch of the hand is so…loving. And there's a voice behind the hand—it soothes me with one caressing word.

Peace.

I ask, *what is the battle about?* The answer from the voice is unbelievable.

They fight for you.

Before flying away, I had reminded Dr. Brandon Lader of something we had both tried to prove long ago.

"Brandon, there's still no solid proof that Harmonic Resonance is taking place. If you want to prove something, prove that this activity is not just some fluke event. Find another example in history that makes sense and that will tell us what to expect." I'm probably transferring a lot of frustration undeservedly toward my friend, so I pause and switch to a more reassuring timbre. "You're the research wizard—while I'm gone, work your magic!"

That is why at this very moment, bleary eyed Brandon has been up for 20 hours straight, examining photographs, sensor readings and information that have been torn apart and analyzed thousands of times before. But Brandon is looking at the information from a new perspective and now he forgets his fatigue—suddenly in front of him on a computer web log, he finds exactly what we need; in the annals of history of the planet Mars; and the Goto Galaxy Supermassive Black Hole.

Entry Seven

EVOLUTIONAL ECHO TRACING – DEVELOPED BY DANIEL ADAMSON, M.S.P.

Hypothesis: If plural images of one entity can be demonstrated at the subatomic level; then the same cause and effect should be evident as amplified phenomena in the quantum universe.

Observing the universe from a quantum perspective assumes quantum results to be accurate and proven. These observations are in fact flawed by space and time curvature, dimensional shifts, as well as by the ego of man. Therefore, our outcomes are exponentially incorrect.

When examining the universe at either the quantum or subatomic levels, we observe multiple episodic echoes of the original origin event— each appearing unique because of its observed location in time, space, dimension, and socio-scientific climate—distorting any conclusions to the point of being worthless.

Conclusion: <u>The above-mentioned distortions suggest that what we are seeing is not what is actually happening.</u> Starting with pure scientific principles—abandoning theories and relying only on proven measurements and formulas—we should be able to follow the trails of these echoes to their origins. <u>Just as in a canyon—using the final report of an original gunshot— Evolutional Echo Tracing can verify the true origin of a quantum occurrence by backtracking its original signal.</u>

NAVEH SHAANAN, ISRAEL

I awaken with a THUMP. "We've landed." It's Fiz standing over me with the SAT Phone in his palm, extended out to me as if it were a treat of some type. I rub my eyes and in doing so my hands also brush over the two-day growth of beard on my face. I suddenly crave a long hot shower. Fiz continues to hover over me without a word and I realize the SAT Phone is blinking green, indicating there's a live person on the other end. I take the offered instrument from my mentor and put it to my ear as we taxi to an unfamiliar airport terminal. "Hello?"

"Danny, boot up your computer, I've sent you some information and we need to talk about it now!"

Brandon sounds the same way he did when he let me know he'd just achieved Level Nine of Doom. While I fumble with my laptop, he speeds on. "Listen, I was looking for correlative factors that would justify what we're seeing with the synchronizing of tectonic and core resonance. And I found out this has happened before—here and on Mars. Tectonics—crust movement—stopped. Period—on both planets! Current theory suggests that stuff stopped moving here on Earth because the continents bumped into each other and so had to reverse direction, but that just doesn't make any sense. The reasoning for Mars was that it was smaller and cooled faster and had more iron in its core and blah, blah, blah. Meaning nobody really knows why!"

"Brandon, how many caffeine thruster drinks have you been sucking down?"

My friend ignores me, "Whatever happened, Mars never recovered and that's why it died—its core and its crust became synchronous: No tectonics, no internally generated heat; hence no global warming effect—no life. Every grade school science teacher knows that stuff, but no one…_no_ _one_ considered that the two planets—Mars and Earth—actually experienced tectonic atrophy at the same moment for some connected reason. That's when I went back and looked at Goto."

"…Goto as in the galaxy Goto?" Fiz has patched the SAT Phone into the speaker system and is eavesdropping. It is he who is now curious.

"Goto," Brandon continues, "as in the galaxy with the largest and oldest supermassive black hole ever documented. There was something I remembered about that site I wanted to check out. You should be seeing the information come up now."

And there it is on my laptop screen. I read aloud with Fiz looking over my shoulder:

"In 2009, astronomers discovered a galaxy that was very similar in composition to the *Milky Way*, but for a few twists. At the heart of Goto is a black hole over one billion times more massive than our sun.

"The galaxy and black hole must have formed very rapidly in the infancy of the universe', said University of Hawaii astronomer Tomotsugu Goto, one of the researchers and the namesake of the find."

Brandon jumps in. "Goto also mentioned surprise at seeing that size of galaxy and an accompanying black hole, that early in the stages of the universe. We're taught to look at black holes as the end result—dying stars turning in on themselves—not as a birthing event. The existence of the Goto black hole argues that they've been here since the beginning."

"And to protect our pride, instead of trashing old theories on how the universe works, we've had to make up conflicting theories to justify the paradox and hope no one notices." That's me getting on my soapbox.

"But no one does notice because everyone's busy covering their backside with their own conflicting theories—after all, we must keep the grant money flowing." Brandon is firing on all his cynical cylinders.

"Everyone but us," Fiz is walking back and forth in the limited space allowed by the jet cabin. "So, Quartermaster, how does this information relate to Harmonic Resonance on Earth and Mars?"

Brandon eagerly answers. "Depending on which research you read and whose data you believe, Goto's supermassive black hole was formed around the same time Earth was just settling down into a predictable planet. If that's so, there would have been evidence of the same kind of synchronizing resonance we're seeing now. I programmed a computer model using the assumption that Mars and Earth both ceased tectonic activity at the exact same moment due to the influence of some intense form of gravitational force. Then, taking into account the distance in light-years from Goto, I asked the computer to look for any recent Doppler inconsistencies since the discovery of Goto—assumed errors which observers would have dismissed as equipment malfunctions or inaccurate logging..." Brandon is speaking and thinking at rocket velocity. He catches his breath and charges on. "... Danny, you're process works."

"What? I'm sorry, I don't follow…" *Maybe I was sleeping—I thought my friend said…*

"Evolutional Echo Tracing—it works!"

Fiz is shaking his head. "Quartermaster, slow down. What has E.E.T. to do with tectonic shutdown on two planets and the influence of some obscure galaxy?"

"It's NOT obscure. That's the whole point. When I ran the model for Goto, a Doppler signature was generated. It was the same signature as the one we were shown from the Hubble Group in that meeting yesterday. Not just similar—it's an EXACT MATCH!"

I'm in Doubting Thomas mode now. "You're saying the largest supermassive black hole discovered is somehow also V4641, the smallest microquasar found?"

"They exist in separate places at separate times, but they are the same phenomena." Brandon pats the top of the pile of computer printouts before him to emphasize his conclusions.

"That can't be…" Fiz holds up the palm of his hand to stop me from completing my sentence which gives Brandon enough time to charge ahead uninterrupted.

"No, it can't be. You're right! And on a crazy hunch, I tried to prove that out by using your formula for E.E.T. to follow the rabbit trail. They're echoes, Danny. They're the same! Goto is the Milky Way but reflected from eons past."

"But if that's so, then Goto's black hole would be shifting in position and demonstrating the same peculiarities as V4641." Fiz is bending over the table as he speaks, scribbling on a small pad of paper, what looks to be a list of facts Brandon has just given us about Goto.

"It is—excuse me, it was! That's the crazy thing. Goto no longer exists—it's historic, not geographic. But once you take time out of the equation, it makes perfect sense. What happened there, then…is happening here, now. It's like looking into a galactic mirror."

I'm still not convinced. "Brandon, besides using Evolutional Echo Tracing, is there any way to prove this…is there other supporting evidence?"

"Danny." Brandon puts on his wounded puppy dog act. "Don't you know me well enough by now? I'm sending you another link now. Look at the latest data from *Spirit*.

"...*Spirit*—the old Mars rover *Spirit*?"

"…The same—which is still faithfully operational and sending back telemetry."

I look at the NASA site from the Jet Propulsion Laboratory at the California Institute of Technology that Brandon has just pointed me to. Lo and behold there is a complete listing of activity for the Mars *Spirit* rover. At the top of the page in bold lettering is a news release that probably only a few people have yet bothered to read:

POSSIBLE SEISMIC ACTIVITY DETECTED BY *SPIRIT* ON MARS

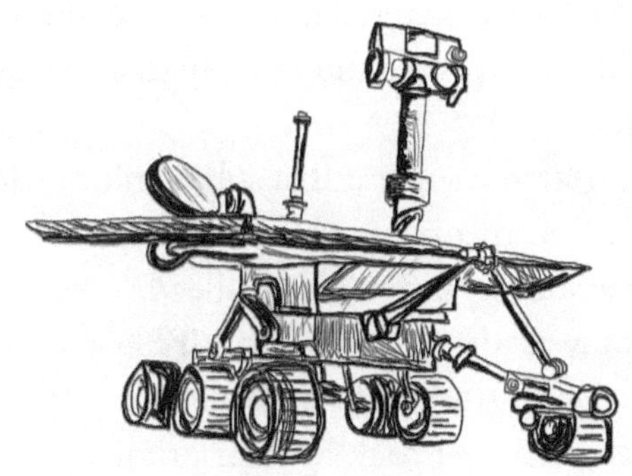

The article proceeds to explain away its own headline by blaming poor little *Spirit* with an unexplained malfunction. After all, everyone knows that there can be no tectonics or volcanic activity on a planet whose crust and core are fused together.

Brandon becomes a reader of minds. "Yes, Mars has come alive again."

"Brandon, I'm not sure I'm following this. If Earth's crust and core tectonics are beginning to die, but Mars' tectonics are starting to awaken; why would we conclude that the same anomaly is causing both?"

Fiz and I have transferred from the jet to a waiting car—an older limousine—not having had to run through customs. I'm silently awed at the clout of the man sitting next to me in the well accoutered passenger compartment. The window separating us from the driver's compartment remains up and the windows on each side and to the rear are tinted so darkly that we had to request of the driver via intercom that he turn on the interior lights. I suspect that we are in Israel, mostly because of the mix of Western and Middle Eastern dress I see adorning the people we pass on the streets—also *Naveh Shaanan* just sounds Jewish.

"Okay, I'll speak slowly so you can follow along. The same anomaly affected both planets—actually all the planets; but because of the size, locations, and structures of each, they all reacted differently. Mars just plain never recovered from the *stop shock*. Earth rebooted with one of those infamous alterations of magnetic north and south along with a strange reassembly of some nucleonic material into nucleic composition. This new event is thus awakening one planet and is likely to at least temporarily put the other one back to sleep."

"Wait. Did I just hear you suggest that subatomic particles were altered into nucleic Brandon, your theorizing that this thing out there created life!"

"Not theorizing at all." Brandon plows ahead. "I started with a query. Your E.E.T. concept was designed to identify big events—origins in quantum space. But using the same approach, we can also trace micro-reactions at the subatomic level back to their origins. I ran the computer model again, this time looking for neutrino activity related to V4641 and Goto. Then I compared them with the neutrino activity found in common strands of D.N.A. and R.N.A."

"Brandon, nucleic acids don't produce neutrinos."

It's Fiz who replies. "Child, hush. Quartermaster, how can you distinguish between neutrinos generated from D.N.A. or R.N.A. activity and those from solar or deep space events?"

"Easy, the charged particles from the decay of proton and neutron reactions—what we call Standard and Muon Neutrinos—haven't matched up in number to what researchers projected.

"For years, physicists have been trying to justify the energy loss in nuclear reactions—which is how the whole search for neutrinos started and why we've hypothesized that there was a third kind of particle—*Tau*

Neutrinos—sucking off the energy. But Tau Neutrinos aren't energy suckers, they ARE the energy. That's the whole point. Nuclear reactions in the sun and beyond have been bombarding us constantly: We absorb some of that energy, but we also react to it…like an echo. I found, using Danny's formula, that there's more energy coming out of Nucleic Acid - D.N.A. and R.N.A—than there is going in. In other words, Tau *neutrinos* are organic neutrino babies created from inorganic neutrino mommas and papas!"

Fiz leans forward to speak pointedly into the SAT Phone. "If you have proven this, it changes our entire concept of molecular reactions."

This is so far out in left field that I give up trying to chase the ball. That Brandon would use E.E.T. to explain the very origins of life is totally absurd. I didn't design it for that purpose so it should certainly not be used for that purpose…*should it?*

"The picture is still not complete." Fiz is still jotting down notes, focusing on the pad in his lap as he speaks. "We will need someone else's input—someone very…different—to help us sort this out."

Just then, the limo comes to a halt and the rear passenger side door flings open. The light coming in is blinding and silhouettes a grizzled figure who shouts in booming bass guttural tones, "Fitzgerald! You have not changed an age! Praise the Eternal, how is life my Talmid?"

NAVEH SHAANAN, ISRAEL – THE TECHNION-ISRAEL - INSTITUTE OF TECHNOLOGY

Fiz drops whispered bits of information in my ear to help me acclimate as we cross the threshold into a large auditorium. "We're in the Technion-Israel Institute of Technology. Everyone here just calls it the Technion, but I have always known it by a more personal moniker—*Mishkan*—translated, *The Tabernacle.*"

Only minutes ago, we had hung up with Brandon and our eccentric tour guide introduced himself to me as I exited the limousine with an engulfing hug and by simply stating his name, "Moses Folzman," That was apparently enough, for our football linebacker sized host then started walking at a brisk pace toward a set of doors into a long green hallway. Fiz and I followed without a word.

Folzman now continues leading us down the auditoriums' center aisle explaining current events as we progress rapidly toward the stage. "Your call caused quite a stir, Child. We have had to adjust many things in preparation for the meeting, but everything is coming together."

I'm about to explain that I didn't call him and then catch myself, wondering why this high energy bushy grey bearded bear of a man is addressing me in the same manner Fiz does. Then it hits me. I'm not the one he's addressing. Now I am in shock—*who would dare call Fiz, 'Child'?*

Incredibly, Fiz responds as if this is the norm. "We have just found out some other information that will also help confirm what you've been working on here, Moses. It is almost The Moment."

This statement stops Moses Folzman dead in his tracks—Fiz and I have to skid to a halt to avoid colliding with his massive body. He does not turn back to speak to us but looks up at the stage and before us and whispers, "…Almost The Moment. Prepare us, HaShem."

Now Moses spins himself around to face us. "I must make a presentation here in fifteen minutes to the faculty and student body. Sit and be prepared, I may call upon you for input." With that, he leaves us by the front row seats and rapidly exits out a side door.

"Fiz, can you please fill in a few more blanks for me here?"

"Sit, Child and learn."

THE PAST

This place had given birth to the scientist within Fitzgerald E. Hindeland. Founded in 1949, in the midst of the battle for the founding of Israel the nation, this location was chosen to create the infant nation's first nuclear fission reactor. Fiz's parents taught here and here he was nursed on applied astrophysics, quantum mechanics and…theology? Apparently, one cannot acquire scientific credibility in this corner of the world without a full immersion into Hebrew numerology and a complete investigation of Talmudic precepts. Enter Fiz's mentor, Ph.D., Atomic Physicist and

Rabbinical Studies Master, Moses Folzman - the only known modern day semicha (ordained) rabbi bestowed with two titles, *Mashgiach* (spiritual supervisor) and *HaGaon* (genius).

Reb. Folzman left the yeshiva to do battle with the scientific community. He did so in a very unorthodox manner by entering the prestigious Technion program and acquiring his Ph.D. within two years, then challenging the entire academic staff to an oral debate on the spirituality of physics. Two of the Technion professors asked to join on his side of the presentation and Reb. Folzman welcomed their support. They're names? Mama and Papa Hindeland.

The short version, shared with me by Fiz is that he, as a ten-year-old boy, sat in the gallery and watched Reb. Moses Folzman, along with his parents, soundly thrash the remaining staff. They compelled the others with incredible arguments connecting Biblical tenants to scientific principles in such a convincing way that the three were asked to oversee the expansion of the newly formed College of Astrophysics. Folzman and the Hindelands accepted and immediately began development of the world's first Sonic Black Hole which they successfully supervised to completion. In gratitude for the honor of working on his team, Mama and Papa H. offered a sacrifice at the altar of Reb. Folzman's department: Their son, Fitzgerald E., became the wunderkind understudy of this Subatomic Sage.

Convincing Fiz to follow in their footsteps proved no contest. As he explains it to me now, "When I saw the three of them humble an entire board of academic lords, I realized nothing human-made on this Earth is sacred. I was inspired to discover just what is holy in the universe and there before me stood the one man who could at least point the way."

From that day forward, Fitzgerald Hindeland served as the devoted protégé of the planet's only designated Physiotheologist, Rabbi Moses Folzman—known to most here by his pet name—The Crazy Prophet.

SOMEWHERE BETWEEN HERE AND THERE

Molecules—such giant, cumbersome things: If you listen, you can hear the resistance of their electrons as they clamor by. Why so loud? Without their orbits, the plan would be incomplete. But look more closely—at the spaces within the spaces. The invisible reveals the truth and it all sings—a chorus of one vibrant chord. So beautiful; but its song must be silent until all is ready to be revealed: Now it shall be a-ruk-ah…Finished.

NAVEH SHAANAN, ISRAEL— THE TECHNION-ISRAEL INSTITUTE OF TECHNOLOGY

"I have assembled you today to explain the reason for my recent absences and clandestine activities, but before doing so, I want you to welcome back, my esteemed disciple, Dr. Fitzgerald E. Hindeland and his disciple, Professor Daniel Adamson, whom you will recognize as the author of the incredible process of Evolutional Echo Tracing."

The auditorium of colleagues immediately comes to its feet in deafening applause and cheers. I cock my head toward Fiz with my best *deer in the headlights* look. He smiles, takes my arm, and stands pulling me up with him. We turn in tandem to face the multitude but I simply stare down at my feet. I'm wearing the same sneakers I've had on for the past four days—the same pair I was wearing when Misty slapped me a millennia ago. All of this is so not-right.

The applause runs for…ever and Moses Folzman finally raises his hand—he too has been clapping vigorously. At his signal, the entire room quiets, and seats itself. *The absolute power of individual awe and respect,* I think to myself.

"Centuries ago, in the city of Padua," Folzman begins, "a rather humble Italian mathematician and philosopher became more curious than most. Why this particular individual was inspired—how he came about the skills necessary to assemble the device he would use to prove his point—is more legend than reality. But little can be argued about how his astounding discoveries changed our ways of thinking—so profoundly in fact that all physics as they were understood, even the religious dogma of the time, had to be reexamined and adjusted. The world was ill prepared for Master Galilei. I speculate that Galileo himself did not anticipate the effect his reporting would have on society and his own life. But then, few of us are ever properly steeled to receive enlightenment."

"This is Reb. Folzman's *M.O.,*" Fiz had warned me when the Rabbi was walking up to the podium, "You are about to experience the consummate weaver of parables."

Reb. Folzman is still talking. "…If one digs a well to find water and instead discovers gold, does the digger not rejoice in his prosperity, then use his blessing to facilitate his original quest? Doctor Hindeland and Professor Adamson are here to remind us of that original purpose and, in fact, enable its culmination. Their research has uncovered disturbing evidence affecting the quantum and the subatomic universe in ways yet to be properly explained. The opportunity now exists to rethink our methods—to begin anew, and certainly quickly, to find answers to this mystery."

Before the whole planet falls to pieces and us with it, I think to myself. But the real question still remains. *Where has V4641 gone and how can this strange monk of a man, garbed in a prayer shawl and unshaven locks, help us find it?*

"Misty?"

"Hi Daddy!"

"Sylvia! Oh, I'm so glad you answered mommy's phone…how are you honey?"

"We're playing in grandma's back yard! I miss you daddy, when are you coming to see me? Can we come home?"

"So many…questions. Soon baby—very soon!"

"Okay, Jake wants to say hi daddy—I love you…"

"Sylvia?"

"Daddy! Grandma Adamson has tractors just like the ones at mommy's old farm, but they're little, not like the big real tractors!"

"Yes, she does. They used to be my tractors…"

"…She says they're mine now!"

"She's right! Are you taking care of Mommy?"

"I'm the man! Mommy says so, just like you told me too. I'm the man!"

"You <u>are</u> the man…Doc. I'm so proud of you."

"Mommy says hi, we've got to take baths now—yuk! I love you daddy, bye!"

"Jake? I love you too. Let me talk to Momm…"

CLICK.

To call it a dining room would be like calling a water closet a spa. It is more of a small study than anything. Perhaps 'miniature museum' would suffice as a descriptive if it weren't also for the holiness of the relics and placement of artifacts…as in a place of worship.

And then, there's the table—not just any table mind you—it's composed, it seems, from one piece of naturally smooth stone—altar like, the surfaces not having been worked or roughhewn by human hands; unfinished around the edges—that rests solidly on two smaller stones as its base. *How could such an immense object have been moved in here?* The whole room smells of ancient sand, causing me to sneeze repeatedly.

Fiz follows my gaze and leans over to quietly instruct, "The stone existed on this spot before our history was written. The room was built around it."

That really only invites more questions: Why was it fashioned, when? Was the table the reason for the room? Was the site for the Technion itself reasoned on this very object? Fiz offers no further explanations.

Sardined into this intimate vestibule are nine others beside me. We've been invited to this late-night dining experience for open dialogue with various world influencers who are apparently sitting with us. Besides Fiz and Moses Folzman, I've only been properly introduced to two of the others: One of them is Darius Mede, whom I met first during the web conference with our very own U.S. Commander-in-Chief, on the trip here. The other is Dr. Elizabeth Fielda, President of the Technion.

The remaining guests, I'm told by Dr. Fielda, are interested parties who are eager to contribute in any way to see our efforts come to a successful conclusion. She points out Dr. Ravi Kumar from The National Physical Laboratory of India in New Delhi and also Brenda Anders, from the Green Order Coalition. Dr Fielda does not bother to introduce me to the other three and I get the sense this is purposeful—possibly even a warning for me not to offend them by attempting to cross the barrier of familiar courtesy. It's a political cauldron we've been tossed into, the food being served is only for fattening the main course—us. The fire is just now being turned up and the stew will soon be boiling.

Dr Fielda clinks her wine glass with her knife to begin the festivities and invites everyone's attention toward Fiz. She requests, "Fitzgerald, will you please invite The Eternal to this feast?"

Fiz and prayer? I've never considered the two as complementary. I notice out of the corner of my eye, as I respectfully bow my head, that our Indian guest, Ms. Anders, and Chairman Mede seem visibly uncomfortable with the request. All others in the room have politely folded their hands and appear to be contemplating their respective navels as Fiz begins.

"…Almighty. We are nothing in your sight and yet You chose this place and these people, this land, and this bounty to bless. We are Your 'chosen', we honor and worship You as The One. Bless this meal and nourish us, strengthening our bodies for the service You require. It is so."

"Imagine God in this very room among us" chuckles a reedy voice at the opposite end of the table. "What manner of things might occur if that was a reality?" Darius Mede is now sipping his glass nonchalantly, head turned slightly to one of the 'unnamed' sitting on his right. He had made the comment subtly—with just enough volume to carry down the table length—yet not enough to appear as if intended for everyone to hear.

"Why imagine God?" Reb. Folzman, The Crazy Prophet, is not one to pass up a debatable moment. "Why not see Him? Recognize Him? Touch Him? Who would want to simply imagine the Creator of the universe?" He leans back in his seat, fingers of both hands touching at fingertips with both index fingers now pressed to his lips. His eyes are the key to his concentration though—they bore laser channels straight through the head of Mede.

"Oh, the argument of theology—how quaint," exclaims Darius, now invited by the query to speak. Let's see:

> Man wants to explain the universe so he conceives a superior being to make things acceptable no matter how strange the circumstances. The superior being then makes the strange circumstances acceptable—man complicates the acceptable by fighting with other men over the possibility of other superior beings equal or better than the first. Man creates stranger and stranger circumstances to see which superior being can out do the others. All men start fighting against all superior beings because they can't seem to make the strange circumstances acceptable according to man's expectations.

> The superior beings give up and disappear. Since they were man's invention in the first place, this is easy to do and no one tries to stop them."

"EXCUSE ME, I'm a vegan! I just can't comprehend why you people actually violate these poor creatures in this manner!" This is Brenda Anders and she obviously believes this pronouncement important enough for the whole table to hear and to interrupt Mede's logic lesson. The server, who has offered her a portion of lamb for her plate, sheepishly retreats with an apology.

"Forgive my impertinence, Dr. Fielda," Mede offers graciously with a smirk on his lips. "Of course I realize the significance of a god to you and yours—I mean no disrespect—but can't you see? By inviting him in—even though there is no evidence he has arrived—it immediately demands the respect and attention of all in the room, as if some magical potion was just released and, unless we all believe in the spectacle of it all, your deity will wreak havoc. I believe it is man's choice to let chaos reign, not by dictation from some third party."

Moses Folzman reenters the ring. He has slowly cut a thick piece of mutton during the ensuing dialogue and, arm bent with elbow on the table before him, holds the lamb laden utensil in his left hand as a baton to emphasize his words. "Mr. Mede and Ms. Anders, how tragic that we offend your sensibilities, but that is the truth of it, isn't it? I offend you and I should not speak my heart out loud or practice my dietary customs in your presence. What an effective way to silence the opposition! I would ask a question of you, though hopefully it won't also offend you."

Mede nods his head curtly allowing permission; Anders attempts to assassinate Folzman with her eyes.

"If you are offended at the idea of having to consider the existence of God, do you think God might also be offended at the idea of having to consider that He doesn't exist? What consequences might there be if you are wrong and it is we who are the created?"

Someone's fork pings against their plate. No other sound is evident.

"I can see that I am surrounded by friendly banter and intriguing concepts in this group," Mede finally acknowledges with a guarded grin.

The Rabbi smiles right back. Then, instead of continuing with Mede, gives a glance to each person seated—asking no one and everyone, "By the way, have you ever met God person to person? Of course not—few have and lived to tell."

I was preoccupied with cutting my own lamb when the Rabbi began his homily, but his words now begin to penetrate…*too confidential…too familiar.* I look up and realize the entire focus of interest has changed. I sense the room of eyes—every pair of them—focused on the same object as Reb. Folzman's. His piercing gaze is aimed exclusively…at me, plunging into the depths of my soul, his words and his intent now demanding my attention.

"Yet I know who God is. How can this be? He is after all, so distant from us—separated by our imperfection and unwillingness to love Him." The words of the Rabbi are thieves in the night, stealing concepts and thoughts from my past and somehow rearranging them to my discomfort. "I'm intimately familiar with El Shaddai because He has already sacrificed dearly on my behalf, having paid a heavy price, and yes, a book has been written about it."

Folzman's patient exploration of my inner condition continues. "By all the measurements and clues that nature and reasoning provide, little if any science is necessary to figure out The Eternal exists—most any child can do it if they are just pointed in the right direction."

I've forgotten my lamb.

The strange dinner dialogue ends awkwardly with Dr. Fielda responding to some secret cue from Fiz or Reb. Folzman or maybe Jehovah himself, I don't know. She announces abruptly that on such a lovely evening it is time to move to the porch for dessert and star gazing.

I mechanically push my chair back to exit until I realize that three people are still staring at me with deliberate interest. Fiz, Reb. Folzman and Mede show no signs of receding and a sideways shake of Fiz's head tells me I'm also to stay anchored in this place. Then Folzman, suddenly not seeming crazy at all, turns to Mede and inquires casually as he takes a sip of wine, "So what's your visit here really about Darius?"

Darius Mede puts his hand to his chest and manages to portray an almost infant-like innocence. "Am I not allowed to visit old friends and seek their counsel?"

"We haven't claimed friendship for a very long time."

"To your question then," Mede concedes. "There are other motives in my being here. I hope to convince you they will result in astounding rewards for yours and my interests. Please dismiss your pupil so we can discuss this in more detail." I feel suddenly as one who discovers he has not—as previously thought—advanced past diapers.

"He stays. And he will have access going forward in any discussion or information." Fiz states, not to be denied.

"Important is he?" Mede lets the silence hang for a good thirty seconds before again speaking. "Very well, but before I tell you what I have and what I want, tell me more about this…principle of yours Mr. Adamson. It seems rather simplistic—is there actually a tracing method or formula to substantiate your assertions?"

What was it that Fiz encouraged when someone feels convicted? 'Dwell in the moment'. Okay, this is me 'dwelling'—I'm about to bust open Mr. Mede's head with a little…make that a <u>big</u> physics controversy. "There is a segment in the E.E.T. formula that reexamines Einstein's Theory of Relativity, setting aside the space-time curvature theory part, while keeping the very provable principle of mass linked to energy."

"Set aside? You suggest that you have a better explanation than the Master of Science?" Mede squints his eyes suspiciously. "So how would you connect the two—time and space?"

Oh boy, here we go…I jump into the fire with my own hot question, "Who says they are connected? For that matter, who first came up with the notion that time is a physical element rather than a mental convenience used to explain motion? Time is a theory rather than reality, why try to explain it at all?

Mede pulls himself to his full height—I'd say about 6'2"—and glares down at me. "Don't patronize me with cleverly couched postulations. Tell me how you came up with your idea of Evolutional Echo Tracing and don't worry about throwing out heady terminology—I'll be able to keep up with you."

I don't doubt him a bit. The guy might be obnoxious and arrogant, but he certainly knows his stuff, so I get to the bottom line. "In tracking neutrino signatures, a curious effect shows up. The actual particles show up in multiples, but when inspected more closely, it turns out there is just one particle observed at different points."

"Points of time—is that the echo effect?" Mede presses me.

"Not exactly: Although the particles are obviously in motion, there is not a time sequence associated with the motion. The echo is motion related, but instantaneous and…timeless."

"I'm sorry, I don't understand. I thought that time is motion?" I bet Mede understands perfectly and is goading me.

"Einstein himself struggled with the same question," I respond. "He had a conflict to deal with—space is finite, time is infinite—and he had to somehow make the two compatible.

"The problem is complicated when trying to justify four or more dimensions where curves may run in opposing directions. Kind of like when two people who are absolutely compatible live together in total harmony for a period, then start to have affairs with other people. Where'd the love go?"

Fiz is smiling and the Rabbi raises an eyebrow at this last analogy, but Darius Mede is not in the least bit amused. "You have yet to convince me that I should support you in any way."

"Actually, the support we need comes from other sources." I shoot back. "In order to figure out the reason for the strange behavior of V4641 and determine why the planet is acting so strangely, what I'll…what we'll need, is access to data that is protected as sacred by the institutions that hold them. Also, as new geophysical or astronomical activities occur, we'll need to travel to sites quickly to observe and measure."

"Observe and measure? So, you're not trying to save the planet from utter destruction?" Mede says this with such utter sarcasm that I wonder if he believes any attempt to alter physical conditions is worthwhile. Now he turns to Fiz, whom I now suspect he's been indirectly addressing the whole time and speaks in that special tone politicians save for a speech in which they imply money and influence ready to be shared…if only the constituency will vote for them. "Because of my affiliations and the resources available to me, I have been an active contributor of the NASA project you know as Hubble and a number of others—to the point that their funding has primarily come from me. I even have a bit of pull as to whether or not certain discoveries and data are disseminated out of their revered halls."

Now I get it. This man holds the keys to the treasury.

"The devil deals. I'm not comforted or flattered," says Folzman. "Why would we want to partner with you?"

"The question is—why would you not? Mede leans back in his chair and explains. "I ask for nothing in return. All I require is immediate and unrestricted access to the information that is already mine to have anyway. You would simply provide the convenient…assemblers of the puzzle to which I hold the many pieces."

The Rabbi has made it back to his chair and that appears to be Fiz's cue to stand. He does not move from his place but examines everyone seated and then speaks deliberately. "Strange bedfellows indeed—perhaps there is a way to make sure all benefit here." Now he looks directly at Mede. "We'll provide you with our results if there are no questions asked about our needs up front. What we ask for is what we get—no approval process, no inquiries, just a blank check."

Mede smiles coyly. "Gentleman, I believe we are strangely in agreement."

Entry Eight

NAVEH SHAANAN, ISRAEL – THE TECHNION-ISRAEL INSTITUTE OF TECHNOLOGY

There are four people now gathered around the screen on our side of the world: Me, Fiz, Moses Folzman and Darius Mede. Fortunately, Brandon Lader the Super Researcher, hasn't stopped at just pointing out conflicting data and he has worked up some new ideas of his own.

"Danny, I apologize—hope this doesn't hurt your feelings, but E.E.T. is not the answer in and of itself. We've been so obsessed with trying to figure out the trajectory of V4641 by looking backwards at where it was and where it's hiding currently, that we've neglected one crucial aspect. Why not figure out to where it's heading?"

"Hold on. How would you be able to do that?" Mede asks this accusingly while shaking his head, implying he believes this ability not possible for simple folk such as us.

"Do you know that it was Galileo who suggested there were harmonics in space and that we should be able to hear their music? It was actually his father, Vincenzo's idea—of course you know he was a renowned music scholar." Moses Folzman is in story mode and we've learned to listen. "It was this speculation that led eventually to the first radio telescopes. The universe sings, we just have to tune in to the right frequency."

"…Right!" Brandon is excited that someone else actually understands the way his brain works. "So, I tuned in to some of the radio telescope data for Alpha Centauri, Barnard's Star and Wolf 359—the three closest star systems to us. Then I went back in the records to see if there had been any significant frequency changes in them and also on Sol, our sun. Amazingly, all the systems registered changes. All the variances occurred at the same exact time, back in September of 1999."

"The time when V4641 acted up," Fiz asks?

"The same," his Quartermaster proudly announces. "So, I compared those readings to current frequency outputs and there is a source, right here on Earth, that is producing those same frequency readings right now. All we have to do is go to that source and use it as a kind of reverse transmitter to signal back to V4641. My guess is that the source here will help tell us exactly where V4641 is, where it's headed and possibly when it will arrive."

Now I'm intrigued. "And where is it that we need to go to tap into this transmitter?"

MAMMOTH CAVE, KENTUCKY

Three hundred, forty-seven feet below the Earth's surface, Brandon and I have descended into a well-known attraction and treasure trove of geologic wonder. It's a chamber, scientifically designated as Station D6 of the New Entrance, bearing 084.5 x 264.0. Tourists know it as the *Frozen Niagara* formation located in the extreme southeast region within Mammoth Cave. Actually, we have climbed below the unique feature named for its resemblance to the famous waterfalls and are at the lowest geophysical point in the caverns—at least the lowest point where we can port the equipment we've sequestered for this adventure.

It's fairly well-lit here thanks to the engineering prowess of the National Park Service who provided electrical power and egress via a metal stairway connecting the upper levels to our present residence.

My companion and stalwart Quartermaster for this project, is desperately trying to figure out if the gadgets he has assembled in this chamber are up to the task of answering our questions. While I'm waiting for him to flip switches and adjust amplitudes, let me expand the picture a bit.

I had flown from Tel Aviv to Louisville, Kentucky by way of a special supersonic transport provided at the courtesy of the Israeli government. At Louisville, Brandon, met me with a HUMVEE, kindly provided by Uncle Sam, and we drove the remaining ninety-four miles to a special *Employees Only* entrance for Mammoth Cave. Here we have unloaded over 400 pounds of equipment that Brandon managed to cram into the back end of the HUMVEE and have hand carted it down into the belly of the caverns to our present location.

With relatively low humidity, these caverns are the ideal location for us to be camped. The Mammoth Cave System is just as the name suggests—it's the granddaddy of underground canal interchanges and if untangled, would represent a string well over 369 miles long—more than ten times the capacity of any other dry cave system.

In our case, the important factor is resonance, not depth. We need to listen to Mother Nature…the old-fashioned way; through its song sung as vibration through rock. Another way of looking at it would be to think of setting up an antenna to receive a signal. Stretching a wire straight up and down between two points is just not as effective as taking the same wire and crisscrossing it multiple times in different directions.

"Rainstorm approaching," Brandon says to the uncaring apparatus before him. This would ordinarily be of no concern, Mammoth being a dry cave system with very little moisture leakage from the outside world. However, Brandon's research indicates that this particular region of the Earth's crust may be in the early stages of expanding outward as a result of internal pressures related to Harmonic Resonance. Because of this *skin stretching* trick—we're concerned that fissures have developed which will let <u>outside</u> things—like rain—<u>in</u>.

"Tarps—I need more tarps," Brandon commands to the ceiling of the cavern. Quartermaster will not be satisfied until the entire cave system is vacuum sealed. He disappears into the vaguely lit recesses of the cavern. I can only follow his movements by visually tracking the bobbing, weaving motions of his flashlight interrogating the cracks in the walls and upper dome.

Then I hear him mumble, "What in the…?"

I also hear the noise that has caught my partner's attention. Hardly a noise at all, it's more of a subtle…rustle, like fall leaves dancing with the wind on a hard surface. The metaphor is romantically soothing, but the increasing tenor of this eerie intrusion prickles my senses in a bad way. I'm thinking the approaching weather has unsettled the creatures that worship in this subterranean sanctuary.

"Cave crickets," Brandon shutters.

This will be our greatest challenge, not because they pose any threat to our instruments, but because—more than any other creatures of the galaxy—Brandon is most innately terrified of crickets. It's a childhood thing—those details unimportant at the moment—the resulting transformation of behavior in Brandon is what I have to deal with. He is reverted to near infancy—'fetaling' into a half squat, half tuck—trembling with arms wrapped and securely clasped together around his knees. His head darts from ceiling to wall, back to ceiling, then to floor—he is a captive, turned to inert jelly by unresolved fear…

…We've done this before: The first time on a camping trip in Mexico as part of a geological survey for fourth year student credit. That time also involved a midnight downpour, well, more of a raging thunderstorm. Then there was also no place to escape to—it was either survival in the tent or drowning in the deluge. The critters knew this too and it was the enterprising crickets that discovered the small hole in the tent fabric. First one, then another, then they radioed out to their counterparts preparing for a full force invasion. We didn't detect them at first. A near strike of lightning woke us both from our deep slumber and another flash outside lit our shelter just enough to suggest that we were not alone. Brandon informed me of our guests' presence by means of a very feminine scream.

I shone a flashlight on him and illuminated the same body posture and response then that I now see of my friend. I figured at that time, everything would be OK once I rid our tent of the infestation, so I had first searched out the trusty duct tape and mended the tear in the tent. Then I proceeded to capture the vermin in a zip lock bag, hiding my captives from Brandon's sight as best as possible in the limited space.

Once all the other occupants were detained, I tried to bring Brandon back to a state of reality. Nothing worked—snapping fingers in his face, shouting his name, explaining, and assuring him that the terrorists were gone—even a healthy slap on the right cheek failed to revive my pal. After twenty minutes, I had worried the hysteric coma might be permanent so I improvised.

I grasped the baggy of agitated crickets, cracked the seal, and carefully reached in with thumb and index finger to extract one specimen. This in itself had been no small task as, I too, dislike insects. My friend was at risk though and desperate times demanded me to hold the squirming insect directly in front of Brandon's glazed stare, shout his name while simultaneously pinching the creature with enough force to cause it to explode—guts flying over both of us.

Whether it was either witnessing the execution of his foe before his eyes or the shock factor of cricket crud splattered across his face, Brandon responded, blinking once. Then, by the light of another nearby lightning strike, I saw panic again starting to build in his facial expressions as he glanced at the baggie full of crawling culprits. I quickly took the bag, unzipped the tent flap, and tossed it out into the torrent. Before I could properly reseal the opening, our tent floor was flooded from the rising water. My tent buddy seemed oblivious to the pond in which he was sitting and I didn't mention to my recovering sidekick, the entrails decorating his body. Nor did he ask, instead collapsing for the rest of the night into an exhausted heap onto his very soggy sleeping bag.

...That was then—this is...different. Mexican camel crickets are known for their aggressiveness and formidable size, but they are mere pests when compared to their North American cave counterparts. These bruisers have a body length of three to four inches matched to legs approximately six inches in length when fully stretched. Picture thousands of these curious nibblers scavenging about, probing with waving antennae and articulating mandibles in the darkness—creating not only the strange noise that originally drew our attention, but also a wave illusion on all surrounding surfaces. Their coloration is exactly that of the limestone—the chamber now appears fluid and breathing...seeming on all sides to be moving, approaching...approaching what? Us.

BALTIMORE, MARYLAND – GREEN ORDER COALITION HEADQUARTERS

I'd like to be just about anywhere else, other than Mammoth Cave at this moment. Anywhere else would even include the offices of the Green Order Coalition where many more lights exist than do in these caverns. They burn brightly to help with the late-night special project mandated by Brenda Anders, founder, and president of T.G.O.C. We've met her once before. She's the high maintenance drama vegan who attended the Technion dinner at the invitation of Darius Mede. By some strange new skill set—acquired after my spiritual cell phone encounter—I find myself able to observe the goings on at T.G.O.C. without leaving the confines of my not so comfy cave home.

It seems Brenda is concerned—extremely concerned—as she is seeing a pattern develop. Brenda is not a data analyst and by no means a statistician—she's hired others for such menial tasks. But she does care deeply for her planet and its inhabitants—all of them from the smallest microbe to the largest whale—and recently she had read reports from her statisticians, data analysts and, most importantly, from several key monetary contributors, that suggest there is a downward trend of support for environmental activism. People are frustrated with the conflicting information bantering about. Is the planet cooling or is it warming? Is there less ice in the Polar Regions or is one section of ice replacing another by some strange natural method of balance? Her sources are now suggesting there are a growing number of people resisting the idea that carbon dioxide is a pollutant which must be controlled. One group even cites evidence that global plant-life is flourishing due to increased carbon dioxide emissions. Hogwash!

It is and always will be Brenda's duty to help the public become more aware of humankind's effect on the ecosystems of Earth. Community awareness had become her mission in college when finally, she accepted the reality of what high school and college had taught her –she was not the dating or sorority type. Then she discovered her gift for instigating change and fighting for causes she believed in. At six foot five and 186 pounds of lean but healthy disciplined muscle, Brenda was an imposing figure and she learned quickly that few men would stand toe to toe with her in a confrontational discussion. All she had to do was stand up, stretching to her full height and begin walking purposefully, straight toward her adversary as she talked. It seemed the closer she got, the less willing they were to push their points. It also helped that her voice was somewhat high pitched, enabling her to easily out yell any other argument. Brenda didn't need to be exact on her facts—she just needed to have lots of information that favored her position at her disposal. She would expose her points one after the other, in well memorized fashion until those who disagreed grew weary and acquiesced.

On this set of skills, Brenda Anders has built one of the largest and most influential environmental groups in the world and is now imposing her will on not only industry and public concerns, but also on government entities. There was no accident in the naming of her brainchild—Brenda is interested in the brass ring. She wants influence over every aspect of corporate and civic interests—this is her planet and she intends to keep it that way.

That's why, when her resources suggested that something needed to be done to reenergize public interest in climate change, she kicked into high confrontational gear. Calling all her minions together, this maven of ecological causes explains the situation in her usual style.

"There are those out there that would suggest humankind is not the party responsible for the climate crisis we are now facing. What's more, they are promoting the idea that we are simply experiencing climate cycles. They have tried this tactic before and failed. They are wrong this time too and we will prove them so."

With that being said, Brenda now requires the entire staff of her empire to put aside all personal business and plan to live at T.G.O.C. headquarters for the duration of the weekend. This isn't an inconvenience to most because Brenda possesses another gift—she attracts and hires the lost souls of the world. A typical psychological profile of one of her subordinates might include words such as 'atypical' or 'has difficulty relating in social settings'. Brenda herself is married to her Cause and she expects her Cause to come first with anyone she hires, so she carefully selects and nurtures odd personalities that fit quite nicely into the puzzle that is T.G.O.C.

That's why the lights are now burning brightly at T.G.O.C. headquarters, but it does not explain why Brenda's temper is solar flaring. "What do you mean it's improving? Do you realize how ridiculous that sounds?"

Brenda's team of environmentalists cringes before her as she explodes. Preferring to stage her meetings whereby she stands and others sit—better to be able to watch and impress others from a higher altitude—she is doing so now as the senior man explains to her that carbon levels worldwide appear to have been decreasing at a noticeable rate over the last five years. Brenda is concerned.

"Your findings are wrong," she determines. We all know that the increased impact of humans' presence on this planet is being profoundly felt. Increased carbon emissions are a fact—recheck your information." The messenger, being shot directly in the ego, quietly nods, and says nothing more.

"Well let's move on. What is this report on the expanding of the Earth's crust in some locations?" The report is on the podium next to her, but Brenda wants the details translated rather than having to digest and spit out the scientific jargon herself.

Another researcher gathers courage and explains the information that was now flooding the World Wide Web concerning a recent meeting of scientists. Measurements of the planet's crust suggest that something may be causing sections of the world's skin to bulge out seemingly in every direction. The brave soul who has spoken up emphasizes that the evidence is speculative at best, but it's too late—Brenda's interest is peaked. A faint connection is made in her memory relating this activity to the recent meeting and conversations she participated in at the Technion. "What are the possibilities of damage?"

She smiles as the predictions are read to her. When the word 'dire' is mentioned, it causes her to nod her head and clap her hands. "That's perfect. We'll use <u>that</u>!" All others in the room look back and forth at one another, puzzled as to what <u>that</u> is and exactly what they are going to use *that* for? Brenda senses the confusion and elaborates.

"Don't you get it? The pressure on the Earth's crust is measurable and condemning. Nothing other than our negligent misuse of natural resources can be responsible for such unusual global phenomena. I bet that the expanding crust areas are in highly populated areas and in locations where oil exploration is uncontrolled—they would have to be—it has to be because of our industrial abuse of the planet!"

Brenda's team is not sure how she knows that this has never happened before, but they do know that, once she has come to a conclusion, additional discussion is unnecessary. Without dismissing the meeting, the president of T.G.O.C. walks quickly and purposefully out a side door. Glances are exchanged, papers are shuffled and silently everyone heads back to their respective cubicles. When the last two women researchers leave, they turn out the lights of the room, close the door and head down the hallway. One looks at the other, shaking her head and says, "That was different."

MAMMOTH CAVE, KENTUCKY

"...Different, but the same," I hear myself saying to no one. Brandon sure isn't listening—he remains in a trance. I push away my own panic and walk to an undulating crevice, delicately reaching out and nabbing a beast. This one's a female. I know because an entomologist once described to me the extra appendage. It looks like a six-inch stinger—inherent to this species.

"Don't worry," he had assured me. "It's harmless really—they use it to deposit their eggs in small crevices."

I'm not sure my entomologist friend had ever grabbed a female cricket in the wild before. I'm discovering now, another use for the non-stinger as this nasty little girl uses it to whip and slash my exposed palm while additionally spewing eggs in an abortive attempt to distress her enemy into releasing his grip. Very effective—I drop her immediately—regain my composure and reach rapidly for another. Unfortunately, my next prey is also a female—unfortunate for her too because, this time, I hang on despite the abuse rendered to my hand.

Mrs. Cricket is not ready to give up. I hear what sounds like the clicker of a ballpoint pen being repeatedly depressed. I visually examine my captive and am treated to the sight of massive mandibles attempting to grab the foreskin bridging my index finger and thumb—fortunately, the target is just out of reach.

"Brandon," I shout and reenact my big-tent bug squashing performance of years past—the carnage this time, much more extreme—the impact on Brandon however isn't anywhere near as effective. One of the creatures has the nerve to boldly hop onto my friend's face and do an antenna sweep of his nose before catapulting to some other interest. Brandon remains inattentive. Now I reach deeper into my resolve. "Something more," I think out loud in a frighteningly grizzled voice—its echo haunting me from all directions. I clutch yet one more encroaching cricket—another female, there are no men to be found here! *Good grief, how do these things reproduce?* This time I pay no attention to the animal's defensive attempts.

"Brandon!" I scream his name this time and do something even I don't comprehend, thrusting the wriggling insect body into my mouth, immediately biting down. I'm not sure if the intestinal expulsion of Mrs. Cricket number III does the trick; for at that same moment a fountain of water floods down from the roof choosing our exact location to shower. Then again, Brandon may have been revived by my overt act of vomiting a blended mix of bug innards and the hamburger I ate three hours ago directly into his face. Regardless of which cure worked, he comes to and, thankfully, the creepy cave dwellers find the rushing torrent inhospitable.

They retreat a safe distance away allowing me the opportunity to reach out to the strong soul of my colleague.

"Brandon, listen," I bellow over the wash of our cavern baptism. "I can't begin to do this alone, there's ugly stuff out there—no, don't look out there, focus on me—I need you. Kill the fear—don't let it take you. Kill it and win!"

I've found a mantra and keep repeating the phrase. Every time he tries to look beyond me into the darkness I pull his eyes back to mine with my insistent voice, "Brandon, kill it and win." Now I nod my head up and down in concord with the words and slowly his head begins to nod as well. Distantly at first, his pupils seem to center on my lips and his mouth starts to mimic mine. "Kill it and win."

All I can do is to continue my chant. Brandon's voice becomes louder, gradually more confident, "Kill it and win." Suddenly he stands up in the rush—water purifying his resolve. I stand to face him, both of us safe in the protection of the turbulent froth. He finally speaks in his own words, with his own voice.

"I'm good—it's done." That's it, simple as that. Brandon now looks out beyond me one more time at the vanquished legions, shaking his head back and forth with a disbelieving smirk on his face. "Cave crickets," he chuckles as if to say, "I was afraid of those?"

On the other hand, I need to throw up again.

BALTIMORE, MARYLAND – GREEN ORDER COALITION HEADQUARTERS

I take a temporary mental leave of our underground adventure to drop in again on the Green Order Coalition offices…

"…I want a full media attack on military and industrial research having to do with seismic stuff." Brenda Anders's folks again exchange glances because seismic stuff covers a lot of territory. Thankfully, she explains. "…Any deep weapons testing, sonic experiments on the Earth's crust and most of all, I want to call for a complete halt to all oil and gas exploration and drilling."

The whisper of air coming through the HVAC ducts in the room now sounds like a roar. Brenda allows the silence to underscore her dramatic plan for a moment longer, then moves on.

"I want the Governmental Relations Department to call our contacts immediately within all government offices—I don't care what time it is—this is a crisis and they need to know it's a crisis. Call them on their cell and home numbers, don't leave this to an email blitz, make it urgent. Research—go find everything you can over the last ten years on seismic activity whether it seems to be related or not. Public Relations, work with Research on this and whatever they find, make it relate."

The room is filled with the clicking of laptop keyboards and the scribbling of styluses on computer tablets. The sound is a majestic concert to Brenda, but the music must be broadcast to be effective.

"Before any of you do anything on this though, I want each of you to compile a list of at least five family members and or friends. Contact these people with this message:"

> "I don't want to worry you, but I just found out through a very reliable source, that there is a global crisis being covered up by governments and industries. if not corrected immediately, this will destroy life on the planet within one to five years' time. Please keep this information to yourself, but I'm telling you so you can start putting your affairs in order."

"Get to work now. We've got a world to change!" The room empties in a flood of escaping people. Brenda smiles and speed dials a number on her cell phone that connects her immediately to the one person on the planet to whom she would willingly give her soul. His voice, answering on the other end of the line, excites her in ways she dares not confess.

"Darius Mede."

MAMMOTH CAVE, KENTUCKY

Brandon and I are busy too. Fortunately, the water pouring down from above is localized to one crack that has opened up. We've made sure the equipment is out of harm's way and functioning properly. Now the only thing left to do is to initiate the signal.

What signal? When Brandon discovered that the planet's core rotation was resonating in sync with that of the crust, he also noticed something discrete. No one else studying the information (including me) had picked up on the fact that the resonating signals were not only consistent; they also paused in consistent cycles.

"What I mean to say is," Brandon tried to explain to me at an earlier point, "there seems to be a well-timed lag and it suggests something unthinkable. The consistency of the resonance indicates that the delay seems planned."

"Planned?" I was slow on the uptake.

Brandon patiently elaborated that the findings suggested someone 'out there' was sending a signal and is waiting for a response. I had seen this in a favorite sci-fi TV episode once and said as much to Brandon. This was not good science.

So tonight, along with all the other data we're hoping to collect, we are also going to run a tiny experiment. Based on our seismic studies, we think we have calculated that the resonance period is missing a sequence—kind of like one of those stupid test questions from school where they ask, "For the following numerical sequence, predict the next logical number that should follow in succession: 1, 2, 4, 16, 256, _______."

We think we've found the equivalent of 65,536—the next number in the sequence—creating a pattern we can use to…speak back to V4641. If our pattern is close enough to the radio frequency we were hearing from V4641 before it vanished, then we'll simply…answer.

Brandon has rigged a seismic resonance projector on-site to emit what we think is the missing sequence in the signal. We'll literally be using the tunnels of the cave system as a broadcasting antenna. If we're not crazy, then the vibrations we generate will create a harmonic signal in the Earth's crust like the one we've been receiving in different forms over the past few weeks. And if our little exercise bears no results—no harm done; the real value is in all the other information we'll be collecting.

Brandon nods to me that he's ready, so I start watching the readings on my laptop. We also have speakers hooked up in the chamber to translate the resonance into something audible—there's nothing like some good Earth vibration music to soothe the soul. He tells me to press the "activate" key on the computer and when I do, the strangest thing happens…

…What we are yet to discover is that the strangest things are happening everywhere: An electromagnetic spike shuts down the Hubble Hive and the computers at MIT; earthquakes at Naveh Shaanan and other parts of the Middle East, collapses structures including the stone table at which I recently sat; torrential rain and devastating floods begin to ravage typically arid New Mexico and West Texas; hail twice the size of softballs cover the Dakotas; and a freak meteor shower boasting boulder sized projectiles randomly crashes through homes and buildings throughout Europe and Asia. Across cities, towns, countries, and continents—multiple tsunamis, animal stampedes become the norm of the moment.

…But right here beneath the Frozen Niagara in Mammoth Cave—the strangest thing of all—the crickets have lined up. No, that's not a very accurate description—the crickets are gathered into thousands of patterns, shapes, and formations. Some are geometric, some hieroglyphic, there's even one that looks like a…man's face? All are perfectly aligned and now Brandon—being the quick reactor—is snapping pictures of our private cricket art show.

There is a throbbing sound emitting from the speakers and various background sounds behind it when the inbound V4641 signal appears to be speaking; when the outbound signal cycles, Mrs. Cricket and all her girlfriends start vibrating their *egg-whips* on the limestone. Look at that—there are male crickets! They distinguish themselves now by standing at attention in their appointed places—smart guys.

Strange—The cricket forms…and the structures within the cavern appear to be…blurring? If I didn't know better, I'd say they look as if they are losing their shape. I'm also having trouble determining where rock begins and equipment ends. Brandon holds his hand and arm up to a light and I can see right thought the flesh. For that matter, I'm beginning to see right through all of Brandon and then I look at my own hand and it appears to be disappearing.

"SHUT IT DOWN!" I hear Brandon yell over the increasing amplitude and I find myself torn, almost unwilling—I'm fascinated by what's happening; to the point of being strangely compelled not to stop our signal. Then again by the looks of it, I won't be here long to appreciate the show if I don't flip the switch off fast. So, I do.

Turning off the signal sequencing equipment has stopped nothing. Well things do become clearer—My fingers are no longer translucent—but the whole place continues to vibrate and vibrating caves are simply bad places with which to be associated. The first rock from the ceiling hits the floor—a pea sized stone really. The White Niagara is swaying—that can't be good. Not good, especially because our bodies and two million dollars of equipment are positioned directly beneath the structure.

"Brandon," I yell above the increasing din. "Have you uploaded?" He nods, understanding my concern and holds up his laptop to indicate that he has disconnected from the system after transmitting the data to the U.T. Austin computers. And now his presence is obscured by raining debris. The ceiling above is becoming a limestone downpour. I have little choice but to run up the stairway housed in the metal gantry connecting our base camp to the main cavern level. The alternative is drowning by rock in a White Niagara deluge.

The mineral-hailstorm hitting the stairway is deafening. I'm waiting for something bigger than a grape-size nugget to smash my skull, rendering me unconscious—the sting of the attacking rocks causes me to wish for a quick ending.

Somehow I reach the top of the stairway and dive underneath an overhanging ledge that is the only umbrella available against the onslaught. I hold no hope that the covering won't also collapse. Something soft and bulky lands next to me and I prepare to be crushed until I hear it speak.

"Crap!" The soft and bulky thing shouts. Brandon has followed me under my questionably protective awning and now there's a second rumbling that seems to be growing out of the first. I look over to see the White Niagara, the stairway and directly across the cavern from us, the only known exit from our cascading tomb, all disappear in a total collapse of mammoth-sized boulders.

And a strange, confusing observation comes to me in that moment when the light disappears—one that wouldn't have occurred to me five minutes ago. We are alive.

ROCHESTER, NEW YORK – THE CHESTER F. CARLSON CENTER FOR IMAGING SCIENCE AT THE ROCHESTER INSTITUTE OF TECHNOLOGY

At the Hubble Hive, Spencer L. Lynd, Ph.D., and his cohorts are desperately trying to reboot. Their entire system of computers and equipment had simply shut down when the Electromagnetic Pulse hit them. Even the emergency lights and backup systems have become inert. Then, as suddenly as it had all started, the lights come back on.

One by one, the hard drives whir back to life and monitors start displaying cryptic operating system code indicating that the circuit brains of the units are checking and cross-checking themselves for damage and errors. One particular component piques Spencer's interest. The Trinity are back online and he is thankful. But the images that his three screens now display are beyond even his brilliant mind. Before him are three live images of 'Sol plus One-C', the section of our galaxy immediately adjacent to our Solar System, a scant 2.14 parsecs away from our planet in the direction of the Magellanic Gas Clouds. And there in plain sight, for anyone interested to see, is the radio telescope image of V4641.

Entry Nine

"To tame the untamable was the first ambition of humankind."

—*Reb. Moses Folzman, Ph.D.*
Mammoth Cave, Kentucky

"Now what?" Brandon asks the darkness. His question inspires me to feel with my hands—the only available method for a personal body check. I can't seem to find any missing parts and there are no large amounts of liquid oozing from anywhere. Assured that I'm not going to die in the immediate future, I begin to grope further away for the one item I had held in my left hand when I had started my rapid ascent. My finger locates something not stony in texture and I trace its outline until I feel...there it is—thanks be to the inventor of the flashlight.

After a period of radical physical change, you still remember the historical landscape a certain way. There was a slanted path here, a crevice there, a well-kept image in my memory—and then with the simple flip of a flashlight switch, a totally new vista surprises me. My recollection is disappointed. The path is now more of a smoldering rock mound thirty feet high. The crevice—who knows where that went?

The light suggests more unknown than known, less opportunity than obstacle, piles of limestone and traps of twisted metal in a place of continuously moaning, shifting structure. Newly formed canyons wander into smoky nothingness, fogged and impossible to determine where they lead or how deep their peril. Our life jacket in this sea of uncertainty is the six-volt lantern held tentatively in my badly bruised hand.

"Turn it off for now," Quartermaster Brandon orders, vocalizing my thoughts. "We'll need that to get out of here once we figure which way is out."

Fear starts to creep up on me in the darkness. "That's the question isn't it?" I'm not able to hold that comment in and I know the panic is evident in my voice—I can hear its tremble. "Is there a way out?"

Brandon is far more cool under the circumstances than I. "Oh there's a way. The question is just how we'll find it before the lantern battery drains?"

Another pebble assaults my forehead and I'm ready to launch into a high-powered *rant*, but something else first begs attention. A familiar sound—clicking?

"The crickets," Brandon reminds me. "Turn on the light a sec."

Effectively distracted from escalating my panic attack, I do as I'm told and sweep the beam toward where I think the noise is emanating. There they are—all proceeding, most definitely in one direction. As I remember it from the old cavern picture in my mind, they appear to be migrating east.

"Follow them!" Brandon commands, getting to his feet, grabbing the light out of my hand, and moving after the retreating insects—I have little choice but to rise up and join in.

It has seemed more like days, these past six hours. Brandon and I haven't talked much on our trek, trying to conserve energy. My only awareness that he's still following me are the occasional grunts and clacking of rocks pushed aside that I hear behind me as we slowly probe into the unfamiliar recesses of Mammoth Cave. He had given me back the flashlight once I had started moving with him out of the main cavern, following our cootie escort.

The earthquake has altered most everything. In many places the strewn debris has made access to exit ways impossible. In other cases, new corridors with questionable stability and destination present themselves. We cough and wheeze our way toward a hopeful escape—the air quality down here being less than stellar. *Still, we are breathing*, I rationalize to myself thankfully.

Too much of my time has been spent either in a crouched position on all fours or sliding painfully on my back into a sandwich of rock face, not knowing if I'm just squeezing my body deeper into a wedge going nowhere.

So far, mercifully, our six-legged guides have led us through the gauntlets into ample chambers to negotiate.

The crickets are definitely on a quest—there's purpose in their journey—not one of them seeming to veer from whatever unseen trail of breadcrumbs they pursue. I've been trying to discern a sensation of progress upwards toward the Earth's surface. But after hours of climbing, crawling, and tumbling through the quake zones, for all I know they're leading us to Hell itself. The lantern is so dim now that I can't see any farther than five to six feet in front of me.

"What's that?" Brandon asks. Nothing new, other than the next pile of rocks is apparent to me...except a sound. Something behind the cricket clicking—a familiar trickling sound—it seems so long ago, was that yesterday that I heard it outside these walls? Running water! "To the right," he directs and sure enough that's where the crickets are leading. The cave floor is smoother on this path so I'm hoping maybe for a main passageway with a door that has a nice rectangular box above it marked in red letters—*EXIT.*

The water sound is closer now and I can stand up in this place—the joints in my back and neck revolt. And there in front of us, I see it, an underground river—more like a big creek actually, but it is moving—which means it has an entrance and exit point from this place. The question is which is closer?

"Here" Brandon is now beside me, holding an object with his extended hand in my direction. I take from him what looks like a folded pamphlet of some sort, glossy by feel and made of heavy paper. The light in my hand barely reveals the lettering. I unfold the pages and discover...

"A MAP!" I shout a little too dramatically. It's one of those tourist pamphlet maps that detail the underground points of interest and has a handy little legend indicating direction and depth. "Where did you get this?"

"Had it in my back pocket the whole time, but I forgot about it. Wouldn't have helped anyway until now—the passageways on this were all blocked, the path that got us here was way different than what shows on the map."

"Okay, where's *here?*"

"Well, that's the other interesting part. I didn't forget that I had a compass on the handle of my old knife." Quartermaster Brandon never went on any hunting excursion without his trusty Swiss Army Knife that his dad gave him when he had joined the boy scouts. "I didn't mention it before because it didn't seem relevant—there was only one way to go until now."

"Brandon, where is <u>here</u>?"

"We've been gradually trending East and South," He explains, "away from the main body of the caves. As close as I can figure, this is a new branch that probably connects the Mammoth system with the Horse and Hidden River system."

"Great, didn't happen to bring the map showing the new, 'improved by earthquake' Mammoth Cave system, did you?"

Brandon ignores my sarcasm. "If this is the Hidden River we're standing by, it should lead us out of the caves. The only question is which direction is going to get us there more quickly—upstream or down. As I remember the cave entrance, it's closer to where the river leads into Horse Cave and we can't be too far into that system, we just can't have come that far off of the Mammoth system. So, I think we head up stream."

The thought of working against the current in our present condition does not excite me at all, but suddenly, the lantern battery finally gives out and we're left to consider our options in total blackness. Now any direction at all will do just fine as long as it leads out.

We both have reached into our pockets to see what other accessories might lend themselves to our journey. My cell phone is still intact, but the battery died long ago. In Brandon's shirt pocket there's a plastic zip lock bag which we now use to seal up my phone, our wallets, and the map. All is now ready for our aquatic adventure escape from the underworld. We don't seem to have anything else on our persons of real value so the only thing to do is plunge in.

"Careful," Brandon warns. "Don't know how deep this is."

Of course I know to be careful. I'm the underwater expert here—the nerve of him. "That's OK. You jump in first." And he does. I know this because I hear two sounds. The first is a splashing sound as his body meets the resistance of the water-flow. The second is...

"Oh my...whooooh...c...cold! Hold on to the side, I...can't...feel the bottom. Whoooh!"

It would have to be cold—this is a spring fed system. And that is my second to last intelligible thought. My last intelligible thought comes as I ease into the frigid recesses and quickly realize that I'm going to die.

There are things in my past I haven't confessed before now—some far worse than others. But I want to focus on one of the 'less worse' things, having to do with a church I attended as a kid. I went there because—at a time before I dreamed of exploring the universe—I had dreamed of being a rock star and this particular church had a need for a guitar player. Great fun, until I was also encouraged to go to confirmation classes to learn all about the Bible. Fine, I was just curious enough to try it. The problems—all of them come to think about it—started there.

Confirmation class was taught by a very serious, uncompelling man of the cloth. In my mind, I can picture him only in the traditional garments worn at that time—Black shoes, black pants, black clerical shirt and of course, the beacon of clerical authority, the small white tab affixed into the collar. He was all of five foot, seven inches, one-hundred and forty pounds, when soaking wet, with black-rimmed glasses guarding whatever emotion his eyes might have betrayed—all of this crowned by an egg-shaped head with four or five strands of hair still securely attached. His expressions were thoughtful, but flat, telegraphing to me the immediate sense that he had been asked to teach the class rather than having volunteered.

I can't now bring to mind his first name, but his last name was of good German stock. Fale. Pastor Fale. It wasn't till much later that the phonetic irony of his title and last name—placed together—hit me. I realize now that I had almost sung his name out as an audible jab, separating out each syllable—*P a s s e d - o r - F a i l.*

This man for whom I then had so much disdain, has turned out to be one of those *secret whisperers*; the ones that say something—maybe they don't even realize how profound their prattle—and the information floats out as a seed on the wind seeking fertile soil.

...The seed of Pastor Fale? We were arguing (he would have called it a discussion—I was picking a fight) about the origins and development of things from a Biblical perspective—you know, six days and a garden vs. <u>Real</u> science. I knew what I knew. There were dinosaurs, fossil and geological records, geeks with calculators and slide rulers on TV that had convinced me beyond a reasonable doubt that Einstein and Darwin were the true gods.

Pastor Fale believed differently. "I know what it looks like to you, but there are things we just can't explain or understand happening even now. Try to see them, do not trust the world, it's a lie."

I also remember having a sudden surge of pity for such a naïve individual. Then, the universe shifted, as did the topic. Somehow we got onto the vastness of creation and greater mysteries including one of my favorites: Singularities. At that time, I wasn't educated to any real degree on the topic...but I believed in those mysteries strongly. To my shock, so did Pastor F.

"Conservation of Energy is one of the most basic laws of science. It states that energy cannot be created or destroyed; only changed from one form to another."

I don't know why this particular tidbit from one of Fiz's many lectures comes to mind now, but it is somehow comforting to remember the very safe and warm environment in which the words had been spoken, so I let the old memory continue to play out. If nothing else, I find strength in the recollection of my professor's brilliant confidence.

"The universe could not have created itself using natural processes. After all, nature did not exist before the universe came into existence. Something beyond nature must have created all the energy and matter that is observed today. The logical conclusion—a SUPER-natural force created the universe."

The darkness and freezing water conjure up other classroom apologetics. I must be on the verge of a total thermal shock as I can hear very clearly, the words of Moses Folzman, who had invited me to sit in on one of his class lectures prior to my flight back to the States.

"There was a young man named Darwin who believed he had found the answer to the origins of multiple life forms on earth in the guise of specific species. This articulate scholar said that, if the fossil record did not blend together by small steps, his theory would fall apart. Darwin hoped the missing transitional fossils would be discovered."

Perfect logic, I remembered thinking at the time. *Darwin was a true student of science.* And in my mind's eye, Reb. Folzman signals me to hush as he continues to parable a great question of life.

"But after 150 years of searching to validate Darwin's theory, 99.9% of the transitional fossils still do not exist. For example, there will be hundreds of fossils of one species, then there will be thousands of missing links, then it picks up again with hundreds of fossils of the next species. Any reasonable person would think those thousands of missing links never existed."

Of course, I think in the blackness, *that's the continuing quest.* This time the Rabbi frowns at me and moves on.

"Darwin himself concluded that life is too complicated for all living things to have evolved from a single-cell creature (a germ). Small changes help living things adapt to changing conditions, but changes just go so far and then stop, as in dog breeding—dogs don't turn into cats. Something else has to be at play."

Wait…what? Darwin concluded that? It would mean…I'm confused… What is the 'something else'? I never receive an answer. Instead, Fiz's image floats into my awareness and we share wonderfully warm coffee as he raises another difficult conundrum.

"If the universe is expanding, into what is it expanding? If the universe is 'stretching' how is the space-to-stretch provided? If there was a Big Bang, what was the substance or non-substance that existed outside of the 'first mass'? How was it defined and how did it exist without mass?

Why are these memories coming in succession? What makes them important? What connects them? And then there is one more voice that pricks my conscious mind. It is my father's.

All will soon change. .

Brandon…breathing funny…short rasps, like…reverse cough—sucking in more…letting out less.

"Are you OK?" He gasps. "You sound like…dog barking backwards. Try…catch breath…

"You making no sense. I not…dog. I cold…dead."

"Light. Up—left!"

"You…no sense." Light?" *I not think good…oh, end of tunnel…light… death…heaven.* Dead. Pastor Fale grabs me out of the water. *I'm free. Dead.*

"Crawl up toward light," God or Pastor Fale commands. He's behind me now—pushing up, more up. Pastor Fale and me on all fours, stop, tired, dead—crawling dead. Rocks all around—all over—scraping head, bleeding back…light brighter, warmer—*I will go there.* Pastor Fale taking me to God's place for hot coffee—*extra hot please.* Noise—*what noise—like cars on a road, passing by? Are there cars at God's place?* Light is too bright. Can't see, only feel, rock, more rock, tired of rock, hate rock, soft wet… wait…grass? God grass, God's place. Here.

And suddenly the words of Pastor Fale come back to me brighter than the outside light assaulting my eyes—words he spoke to me that I had hidden away. His meek wisdom had tickled my consciousness, steering me on a course of discovery that now is redefining all I thought was real and fantasy. There he is behind the light, saying it all again as if for the first time.

"I'm fascinated by the simple depth of what God put into place, speaking matter into existence. Everything looks and feels and seems complex, but the truth is that we are nothing—even our science—and God is all. Everything: dinosaurs, atomic structure, even you have purpose… all things from nothing because God spoke it. Black holes? Yes, they seem amazing, but don't be confused by the phenomena—instead, consider the purpose. It isn't about how matter is absorbed by a black hole or even where that matter goes once in the black hole. What matters is what the matter becomes—what purpose will it serve for God?"

He 'got' it. Pastor Fale 'passed' and he has unknowingly passed his achievement on to me! Up until now, I had failed to get it, but the <u>past</u> doesn't matter—only the <u>now</u>.

Laughter—REAL laughter—starting with a small hiccup growing into a full gut chuckle and cascading into free heaves. I like the sound—Brandon is alive too. Is that funny? Why is he laughing?

"Look over on the other side of the road," he points while still snorting. We're lying in a grassy section just outside the rim of a sinkhole created by our earthquake. The grass and new cave entrance are maybe 30 yards off of a secondary highway. My eyes catch the movement of traffic and are then drawn slowly up a cliff face on the opposing side of the road. At the top, a tall chain-link fence boasts two large signs. The newer, less worn billboard reads:

LAND FOR SALE OR LEASE

The second sign is much more designed, sporting a ghoulish logo and scripted lettering saying:

WELCOME TO GOLGATHA FAMILY FUN PARK

I look at Brandon who is now wearing a cocked grin and then we both spew out guffaws which are strangely mixed with tears.

Entry Ten

The trend appears to have swung toward everyone trying to make quantum physics work at the subatomic level. The better approach may be in trying to make subatomic physics work at the quantum level.

—Subatomic Quantum Reverse Effect position proposed by Profs. Fitzgerald E. Hindeland and Moses Folzman

AUSTIN, TEXAS – UNIVERSITY OF TEXAS COMPLEX, QUANTUM SYSTEMS DEPARTMENT

Since hitching a ride back to our surprisingly undamaged HUMVEE and then arranging post-haste transport to the University of Texas, Brandon and I have had miniscule nourishment and less sleep. I'm simply too exhausted to move from my seat, but Fiz reads my mind and has a fresh hot cup along with a doughnut ready to meet my extended hand. Suddenly I'm reminded again how little I've eaten in two days and wolf the doughnut down in two bites. *I will live.*

The Rabbi has also flown to Austin and is sitting in one of Fiz's comfortable lounge chairs cradling a steaming cup of coffee. He and Fiz have now set up shop in the Physics Building with a computer server completely dedicated to analyzing the interactions between Mother Earth and V4641. Fiz is firing off information in bullet point staccato, trying to bring us up to speed.

"We received cell phone text reports about the US *Grand-quake*, as the media has dubbed the occurrences, and also the larger ones in the Middle East. We too experienced some strange physical anomalies while flying over here and Darius Mede in Geneva called to report some incredible oddities going on throughout Europe…"

Moses interrupts his colleague. "I think no one has briefed Daniel or Brandon on all the other happenings while they were on their spelunking holiday. Perhaps we should replay the news broadcast we recently recorded?"

Fiz nods and without further explanation, enters a command on his smartphone which opens a Bluetooth connection and casts an image to the plasma TV screen on the wall. There before us unfolds a newscast presented by a well-known broadcast anchor from my very own employer, N.H.Q. The news anchor is standing outside the N.H.Q. corporate offices which are shockingly engulfed in flames. He describes in the calm and informational tones acquired through the long practice of his profession how he had been on assignment in Atlanta and during the film crew's drive back, just as they neared the N.H.Q. building, their van had been rocked by a huge explosion.

The film crew must have been working on automatic pilot. To their credit, the shock of the scene before them wasn't interfering with the skillful duties they now performed. Someone on the crew had the snap to access the World Wide Web and started feeding the newscaster information about global catastrophes and seemingly paranormal events that had begun to occur at nearly the same time—a time well documented because of man's obsession with clocks.

But before the exact time is shown on the monitor, I already know. It happened at 5:32 pm Central Standard Time or 11:32 PM G.M.T., the exact moment when Brandon's laptop registered that I had pressed the command key to begin our fateful experiment. I'm convinced that my single act had caused the world to crumble.

An old nursery rhyme invades my thoughts. *Humpty Dumpty sat on a wall…*

Misty, please pick up…
"Hello? Danny? My God, are you OK?"
"I'm fine. Brandon and I are in Austin at the University."
"I saw the reports on Atlanta and…"

…All I hear is sobbing on the other end. I realize now that she had no idea where we had been at the time of the catastrophes and I decide to keep the answer simple. "I've been safe (*liar!*) the whole time. I'm more worried about you and the kids. How are you, how's my mom?"

"There were ferocious winds here and the power was out for about 12 hours but no permanent damage. Danny, what is happening?"

"We're here with Fiz right now trying to figure that out. All I know is that I want you all here. Please, no arguments or fighting. I love you and need you with me as soon as possible. *Please!*"

"Is it safe to fly or should we try to drive?" There's no hesitation in her voice.

I sigh in relief and continue. "Fiz is having a special jet sent for you. Just pack clothes, everything else will be here for you. Tell mom that she needs to come to help take care of the kids—that should convince her."

"Danny…I'm sorry, I thought…"

"No!" I yell through the phone. "Don't you dare apologize—you were right. I have been so absorbed in my own little world that I couldn't… wouldn't share it with you. I'm the one who needs to be begging you for…"

"Danny," she whispers me into silence. "I'll be there soon. I love you too much to look back on what has happened. Let's look together at what will happen."

…All the king's horses and all the king's men couldn't put Humpty together again…But Misty can!

As I hang up the phone, Fiz motions from the doorway for me to walk with him back toward his office. He informs as we travel, "When you were gone, there was one more thing we discovered that you'll want to know about." Before he can go into detail, we open the door to his office and almost collide with a highly energized Brandon who was apparently headed our way.

"Danny," he squeaks excitedly. "They've found it again! They've found V4641!"

I try to appear interested about the Intel now being fed to me regarding the rediscovery of the unpredictable mini-quasar by the Hubble Hive. Fiz recognizes my lack of focus and interrupts Brandon.

"Keeper, what is it? Are you worried about your family? They'll be here soon."

I shake my head. In my mind I'm replaying a much earlier event when a certain doctoral student had decided to play god and caused an underwater avalanche because of his arrogance. Why hadn't I learned the lesson then? Why did I think I could control nature this time using similar techniques? "It was me." Everyone in the room eyes me in question. "I caused all of this. It was my experiment that started the chain of events that triggered all of the chaos and…deaths. It was…me pushing the stupid button."

"Is that what you think?" This is Moses. He lifts himself from his chair, walks up in front of mine and commands, "Stand up!" I look at him confused, but he simply repeats more authoritatively, "STAND UP!"

This time it registers and I begin to comply, but just as I come out of my chair he places his hand on my chest and pushes me back. I look up at him, now totally stupefied. He simply remains standing in front of my chair, demanding my attention. "Tell me Child, was it me who caused your plummet back into the chair?" Before I can reply he continues. "Or was I an agent of some other mystery at work? Could you not argue that gravity was the cause of your fall and that my action was only a convenient catalyst? If we dare to live in the world, do we not need to explore these mysteries? Is that not part of The Eternal's greater purpose for us?"

I have no good reply to his argument, but I'm feeling pretty sorry for myself and defensively open my mouth anyway. "I appreciate your trying to help, Rabbi, but you're just inviting the 'Which came first, the chicken or the egg' question."

"Actually, I'm inviting the 'Why did the chicken cross the road' question. So answer Child. Why did the chicken cross the road?"

I know this one. "To get to the other…"

"No! You and most others who claim to be dedicated observers have missed the very point you ironically preach about in your articles. You can't suppose based on the unseen—you do not know the inner thoughts or purposes of things. You must deal with the concrete. The chicken crossed the road because his feet were moving in that direction!"

Moses now squats down, places his hands on my knees and peers directly into my soul. "What caused these things to happen, is yet unknown. What we do know is that they happened at the same time you were running your experiment and there may be a connection."

He's making sense and suddenly my higher brain functions awaken. One phrase flashes as a neon sign in my brain. I blurt it out, "Chains of Inference."

Brandon jumps in. "Yes! The relationship between evidence and factual proof—just because we see something occurring, we can't just make up…theorize its cause."

The Rabbi brings the discussion into tangible focus. "The chicken is crossing the road. We cannot probe the animal's mind to know what drives it or how the action began. And yet we try to theorize its purpose and by doing so, begin a chain of inferences that leads us down a specific path. How can we know that path is accurate unless we prove the original theory to be accurate? What if the chicken isn't trying to cross the road? What if the road just happens to be in the way of some other interest?"

I'm trying to keep up with all the metaphors and personification. "So are you saying V4641 is doing what it's doing because there's some kind of intent?"

Moses shakes his head while smiling. "Child, this conversation has been centered on you. Why did your reasoning jump to the subject of our little quasar?"

I *have no clue as to why!* "Isn't that what we're trying to solve here: How an anomaly from the center of the galaxy suddenly and inexplicably blinks out, starts strangely affecting physical conditions in our solar system and then just as suddenly appears seven light-years from us, literally in the next neighborhood over—sector SOL plus One-C? That's the puzzle, isn't it?"

Fiz has been strangely quiet, listening and patiently sipping from his preferred drink—a glass of club soda with a slice of lime. My question prompts him to jump into the discussion. "We've been considering the problem from only one dimension—not only should we be using a telescope, we need to be putting V4641 under a microscope.

Moses nods, "Copernicus and Galileo observed the universe from afar. Newton was lucky, the apple was right there to see. The world of sub-atomics is still right at our fingertips and we have to reach out deeply to touch the quantum universe. I believe we have wrongly concluded, by the design of our theories and hypothesis, that the two are different. Why don't we go back to the beginning and identify the principles on which our universal laws are based?"

"Stop! Identify principles—are you serious?" Everyone eyes Brandon whose crimson complexion gives him the appearance of a volcano which has recently erupted. "I've just traveled back and forth between three states, was almost buried alive in a cave and nearly froze to death in a subterranean river. I'm not in the mood to sit around, listening to people hypothesize and ponder the mindset of poultry or review the laws of scientific structure all day long. We have got to start putting facts together rather than picking them apart. We are missing some critical data here!"

Fiz looks at him quizzically and asks, "Such as?"

"Such as what was going on back at the cave when things began to vibrate and I saw Danny and most of my equipment…and me, become translucent. If the resonance burst had continued much longer, I think we would have started to vaporize. I know it sounds crazy, but I saw it happening. Danny did too! What explains that?"

Fiz and Moses look at one another as if daring each other to speak first. But neither seems to have an answer they're willing to yet share. So it's up to me and once again, my mouth opens to betray my thoughts, "The Hutchison Effect."

Fiz squeezes another lime into his club soda. "I seem to remember something about a man named Hutchison—Canadian I believe? Wasn't he labeled a mad scientist of sorts, claiming to be able to alter elements without heat?"

"The same," exclaims Brandon—John Hutchison was a modern-day alchemist—his experiments could never be properly replicated in a lab—a total nut job."

"Actually, we may have simply not had the proper laboratory in which to reenact his work." This statement emanates from Moses Folzman, the diehard subatomic guy in the crowd. "And more profoundly, the Hutchison Effect is all about molecular manipulation using resonant frequencies—no one has ever produced a quantum reaction that also affected microphysics. If we can somehow validate his work…"

I look over at Brandon who has simmered down a few degrees. Not only that; he's nodding his head agreeably and I believe I can see the Nobel Peace Prize reflected in his gaze.

Fiz is stirring his concoction in the glass before him with his finger, not looking up. "So, Keeper, tell us more about Mr. Hutchison and his work."

I explain that Hutchison accidentally stumbled on some unexplainable laboratory phenomenon. He was able to levitate objects, liquefy metals at room temperature and merge incompatible materials such as wood and metal together.

Fiz is back to his electronic whiteboard, scribbling and talking in rapid combination. "We know that the state of matter can be changed—from solid to liquid, to gas and to plasma—water is an elegantly simple example, which when heated, changes from liquid to gas and when cooled, a solid block of ice.

"On the other hand, finding the right resonance frequency—the harmonics of the molecular bonds—would be indeed a much more efficient way of rearranging what we think to be non-arrange-able." *Did Fiz just make up a word?*

"…Which is what happened at Mammoth?" I can't tell if Brandon is asking this question or answering it.

Crazy Profit moves up with Fiz to the e-board and also grabs a stylus to make notes. "The Hutchison Effect included liquefaction of metal without heating and burning and scorching structures; using a frequency source to cause objects to morph into a liquid state."

...My turn. "According to Hutchison, once the frequency source is switched off, objects would be merged into one solid structure. That was Hutchison's claim to fame. He provided proof of his experiments in the form of strange combinations of metal/wood artifacts, created in his lab, which have not been seen or produced since."

"Hold it, that's the flaw. We couldn't have been seeing the Hutchison Effect." Brandon seems almost proud of this proclamation. "When we started *phasing out* in the cave and you switched off the resonance generator, we didn't 'merge' with the rock or the stairway or any surrounding structures."

"Yes." I agree with my friend while picking up another doughnut. *Why am I so hungry?* "But Hutchison used standard radio waves to produce his outcomes. We generated a single high frequency wave aimed outward. And we used a resonance pattern captured from an outside source that we still don't fully understand. Our response signal to V4641 triggered something similar to, but beyond a Hutchison moment. His experiments were just primitive, that's all."

"...Which made your experiment all the more foolhardy and dangerous," Fiz comes over and sits between me and his Quartermaster to complete his thought. "You were certainly more successful in your results. I fear however the ultimate outcome would have been much less... constructive. Based on the changes in atomic structure that you were experiencing, had you not shut the experiment down, you may have been even further 'molecularly altered' than you had already become."

Both Brandon and I look at one another and then at Fiz in disbelief of his claim. "Molecularly altered?" We ask in unison.

"Indeed, and I can prove to you that what I'm suggesting is fact. But to do so, I will need a lock of hair from each of you to extract a D.N.A. sample to examine with our electron microscope.

"...Why not?" Brandon exclaims sarcastically. "If I'm going to disappear anyway, I should at least leave something behind to be remembered by!"

As Fiz surveys Brandon's and my sample D.N.A. material, we can see what he sees on the super-sized plasma monitor positioned on the wall of the University's laboratory. "I've placed two samples of Brandon D.N.A. side by side—one from before your adventure and one from after."

"How did you get a sample from before my…"

"Hush, Child." Fiz will not be distracted. "Look at this gene sequence here. There seems to be an alteration."

Now Brandon is insistent. "Alteration—my genes are altered? What exactly does that mean?"

Fiz takes his eyes away from the microscope and looks back at us. "Child, behave! I am an Astrophysicist not a Geneticist. You are fortunate that I can even work this contraption. My point was to only show you that something is at work here. I have no explanation as to how it is affecting you."

"Perhaps I can assist." Moses moves over to the microscope and Fiz stands to offer his seat at the controls. The Rabbi glues his eyes to the view-caps, adjusts the focus with his left hand and then says one word. "…Transposons."

I know this one from my Junk Science research articles with N.H.Q. "You're saying that something has invaded our bodies?"

Moses Folzman continues to stare into the depths of our bio-molecular structures and speaks in a distant, removed voice. "Transposons are by no means attackers, but rather, joiners—changing rather than breaking down genetic relationships. They've become the very hand in mutagenesis— improving crop production.

"Great! So what have we turned into, Teenage Mutant Ninja Turtles or a better form of asparagus?" Brandon is now up and pacing. I've not seen him this animated and impatient—ever.

Now the big man lifts his head from the microscope and faces us directly. His stare is strangely chilling. "We must acknowledge the observable. As I look at the changed sequence in Brandon's D.N.A., I must conclude that they are affecting his personality."

"Yes," Fiz inserts. "That would explain the increased energy level and the shortened patience level."

"What are you talking about? I am NOT impatient! Can you please make whatever point you're trying to make so we can get back to solving our intergalactic quandary?"

Both Moses and Fiz continue to review the monitor, which I can also see has a different header attached: SUBJECT—ADAMSON, DANIEL.

My mentor looks at me in the same way the Rabbi did just a minute ago. The sensation of my whole being placed under their lens, gives me goose-bumps. Fiz speaks for the both of them. "You, on the other hand, Keeper, seem to be affected differently."

Oh, oh, "How so?"

Fiz takes his eyes off the screen and walks back to me, standing and putting on his reading glasses, but nudged down to the tip of his nose so he has to look over them as he examines me in my chair. There's a printout in his hand and he keeps glancing at it. "There seem to be nuances in your D.N.A. that are, well, more complex. Your actions, your behavior, your appearance are all modified."

Now the Rabbi also comes over to stand before me and starts another story. "In ancient times there were people on earth that were extraordinarily gifted. They are mentioned numerous times in the Hebrew Bible and also referenced in many other texts. They were of larger stature, sophisticated in culture and were considered great rulers. No one really knows where they came from, but it has always been conjectured that some physical event, either on Earth or elsewhere affected many species. These Super Beings were called by many, *Sons of God.*"

"…Of course!" Fiz is much too excited. He bends down, pushes his glasses up to the back of his nose and eyes my face from a distance of less than six inches. I am hating this—a lot. "…The Nephilim! You are right, Moses, this could very well be the precursor of a new occurrence."

I literally push my mentor back and stand rapidly in one fluid motion. I'm feeling very alert and very tuned in to all around me, but why does everything seem to be moving subtly slower than me? "What are you talking about? There's nothing different. Look—same hands, same body, same face. Me!"

"You are taller." This is Brandon now evaluating me. He's supposed to be defending me, and for him to join in my anatomical dissection is too much.

"You're crazy! I'm too old to be growing or mutating or whatever it is you're suggesting."

"I'd say about two good inches of growth." Fiz is jotting things on his tablet. "And I noticed far more than normal strength when you pushed me. Child, when did you develop such an appetite for doughnuts?"

I glance at the box next to me and realize I have been eating one after the other while trying to follow this conversation. I've never been a big pastry eater, but now I find myself wanting more—I'm still hungry! I also now observe that my pants seem too short.

"He is also quicker—mind and body. Notice his reflexes..." Moses quickly tosses a pencil my way and I catch it even though I'm looking away from him. *Did I actually hear the pencil flying through the air?* "...and his powers of deduction have improved."

"I'm right here! Stop talking about me as if I'm some sort of specimen." I know something of the Nephilim as well and bring the knowledge to bear. "The ancient super-race you're talking about was simply a result of progressive generations of good gene combinations being blended. That's all there was to it. I am no superhuman! Next you'll be telling me there's some kind of strange correlation between my so called 'modifications' and Brandon's work on Tau Neutrinos."

Everyone has stopped what they are doing and are now eyeing me again. The look of scrutiny on Fiz's face is highly unnerving. Fiz aims a gaze at Brandon who looks puzzled at first and then appears to have an epiphany of his own. "The new RICH Counter? Of course! Why didn't I think of that?"

"What are you talking about?" Equipment is not my forte and apparently a RICH Counter is something that exists in this room and can work some magic to help us.

Fiz elaborates as he moves to another console and flips a switch. There is an electronic hum emanating from behind a wall somewhere and its cadence increases as he adjusts some dials. "The RICH Counter—an acronym for **R**ing **I**maging **CH**erenkov Counter—one of which actually resides in the basement of this very building—is what is used to detect localized Tau Neutrinos and so it has not been of particular interest to me until now."

"And now you're interested because?" *Why do I fear his answer?*

"Because this particular RICH Counter can detect neutrino trails in as small a space as say…a human body. As a matter of fact, I am running a Tau scan as we speak and I am narrowing the focus down to this room only. Quartermaster, would you please activate the other monitor over there?"

Fiz is pointing with one hand to another large plasma screen on the opposite wall. Brandon stands up and walks over to a panel on the same wall, presses a button. What now appears on the screen looks like a Technicolor light show that one might see on a ride at a certain theme park in Florida. Streams of light trails dance in front of us.

"Those are actual neutrino trails that you are looking at." Now Fiz walks over and uses his laser pointer to pick out the curiosities on the screen. "These are computer generated images—the differing types of neutrinos are identified by color variations. The Standard Electron trails are yellow, the Muons are red and the ones we're looking for—the Tau—are blue."

Fiz moves a joystick on the console and the images shift. "I'm scanning around the room now; see how many more yellow trails there are? The Standard trails are more prevalent because the majority of neutrinos passing through Earth come from the sun, which generates trillions of Standard neutrinos daily."

The multicolored trails on the screen appear to be streaking through and around distorted objects that are not easily identifiable because they mostly appear as blurred and darkened static…with one exception, which Fiz now centers on with his joystick. This object on the screen seems to be emitting blue light. All the blue Tau trails on the screen appear to orbit it, pass through it, and return to it over and over again. Suddenly I feel a tingling in my nose.

I follow through with the urge to pinch and rub my nostrils. On the screen the image instantly changes, the blue object moving and adjusting in an odd gesture that seemingly mimics my movements. An odd curiosity overcomes me and I throw my arms back to release a huge yawn. The bright blue blob on screen also stretches and yawns—streams of energy aligning their orbits and trajectories in sympathy with the action. Now I stand up almost hypnotically and walk toward the screen to examine the image more closely. The image obliges by walking towards me. I reach up with my index finger to touch the blueness, half expecting to have the blob on screen jump out and become part of my reality. Instead, the blurred image of an arm with an extended finger meets mine at the surface of the monitor. Me and my shadow then make little circles on the surface in unison, changing directions and motions simultaneously. I spin around with a sense of unease and face the others in the room. "What is this? What is going on?"

Moses walks over to me and places his hands on my shoulder. He is smiling, a warm, reassuring gesture and his touch is comforting-soft—I really need to hear him say that this is a dream.

"Do not be afraid, Child. You are simply…growing."

"I think his voice is getting deeper too," Brandon comments. Fiz and Moses both nod and grin.

GENEVA, SWITZERLAND – WORLD TRADE ORGANIZATION GARDENS

While I'm watching myself on Smurf TV, in my strange new mind, I can also see the sun is just setting at another location on the planet. Two individuals walk down a shaded garden path behind the expanse of the World Trade Organization Headquarters. Darius Mede speaks while Brenda Anders, president of the Green Order Coalition listens with rapt attention. "Your conclusions about the global distortions are remarkable, I'm glad you've brought them to my attention."

Darius takes her hand in his. The touch and the cooing of his voice cause an immediate change in her visage. Brenda Anders closes her eyes and her face becomes flushed with color. She is trembling slightly. "I only want to help."

"Yes, I know. And I need your help very much." Mede is silent for a moment and then continues. "The timing will be crucial for our next step. In one week, the World Trade Organization will be meeting here and we must be ready to show our strength. The very survival of our planet and its beautiful resources may be at stake."

Trance-like, Brenda responds. "It is beautiful, isn't it? I want so much to keep it safe. What must I do?"

Mede stops walking and places the palm of his other hand softly on Brenda's cheek. She releases a breath and leans slightly back with her eyes closed. Darius places his lips close to her ear and whispers softly. "The governments of the world are greedy and do not understand the peril we face. New, stronger leadership is necessary to save us. You must let your followers know that the recent cataclysmic events herald the end of life as we know it. We cannot wait any longer. Have every-and-anyone who can, gather here in Switzerland for a demonstration during the meeting. Those who cannot be here need to gather in the capitals of the world and before their city and local governments. They must insist on a governmental shift in power."

Brenda whispers back. "What governmental shift?"

"Someone must take charge who knows what has to be done. I must assume that responsibility, whether I want to or not."

Tears are now welling in Brenda's closed eyes. "You must. I will help, I'll do whatever you want me to, but please, you must lead."

"For this to happen, I'll need your help one more time, beyond the excellent ways you've assisted so far."

"What else can I do?"

"There is a certain relationship from your past that we must now make use of—a person with whom you were once very...intimate."

Brenda's eyes open immediately at the reference to her past, and at the suggestion, she now backs one step away from Mede. "Darius, please, no. I now have feelings only for you. I...please don't ask me to revisit that time."

"Brenda, I'm not jealous, please don't be alarmed. I would not even ask if there were any other way." He gently pulls her closer to him, stroking her hair as he coos, "You are the only one who can do this for me. I need you so. It is as difficult for me to ask this of you as it is for you to offer it to me. I will be grateful beyond anything you can imagine."

Brenda Anders feels a tremor, but it has nothing to do with the physics of Earth. "I...must do this?"

"You must."

"Then I will, only for you."

Entry Eleven

Ockham's Razor—One should not increase beyond what is necessary, the number of entities required to explain anything.

—William of Ockham –
Franciscan Monk, 1285-1349

SOMEWHERE INSIDE DANNY

The planet is clearly visible from here, *but everything else seems a blur—out of focus. I need to light everything up. That's it. Light! But not just any light: Brilliant and blue, like the planet, like me. If I can shine my blueness onto everything else…there will be no other need. But to do that I must disappear—I must diminish so that the blue increases.*

The armies see me now and rush toward me. Somehow I know that one army, the enemy, wants to extinguish the blue light, the other wants to guard its shining. And there is the dragon. Have I noticed before that it flies with the guard?

The dragon reaches me first—its silvery skin also begins to shine blue. Our combined blueness blinds the attack-army and our guard overtakes them. As the onslaught progresses I see that behind the enemy, another form takes shape. It's another dragon! This one is red in color and seems to give confidence to the enemy. They are as fiercely determined as is the guard and it seems that neither army can advance.

AUSTIN, TEXAS – UNIVERSITY OF TEXAS COMPLEX, QUANTUM SYSTEMS DEPARTMENT

Professor Moses Folzman has arranged to teach his Technion class via webcast and has invited all of us to observe. As typical, he has the rapt attention of his audience even though to most, he is only an image on a screen thousands of miles away. I sense the power of his words and his presence in a very personal and exciting new way. It's as if the whole room oscillates with his aura. I can feel it through my feet…and it's increasing. The water glass on the table begins to vibrate and dance, before me. The blinds on the office windows start to rattle. I look up at the TV monitor that is showing two images at once: Moses at his podium and a fisheye view of his students at the Technion, diligently taking notes on his oration.

Except now, one by one, they stop writing and begin looking around the room. Books start to hop and then appear to bounce off their desks. There is a rumbling noise and I can't figure out where it is coming from except from everywhere. Ceiling tiles pop out and start falling and I too am thrown to the floor from my chair. But the floor is not a safe place as it is moving, seemingly in all directions at once. Test tubes shatter, beakers explode, glass and objects defy gravity as they hurl back and forth across the room. *Oh good,* I think in slow motion, *I'm so glad this is a dream because if it were real this would all be very bad crap.*

"This was not like the other quakes. This was…an entire event." Brandon has his laptop open and is reviewing data streams from R.I.T, other universities, and scientific refugees whose internet chatter has now become his lifeline to the outside world.

"Explain." Fiz gives the command while picking up books and placing them in stacks. We had gone outside to determine the damage and it appears the structure of the building is still sound (thankfully the architects and builders of the U.T. Physics Building had done their jobs very well!) though the walls strangely appear to be leaning—telltale cracks in the plaster and veneers suggest not all in our cozy little corner of the world remains plum.

Somehow the power is still on so there's no need for the backup generator, yet. As a precaution we've checked the supply of kerosene which is stored on the upper maintenance level and if that time does come, we should have plenty of fuel to keep the facility functioning for at least several weeks.

"The mantle of the Earth is expanding out," Quartermaster says.

"Which section?" I'm in anxious mode, not only concerned about this recent cataclysm and Brandon's weird claim about mantle expansion, but also to know how fares my family. I can hear the demanding tone and tension in my own voice."

"All of it."

Now I put my other concerns aside. "What you're suggesting is impossible."

"We know," Brandon stops me, "but it is happening regardless, exponentially across the globe. We've verified it at strategic stations in numerous countries."

RANDOLPH AIR FORCE BASE, SAN ANTONIO, TEXAS

Because of the extensive damage to major airports across the country and throughout the world, commercial air travel is now highly restricted. But Fiz has connections and he has arranged for my mother, plus Misty and the kids, to be flown in by special transport to Randolph. With the freeway system being compromised so badly, it takes us nearly as long to drive to the base as it does for the plane to fly them from Virginia to Texas.

Brandon and I arrive in our extended cab HUMVEE just in time to see the wheels of the specially equipped late model 787, touchdown on the hastily repaired runway. The behemoth aircraft taxis up to our location on the tarmac and a very official acting marine is the first to disembark down the stairway. He approaches and then stops abruptly, ten paces away from us.

The lieutenant—I now can make out the insignias on his uniform—salutes smartly and announces, "Dr. Adamson (he must have been briefed on what I look like because he skips over part about seeing my credentials), we will be prepared to make the next leg of the trip with wheels up at 0600 hours tomorrow morning."

Before I can ask him about exactly what next leg to which he is referring, he turns sharply again and parades back toward the plane where I now see my mother being helped carefully down the stairway by Misty. I also start trotting that direction without looking back to see if Brandon is following. Somehow, Jake and Sylvia have both squirted past the two women and have made it down the stairway to come charging into my arms. They are both so excited that they can't stop talking as we walk back toward their mother.

"Daddy, that plane is bigger than grandma's house and our house put together." "They let us run up and down the aisle." "They have a control room that they let us play in and pull knobs and switches and I got to fire a real simulated laser cannon!" Now they look over my shoulder and see something far more exciting than their father's arms. "Unky B!" Squirming out of my grasp, they charge and almost knock my best friend down with their assault.

I turn again toward the plane and Misty walks rapidly toward me. We meet in embrace without a word and I give her a long deep kiss which is returned in kind, followed by tears and gasps of words between more kisses. "I'm so sorry." "I'm the one who…did I hurt you when I hit you?" "God, I missed you." "You look different somehow, have you gotten taller?"

"Okay gang," my mother takes charge, "you can all get reacquainted later. Right now, do you think we might be able to find a place to let the children burn off a little of this energy they've obviously stored up? And for that matter, I could use a big cold glass of anything. It's eight o'clock in the morning and hot as blazes out here."

"Welcome to Texas, Mom."

On the trip back to Austin, I drive. Misty is up front in the passenger seat while Mom and Brandon sit in the mid-section of the HUMVEE. They act as a buffer to the kids who crawl around exploring the back section of the vehicle. This arrangement gives my wife and me precious time to catch up and heal our relationship.

"How long do we have?" Misty has always been a Get-To-The-Point kind of person.

"Depends on who you talk to: Fiz and Crazy…Moses Folzman think things are changing way faster than most of the other research teams who are…"

"I mean us. How long do you have with the children, your mom and…me?"

We are driving down a highway strewn with debris that hints at the broader end-of-world landscape surrounding us, but Misty is concerned with only the importance of our time together and nothing else will interfere. Forget the fact that even now a small tremor vibrates the HUMVEE and an ancient pecan tree off to our right topples over.

"I don't know," I answer honestly. "I think I'm going to have to fly somewhere…classified, tomorrow. We have tonight for sure."

"Good, what you're doing is obviously important so I don't want you distracted. If we need to stay elsewhere or be out of your way, I totally understand and the kids will too."

"You won't distract me. I've been more distracted by your not being near me. There's…a lot I need to share with you about what's happened." *Do I dare tell her…will she have me committed?* I motion for her to lean my direction and I whisper in her ear so that my mother can't overhear what I'm about to say. "I've been speaking to my dad…as if he was still alive. I can hear him at times as clearly as…I can hear you now."

"You're mom's been talking to him too."

I jerk the steering wheel and have to fight to control the HUMVEE to keep it on the road. When we are running straight again, I say loud enough for everyone in the back to hear. "Sorry, I…almost hit some wreckage on the road—everyone OK?"

"Do it again daddy!" I see my mother's face looking back at me in the rearview mirror shaking her head back and forth. I shake mine in agreement. Now I again look over at Misty and she places her index finger to her lips. Obviously, she had just shared something that is to be kept secret. I wonder exactly what my parents have been chatting about and, for that matter, just how many other people my father has been broadcasting to? I stay silent for a moment, half expecting him to respond, but…nothing.

"What can I do to help?" Misty has always helped me out as a quasi-research assistant. In addition to serving coffee back in the college years, she was also a student in the University of Texas biology department—even having had aspirations of becoming a veterinarian prior to meeting me. She also has a knack for finding internet sites that relate to the odd kind of stories I need to support my Junk-Science habit. I'm tempted to invite her to the physics lab but think better of it.

"Right now, the best place you can be is with the kids."

"Hey buster, who do you think you are?" I'm shocked as my mom speaks out in defense of her daughter-in-law. "She's been with the kids. She's played with the kids and fed the kids and listened to the kids and the kids are fine. I'll handle the kids if they need handling. Your wife on the other hand is <u>not</u> fine. She wants to contribute. She wants to be helping her man. Let her help!"

"Yes ma'am," is all I can muster. Misty is looking down and I can see her trying to hide the smirk on her face from those in the back. I think for a moment and then respond to my bride. "We could use an extra pair of hands researching details from other sources."

"Great. Count me in." She flashes me her special "I love you" smile and I somehow know that nothing can hurt me now.

SOMEWHERE IN WASHINGTON DC

There are other alliances being forged at this moment too. Three people now meet in private—four if you include my invisible presence at this clandestine meeting. I'm just beginning to get used to my "fly on the wall" perspective.

Darius Mede has somehow connived himself into the President of the United States' busy schedule. He has invited the other person in the room who jumped at the chance to participate. It's none other than Professor Winston Wire-rim—the face from the first video conference we held only a few weeks ago. Winston was the one who had tried foolhardily to discredit me before my peers and my protector, Fiz Hindeland. Now he stands in the flesh before the leader of the free world.

"The world is coming apart at the seams and you want to discuss politics? Are you so blind you can't see the bigger need outside of these walls?" This is our stalwart Commander-in-Chief speaking. He's reacting to a proposal introduced by the head of the World Trade Organization. Mede doesn't flinch at the reprimand and simply responds.

"Mr. President, of course the situation appears dire, but I assure you that Dr. Torin's findings confirm my own. As the head of the Department of Astrophysics at M.I.T., I would hope you would agree with me that his credibility should not be in question. There certainly is a terrible change that is taking place, but it will not be the life-ending event many have led you to believe it is."

Well, now we all have discovered several of the secrets of the universe: Winston's last name and position in life, along with his bodacious title! Darius Mede has planned this encounter carefully and speaks convincingly. "I have other researchers as well working on their own time to make sure that the data coming to you from Austin is corroborated.

"I believe you'll find the documents I'm sharing with you to be highly revealing. It seems that another very reputable organization, the Green Order Coalition supports the idea that the catastrophes we are experiencing are not the result of some galactic devilry but are the Earth's reaction to a combination of mankind's hydrocarbon drilling activities and our environmental abuse. The world is literally fighting back."

The President is pacing now, impatient with the length of this meeting. Mede looks toward Winston who pulls a thick sheaf of papers from his briefcase and nervously lays the pages on the President's desk. "Uh, this report clearly shows the correlations between man's influence on his environment and the escalation of the current anomalies." Winston takes off his glasses and earnestly turns to the President. "Sir, I will be glad to show you…"

"Look," the President interrupts, "I wasn't born yesterday and I know that correlations can also be coincidental. Otherwise, we should outlaw breastfeeding because it leads to death—everyone who is breastfed dies."

Mede smiles again. "An interesting point Mr. President, however, this is a much more serious conclusion. Are you willing to take the risk of ignoring these findings?"

The whole time that Mede speaks, Winston is nodding his head like a bobble-head doll. The President is watching this and becomes annoyed. "It appears you have your own agenda and following as well, Darius. I appreciate your efforts, but I do not report to you or your organization. I report to the American people and my responsibility is to them. I'll take your information under advisement and, as promised, share our data openly with you. We will, at some time in the very near future, have to decide if a global response to these occurrences is appropriate, but that will come after I am appropriately advised by my Cabinet and Congress."

Mede narrows his eyes a moment—then relaxes. "I understand Mr. President. Just do not delay your decision too long. There are already reports of world-wide panic and unrest. We should be preparing now, not later, for a unified reaction and perhaps even a coordinated global governmental response to the threat of anarchy that exists. We may have to proceed with or without the support of the United States."

"If you're suggesting that you're going to use this crisis as a ploy to wrestle government control out of the hands of our country's elected, you will find a worthy foe in the form of the American people. And as their President you will also find me a staunch obstacle to your plans."

Mede chuckles in a dismissive way and looks directly at the President. "Sir there is no need for threats from anyone. I merely state the obvious—there are forces that appear to be tearing our world apart and the populations of the planet are in upheaval as well."

"By the way, I have already taken the liberty of sending the information to Dr. Hindeland's and he has not responded, so I must conclude that he..."

"You need not conclude anything. I've asked Dr. Hindeland to report to me, not to you and I'm sure he will do so when all data is corroborated. Meanwhile, I agree with you that this is a serious matter deserving immediate attention and that we must not let our differences interfere with our solutions. From here on in we should make sure that all information, including actions being taken socially, governmentally, and scientifically be shared openly and rapidly. Our response should not be one of panic, but of rational intent. Are we clear on that, Chairman Mede?"

"Certainly, Mr. President—crystal clear. I would even offer for myself and Dr. Torin to fly to Austin to help with the research and to make sure we understand what progress is being made on all fronts."

"I would suspect that Fitzgerald would be a bit nonplussed by having a team descend on his domain so I'll recommend that just you go, Chairman Mede. Dr. Torin, no offense to you, but I'm sure your efforts might be more effective at your own facilities, sharing your findings as they further develop?"

It is framed as a question, but Winston is bright enough to understand the command implied within. "Yes sir."

The US President stands, signaling the end of the meeting and Torin follows suit, but Darius Mede is not finished with his agenda. "Winston, will you please wait out in the foyer—I have one more point of confidentiality that I must convey to Jack." Winston nods and vanishes through the door.

"Chairman Mede, I don't recall us being on a first name basis."

"My apologies sir, I mean no offense, but I think this last point to be a very difficult one that requires your full attention and should enhance your willingness to see that Fitzgerald and his crew cooperate with my efforts."

"Quit dancing and get to the point."

"Well Mr. President, frankly the point of this discussion has to do with your wife and an extremely…intimate relationship she once entertained with another woman who happens to be a very close friend of mine."

Entry Twelve

"It isn't true to say that all laws of physics break down at a singularity. You can imagine the problems though—how do we interpret an infinite mass or infinite energy or infinite force? Usually, we assume that there is some new set of laws or some new way of looking at the problem that makes the apparent singularity go away."

—Brent Nelson, M.A. Physics,
Ph.D. Student, UC Berkeley

AUSTIN, TEXAS – UNIVERSITY OF TEXAS COMPLEX, QUANTUM SYSTEMS DEPARTMENT

"False Prophet," Fiz yells. "The man has no intention of cooperating. To him this is another chance at a power grab and he'll manipulate data and circumstances to that end. All you have to do is read the ridiculous report from Torin and the Green Order Coalition to see that."

Moses Folzman is chuckling to himself as he doctors a cup of tea at the table. I've seen this ritual now many times and am still amazed. He adds an equal amount of honey and lemon juice along with three teaspoons of sugar to his concoction. Every time I see him consume his secret formula; I half expect him to explode in a sugar rush. The aroma of honey and citrus surrounds the Rabbi and serves as his surrogate presence, lingering even when he is absent from the room. Now Moses speaks. "Are we so different? Has not the entire scientific community for years been guilty of piling theory on top of theory without concern for the absolute validity of the original premise? We all have our false gods that we have worshiped—we have all become manipulators of our dreams rather than followers of the Eternal Spirit. To turn away from the sin of what we have constructed—to seek the greater truth—means sacrificing everything we claim to believe in."

The Rabbi stands up, walks over to Fiz, and places his giant paws on his student's shoulders. "So, what is it we are to do about this, Talmid? How can we prepare for the inevitable?"

Fiz is silent again; reflects for a moment, then thinks out loud, "All we supposedly know are three things—Gravity, Mass, Energy. We know them not because we can prove them—**they prove themselves**."

"But even within the facts we depend on, there hides a mystery—as of yet we don't even have valid witnesses to the origins of these three things we know so well." The Rabbi seems to be going around in circles with his reasoning and I'm becoming frustrated by his challenging of even basic scientific principles. If we can't depend on the very foundations of our science, on what can we depend? As I listen to him, a strange request comes to my mind.

Moses, lead us through the wilderness.

He speaks again as if to oblige. "After Daniel and Brandon initiated their experiment in Mammoth Cave, they perceived that their actions set off a chain of events. In fact, they were merely part of the chain itself. What if we were to begin with the idea that the chain originated elsewhere in another time and another place? Would that affect our next decisions?"

Moses smiles at me and is silent for a moment. Then he says, "Let me ask you a question. As your explorations draw you closer to the center of the beginning, what do you find there? Is it yourself or something else?"

I absolutely have no idea where he's going with this, but I do know the answer. "I'm not the center of the universe."

"A profound discovery in and of itself!" The Rabbi seems very pleased. "Is the universe an accident of coincidence—atoms and molecules somehow assembling from nothing to become something?"

I think I know the answer to this one too. "That would be improbable."

"Not improbable: rather; impossible! Where is your manhood, boy? Even now you hesitate to commit to what you know to be true. Something cannot come from nothing—that is the very foundation of science and life, for that matter. That is the law we must start with! Do you accept this or not? Take courage and answer!"

I have a sensation of being an animal trapped in the corner of my safe little cave, about to be captured. I have to decide this moment whether to attack to protect my tiny kingdom or "I agree, something can't come from nothing."

"So?" Moses asks this as he pulls up a chair and sits directly in front of the one I'm sitting in and places his hands on both my knees. His grasp is firm, I suspect in the way a trainer's hands would be to a wild mustang who is about to have a halter and bit placed over his head. Yet he waits for me to give him permission.

"I…okay, there has to be something that…marked the beginning of the universe."

"Go on." Folzman is not going to let me off that easily.

"And there would have to be some way that matter would be brought into existence. It would not just come from nothing."

"Are you suggesting there is a force out there capable of such an impossible feat?" I hear sarcasm tinged in the great professor's voice and look helplessly over at Fiz only to see a smirk plastered on his face. He is enjoying this far more than I am.

Suddenly I think of an 'out'—a way to skirt the issue. "The Scientific Method tells us that we must have solid proof of something's existence. I can only speculate as to what was before the universe and we've agreed in this room that we're not going to speculate or theorize." *There, that should shut him down!*

"But I'm not asking you to define the force, just to acknowledge something must exist. Just as we have done with gravity. We cannot define it, yet we do not float away. These things exist even if we cannot completely understand them. Do you agree with that?"

"I agree, but still I resist. *Why?!* Then another thought hits me—this one has nothing to do with our origins, but rather the makeup of all we know. There remain innumerable mysteries such as what we are discussing now. Again, my mouth takes on a mind of its own. "I'm starting to think that…based on what we've encountered, the universe is actually a deception…where the mysteries are the norm and the things we see are only distractions?"

The lights flicker and a small tremor vibrates the glass windows. We all intuitively grab for our beverages to make sure they don't spill. I note mentally that everyone is now getting used to the quakes—we're adapting behaviorally. As if to prove my point, my cell phone buzzes signaling a text from Misty who is camped out with the kids and my mom at a local hotel. It reads: *We're fine, don't worry.*

I look up from my phone to see everybody staring at me. Both Fiz and Brandon walk over and pull up chairs next to Folzman, the inquisitor, to face me. They say nothing—just stare at me. There's nothing left to do except to fill the void. "Maybe the distractions are intentionally placed to keep us from focusing on the reality…the hidden truth. Or maybe that truth is set out there to be discovered, but only at the proper moment?" I'm having problems with my own thoughts. I may have just admitted to something I've been resistant to—the acknowledgement of a Supreme Being who is more than just an invisible construct of the human mind.

The Rabbi nods his head and also stands up. Everyone knows a parable is about to unfold. "There was a computer programmer who was a virtual wizard at what he did. His ability to write code and understand process language made him a legend in the industry. One day, the owner of his company comes rushing in saying, 'I need your help quickly! The recent code you wrote was used for a well-known website and there seems to be a problem with how it appears to Web users.'

"'Let me see,' says the programmer. The owner pulls up the Website and there appears a beautiful green glade of rolling hills and row upon row of cemetery tombstones ranging into the distance.

"'I see no problem,' responds the programmer.

"'I asked you to program a picture of the most perfect natural spot for people to come and relax,' exclaims the owner.

"The programmer turns to him and replies, '…Relax? I couldn't find an adequate definition in any computer reference, so I looked up the word *REST* as an alternative. There I found a reference to *FINAL REST* and in that definition I came to imagine the picture before you.'

"'I'm telling you this because we all define our ideas by the environment in which we individually exist. If you are asked to consider or solve a problem, you must be careful not to exclude the universe of answers that lies outside your own. What's more, when presented with an alternative, no matter how compelling, we resist because we are so entrenched in our existing perceptions. True faith in The Eternal's supreme power is the most difficult and therefore most cherished level of awareness one can achieve." Moses leans back in his chair to signal the end of the story.

"Which leads back to the point I was trying to raise: What if all we see is one thing? I mean—nothing distinctive unto itself—it's all really connected."

Brandon shakes his head, "You're not trying to expound the 'We're all a part of God and God is a part of all of us' nonsense, are you?"

"No!" I'm surprised at my own impatience with my friend, but I've got to try to work through this to have it make sense to me. "What I'm talking about is that whatever or whoever created the universe is the First Thing and that nothing else could exist without the First Thing."

"Of what 'First Thing' are you speaking?" With his typical air of importance worn on his face, Darius Mede enters the room—freshly arrived from Washington. Fortunately, the President has warned Fiz of the man's arrival so we are not surprised at his grand entrance. Mede carefully places his suit jacket on the hanger attached to Fiz's door, as if he owns it, and then walks over to stand just outside our seated powwow. There he waits as if expecting us to re-explain our entire conversation. I decide the best reaction to him is to continue right on from where I left off. I too stand up and walk to the whiteboard. "We create theories and laws for things unexplainable— adjusting and redefining the phenomena to meet our explanations, thus attempting to alter the phenomena to prove our theories and laws."

Writing while talking helps me better articulate my thoughts. So, I list the following:

Must...

...a Singularity obey finite physical laws if it is infinite?

What if...

...there is only one Singularity manifesting itself in different forms?

...we are creating laws to explain a mystery that cannot be explained?

...the Singularity is the one and only constant in the universe?

What if…

…we are altered by the actions and definition of The Singularity, not the other way around?

Interesting—everyone is writing on their pads and e-tablets—are they copying my words? Is what I'm laying out that important?

Fiz sets his tablet down, walks over and intercedes on my behalf. First he goes to the board and above my scribblings he writes a title: <u>The Cause-and-Effect Conundrum</u>—then he elaborates. "We have gathered firm evidence using Evolutional Echo Tracing—including what Quartermaster discovered, identifying the Milky Way and Goto galaxies as mirror images. Based on that evidence, we have to conclude that many, if not <u>all</u> of the galaxies, star systems and deep space objects…maybe everything we see, is merely a reflection of…just One Thing."

Mede is looking at us as if we've just arrived from another world.

The silence is deafening so I nervously fill it. "We've been missing a key element when we look at the evolution of the universe. The force and speed at which everything came into existence created a very warped picture. Space literally was and is being curved by the energy of this rapid movement and our senses perceive the motion in multiples, where actually we are seeing something more along the line of mirages on a desert highway— shimmering false images created by an immense energy release."

"Are you insane?" Mede verbalizes what I myself am already thinking about what I've just spouted.

Fiz smiles, sits down again, leans his chair back, stretches his arms out behind him in yawning mode and then sits forward, "Danny, there is a very simple way to test your hypothesis."

We all wait for him to fill the dramatic pause that hangs in the air.

"All we need to do is select the four most distant objects we know to exist in the universe and run an Evolutional Echo Tracing on each one."

"…Of course!" Moses bellows this exclamation as he rises to his feet. "If Daniel's speculation is correct, then all the objects will point to one location. That location will be the point from which all other matter was created—the source of all things. Whatever reality we find there will tell us what reality actually looks like!"

Brandon is shaking his head. "Excuse me, but I'm not getting the importance of this tangent."

"Exactly," chimes in Mede. "What has any of this to do with the cataclysm happening on this planet?"

"…Or with the strange behavior of V4641," adds Brandon.

Fiz is still smiling. "Humor us gentlemen and I believe you will have your answer shortly. What harm can be done?"

V4641 SOL PLUS ONE-C – REGION OF THE MAGELLANIC GAS CLOUDS, 7 LIGHT-YEARS FROM EARTH

I wait—The Eternal waiting for them to stop waiting. It is almost the end. It is almost the beginning!

AUSTIN, TEXAS – UNIVERSITY OF TEXAS COMPLEX, QUANTUM SYSTEMS DEPARTMENT

"Let me understand what you are trying to prove…"

"Not trying, Darius—you yourself validated the formula and the procedure. We all are witnesses to the results." Fiz as usual, has taken the lead in defending Brandon who has just finished running an Evolutional Echo Tracing Sequence on four distinct objects known to be at the outer reaches of the universe.

Mede is not happy with the results. "You are saying that this echoing process of yours has identified the very pinnacle of the universe as none other than V4641? And then you would have me believe that this puny and unstable object has some higher purpose and has come on a celestial quest to visit us? Do you realize how preposterous that sounds?"

It's Moses' turn to reply. "As odd as it seems to all of us, the data supports an intentional path on the part of V4641. Whether or not there is a consciousness involved is speculative. Conscious intent is certainly plausible if you view the movement in terms of behavior instead of just a physical event."

"Plausible? Now who is jumping on the theory band-wagon? I thought you and your converts were trying to do away with theories? Now you're implying that there's a god-figure hiding out there. Are you suggesting Intelligent Design in all of this?"

"…A good point!" Mede looks surprised as Moses shouts this exclamation. Moses Folzman takes full advantage of his antagonist's stunned silence. "So Darius, if there were no Intelligent Design at work in the universe, describe what you think we are looking at based on these results?"

Darius Mede is really off balance now; I can see it in his eyes—how did the question get turned back on him? He glares at Folzman and finally replies. "I will not get caught up in such a ridiculously speculative discussion. We have to deal with the immediate need."

"Perhaps you are correct. We should not be hypothesizing—we should be busy with the truth. As Pontius Pilot once asked, *what is truth*? So, Darius, what is truth?"

Now I'm interested. I want to hear this quasi-world leader/scientific guru's answer because…well, I'd like to know—what is truth, too.

"…The truth?" Mede looks angry. "I am not concerned with truth; I am concerned with results and right now you have nothing to offer in the form of results! I offer suggestions and means to control our circumstances while you offer bizarre ideas about mirrors and invisible mad scientists hiding in the heavens. It flies against everything we know to be reality!"

"…As does everything happening around us. Does the fact that none of these occurrences make sense cause them to be any less real or true?" Fiz is becoming impatient as well.

"No, but you are chasing phantoms instead of facing the problems head on. I've provided you all the information I've accumulated from two highly credible sources that suggest these anomalies are man-made and…"

"…And neither your World Trade Organization nor the Green Order Coalition sources you've sent us offer specific proof of any cause," Fiz moves toward Mede as he speak, "they only point to coincidental speculation about man's so-called abuses…"

"…So called!' Mede steps toward Fiz. "I'll have you know…"

"Gentlemen, please!" It's Moses once more to the rescue. He actually has to stand between Mede and Fiz who have come nose to nose and are trying to shout each other out of existence. "I'm not sure we've given Daniel a chance to completely articulate his thoughts. Maybe he will not be able to clarify his idea, but then again maybe he will. Let us take that chance. Daniel, please benefit us with your understanding."

Moses Folzman should have gone into politics, but now it's my turn to take the podium. "Whether we want to admit it or not, the complexion of our existence in the universe is being radically changed, both here on Earth and in nearby sectors. Boiling it down to the simplest equation, we have to look at what all our observations have in common."

"And that is?" Fiz encourages me to keep going.

"Earth, quite likely our entire solar system and V4641, share some kind of unique attraction to one another. That being said, we also need to admit we know a whole lot more about Earth than we do about V4641. That could be to our advantage—it might even help us determine what we can do to understand and possibly resolve our problems."

Mede is now curious. "Explain our advantage."

"Knowing as much as we do about our home, we can use all that material as a baseline. We then assume that the changes we have been experiencing as of late are all attributed to V4641. We compare those differences to what we know of our baseline and in doing so; we map the characteristics of V4641—simple cause and effect."

"That's a mini-quasar out there!" Brandon is pointing off into space. "It's sucking in matter and in space terms—it's real, real close to us. What more do we have to know?"

"We perceive a singularity as an object that's infinite." I struggle to paint the picture I'm unraveling so again I go to the whiteboard and grab a writing stylus as I ramble on. "In other words, a singularity doesn't really exist unless it exists everywhere at once. This kind of formulaic voodoo doesn't settle well in our brains.

"Because of this incongruence, we have a choice: Either try to make singularities fit our current understanding of physics and the universe or we flip the equation." *There, I've said it. I dare someone to ask the question.*

"Flip the equation?" I had expected Mede to be the one to ask, but surprisingly, it's Reb. Folzman with the curious look on his face and query on his tongue.

"We have started out with a very 'inside-out' perception about our physical origins," I suggest. "We should begin with a new question. What if the singularity came first and we came second? In other words, what if we and our universe are a result of a singularity, not the other way around? Could everything we are and see be an echo of a singularity event?"

"You're implying we are not real, we're just a reverberation of some original noise?" Mede has joined the discussion again. His timbre suggests absolute doubt of my capability to hold any kind of rational discussion.

"Actually I'm suggesting our universe is the mirage. Instead of us having been blown out of some kind of Big Bang, we actually remain inside the original…Singularity Event. What if we are a part of, not separated from, a singularity—more accurately, The Singularity." I write the phrase on the board as I'm talking. "There is only one of its kind—we are on the inside looking out, not the outside looking in. That's why our theories— even our absolutes—appear confused and incongruent."

CLAP, CLAP, CLAP, CLAP. It's Mede, now rising to his feet and applauding, shaking his head back and forth. "Congratulations. You've done it. You've managed to find a way to discredit every solid scientific fact we know and replace it with one gigantic new theory that is totally not provable. And in doing so, you get to create your own world and everyone will just smile in awe as you do it. But I will not stand here while our world crumbles and simply let you pretend it's not happening."

"Why are just our physical origins in question?" This is Moses again. I think he's just ignoring Mede—he also stands and walks up to the board with me. Moses puts out his hand and I give him the stylus while he speaks on. "If we are going to rework the way we view our universe, why should we assume the physical universe is all there is to see? For once, let us infuse into the equation the thing most of us already live by, but are unwilling to justify scientifically—there is a spiritual component, an unseen, but known dimension. It affects and influences, even directs all of what we are. What if this Singularity you speak of is that unseen component and what if it does have an intentional spirit about it? What if we are…not alone?"

"<u>You are mad</u>! Moses Folzman, you of all people know…"

"Shut up, Darius!" Fiz finally comes out of his own contemplation. "If you have better ideas other than just that Green Order Garbage you've been spewing, then give us your insight. If not, we have work to do here and we would appreciate your constructive input."

I'm not privy to whatever history has happened between Fiz and Mede, but the head of the University of Texas Quantum Systems Department apparently has some kind of power over the chairman of the World Trade Organization. The latter sits back down in his chair without another word and remains there—silent and fuming.

Fiz continues with a frustrated sigh. "Perhaps now would be the best time to take an inventory of both what we know and what we want to know. Quartermaster?"

Brandon is the obvious choice to itemize the circumstances. His mind works in bullet points and formulas. "We know that the resonant signatures of Earth and at least one other planet in our solar system are changing. We know that the core and the tectonic plates are beginning to resonate in unison. We can't explain how those two are connected. We know that V4641 has been in motion—we don't know how, we don't know why. We know where it is currently but can't assume it won't move again and where it might head or what connects its behavior to our planet's behavior."

Everyone looks toward me now. My brain doesn't operate like Brandon's. I see things less box-like and look for trends rather than seeking ways to arrange things into tidy packages. So that's how I proceed. "We apparently have to reset our definitions and presumptions and start with the understanding that we exist in an infinite state—not limited by the laws we thought confined us."

The ground beneath us tremors once again.

Entry Thirteen

"In the 1960s and 1970s, the National Aeronautics and Space Administration spent millions of dollars to focus on possible contamination from space microbes that may exist in the vacuum of space—you see, they too had read War of the Worlds by H.G. Wells. But if you were to ask anyone in NASA at the time exactly what microbes, germs or other invisible beasts exist outside of our protective sphere, they would not be able to tell. These cautious scientists based an entire protocol of decontamination for returning astronauts, solely on a suspicion and thus proved one great truth…

"—We don't know what we don't know,
but we do know what we fear. And what we fear is:
What we don't know will likely be the end of us."

—Reb. Moses Folzman, Ph.D. –
Commencement address to the
1998 graduating class of the Technion.

US AIR FORCE DELTA TANGO 131 – SOMEWHERE OVER MEXICO

The drone of the engines lulled me to sleep for a few precious moments, but only a few—now I'm back, uncomfortably awake. After my family had disembarked from the 787 that had carried them to Texas, the assigned military crew had begun its transformation. From passenger transport to cargo beast, it is now filled to the brim with specialized equipment for its next quest. Only two seats are left in place for me and Fiz. We are located in the emergency seating section—wedged into the two window seats on opposing sides of the cabin, cocooned in by our luggage and a menagerie of equipment. These also happen to be the seats in the plane with the distinct characteristics of not being designed to recline. In order to get what sleep I have, it was necessary to prop my feet up on a wooden crate in front of me and lean over towards the window—using a small scratchy blanket, that I managed to scrounge from an overhead bin, as a pillow.

Fiz on the other hand has somehow positioned his legs into a full lotus position and appears to be deep in a trance state—his facial qualities remain peacefully relaxed. I can see his lips moving and try to listen to what he's saying over the engine noise and creaking of the cargo. I catch only snippets, "…we look to you for guidance…the world groans in waiting for your word…please forgive my arrogance and rebellious nature…" I realize now that I'm eavesdropping on his prayer time and guilt compels me to focus my attention elsewhere.

I know how we came to be on this journey, but I still find myself asking, "Why?" There is some unexplainable comfort in replaying the events over again in my memory...

—Our efforts in Austin had seemed to take a sharp left-hand turn when Fiz decided it was time for a call to the President of the United States, along with his Cabinet, to brief them on our progress.

"We received your data stream and are not quite sure what to do with it…the information is not conventional." These words were spoken by the Secretary of The Interior.

Fiz addressed the plasma screen on the wall that has somehow incorporated all our faces, itemized as in some kind of strange internet dating site.

"Mister President, we have made significant headway, but please understand, there is and incredible amount of information to accumulate. It is difficult to assimilate—we hardly know where to start."

"The word *hardly* would imply that you do know where to start." This was the Secretary of The Interior again who was obviously still trying to take charge.

Fiz simply replied, "We do: The Challenger Deep." He went on to explain that the Challenger Deep—the point at which the planet's core and crust are most vulnerable—will also offer us the greatest and most immediate look at what is physically changing everywhere else.

Darius Mede was with us on our side of the web conference and was amazingly supportive. Prior to this meeting, a temporary truce between Fiz and Mede had been negotiated by Moses Folzman, who suggested that we tackle two fronts simultaneously. Looking for immediate solutions to the geophysical trauma ravaging the planet, we also continued to closely monitor and identify any correlated activity suggesting connection between the Earth's crust's expansion and V4641. It was Darius Mede who had initially observed a consistent pulsing radio wave rhythm emanating from the mini-quasar occurring every seven hours. It corresponded exactly to the continual tremors that were now occurring consistently, every seven hours, around the globe.

Fiz then segued into the more complex subject matter of how a mini-quasar could travel across the galaxy to visit us. "Mr. President and members of the Cabinet, our research is bringing us to the conclusion that V4641 is…there is no better word…integrating with Earth and the surrounding area."

"Integrating…please explain," the President commanded.

Fiz pressed on, "Simply put, we are observing a direct correlation between our planet's activity and that of V4641. This quasar affects the pressure and gravity of any object in its sphere of influence. What we need to find out is how it does this and how far reaching are the effects."

The President asks, "How far reaching do <u>you</u> think the effects could be?

"Mr. President, ladies and gentlemen, we must look at the most immediate issue. All the mysteries we are researching will be meaningless if we do not find a way to survive. We believe the Challenger Deep is a significant focal point to discovering our survival solutions."

…And that's how, after bidding our colleagues and my family farewell, Fiz and I became the chosen delegates on our way to a rendezvous with a research platform in the middle of the Pacific Ocean.

THE RECENT PAST

Oh yes, there were two other significant conversations that took place prior to our journey. I was packing a duffel bag of essentials and heard my cell phone rattling, in vibrate mode, across the room. I ran and caught the call to be greeted by a familiar, if disquieting voice.

"How's my number one Science Editor getting along?"

"Mr. Trimble?"

"You sound surprised, Danny. Am I not entitled to check in on you from time to time?"

"Yes sir. I'm actually flattered you've taken the time to call. I just thought you'd be focused on the damage to headquarters and to covering the events unfolding."

"There are other people taking care of those things for me, but you…I can't tell you how excited I am for you finally going to the Challenger Deep! I'm sure you can't speak openly now for security reasons. I just want to encourage you and let you know that we will support you in every way possible, no matter what happens."

No matter what happens? What might happen?

"I've assured some strategic organizations where I have influence—such as the Green Order Coalition and the World Trade Organization, that you are the man to help with real results."

Great, my boss is in bed with Darius Mede.

"Danny, all I ask is that you keep me as informed as possible. Any progress we can show toward some kind of 'fix' will go a long way in quelling the fears of the worlds' population."

It was not one minute after I disconnected with Jonathan Trimble that the second conversation took place—the voice revealing itself to me clearly and distinctly as that of my father's. *Your joy is about to be completed, you will soon see the light. Be ready to believe!*

US AIR FORCE DELTA TANGO 131 – SOMEWHERE OVER THE PACIFIC OCEAN

A feeling of overwhelming loneliness has come over me. I'm thousands of miles above the earth and equally distant from any significant land mass, surrounded by countless crates and boxes that symbolize the vast storehouse of problems we face. I'm reminded of my inability to solve the puzzle and it presses down on my consciousness like a hungry animal. I close my eyes, trying to force away the melodramatic images; when I open them, there is a new face before me—Fiz.

"You heard Rabbi Folzman's challenge in his web-lecture to his students regarding the need to commit to a choice. What do you think?" Fiz is in Confrontation Mode. He has climbed over some equipment in order to sit next to me, obviously in the mood for a conversation—I have no choice but to respond.

"I think he was passionate, but I'm not sure those in his class appreciate the depth of…"

"Enough!" My professor stares at me in a way I've seldom seen him do before. "Stop examining, stop speculating and evaluating—stop tearing apart. Child, what do YOU believe?"

Maybe I'm tired of hospital beds and having strange animals coming to my assistance and having my body rearranged molecularly. Maybe I'm just weary of riddles I don't understand or can't comprehend, and certainly I'm just plain sick and tired of carrying the burdens of the world on my shoulders.

So, I lash out. "You expect people to process and accept what you've had years to assimilate? I'm supposed to just accept unquestioningly every bit of what you propose, yet it was you who taught me to doubt <u>everything</u>!

"I don't know what I believe because there's too much to believe—I'm not sure what's real and what's theory anymore. Frankly, I'm at a point where I don't <u>want</u> to think, I don't <u>want</u> to believe in anything. I want you and the whole world to leave me alone!"

There's one very specific thing I don't <u>want</u> to believe. I don't <u>want</u> to believe I just uttered these words to this man who shaped so much of my life. Another word creeps into my thoughts—it causes tears to well up in my eyes. The word is *shame*. "Fiz, I'm sor…"

Before my apology is completed, Fiz places the index finger of his left hand at my lips. He puts his other hand on my shoulder and pulls me toward him. Now he embraces me completely, warmly, lovingly. My sobs betray the insecurity within. Fiz continues to cradle me in his arms, allowing my release to be complete. In this moment, there is no concern for others or the world and I remain with my head buried on his shoulder, my tears helping to cleanse away the confusion. All I need is something—<u>one</u> thing—to make sense; to fill the void created by the sucking away of all things unimportant.

Fiz pours words into the maw of my emptiness. "If there is an all-powerful, interacting, sentient *Presence* that invites an intricate relationship with us, then shouldn't we focus <u>all</u> our attention on it? Shouldn't it become the primary thing we allow to attract us—draw us in—creating a Spiritual Singularity?"

I'm having trouble with this concept and I'm annoyed that I can't stop my crying.

Fiz will not let go. "Relationship is a word that does not seem very cosmic. It suggests something more intimate—more personal."

What is he suggesting? "Fiz, if the V4641 phenomenon and all of the geophysical acrobatics happening on this planet are by the hand of God… okay. But that explanation allows no one else to be blamed for <u>not</u> finding a solution. What if you're wrong? What if all of this is some cosmic accident?"

"What or who you choose to believe is in control of this situation— any situation—will forever define your existence. How do you choose to exist, Danny?"

There is no time! I hear the words and know they are more than just my father's voice—it's a bigger message. I've denied for so long—speculating God away—refusing to consider the implications of a Supreme Being's existence. But now, *there is no time.* I have to choose. My not wanting to choose before has been purely avoidance behavior rather than a choice—a walking death of indecision. I can't go on like this. *There is no time.* I must, I…desire to be awake…<u>Alive</u>! I turn and face my mentor and speak in what sounds to me to be an alien tongue. "God is God and I am not. I want Him with me!"

V4641 SOL PLUS ONE-C – REGION OF THE MAGELLANIC GAS CLOUDS

Molecules burst from the impact, a consuming fire flares all around an eruption unlike any other—how can it be explained? No force anywhere—except The One Which Created—can appreciate its power and beauty. Behold the birth of awareness—the revelation of light upon darkness. I am once more in love!

Entry Fourteen

Deep calls to deep at the roar of your waterfalls; all your breakers and your waves have gone over me.

—Psalm 42:7, The Bible

11"21' NORTH LATITUDE, 142" 12' EAST LONGITUDE, PACIFIC OCEAN – EAST OF THE 14 MARIANA ISLANDS

"Sampson to Zorah, Sampson to Zorah, testing one, two, testing…" Steve Billings, the same who co-piloted the Alvin III on our ill-fated test-run, is going through the launch list prior to our plummet into the ocean depths. He is in the proper seat for him this time—the Pilot's chair. I'm not sure why he accepted the offer to go with me considering our last experience together. Then again, no other manned submersible has revisited the Challenger Deep since the Trieste. This will be one of those <u>big</u> moments for the stalwart pilot.

Right now, we are literally hanging from a gantry off the rear of our launch and command ship, the Zorah. Steve appears very comfortable in the Sampson—he has rechecked the settings of the instrumentation at least four times—but this vessel gives me no great sense of assurance. The Sampson is very new in its fabrication, yet very old in concept. It's a bathysphere—not like a submarine or a submersible—in that it remains tethered to a mother ship and has to receive electricity and atmosphere from the surface.

Compared to the Trieste and Alvin III, this thing is a veritable RV. The lightweight yet super high tensile composition allowed its designers some greater latitude. They widened the cockpit to allow more room for instrumentation and included swivel bucket seats complete with easy release restraining harnesses to allow greater access to the rear for observation purposes. Cup holders are even notched into the center console. Unfortunately, I also notice that the chemical *port-a-potty* in the back is still…a public affair. Guess observers inside and out will just have to close their eyes and nose.

The unique hull construction is what makes this craft so interesting and unsettling. Other than the deck flooring and some inner support girders, the entire affair is constructed of a newly tested ultra-strength polymer compound. The US Navy first discovered that, the deeper the ship made from Pressurized Polymer submerges, the stronger the molecular bond. It's the ultimate—if somewhat pricey—deep water submersible construction material. Did I mention that in its most refined state, it is virtually transparent?

Hence the birth of the Sampson; hence the port-a-potty predicament; hence the delicious irony of a submersible fishbowl occupied by two people descending to the ocean floor: Adding in my deep-water phobia, the word *vulnerable* doesn't quite capture my frame of mind.

I've calculated our ultimate destination, The Challenger Deep, to be the ideal location because of its characteristics and location. There, we'll be able to determine if V4641 is affecting us through high levels of neutrino bombardment and to see if the current "Earth hiccups" are associated with its approach.

There is the other purpose—my very selfish purpose—of finally being able to visit the one place on the planet I have longed to explore. We'll be observing firsthand, the deepest, most mysterious region of our world.

There is a beeping sound emanating from somewhere in the cockpit. Steve looks at his watch, shuts off the annoying alarm and exclaims, "One coming." He reaches for a hand-hold and I scan the surroundings for loose objects. I grab an unsecured toolbox that is balanced on top of the console just as another seventh-hour-tremor runs through the ship— only out here, in the middle of the ocean, the passing effect results in a churning ten foot wave which causes the ship to roll and pitch as if riding a small rollercoaster. I look out through the cockpit windows to see that everyone else has also prepared for the ride in similar ways, bracing and grabbing for precious cargo. It's amazing how people are now acclimating to the new conditions of our existence and it causes me to wonder at our behavioral adaptability.

Steve excuses himself and climbs out the hatch for a final check of the tether connections. I'm alone. The discomfort of this setup along with the risk involved and the urgency of our mission cause me to do something I've not attempted in a long time.

I start off with a non-vocal inquiry…*God?*

The lack of response is not surprising. The Supreme Being is being kind—had He answered verbally, such as in the recent conversations with my dad, I'd be climbing out of the hatch and checking myself into the nearest mental health facility. Still for some reason, I ask again…*God?*

I'm not sure what else to say, so I just start talking out loud. "I…haven't done this for a while," *get to the point* "I've doubted there was anything personal between us. I haven't focused on You because…why do I need to? Aren't You capable of taking care of Yourself?"

"Me? I've been…okay—there's been no need for You to…<u>no</u>, that's not true! I hated my father leaving—we weren't finished yet—the timing stunk!" *Where is all this coming from?* "For that matter, the more I searched for answers from You, the more I saw the hypocrisy of churches and of those who claimed to be Your messengers. Even Your Text seemed full of errors and legends instead of revealing paths."

I'm rambling—an image of a sanctuary pulpit comes to my mind. *I get it—look at me preaching to The Eternal.* "I apologize, God. It's just…this is like starting over. I…" *What do I want from God?* "…I want to…" *Wait, wrong question—<u>selfish</u>!*

"God, what would You have me do? I'm a scientist at heart—I know that's what I am! And so my skill is in doubting everything—even You."

"But that means…I should doubt myself too. Maybe I've depended on things that look good but aren't provable—not *truth*. Maybe I need to trust in something…no…trust in <u>one</u> thing that's constant and certain even though everyone else suggests…that You…cannot be. You are! And if I trust in You as the *truth of truths*, I'll know what to look for in the depths of the oceans and the vacuum of space…and in my heart."

"What did you say?"

I know I've just jumped out of my seat—my head hit the overhead readout. Steve proceeds to climb back down into the cockpit. He obviously had heard the end of my celestial chat. "…Nothing—just thinking out loud. Are we ready?"

"As ready as we'll ever be." Pilot Steve holds out his hand for me to shake. He has a firm grip. Looking again at me as if he's searching for something deeper in my psyche, he simply says, "Let's do this." He radios the launch crew of the Zorah and gives the command to lower us away—then looks at me and says, "You know God didn't create us to doubt, but he did wire us to question. The secret is in knowing the difference between the two."

DEPTH 0 FEET – EPIPELAGIC ZONE.
DIVE TIME: 0 HOURS, 15 MINUTES

The trip to the bottom begins with anticipation and then comes the tedium of descent. The human body can only adjust to so much pressure changing in a given time so it's best to go slow. Bring a good book along to read—where we're going is seven plus hours away, straight down and there's little to do along the way.

After the first 200 feet under the water's surface, there's just not much to see—lack of sunlight penetration pretty much takes care of that—so my thoughts wander. I find myself bemused by the fact that a ship—which is always considered feminine by her occupants—would be dubbed "Sampson.. Right now, I need all the comforting I can muster so I'm grateful to whoever chose the name of strength in spite of the contradiction.

The Sampson is highly unique in another way. Because of the plastic composite design, this lady is extremely quiet. Yes, there is the occasional popping and pressure causing cracking noises, but they are few and far between and not nearly as loud as they were in the Alvin III.

I have to depend on the need to yawn and chew gum—allowing my ears to adjust—to know we are going down. Adding to the flavor of the gum, there's a salty taste on my tongue and the smell of brine in the air—reminders that at any moment, if the Sampson were to develop a crack, we will be quickly crushed to uncomfortable proportions.

Steve continues to study the instrumentation. He also must make sure that the air we have in here is breathable. If the re-breather were to malfunction we would fall peacefully asleep, merrily sucking in our own carbon-dioxide until our hearts and brains ceased functioning. I busy myself with reading material that I downloaded onto my smartphone the night before—reading which has nothing to do with the mission—a distraction for my claustrophobic nature.

"What are you reading?" Steve asks.

...So much for personal privacy. "...Nothing much...just...some Biblical passages."

"Good, we may need some guidance down here—pretty dark in the abyss."

Steve now becomes a little more serious, swiveling his seat to face directly at me as he speaks. "Look, I have no idea what's down there or what's going on. Whenever I'm headed into an unfamiliar situation I want to know that whoever is with me is 'the real deal'. If things get... complicated, I need to know you're not going to panic on me. I guess what I'm saying is that I need to know if you're spiritually strong."

...Spiritually strong? What in the world does that mean? "Yeah, I'm good."

"Good?" Steve seems surprised at my choice of words. He looks at me skeptically.

I decide that keeping the conversation going from my side might avert him from asking me more awkward personal questions. "You don't have to worry. I've been through some pretty strange circumstances lately. I won't fall apart on you. But I do have a question."

"Sure."

"You're a pilot of deep-water vessels—aren't MOST of the situations you face, unfamiliar?"

"To a degree, but very few dives I make include unpredictable factors— we try to plan them out pretty well. There was one a number of years ago where some guy had me start an underwater landslide..."

"Point taken and...sorry again for that."

"No need for the apology. Besides, that experience taught me a lot about you. You're unorthodox, but trustworthy - I think you do hold up well under pressure...no pun intended."

Farther and farther down we go. I don't know why my thoughts drift to Brandon, but I feel a sudden concern for his well-being.

I've come to know Brandon as an enigma. He maintains his *grunge look* as camouflage. Effective too—most people would not consider this fully bearded, sandal and tie-dye shirt laden throwback to the 60s for what he really is—a supremely disciplined obsessive compulsive *clean freak*. To say that he's tidy would be like saying a shark likes a little meat now and then. Brandon is the personification of the laboratory environment.

As his best friend, I know an additional curiosity about this genius that is seldom shared. His appearance is a purposeful ruse of rebellion. Fiz's nickname for him—Quartermaster—is deserved for multiple reasons, as Brandon Lader, Ph.D. is also a decorated war hero.

It seems that Brandon had acquired his standing at U.T. based on a full military scholarship from the US Air Force. For a brief period after I was ushered out of university life, Brandon was called up for active duty to assist in the development of advanced drone technology. Many of the design improvements were of his creation and Tech Sergeant First Class Brandon Lader was obtaining quite a reputation in his battalion. However, when not on maneuvers, he refused to put on the standard issue combat boots that are required for every soldier to wear on duty. Brandon had been reprimanded on numerous occasions but insisted that a recurring toe fungus required him to wear sandals at all times for 'ventilation' purposes. The Air Force was not impressed by his reasoning and, regardless of his valuable qualifications, was preparing charges for insubordination.

One day, an enlisted technician who worked in Brandon's group walked into a test hanger with an armed shoulder-mounted rocket launcher claiming to be an instrument of his god for the destruction of the evil presence represented by Uncle Sam. He demanded that all the personnel in the hanger, including Sergeant Lader, raise their hands in preparation to be sacrificed in the name of Allah.

What this clandestine jihadist failed to realize was that Geek Warrior Brandon had an ability to multitask in a very unique way. Prior to this unfortunate intrusion, he had been crouched on the floor of the hanger, reassembling a remote-control joystick motor for an attack drone that was now mounted on a gantry ten feet above his head. This particular drone had an additional feature that Sergeant Lader had improvised into its fuselage—a fifty caliber machine gun on a swivel mount that just happened to be pointed in the direction of his tormentor.

Keeping his hands in the air as requested, Sergeant Lader slipped off the sandal from his right foot and used his toes to manipulate the recently repaired joystick so that the drone's machine gun was aimed appropriately. Then with a delicate tap from his big toe, the armament was engaged and the once threatening attacker immediately became…disarmed.

From that day forward, until his release from active duty, the Air Force turned a blind eye toward Brandon's disregard for their dress code.

So I know well that he is very capable of taking care of himself. Nevertheless, I decide to put in a prayer on Brandon's behalf.

DEPTH 8000 FEET – BATHYPELAGIC (MIDNIGHT) ZONE. DIVE TIME: 3 HOURS, 48 MINUTES

Maybe there's no time according to my father, but there seems to be lots of time down here. Dangerous time: time to think, time to remember back to what were better times…

—When we started out at the lab together, Fiz had quickly identified the perfect capacity for my friend Brandon: He was given full autonomy for the department. But Fiz went further and gave him his unique title. In the navy it's the Quartermaster who is at the wheel of the ship. And without the planning, support and coordination of the Quartermaster/Supply Sergeant, the army simply dies. Fiz envisioned his crew as infantry engaged in confronting the universe. He surmised that without a QM, we would perish.

On the other hand, Fiz had given me the title of Keeper, but it was Misty, one evening at our kitchen table, who defined my inner character.

"Brandon," she began, "is a good work match for you. He's stuck in a pit—not going anywhere—just doing what he does because it's there to be done. That's good for him, but he can't see past the walls of his pit and that's dangerous."

I wondered when and why she had observed Brandon so intently.

"You," she took my hand while speaking, "are in a rut, not a pit. A rut's a good thing actually. Most people try to get out of their rut, but then they either wander around aimlessly, or get stuck like Brandon in a pit and never move. You are methodical, but ever trudging—persistent if not always aware of your true purpose. I get frustrated with you because you often ask too many questions. You get so involved in pursuing each one, and you sometimes forget about your family and those around you who are also on the journey with you. I love you because you will not stop until you have an answer, but you need to remember to involve those most important to you and help prepare them for the rest of the trip."

My soul mate had just finished reading an old book - *RUT Management*, it was called—and the guy who wrote it had apparently nailed the whole pitiful pattern of my life.

I have yet to describe the complexities of Misty's character. I'm not capable of that kind of depth—certainly deeper than where I'm headed now. She is the root beneath me, my anchor, and my source of nourishment to keep me going.

DEPTH 14,500 FEET – ABYSSOPELAGIC ZONE. DIVE TIME: 6 HOURS, 26 MINUTES

As we continue to plummet into the void, my thoughts also run deeper…

"…Are you a mirror or a window?" It was a question Fiz had posed to me on the plane ride to our launch site.

I was clueless to where he was headed with this. "Excuse me?"

"What do you want people to see when they look at you, themselves or a glimpse of something else…greater…inside and beyond you?"

…The question snaps me momentarily back to the present. This is the world in which I exist—dark, impenetrable, seemingly unwilling to reveal its secrets. I turn back in my mind's eye to Fiz who is waiting patiently for a response….

"…A window—I want to be a window. But, I can't see beyond the glass, how am I supposed to point others in the right direction?"

"Silly Child—let there be light…"

…A flash in the murkiness before me brings me again out of my reverie. It must be one of the many creatures endowed in these pressured confines with the chemical ability to briefly illuminate, either for navigation or as a signal to others of its own kind, or possibly as a lure for its next meal. What a diverse menagerie this is. We know so little of it. *If only I had more light.*

DEPTH 35,851 FEET – HADALPELAGIC ZONE. DIVE TIME: 7 HOURS, 39 MINUTES

As we approach the bottom, I'm absolutely conflicted. This is <u>The Moment</u> I've aspired to for the last ten years. But what is it now that I've come here for? Am I here to seek some apocryphal answer as to why the planet and the universe are misbehaving? Am I here for some kind of personal sense of accomplishment or recognition? Is it simply to culminate what I had set out to do once before? Could this venture have nothing to do with me at all? For some reason, that question bothers me most of all.

"This is breathtaking—look!" It's Steve in observation mode. He's angled the vessel so that the nose is pointed downward at a 20-degree pitch. We're both leaned forward in our harnesses by the gravity and I peer out to where his index finger points.

"What in the..." I hear the words come out of my mouth; no completion of the question is necessary. There is no answer. We are looking at a glowing ridge below us, the water temperature gauge reads a balmy 85 degrees Fahrenheit, but I suspect as we draw closer to what is obviously a brand new and highly active volcanic vent, the readings will rapidly climb. The temperature near other such vents in the Mariana Trench is known to approach 572 degrees Fahrenheit—not the most ideal place to take a casual swim. So I'm a little...a lot surprised when I glance again at the readings to see that the water temperature is actually decreasing as we near the glow. Steve is puzzled too and reaches up to tap the electronic display, as if that will actually fix the data. Instead, the temperature reading drops by another twelve degrees.

"Something's wrong," Steve and I speak out in unison.

"I'm going to level off so we can check the systems." Thankfully, my pilot friend is cautious. "Don't want to get us cooked accidentally getting too close to that vent—I don't care what that meter says."

I nod in agreement and scan the other instruments with my eyes. Depth – 10,200 meters; Hydrostatic Pressure – 15,842 pounds per square inch; Trace Oxygen Levels –.0001. All reading as predicted. It can only mean that the temperature sensor is faulty…

…A jolt. A <u>big</u> jolt, on the starboard side—my side—of the ship, rocks the Sampson. My personal oxygen levels and heart rate immediately elevate—no external sensors are necessary for me to detect this. Something tells me to check my watch—*no, it's not the seven-hour tremor.* I turn my head away from the instruments and search outside the cabin, using the two sensors I trust the most—my eyes. They betray me, for what I see can't be real—not at this depth, not in this place.

I turn back to see that Steve is also gape-mouthed, staring at the impossible—a sperm whale that has just brushed against our hull and is swimming lazily before us toward the vent. Actually, not just one, there's a whole pod of whales now reflected in the light. "There!" Steve is now looking portside. I follow his lead and see schools of fish, thousands… more…I notice above us too. Jellyfish, other (*what are those?*)'things' drift over the entire area—all seem drawn toward the volcanic rift.

I refer back to the console and things are strange there as well. I read it out loud. "Water Temperature – Zero; Pitch – Zero; Depth – Zero…" I feel something brush against my right temple. I jerk involuntarily and then turn to see my pen and notepad floating in mid-air. Steve now reaches in front of me to grab his bottled water which is doing slow somersaults before us—the water within the capped container is separated into four ameba-like globs, each independently formed into different shapes and gyrating in random directions.

"What is that?" Steve is transfixed by another object ahead, but nearer to his observation point—long, sleek, very large, reflecting many colors… iridescent, yet brilliantly white with a silver sheen—ever changing, ever the same. Pure…the familiarity frightens me.

"Beautiful," Pilot Steve expresses the obvious.

…Wings—as in my dreams? Maybe not, the more I stare at them, the more they resemble fins…now also a tail, skin-like…not scales…prismatic leather—radiant, alive—it turns toward us. And, as in my dream, the dragon with the broken horn wears a sad expression. There is no smile this time, just an ever-increasing brightness as it comes closer to investigate

us. The dragon abruptly turns again and swims / flies toward the vent. Sampson's hull shudders and we too begin to descend—undesirably pitching to the starboard so that Steve in the pilot's seat is now closer to the strange activity ahead. The instruments continue to register all zeroes, but our motion and the scene before us say a whole lot is going on. Steve and I reach for the tops-side communications switch simultaneously to request we be pulled up—his practiced hand is quicker. There's only one problem—Steve's practiced hand passes right through the toggle switch as if his flesh and bone no longer exist. He tries once more but fails to connect. As a matter of fact, I can barely see him at all, but for the glow ahead of him that creates a halo around my companion. And he is no longer restrained by his harness. Sampson's pilot tries to speak, but no words come out of his mouth. Yet I hear him clearly. *Danny, do you feel it?*

I'm not sure what Cheshire Cat Steve is feeling, but I'm pretty stressed. All I can see of him is a radiant smile. It's only now that I think to look down at my own hands. They too, along with the rest of my arms, legs, and body, seem to be breaking down molecularly. I glance again at the ship-to-ship radio and try to reach for it but can't seem to get my appendages to respond. I look toward the vent (*my eyes still work?*) and realize we are now very close. The animals, fish…things, are all disappearing, luminescing? I can see their skeletons, organs, and inner workings, like goblins from some strange Halloween movie—silhouetted against the light of the vent.

It's not a vent, is it? And it's not light either—not light as I've ever known it. There is no color to it, but all colors at once. It's more like… warmth and beauty…it has texture. The light is spreading out—all it touches becomes the light. I'm becoming the light.

I feel it now, Steve…It's absorbing me…I want to…

Another jolt—this one from above and behind—I try to turn to see what has hit us and realize I'm no longer in my harness either and seem to be free floating in the cabin. The Sampson though has changed direction, backing away and upward from the light-that's-not-a-vent. *No! Let me get closer. There's…*

"…more." My voice suddenly resonates in the confines of the Sampson and I fall hard back against my seat and the console. But there are still other people's thoughts in my head. Steve? Fiz? My father? All? Others? I can't distinguish…all of them are saying the same thing, *Radio.*

I turn painfully and see the Top-side Com Switch. My right arm appears to be broken and refuses to move. The left arm is pinned under me. It's all I can do to push up and pivot, the nerve endings sending searing pain messages from my damaged limb to my brain. I somehow get seated again and reach to the Com Switch with my good hand which I notice has blood on it. I flip the switch and speak unfamiliar words, "Mayday, mayday. Pull us up now!" My head is exploding and I see a drip of blood fall from somewhere above me onto my hand. *I must have hit*

I'm too tired to finish the thought. Before I fall to sleep, I look over to see how Steve is doing, but he's not in his seat. *He must have floated to the rear of the ship.* I close my eyes to chase the dragon in my dreams. *There is so much light here. Finally, I can see!*

Entry Fifteen

And it shall come to pass afterward, that I will pour out my Spirit on all flesh; your sons and your daughters shall prophesy, your old men shall dream dreams and your young men shall see visions. Even on the male and female servants in those days I will pour out my Spirit. And I will show wonders in the heavens and on the Earth, blood and fire and columns of smoke. The sun shall be turned to darkness and the moon to blood, before the great and awesome day of the LORD comes.

—Joel 2:28-31, The Bible

AUSTIN, TEXAS – UNIVERSITY OF TEXAS MEDICAL CENTER

The light is so brilliant, tangible. *I can actually feel its form when I reach out and touch it. I can see shapes in the light, hovering over, I sense their concern.*

"Danny? Can you hear me?"

It's Misty, what a nice dream. I think I'll keep it.

"Danny, if you can hear me squeeze my hand."

The light has hands. How extraordinary. I like it. Yes, I will squeeze. Wait, the light is dimming, changing, I'm being pulled away. Oh, please no…

"Danny, look at me."

It's Fiz's voice and I open my eyes at his command. There is something caked onto my eyelids that makes opening them difficult, foggy. Something warm and wet is brushed across my face and a memory comes to me—my mother washing my face after I had a bad fall and cut my head. The wet…*a washcloth, it's a washcloth*…feels good—helps clear away the crust obstructing my vision.

Although it was Fiz's voice I heard—it's Misty I now see looking down at me. Confusing, but wonderfully comforting. Then I move my head to the right, "Ouch!"

"Good, you can move. Just don't try to do it too much." It's Fiz speaking again and now I focus on his face which is next to Misty's face. They are by my bed in…a hospital room! This I don't like. Tubes and wires are everywhere and they seem to all be emanating from…me. Beeps and whirs and buzzes suggest there are also machines in the room. The tubes must connect me to them. There's a buzzing noise and suddenly my arm tingles at the joint of my elbow. A coldness trickles up toward my shoulder and beyond. Misty is in front of me; possibly two Misty's. She's so shiny, "Can you stop floating away? I want to see you."

"What do you remember?" Misty is stroking my cheek, but the voice is again Fiz's. I really don't want to work right now. I just want to gaze into the eyes of my wife and…love.

"Danny please, it's important—tell us what happened down there." Misty is asking this time; it makes me sad. I thought she wanted to love me too. Where did she go?

"Danny, look at me. Try to focus."

Oh, there she is. Okay, I'll try, but only because I want to marry her "I…can't…explain…it." The images, the light, creatures—all wonderful, frightening—won't separate in my mind's eye. There's just a feeling. "…Joy—pure…perfection. There is nothing more important."

"Try to tell us what you saw—what do you mean by joy?" Fiz is hovering in the water by my bed and is holding my other hand.

"There is life down here, but not like…not like life we know. It's more. There is…I can hear, no, <u>feel</u> someone speaking to me." I'm back; in the Mariana Trench—I can see it all. *NO! I don't want to be here,* my mind screams. *Yes, you do—you want it more than life,* another part of me cries.

"Steve? Was it Steve talking to you?" Why is there such urgency in Fiz's voice?

"Steve is here, yes. He's smiling," I smile too, speaking the words. "Steve knows how beautiful everything is. Ask him."

"Danny, try to remember: When you saw Steve last, what was happening?"

I can see now, the moment surfacing slowly as if held down by the pressures and mystery of the deep. "I…we're floating…going somewhere.

Steve sees it first and starts going. I don't want to go at first, but then… now…" I jerk my arms and legs to get up to go with Steve, but I'm restrained somehow. *How did a hospital bed get into the Sampson?* "I need to tell Steve I'm sorry. I didn't want to leave. Can I see him now?" *Why are Misty and Fiz crying?*

"You need to rest right now." Misty leans over and kisses my forehead.

She's right—I'm so tired of remembering. I don't want to remember now…sleep.

I've noticed since the adventure in Mammoth Cave that my dreams are becoming more and more vivid—almost real. I'm having trouble distinguishing reality from my dreams. That's the whole point of this. I wake up and someone tells me about an event, such as Darius Mede having a private conversation with the President of the United States and I already know. I am somehow aware of conversations and can recall exactly what transpired at times and places where I was not physically present. This spooks me. Sharing this discovery in the entries of my journal seems the safest method of relating the strangeness of it all. This way, later…we can all look back at this and maybe it will make sense.

I'll continue…speaking in the present tense most of the time because… most everything—even my past—seems very much present now. I'm also catching glimpses of things to come and I…No, I'm not going to share that yet…it's…not ready to be shared.

Back to my current dream: This one is just as vivid as all the rest. I don't know when it's happening—it was, or is right now and involves Moses Folzman. He's back at the Technion in front of his class and he is unraveling a mystery—his booming voice conveying the passion of his ideas.

"We have grown accustomed to the idea that everything remains constant and comfortable because constant and comfortable are the norms. Quite the contrary, everything in the universe speaks to change as the constant.

"This is evident even at the microscopic and subatomic levels. For example—when a part of the blood stream experiences infection, white cells attack the culprit. If you watch the process, very specialized white plasma cells actually assemble themselves on site. Their combinations are infinitely complex, we can't adequately define all the ingredients laying about in the bloodstream that ultimately result in these 'antibodies'.

"This miracle, this battle we call Healing that occurs within us, is not unlike the changes we are now experiencing throughout our world and beyond. Something has infected our cosmos—something that is not right. The organism that is the Universe is reacting to combat the threat.

"Yes, yes I know there are those of you who summarily dismiss the idea of an intelligence associated with the vastness of the heavens. I won't argue with you—argue within your own mind and take great care battling with the chaos you discover there. Reason with yourselves, 'How can all this be true—how does a cell know to protect itself; how can a neutron reinvent itself and how can infinity be an accident?' Explore what you find within, do not avoid it!

"Do you doubt there is an Eternal Spirit? Fine, prove otherwise—not by theory or speculation, but by confrontation with the Spirit itself! Peer soulfully at God's extraordinary creation and dare to refute his power. See what will happen—prepare for great disappointment, despair, and darkness to be your companions!

"Then consider what is truly happening rather than what you would like to happen and join in the battle! It is called *healing*.

"I hope, I pray that this discussion bothers you. It should bother you, causing the battle to grow within you. Do not be complacent and dare not think you have discovered an answer to anything. The answer to everything was given to us long ago—it is the questions that we have confused and now must correct. If such a consideration boggles your mind causing you to not know where to start, I offer a beginning point for you. It is the most simple and yet most revealing question of all. 'What if there is a God and I am not him'?"

AUSTIN, TEXAS – UNIVERSITY OF TEXAS COMPLEX, QUANTUM SYSTEMS DEPARTMENT

I'm awake now, I think. This seems real enough. It appears to be the time and place I remember as the actual present and I have just been deemed by Misty, Fiz and Brandon—those I consider closest to me—to be ready to hear what has really happened.

"Danny, Steve is…gone." Fiz has his hand on my shoulder and looks sadder than I can remember seeing him ever before.

"What are you telling me? He's dead? How?"

"We don't know. That is the mystery. When we pulled the Sampson up from the water, after the decompression period, and opened the hatch, you were the only one in the cabin. Steve…could not be found."

Fiz's description triggers a series of choppy video clips to explode in my head. Whales and dragons swimming by, light where there should be none, goofy radiantly smiling faces, an indescribable sensation of freedom from physical laws, Steve evaporating before my eyes, a presence I can't look at because of its terrible power, a desire to be surrounded… consumed…there is no good word…swallowed up by that presence… emptiness when I am pulled back toward the surface…longing—if only I had found the strength—to open the hatch and escape, swimming back to that magnificent place. All I can do is weep. "NO! It should have been me!"

Misty's arms are around me instantly. "Oh Danny, you couldn't have saved him. We watched the video log and there were so many strange things happening, you couldn't have helped him!" Her tears mingle with mine—our faces pressed together in the misery of the moment. She is the safest place where I can be at this moment, but even she doesn't understand. I'm not sad because I couldn't save Steve. I am envious of him, wanting more than this reality here, to be where he is now.

"I have to go back. I have to finish it."

Fiz looks puzzled. "There is no possibility of the Sampson or any other vehicle going back to the Challenger Deep. As soon as you surfaced, the crust erupted down there—caused an 11.9 earthquake, strongest ever recorded, sending tsunamis in both directions. Hong Kong, Los Angeles, Seoul, Tokyo…many others…are devastated."

I'm surprised at my response to him. "Fiz, we don't need to go back in that way. There's another way. We can all go there, but first, I have to go. When is our conference with Darius Mede and the President?"

"How do you know about that? I haven't…" Fiz is looking at me very strangely.

"Danny!" This is Misty and there is worry in her whispered cry. She too looks at me as if I've just landed from another planet. I walk over to the mirror that is part of the lab table and stare into it to try to understand what they are seeing. I'm there, it's still me, but I'm glowing. A soft blue light seems to be coming from inside of me.

"What in the…?" This is Brandon who walks over and turns off the lights. It's faint, but there is definitely a halo around me and the others in the room are reflected in the light. I turn on the cold water tap at the lab station, run my fingers under the water and then sprinkle some on my opposite forearm. The water sparkles with a strange bluish hue.

"Okay, that's just weird," Brandon says.

Fiz puts his hand out to Brandon, but makes a request to me, "Danny, do me a favor and go into the other room and close the door just for a moment, please."

I don't know what the purpose is, but comply. In the darkness, I'm my very own flashlight—it's not a very efficient beam I produce, but it's enough. *What is happening?!*

I hear Fiz's command from beyond the door, "Come back in, Danny." I do and Fiz announces another wonder to consider. "Quartermaster is also glowing. It's not as pronounced as yours, but it is there."

Now Scientific Danny wakes up. *A corollary? Some kind of parallel? What is causing this and why me? Why Brandon, less? Why just us? What makes us different? What is it we have in common?*

Fiz walks around us once without comment. Then he goes over to the light switch and flips it back on, saying only one statement, "I suppose it's time we contact the President."

"Do that again!" The President of the United States commands Fiz, who obliges by flipping off the lights so that mine and Brandon's glow are evident via the web camera. I'm getting a little annoyed with the theatrics and am about to suggest we get on with the business at hand, but the voice of Moses beats me to the punch.

"This is all very interesting, but I suspect it is a result of the increasing influence of V4641 and thus we should be busy trying to sort out its meaning. Don't you think?"

Everyone nods their heads, so the Rabbi continues. "There is only one event that Daniel and Brandon have in common that the rest of us do not and that would be the signaling episode within the confines of Mammoth Cave." Moses walks over to an interactive screen at his location and writes our names down under a heading of Mammoth. He continues to speak as he writes. "Now as to why Daniel's luminescence is more pronounced, I would venture a guess that his encounter with the Challenger Deep had an enhancing effect of some kind."

Fiz walks over to a console by the monitor on the wall and presses a button. "I'd like to play the video log from inside the Sampson when it was at its deepest point in the Challenger Deep." Now my mentor turns to me and shows his concern. "Danny, this may be difficult for you to see—you're welcomed to leave for a moment if you wish."

He already knows my answer, but the offer is appreciated. "This is as important for me to examine as it is for anyone participating." Misty squeezes my hand to reassure me that she'll be right by my side in case my words are braver than my reaction. Funny how no one else involved in this high-level security meeting questions her attendance and I'm certainly not going to bring the matter to anyone's attention.

Our group's images on the video monitor are replaced with a fuzzy picture of two individuals in a darkened environment. The picture is from the console camera mounted above the forward view port, giving us a fisheye view of the Sampson's passengers and the cabin behind them. The quality of the transmission is poor, but the scenario is made clear by Steve's and my voice– this is obviously our last conversation. The time stamp at the bottom of the screen reads + 7:55 hours: making this a short time after we reached the bottom.

What is that? Steve's question haunts me and in my mind, I see him gazing at the water dragon or whatever it was, passing us by. *Beautiful.* I'm squeezing Misty's hand harder now. I hope I'm not hurting her. There is an all too familiar deep oscillation coming out of the speakers that increases and with it, the panic on both mine and Steve's faces. Our increasing alarm is reflected in a strange eerie light coming from somewhere outside the ship. The light steadily intensifies and then I watch as Steve and I both reach for the communications switch. There is a brilliant flash that emanates from Steve's side of the cockpit. For seven seconds by the chronometer reading on the screen, the picture is nothing but white static. Then there's another low-pitched rumble and the picture slowly fades back in, with one significant change. There is only one person on board the Sampson…me…and I'm floating toward the aft portion of the cabin as if in zero gravity. I have somehow come out of my harness, which can also be seen in the foreground of the picture—the buckle still firmly clamped.

For another two seconds there is no sound, then one word is heard......*more.*

When I hear my voice echoing alone through the speakers, my reaction is unflattering at best. I'm glad the camera is not on me in real time as I bend over at the waist—Misty still holding on to my hand—and violently throw up onto the lab floor.

SOMEWHERE INSIDE DANNY

And suddenly I realize I'm dreaming again or whatever this state of awareness is called. I'm in another place as if watching myself and the world from some other vantage point.

Pastor Fale is with me. We are in the cockpit of the Sampson. The good Pastor is floating next to me and asks a question. "What are you missing?"

"I don't know—we've analyzed all the evidence, sifted through the data…"

"Danny, those things are unimportant for the moment. What are YOU missing?"

"I don't understand."

Pastor Fale is glowing brighter, as am I. He hovers behind me now, whispering into my ear, "That's an answer, not a question. What is the question you seek to know?"

"How can the problem be fixed?"

"You're assuming, Danny. To what problem do you refer?"

"Are you kidding me? Look at what's happening around us! The world is coming apart—there is a total shifting of the physics around us."

"Why is that a problem?" Pastor Fale seems very interested in hearing what I have to say about this.

"Because we'll cease to exist—there won't be anything left!"

He places the palm of his hand on my chest. The warmth of it is wonderful. "How do you know this to be true?"

"I…" And there is another jolt as we begin to be pulled to the surface. "I don't know. <u>I don't know it to be true</u>. I'm just…assuming!"

"Truth is discovered through faith. What question does your faith tell you to ask?"

"I know this one…I know the question! **Where is God?**"

Entry Sixteen

All things come apart, but the matter of their existence always has and always will exist.

—Exploding Wedge Principle proposed by
Daniel Adamson for the Memorial High School
Honors Society College Scholarship Contest

SOMEWHERE OVER THE ATLANTIC OCEAN

Again, I find myself far above the fray, isolated and only aware of the turmoil below because of texts and emails sent to me from Austin. The seismic tremors around the world are increasing in regularity and intensity. The governments of the world are literally falling apart—already mobs have seized the capitols of Mexico, most of the Arab states and African countries. Many of the more stable countries of the world have issued military orders to protect themselves against their own people. Even the United States has had to issue curfews and disperse the military to keep the nervous crowds at bay.

Misty, the kids, and my mom remain with Fiz in Austin, because it has remained relatively stable geologically and governmentally. But even there, riots have occurred and the Texas Governor has had to declare a state of emergency including shutting off all trade and travel with its erratic neighbor to the south. The U.T. campus is officially closed for business, though faculty and staff are still allowed access.

I know the campus is a well-structured sanctuary and even has its own highly professional security force for protection. Still, my having to make this journey frustrates me to no end. I want nothing more than to be with my loved ones now.

Fiz has emailed me a report detailing that the World Trade Organization and the Green Order Coalition have combined forces, claiming a mandate to avoid further unrest, and have invited governments to join forces under their protection to find solutions to the catastrophes. Darius Mede has been selected as the new Chairman of the United Nations and there is talk of all remaining countries taking the extraordinary step of uniting under one governing body in order to better make use of their resources to quell the violence and to stabilize the monetary system.

Fiz's last words to me amaze: "The United States Congress is seriously considering joining in this action."

In the midst of all of this, I'm having more visions and seem to remain a glowing reminder to the world that something very strange is happening. Fortunately, my friends and people in high places have kept mine and Brandon's condition under wraps—I shudder at the thought of the media finding out that there are two human lightning bugs flittering about.

I also have been having more conversations with my father and Pastor Fale. I've not, however, held them in the presence of others, not wanting to give my family and friends the impression that I've totally lost touch with reality.

All this is to say that this trip to Naveh Shaanan is much more difficult than the first. "Why am I and Brandon headed to Israel?" I had asked this of Moses Folzman who had called in for a chat with us following the web conference with the President….

"—An excellent question, Daniel," stated the Rabbi who then explained to his pupil, "Fitzgerald, please trust me that I would not request the presence of your two most valued cohorts halfway around the world were it not imperative. There are tests that must be conducted and…mysteries to be looked into…"

—A chill runs up my spine now as I recall his words. What mysteries, what tests? Moses had not elaborated. Fiz had simply agreed and that was that. Arrangements had been made, the jet had been prepped and fueled. I reluctantly bid my family farewell again and we are off once more into the wild blue yonder.

Brandon is snoring away in the seat across from me and I wonder what thoughts are coursing through his mind and a thought that suddenly comes to my mind—*No one is designed to be alone.* The void on the other side of the pressurized window reminds me of the great space that separates me from those I cherish most. As beautiful as the vista may be, it suggests that life is too vast not to be shared.

I look again over at my friend and decide that he has the right idea. Sleep helps the brain function more efficiently, so I close my eyes to seek peace—what harm can there be in a short nap?

GENEVA, SWITZERLAND – WORLD TRADE ORGANIZATION GARDENS

I'm walking with Darius Mede, head of the World Trade Organization and newly appointed Chairman of the United Nations. He's feeling pretty good—I can tell it by his gait—he's strutting. Breathing in deeply the fragrant scent of cedar and European pine, that is this place's natural signature, seems to energize him. I understand now why he spends so much time on these trails.

Mede is almost pleasant to be around. I say that because he whistles while walking, and he's good at trilling. I say he's almost pleasant to be around, however, because he only knows one tune, *Whistle a Happy Tune*. He never varies in his blowing, it comes across as a signature or mantra form him and after strolling with him for a few minutes, I want to gag him. Sadly, gagging is not in the repertoire of strange new abilities with which I have been recently gifted.

Why have I come here? I'm observing. I'm doing my out-of-body thing—I'm getting much better at it.

And along comes another person—ah, Brenda Anders again. She is dressed provocatively in a low-cut burgundy dress with matching high heels. Her stature and awkward gait—due to her unfamiliarity with actually wearing such attire—makes this combination garish in comparison to the refined Mede, who is attired in his typical banker-blue pinstripe business suit. Brenda approaches with a smile and outstretched arms. Mede receives her with a tentative smile and a more reserved social hug and wastes no time propelling the conversation in the proper direction.

"Brenda, you are stunning. I only wish there was time to appreciate your efforts, but we must be quick." A slight frown is the only sign of her disappointment in his less than enthusiastic response to her clumsy attempt at seduction. "Of the 192 member countries in the body of the United Nations, 151 have agreed to the terms of the new Governing Council. Twelve others will most likely join us or collapse within the week. That leaves twenty-nine who will continue to resist. I'm confident though, that I will bypass this obstacle and soon achieve all and more than anyone expected."

Brenda confesses, "You know Darius, I'm almost glad these calamities began. Without such a crisis, we would never have achieved such great strides!"

"…We?" Darius Mede's ego signal is flashing bright red and Brenda is quick to pick up on it.

"You are the power that propels—dear one. I only wanted to share in recognizing your success."

"You are certainly helpful, Brenda. And now there is more to do. The efforts of Fitzgerald Hindeland are interfering with our influence."

Mede offers the threat to his power as candy to feed Brenda's sense of urgency. "I know that you have well-placed sources in the academic communities. I need you to suggest to them the danger this man and his team poses to the outcome of our purpose—perhaps even put out the word that his efforts are actually contributing to the demise of the planet. Certainly, there are those with whom you associate that would help put an end to such an obstruction?"

Brenda Anders is displeased. "Darius, you of all people know that I take seriously the value of any life, even…that man's."

"Of course, I'm not suggesting detrimental actions against anyone, merely that you encourage others to discourage him."

But the damage has been done—the head of The Green Government Coalition had heard Mede's suggestion correctly the first time and his inference has caused hesitation in Brenda's devotion. The purpose, I realize now, for my being transfigured here, has just shown itself. There is something my father has counseled me to do—it has been long awaited and for the life of me, I don't know why I haven't acted on it before. At one time I pretended to have already done it, but that was just an act poorly performed long ago as a child. I must put childish things behind me.

Darius can't see me, but I'm certain he senses some change in the spiritual climate of things—the rustling of the wind or the slight variance in the trilling of the local feathered inhabitants, who knows? A slight sheen of sweat around his collar appears and Brenda too, becomes aware of something uncomfortable.

"What's wrong, Darius?" She reaches for his hand, but he pulls away and looks around without a word, as if to seek me out and surprise me. He can't tell her what is happening because he doesn't know what is happening or what will soon happen—that is the crux of his disability. For all of Darius Mede's self-assuredness and savoir-faire, he is blind to the outcome of his actions—unsure that what he's doing will result in his desired objectives.

This moment and this place have been selected specifically by One more powerful than any of us standing here—greater in fact than all who dwell. I'm here to 'up' the stakes of the dangerous game this empire-building man pretends to enjoy. Why now, why here is not my concern. I have been chosen and for once in my life I will unquestioningly choose to obey. The wind picks up as I put my face close to the ear of the now very alert Darius Mede. He looks around nervously and brushes at the air, having no effect on my presence. Brenda watches in amazement as Darius Mede falls to his knees, the sky strangely darkening above him. I too drop to my knees—*Perfect, of course this is the way it should be!* The power of the moment—not Darius' power, not mine—is everywhere. It is electric—it is full of life—it is deathly. And all the man in the pinstripe suit can do is clasp his hands over his ears, close his eyes tightly and shout upwards into the unseen heavens, "<u>What</u>?"

It is now that I confess my sins to the Almighty, for Him and for Darius Mede to hear. "Father in heaven, I am not worthy of your presence. I am nothing—less than nothing—I am filled with thoughts and past actions that betray my sinful nature."

Darius lets loose a hideous scream. Brenda takes two giant steps back away from him.

I persist. "I ask your forgiveness, even though I know I'm not deserving of any gift from You. I have asked your forgiveness before, but I was not sincere. You have loved me for some reason and have brought me to this moment of true repentance. I thank You for Your mercy."

Mede bends down and strikes his forehead to the ground, his voice screeching repeatedly, "No, No, No!" There is a lightning storm above us now and Brenda has found a nearby tree to hide behind.

Now, say it now! "Creator of the Universe, I know that I can't ask for this of my own and I now know what I've been missing, what You've been trying to speak into me by the power of Your Spirit all along. You've shown me that it is only by Your power, made real for me by the sacrifice of Your son—Your presence in human form, Jesus Christ—that I can be granted eternal life. It is only by my speaking his name and accepting him as my Lord and Savior that my salvation can be achieved."

There is a deep throated growling noise coming from the man into whose ear I whisper. I am not afraid. It is time to begin the ending of this. "In the name of Jesus Christ, my risen Lord and Savior, I ask you to dwell in my heart for all time and by the power of Your presence now within me, I command the evil which now exists beside me, to be driven away for all time!"

A lightning bolt hits the tree behind which hides the quivering Brenda Anders, but her scream is dwarfed by the ear-piercing screech of Darius Mede who now rises to his feet and runs back toward the World Trade Organization offices, tearing his clothes from his body as he goes. Brenda limps on one high heel, not far behind.

And just like that, the skies clear, the birds are back—as if nothing had taken place, as if the whole world slept during the event. Perhaps it did. Perhaps only three people and One other were aware. It makes no matter—it has begun—this age is ending.

NAVEH SHAANAN, ISRAEL – THE TECHNION-ISRAEL INSTITUTE OF TECHNOLOGY

"I don't get it. I expected him to go up in flames, spontaneously combust—explode or something like that." I'm sitting with my feet in a tub of hot water and my body draped with cold towels—the extremes helping me recapture my senses. Apparently while winging my way with Brandon to Naveh Shaanan, my nap took me on another little dream adventure. I entered some sort of Zombie-like state and Brandon couldn't bring me out of it. Pay back, I think, for his two cricket episodes. I remained in said condition even after we touched down—Moses Folzman, Brandon and two Technion students having to cart me off the jet and into the waiting limo. It wasn't until I was brought to The Technion and was doused in ice cold water that I snapped to.

After gaining a foothold in the present reality, I thought it would be best if I started coming clean with Brandon and Moses about what had been happening to me, including…well…everything—even my confession and faith with its strange repercussions to Darius Mede. So what if a Jewish Rabbi and my unbelieving best friend might think me ready to be fitted for a straitjacket?

Brandon just nodded his head and took notes, but Moses Folzman actually hugged me and then ordered the special bath I was now enjoying. Then he sat with me as I explained in more detail what happened during my dream. Finally, I finished the exposé and Moses replied, revealing new secrets for my consideration.

"Daniel, you were doing the bidding of the Eternal. You cannot assume to know all His purpose."

"But why would my verbalizing my belief in Jesus as God make him so crazy? What was that about?"

Moses pats me on the back and walks over to the only table in the room, which has a computer and several massive books on it—one of which he fetches and brings back to the tub. "I believe your actions to be exactly as you described—part of the beginning, not the end of something greater."

Moses pauses, seeming to weigh what he has to say carefully before proceeding. He begins to pace before us as he explains. "What if the sympathetic vibrations you tapped into—the Harmonic Resonance effect as you termed it—affected other parts of you…say, your cell structure itself? And what if these changes are being executed…intentionally, for some future purpose?"

Brandon interrupts. "You're speaking as if there is some kind of space alien out there getting ready to pounce on us."

"Oh no, I'm suggesting much more than that. I'm telling you that we are part of 'It' and that 'It' is much more than organic. 'It' can utilize the organic structures 'It' created, even selectively altering their components as happened originally with the structure of life itself. 'It' exists outside of time and space and soon, so shall we." Moses Folzman, The Crazy Prophet, has spoken.

"Please," Brandon sounds exasperated. "Can you support this with any tangible scientific evidence whatsoever?"

Another great belly laugh from the Rabbi: "My good Doctor Lader, I would not have taken up all our valuable time, were I not able to do so. The Eternal has already provided us with many pictures of what was in the beginning, what is now and what is eventually to come. I have saved much time by not veering from this approach—watching many others experiment and theorize their lives away. I find great comfort and wisdom in listening to—rather than telling my Maker—that which is and that which is not."

Moses pauses again to take a long draw from his specially doctored tea. He is grinning impishly and then says, after a swallow, "Laminin."

Brandon isn't familiar with the term, but I nod my head and respond, "Cell adhesion." The Rabbi encourages me to embellish. So I comply, "Laminins are proteins found in most cells and organs of almost every bio-organism on Earth. To boil it down to the basics, Laminins are what hold one cell of our bodies to the next cell. Without them, we would literally fall apart." And as I say the words, everything comes together. Something had happened at the cellular level to Brandon and me, causing us to figuratively come apart at the seams.

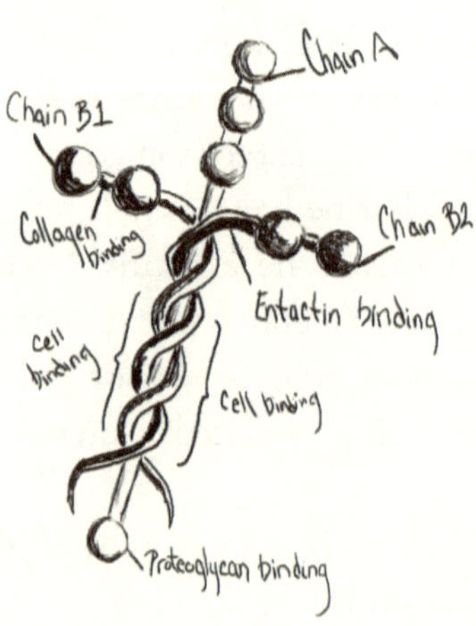

"Have either of you ever seen a diagram of the structure of Laminin?" We both shake our heads negatively and so he walks over and turns on a plasma screen. His voice echoes slightly in the empty room as we stare in wonder at the diagram before us. "Look and behold," he waxes dramatically. "The Eternal paints pictures of pictures so that we may finally understand what connects us to Him."

Then Rabbi Moses Folzman opens the leather-bound tome he has been cradling and begins to read, "From the Letter to the Colossians from the Apostle Paul, Chapter 1, verse 15-17:

> *He is the image of the invisible God, the firstborn over all creation. For by him all things were created; things in heaven and on earth, visible and invisible, whether thrones or powers or rulers or authorities; all things were created by him and for him. He is before all things and in Him all things <u>hold together</u>."*

V4641 SOL PLUS ONE-C – REGION OF THE MAGELLANIC GAS CLOUDS

Some things start in cataclysm—the Universe was said to have begun this way. But is it so?

Could the largest of things known have begun differently? Might the incalculable force of all physically known have been sparked into existence by something less? Perhaps even something as simple as a spoken thought?

What would be the possibilities if such a thing were true? What would it mean? And if that is the way all things began, what might that mean for the way they will be completed? I am ready…LET THERE BE…

NAVEH SHAANAN, ISRAEL – THE TECHNION-ISRAEL INSTITUTE OF TECHNOLOGY

"I've been reading as you suggested. I still don't follow it all, but I'm now cross-referencing with the book of Daniel, Ezekiel, The Gospel of Matthew, Paul's letter to the Thessalonians, Revelations…"

"Good! Good"

Not good, not good! I'm lying on a medical examination table and half expect the hunchback assistant, Igor, from the novel Frankenstein to come addling up to pronounce—*'It is ready master!'* Moses is at a control console in a lead-lined booth attached to the room, our only communication connections being an overhead speaker system, a microphone attached to my neck and a glass portal through which he occasionally peeks. I think he's making sure I'm not trying to escape this madness of make-shift cabling, wires and attachments running to and from my body. Brandon is supposedly in the booth with Folzman, but I have not heard a peep out of him. Perhaps he remembered he hasn't had a jelly filled doughnut in over three days and has secreted out to find one.

I've set my mind on trying to be cooperative, though I have little confidence in this hodgepodge of equipment or its abilities. So I've been discussing with the great Rabbi, the puzzle pieces of apocalyptic prophecy in Biblical text. The conversation helps distract me from my ridiculous circumstances.

"Rabbi, please explain—I've been examining the scriptural writings you've suggested and am more confused than ever. How can anyone possibly make sense of them all or fit them into a logical sequence?"

I'm making him laugh a lot as of late and I hear yet another chuckle emitted through the speakers. "So much you have to learn! Have you read Matthew, chapter 24?"

"Oh, the End Times passages where Jesus talks about the bad stuff coming our way? I remember it."

There is a sound of a latch releasing and then the door to the booth opens. Moses emerges—close behind follows Brandon licking his fingers. *I knew it!* His blueberry-stained lips betray him. Moses assists me off the examination table and over to the desk where Brandon is now excitedly staring at the screen of a laptop and then looks up to speak to me for the first time in hours. "You won't believe what this equipment identified related to your molecular make-up Danny. It's going to take months to figure this all out."

"Hush Brandon, Daniel need not be distracted with such trivial things at this moment—if you would please download the acquired data to Austin. We have little time to waste."

You can't waste what doesn't exist, says a voice in my head—it's my dad again.

"Daniel," Moses commands my attention. "Matthew 24: Break it down for me. What is it really saying?"

I find myself wanting to impress this guy with my recall. So I pull up in my mind, my best recollection. "Let's see, Jesus talks about wars and rumors of wars. Uh, he says something about not falling in with other Messiah Wannabes, then all I remember is that it's going to get real bad…"

"…For nation will rise against nation and kingdom against kingdom and there will be famines and earthquakes in various places. All these are but the beginning of the birth pains. Then they will deliver you up to tribulation and put you to death and you will be hated by all nations for my name's sake." Moses Folzman obviously does not have a problem recalling his scripture. "If you read all books of both Old and New Testaments in their entirety, you will find an incredible constancy of purpose from beginning to end."

"What's that purpose?" I find myself anxious to hear the Rabbi's answer.

"The Eternal planned from the beginning to salvage and reclaim His creation, a creation He knew would fail because of the way He designed it."

"He designed it defectively?"

"That's the nub of it, Daniel. The Eternal is not just anyone and does not design or act like any other. He planned for His success, not our failure. We were the ones who determined a different outcome, but He had to give us that option in order for the end game to succeed."

"…The end game?" Moses has sucked me in.

"…His ongoing plan has always been the creation of an eternal relationship with a group of individuals who self-willingly accept God's love under His conditions."

"I don't see us doing a very good job of accepting the conditions."

Moses lets loose another great laugh as he responds to the obvious. "A terrible job actually. That is why The Eternal threw in a *Ringer*. Because of our hatred of all that is pure, He created within Himself, the one thing we would not expect of Him—the ability to become like us physically, to dwell with us and to be sacrificed. Then he devised a way to be resurrected, so that anyone who accepts his sacrifice and love will be spiritually transformed, having a Messiah dwell within them. By this extraordinary sequence—physics and spirit become one."

CAMP DAVID, MARYLAND

Speaking of a presence within—what about my ability to be present *outside* of myself? This just gets creepier. I'm riding a horse…no, somehow I'm watching a horse—two horses in fact—being ridden and I'm…what am I doing? Am I floating along with them? Is this some kind of moving picture trick in my brain? Can the riders see me? I wave my hands and shout "Hey," but no one reacts. I look at the riders and, oh my word—it's Fiz and the President! Fiz rides? Wait—Fiz jumps! Fiz just hurtled a large fallen tree trunk on horseback at a full gallop. Fiz is good at horseback riding!

The President is no slouch either, keeping up rather nicely with the good professor. The secret service detail on the other hand, is not practiced. It seems the President will not allow a mechanical device like a jeep to disturb the moment, so his guards trot, bounce, and gait awkwardly, not sure how to hold reins and operate their hand-touch earpiece communicators at the same time. Fortunately, there are lots of them so they are strategically preset along the bridal path—none of them having to keep up with the pace of the two men for too long.

Finally, the two equestrians slow the pace and canter into a meadow surrounded by apple trees which have secret service members and cameras hidden in them. The President pulls up beside a particular tree and lithely dismounts. He reaches down and picks up an apple that's fallen to the ground to offer his mount. The mustang gladly accepts the treat and nuzzles the man affectionately. Fiz is now also off his palomino and takes in the moment. There is a scent of spring honeysuckle and hay mixed with the perfume of the apple orchard. There's a gentle wind *how am I able to experience all these things with them?*…and the day would be perfect except for the clouds which do not appear to be rain clouds but composed of smoke and dust. They emit a sulfuric smell that competes with the perfection of this place.

"They started drifting in several days ago," the President explains—catching Fiz's glance skyward. The meteorologists say they are volcanic debris drifting from the west."

"I suspect in another day or so, we would not be able to enjoy this moment," Fiz relays as he also bends down to select fruit for his mare. "I appreciate you inviting me here Greg. And Lord knows I needed a break, but I'm not sure the timing is appropriate…"

"Fiz, I needed to speak with you confidentially and this was the only way." The tanned, chiseled face of Gregory Blueroad, the first U.S. Commander-in-Chief to profess his Cherokee heritage looks very tired—especially in the eyes. "I'm not sure we can hold our governmental power base together much longer. I'm going to need your help, and there may be times when communication will be difficult. I want to get your perspective and also want you to know my wishes." The leader of the free world comes close to his friend. "You know my respect for Mother Earth and for the Great Father—you <u>know</u> I want to do what's best to protect our home. But others will not understand. They are threatened and the population of the world is crying for results. They will demand action even if they don't realize the repercussions."

Fiz has picked a Granny White off a nearby branch and is biting in for a taste. He ties the reins of his horse to another tree branch and the President picks up on the nuance. Blueroad also secures his reigns and the two men begin to walk side-by-side to the middle of the pasture away from prying ears.

"Moses Folzman once shared a parable with me," Fiz recalls, "about another planet inventing the telescope—they peer out at our solar system and see a speck circling a mediocre star…nothing to shout about…probably the blue tint is from ice or ammonia reflecting in the starlight. They observe Jupiter and are in awe at its size and majesty…it must be the dwelling place of a mighty species.

"Looking through a small lens at ancient mysteries does not give us the information we need to make accurate observations or sound decisions—without a witness to original events, there can be no true validation—we must be the voices of reason, encouraging all to look with a larger view at the universe's purpose."

"A witness," Gregory Blueroad considers the concept. "I'd prefer at least two witnesses actually—harder to dispute."

"Two you shall have," Fiz answers cryptically. "I'm going to ask for your trust as a friend in this, Greg. I will do only what needs to be done concerning actions that are from a source greater than us. I won't encourage my team or others to experiment based on theories."

"I'll do the best I can to back you on that Fiz, but I can only go so far." The President offers his hand and the Professor takes it in both of his.

Off in the grove, someone stirs and now a secret service agent begins running toward them. When he reaches the President, without a word he hands his Commander-in-Chief an open cell phone. The President answers, "Hello?" and immediate concern clouds his countenance darker than the grey sky above. He listens intently and then responds, "I understand—do all you can to help and keep us informed. Thanks Bob." He shuts the phone cover and turns to Fiz. "That was the head of the C.I.A. There's a credible threat of military action in Israel—lots of chatter on the internet and several of our sources suggest a large-scale attack from outside the country is about to take place."

Fiz closes his eyes for a moment—then opens them to survey this peaceful setting around him. He looks at his watch and says, "Danny Adamson and Brandon Lader are with Moses Folzman at the Technion."

"I didn't know that. I'll inform our contacts."

"Thank you, Greg. I'd love to stay longer, but now I must get back to Austin as soon as possible."

The two men embrace, then run back to their horses and mount up. Their world has just become an even more dangerous place and they both understand their responsibilities. It would be more time consuming to call for ground transportation than to simply take the trails back to the camp, so the two don't wait for the secret service agents to catch up. As several agents radio their counterparts that protocol has been breached, the President and Fiz ride off at breakneck speed toward the main house.

NAVEH SHAANAN, ISRAEL – THE TECHNION-ISRAEL INSTITUTE OF TECHNOLOGY

I've told Moses about the visions I'm having and about the threat to our security. He has phoned others in the Technion and they respond that the threat is known, but that there appears to be no immediate danger. This new twist does nothing to distract the Rabbi from his theological baiting.

"Daniel, there is one more important scriptural concept you must study intently. It also has to do with the book of Matthew, chapter 24 and its lessons will eventually steer you to several other Biblical sources as well. Jesus says to his *talmidim*…his disciples:

> *"For then there will be great tribulation, such as has not been from the beginning of the world until now, no, and never will be. And if those days had not been cut short, no human being would be saved. But for the sake of the elect, those days will be cut short."*

This is familiar territory for me so I nod confidently in the Rabbi's direction as I speak. "I remember that part. He's telling them that all hell is gonna break loose."

He nods his head back to me. "…In a sense." Now Moses looks at me quizzically and asks the strangest question, "What is the difference between heaven and earth?"

"Heaven is where God lives?"

"Good answer! So, when the last verse says *he will send out his angels with a loud trumpet call and they will gather his elect from the four winds, from one end of heaven to the other*, how do you picture the elect getting to heaven? Is the passage literal?"

Where my head was swimming before, now it's beginning to spin. I remember that there are multiple verses about Christ Followers being gathered up with trumpets calls involved. Will that really happen? If not, what does it all mean?

Now the Rabbi goes for the throat. "We speculate about beings from other planets, alternate timelines, satanic possession, *ad nauseum*. Hollywood, books, and pop-culture are saturated with tales that people believe to be true or that are accepted as being based on real events. Why does the culmination of God's plan have to adhere to some strange manmade accounting of rational sensibility when nothing else has to pass that same test?"

A really good question—in my mind, I hear it another way: *Why do God's actions have to make sense?* "If He can make a universe, can't He do just about anything He wants to?"

"Yes, and The Eternal is just about to do something very Biblical indeed." The Rabbi looks toward Brandon, apparently deciding whether or not he wants to share this information with both of us. He nods as if making a personal decision and speaks again. "I want to warn you. It has become obvious that you are very much the focus of The Eternal's upcoming plans and as such, are sure to become a target for those who would see that plan derailed. The Matthew passage does not say that 'the elect' will not suffer, just that our tribulation will be more…brief. I'm telling you this because I believe your life—all our lives—to be at risk."

It's my turn to laugh. "Good grief, Rabbi, please don't go getting macabre on me. I'm sure there are people out there who would like to see this project disappear, but I can't imagine us to be in some kind of…"

There is an explosion in the distance, but close enough to rattle the sample bottles on the table and shake the building's foundation. Moses is quick to respond. "Brandon, is the data uploaded?"

I'm having a déjà vu moment, thinking about cave crickets and dark places when another jolt rocks us more violently. "It's done," Brandon responds. The lights flicker but stay on.

"Follow me quickly," Moses orders—He leads us to a cabinet and reaches under a shelf to press a hidden button. The cabinet slides to our right to reveal a passageway. "These days, a servant of The Eternal does not exist for long in the Middle East without an escape plan. The University had these tunnels designed into its architecture for just such a likelihood."

As we enter the chamber, another blast knocks us off our feet. I hear objects fly past me and a piece of glass or sharp metal grazes my cheek painfully. Dust and fumes surround us. A barely visible Moses Folzman reaches up and pull a lever which causes the cabinet to reset to its original position, hiding us from whatever might be encroaching into the room. In the dim passage, I see Brandon crouched over and go to him. He looks up, cradling his laptop under his left arm and clutching his right side with his other hand. "Think I caught a little shrapnel," he whispers. "I'm fine."

"Hurry," Moses urges and we make our way through the labyrinth as other explosions and what sounds like gunfire haunt us from the opposing recesses of the concrete walls which now hide us. "Five, one, omega," I hear the Rabbi whisper and now see he has his cell phone out and is speaking to someone at another location.

I assume his words to be code and soon a response crackles over the phone from some unknown location, "Sanctuary, seven."

We half walk, half run through long, dimly lit hallways—turning corners that appear suddenly—and then climb ladders, some going up, others leading down, until I'm totally disoriented as to our whereabouts. The lights in our location flicker and go out entirely. I'm reminded of the changes which have affected me and Brandon because we are both still glimmering in the darkness, the eerie light helping us continue our progression within the winding passageways.

Everything here smells of dirt, old paint, and mildew. I run my hand over the wall and a moist film attaches itself to my fingertips. I rub it off on my pant leg wondering if the stain will be permanent. Moses finally stops and looks up. There is a creaking sound above us and then in the ceiling, a face appears silhouetted by the bright light of day. Obviously, we have arrived at the escape hatch leading from these hidden catacombs to the world above and I hope the man staring down at us from ground level is a friend.

"Halome!" I assume this is something spoken in Hebrew because Moses responds with a barrage of guttural phrasing. I'm pushed out of the way by the big man just as the feet of yet another ladder extends rapidly down on the spot where I was standing. It takes no rocket science to know we must hurry up through the egress. First climbs Brandon –his wound is hampering his progress and I follow below him, encouraging him to keep focusing on one rung at a time. We make it through the opening and Moses climbs out just behind us.

This landscape is even more surreal than that of the tunnels we have just left. It's daylight, but smoke and dust mask the hour and obscure the extended scenery making it impossible for me to get a fix on exactly where we are in relationship to the Technion. I can tell only that we are in an open field. The air is pungent with the smell of sulfur and diesel fuel, telling me that weapons and equipment are in heavy use. Explosions and gunfire all around confirm that a battle is in progress and that we are right in the midst of it. Three Israeli commandos at guard points surround us and I wonder what comes next?

My answer is the thick beating of helicopter blades soon heard over the hills I now can dimly make out to our left. The Israeli version of a Hind Attack Ship appears out of the mist, skims the landscape, and comes to a quick landing near us. The Rabbi and I help the now faltering Brandon through the side hatch while the commandos fire rounds at some approaching figures.

Too fast—Too fast, slow this down! The strange plea runs through my head as the whirlwind of action consumes us—my heart is hammering in my chest. I see one of the figures trying to load what looks like a rocket launcher to fire our direction, but fortunately he and his companions are cut down. The helicopter manages to safely flee the area and I turn my attention to my best friend. Moses lifts Brandon's red-soaked shirt to discover the worst—a serious gash on his right side just below the rib cage. *Too fast!* My eyes struggle for ways to help. *Help what? Do what?*

There is no time, my father reminds.

Shut up! There has to be—I'll find it here somewhere, time has to be here, I insist.

Brandon has lost most of his color and I can hear his raspy, difficult breathing. "Made it," he gasps and smiles with difficulty in my direction. Competing with the stink of sweat and machine oil emitted by the gun ship, the scent of Ammonia is present, emanating from the rancid wound of my friend. Suddenly there's the unmistakable odor of alcohol and antiseptic nearby.

The airship's medic pushes me unapologetically out of the way and begins to work on his patient, sticking needles in and monitors on Brandon's body in rapid succession. An EEG monitor blips away, signaling that a pulse line has been established.

Everything seems so vivid now: The flecks of doughnut in my friend's beard, a smear of blueberry jelly on his lower lip—I remember the first time I saw him devour a box by himself.

"Danny!" I hear him shout and I come as close as I'm allowed by the work going on before me. I move around the working medic and hold Brandon's hand. It's wet like my eyes. There's a tattoo on his upper arm— an Air Force insignia with Latin letters below, *Uno Ab Oto.* I know that phrase…*No one aims higher.*

"I'm right here Brandon. I'm not going anywhere!" I try to keep my voice positive. The tattoo is strategically placed to cover his smallpox vaccination scar. I want every detail, all of it to the tiniest microbe.

"I know, but I am. just want you to know I've been listening too—I want to believe."

"Brandon you're going to be Okay." I look down the length of his body to his feet. His sneakers are strung only up to the middle grommets and double bowed. He likes to be able to slip them on and off while he's working. I've caught him doing it subconsciously as he focuses for hours on a research project.

"Tell me what to say!" My friend pleads through his pain. "…want to meet my maker properly."

I look toward Moses and motion that he should help. The Rabbi shakes his head and mouths the word, *you.*

The medic moves to Brandon's other side and I can now get close to his right ear. It's smaller than the left and a scar runs across the lobe. *Where did that come from?* The chopper blades make it necessary for me to shout to be sure he hears me. "Brandon Lader, do you admit that you are a sinner, not worthy of God's love?" *There's grey beginning to show in his beard—remember that.*

"Yes," my friend coughs. The sound has a liquid quality as if there is something wanting to come out of his lungs and throat that shouldn't be there. *Notice everything—remember it all.* Brandon has a very large neck and wears a medallion on a chain around it. The chain is worn and discolored—there's is one link that looks like it's been repaired with solder.

"And do you repent? Are you sorry for your actions against your God?" *Be who you were meant to be—be the Keeper—notice, take this in.*

"…sorry." Brandon's breathing is becoming more rapid and labored. I remember now, the medallion was his first computer science award medal he won in high school. He's very proud of it—He had once confided that I'm the only one with whom he's ever shared that fact.

"Do you accept Jesus Christ as your Lord, the Savior of your life, through his death on the cross and his resurrection?" *You will have to tell others who he was and why he was important to you.* I fight, sobbing selfishly within my own soul—I want so much for him to be protected from a spiritual death, but I don't want to lose Brandon in the physical.

"I believe Him." Rivers are spilling off my cheeks onto his face, baptizing him with my grief. "Brandon, Jesus now lives within you and I am now your brother in Christ: Your life is saved eternally in the name of the Father, the Son and the Holy Spirit."

I turn to look at Moses Folzman who is now on the opposite side of Brandon holding his other hand—the medic has long since moved away, recognizing the inevitable. The Rabbi's eyes are closed and he is mouthing a prayer while kissing the tassels of his prayer shawl which he has pulled out from under his jacket. He opens his eyes and I see wells of water, deeper than any ocean—the flood of his prayers cascade down his face and spill onto Brandon's arm.

My best friend turns his head slowly to look my way, his eyes looking somewhere beyond me. "I'll be waiting, Danny—see you on the other..." And the EEG blip turns to a steady line. A warning signal sounds and the Medic steps in again, attempting to revive the body by defibrillation and then by injection of adrenalin directly into the heart—to no avail. My academic cohort, and closest ally, has started a new journey without me.

"NO!" I wail. "You can't do this—I can't do this without you. You can't leave!" I bend over Brandon with my hands clenched on either side of his face—willing him, demanding him to look at me.

Moses puts a hand on my shoulder and with his other, closes Brandon's eyes to this world forever. After a moment, the Rabbi comes around the body, takes both my hands in his and says, "Well done, good and faithful servant. I am here for you too—you are not alone in your grief."

I look down one more time and notice that Brandon had missed a belt loop when he dressed this morning. He always misses...missed one or two. *Via Con Dios, my friend.* I bury my head on the Rabbi's shoulder and complete my mourning cry in cadence with the continuing throb of the helicopter's rotor blades.

Entry Seventeen

"We receive enlightenment only in proportion, as we give ourselves more and more completely to God, by humble submission and love. We do not first see the act, we act and then see. And that's why the man or woman who waits to see clearly before he will believe never starts on the journey."

—Thomas Merton, The Ascent To Truth

AUSTIN, TEXAS – UNIVERSITY OF TEXAS COMPLEX, QUANTUM SYSTEMS DEPARTMENT

Since returning to the University after Brandon's funeral, the mood has been sullen. No one wants to talk about him—no one wants to forget him. Reminders of my friend lay about everywhere to haunt us; his computer workstation and his hidden snack stashes; post-it notes stuck everywhere as reminders of projects yet to be finished. Brandon was and still is part of the essence of this place. How can we continue without his contribution?

Misty has done her best to encourage me. She's curled up on the sofa with me, her head resting on my lap, peacefully asleep and softly snoring. How can she do that? Steve is gone, Brandon is gone—soon the world and all of us will be gone, but my wife is at peace. I want peace too—where does it hide that I can sneak up and capture it?

"If you're through with your pity party, I could use your help." Fiz could not have possibly just said that, but I heard the words emit from his mouth. My anger surges and I jump up to take his throat in my hands. I want to strangle him for not sharing grief at the loss of his prized Quartermaster.

And then I realize I'm still sitting—the image of attacking him only a vibrant fabrication of my subconscious mind—Misty's head still rests on my lap. I carefully squeeze my body over and up while finding a pillow to prop her head in a comfortable position. After checking to make sure I didn't wake her, I turn to focus my fury on its target, but Fitzgerald Hindeland is nowhere to be seen. I hear noise in his private office so I walk purposefully in that direction.

When I enter, Fiz is still not to be found. I move toward his desk to see if he's possibly hiding under it in fear of my wrath. *He should be fearful. How could he be so insensitive in the aftermath of Brandon's death? I should* The door to the office behind me swings closed and I reel to see Fiz facing me. He had obviously positioned himself behind the door, waiting for me to enter and then shut the portal to trap me in.

"Good, you do still have life within you. I was worried." My mentor is not smiling as he says this.

"Oh, so you just threw out some casual comment, teasing me about my anguish so you could get a reaction out of me? Great, you've succeeded. Now go write something astounding on your precious whiteboard and leave me alone. I'm not in the mood for this."

"I believe you're the one who came charging into my office."

"And you're the one who closed the stinking door!"

"Your wife is asleep on the couch. We need not disturb her with this."

"Disturb her with what, Fiz—your efforts to save the world or your attempt to get me out of my funk so I can still be your 'go-fer boy' of doom, gallivanting all around the world wreaking havoc wherever I go?"

"Yes, Danny. Let it all out."

"He's dead! You haven't even shed a tear. You are…were as close to him as I was."

"…In ways, closer."

"Typical—got to 'one-up' me. The brilliant Fitzgerald E. Hindeland, mastermind of all things quantum and director of many lesser beings."

"He's dead, Danny."

"I KNOW HE'S DEAD! I told you that. I was there. I SAW HIM DIE!"

"And you saw him live. Far more of his life did we both see and share. Did he live in vain?"

"You mean did he die in vain?"

"I believe I still have command of the English language, Daniel Adamson. I know why Brandon died. My question is far different. Do you know why he lived?"

I fight the temptation to spar with this great thinker…I struggle and lose the battle. "He lived because he was a breathing, functioning human-being…"

"Come now!" It's the Doctor's turn to get agitated. "You can do better than that! You know exactly what I'm driving at and I want to hear you say it!"

"Fine: He was alive to give purpose to the word 'Research'. He was dedicated to his work like no one else and he didn't flaunt his genius, it was a tool for him that he wielded like a surgeon. He loved what he did—so much that he would have…died if someone were to try to take it from him. He was all that, and he was a friend that would do anything, did do anything for his friends. He lived to be what God wanted him to be and he didn't try to be anything else. He was better than any of us."

When I had started, I had closed my eyes, trying to keep the tears shut in. I hadn't seen Fiz sit down. When I open my eyes, he is in his favorite chair again, staring out the window, his face away from me now. But I can now hear agony in his voice as he speaks, "And would you rob him of his joy in life, Danny? Would you have that part of him killed too? He lived for all you just said and for one thing more. He lived for you, his best friend. Your memories of him keep him alive in you. What you know of him is now all that remains. He has left you with a gift—will you squander or honor it?"

I walk over and kneel in front of the man who once more challenges me to greater heights. What I don't expect is what now happens. This great man of science also comes down from the chair, falling to his knees. He embraces me and buries his head in the nap of my shoulder. At first the sound is muffled, but then he lifts his head and a wail comes forth—the sound of anguish long held back, now released from a man born to harbor his suffering in silent dignity. And as he continues to sob in my arms, a new picture of my own purpose comes to life.

I'm changing once again and this time, it appears, Fiz is being changed with me. Part of that transformation includes me assuming a different role altogether. I must take ownership of the responsibilities and duties of the late Brandon Lader, Ph.D. I am now both Keeper and Quartermaster. *How can I fill those shoes…his shoes?*

And a new voice invades my head. I jerk in reaction to hearing the voice of Brandon Lader speak undeniably to me. *Better start praying, Danny. You're closer to the answer than you know.*

RAPID CITY, SOUTH DAKOTA – HOMESTAKE MINE DEEP UNDERGROUND SCIENCE AND ENGINEERING LABORATORY (DUSEL)

And as I wrestle with my inner voices, my "outer sight" also kicks in. I'm once again watching someone else's life experience unfold. What I see happening to Cindy Albertson, member of the physics team associated with DUSEL, is not pretty. Cindy, dedicated as she is, can't help but take a step back in fear. It has nothing to do with me.

What is DUSEL and the significance of this moment?

The Deep Underground Science and Engineering Laboratory is a very curious research facility located in the Black Hills of South Dakota, not far from the venerable Faces of Mount Rushmore. Once the deepest and richest gold mine in the world, things have changed a lot over the years. In 1965, Dr. Ray Davis asked permission to install a first of its kind neutrino detector at the mine's 4,850-foot level. This was where the first neutrinos were tracked. Interest in the mine's unique properties grew from then on and the State funded development of an underground science lab.

These efforts would seem remarkable in themselves, but apparently some other, even more peculiar research was quietly funded as well. It seems that some visiting biologists happened to visit the 8,000-foot level of the shaft and discovered…life. Nothing fancy, only some basic microbes— it seems that these hybrid microbes developed from the viruses and feces left about by the original miners and their pack animals who had once worked the mine.

No one thought that anything could exist at those darkened depths in such barren rock facings. They had all been wrong.

Cindy's team of researchers are trying to figure out just how deep life exists inside the planet and how the hostile conditions, including the 140-degree temperatures down here shape the evolutionary process. They have even brought in other life forms—insects, plants, fungi—to observe if these too can adapt to the strange conditions found here.

She has made the descent many times to the lowest chamber in this once richly laden mineral mine, until recently, when visits were halted as a precaution due to all the seismic activity. Cameras were dropped into the shaft to ascertain what structural damage had occurred and to the amazement of all, there was none to speak of. Volunteers were asked for and Cindy was the first to jump, anxious as she was to see how the experiments she had left at Level 8K were fairing. What she didn't know was that things have been changing even more drastically than anyone could know.

It seems that during the quakes, a number of her six-legged specimens became liberated from their confines and began to roam freely in the darkness. Unknown to anyone, there are mutated viruses down here that have interacted with the insects through their transposons. These crossbred mutants are what confront Cindy at this very moment when she exits the elevator into the lower level and why terror grips her. They are large—about the width of three human fingers put together, but it's their appearance that awes. They have teeth—big ones—that look as sharp as gleaming white needles to the panicked Cindy. The fact that she can see teeth puzzles her. What kind of beasts are these? Her scientific curiosity briefly overcomes her anxiety and she takes mental notes of what she is observing. Their bodies are thick with armor, almost like a war horse dressed for battle. And there are gleaming golden spikes encircling the head of each—maybe the dim light is playing tricks? But it's the tail of the animals that takes her breath. No, not a whip like Mrs. Cricket's: This is a true weapon, obviously designed for one purpose—to apply a barbed sting to its prey.

Cindy's attention is drawn back to the heads of these grotesque monsters. There is something odd and familiar at the same time about these…human…their heads are human, even with humanlike hair flowing out beneath the strange crown of spikes. There is just one word Cindy can conjure as a description—hideous.

The rush of their vibrating wings is the noise of insanity—a clamoring buzz like that of a never-ending cascade of breaking glass. Fortunately for

Cindy, the elevator cage is completely enclosed and, as she carefully steps back in and hurriedly closes the door, only a handful of the creatures are able to follow her in. She presses the button for the surface level and then she presses her body tightly against the back wall. The bugs don't attack at first, but drone about her head searching for weakness. Then it begins—one then another dive in—tails whipping, wings grating, teeth snapping, there is no avoiding and the first barb digs in near the nape of her neck.

That's not so bad, Cindy catches herself thinking, but then the poison reacts. Welts begin to form like blistering, burning volcanoes on her skin as each strike meets skin. *Let me die* becomes her mantra, but death does not answer. Over and over they persist, teeth striking at her attacking hands. There is no description for the agony. Cindy kicks at one insect and manages to crush it against the wall of the elevator—a small victory until the stench of the dead bug reaches her nostrils—putrid acid, stinging her sinuses like gasoline mixed with rotten tomatoes.

An eternity later the door opens and light floods in. The other scientists at ground level are shocked at the tortured scream that flies from the elevator cage and even more surprised as Cindy runs from the confines, continuing to scream until she trips on a step, falls, and hits her head, mercifully knocking her unconscious. Then other screams begin to chorus as the attackers find new targets.

The team of researchers quickly react, finding empty beakers, jars, pots—anything in which to trap their tormentors. Soon the beasts are all caught, but not before all involved are impaled with stings and bites that now give them the appearance of victims who have survived a nuclear holocaust—welts, ugly deep wounds, darkened and swollen appendages abound. Someone gently picks up the limp body of Cindy Albertson and checks her pulse. She is still alive thankfully, but her injuries are incredible.

Others carefully gather the containers holding the angrily buzzing specimens. Pictures are taken, the dead bug is properly cataloged, and packaged and eyewitness accounts are collected from all who are still lucid enough to do so. Then the director of the facility takes out his cell phone to make a call. His hands are too painfully swollen to press the buttons so he has to instruct a helper on the number he wants to call. The voice on the other end confirms that his instructions have been handled correctly.

"This is the White House. With whom may I connect you?"

AUSTIN, TEXAS – UNIVERSITY OF TEXAS COMPLEX, QUANTUM SYSTEMS DEPARTMENT

"I don't care where they are, get everyone together!" The Commander-in-Chief of the United States of America apparently still has some pull because his order results in five different people scurrying out of the room in search of others while his Cabinet Chief dutifully punches a series of numbers on his cell phone, sending a signal that a very important meeting is about to commence and whoever is not in the executive conference room had better get there—<u>fast</u>!

We can see all this happening from the plasma screens at our individual locations: Moses, who remains in Israel—still cleaning up after the attack at the Technion; Misty and me down in the UT Physics lab; and Fiz, sitting at the desk in his office, performing an incredible task—feeding Jake and Sylvia, my children, spoonfuls of ice-cream while they, and even Fiz, giggle uncontrollably. My mom is resting in another room, excusing herself from childcare duties because grandmothers have that option now and again. even if it means dispensing those duties onto a renowned physicist who is about to have a video conference with the President of the United States.

"Mr. President. I'm engaged with my young charges so that Professor Adamson, and his wife Misty—who is skilled in biological dissection—can focus on the task at hand. Master Jake and Miss Sylvia have assured me they will not be a hindrance." Fiz looks toward my kin in mock sternness and they shake their heads in obedience. Then Fiz sticks his tongue out at them and they all three launch once more into stifled giggles.

The President is simply not in the mood. "Where is Mede?"

I handle this one. "Sir, Darius Mede is not responding to our calls."

"Then perhaps you would be the best one to begin this meeting, Professor Adamson."

"Yes sir. Let's begin by bringing everyone on the web conference up to speed." Suddenly, images of the Secretary of State and two other Cabinet members appear on screen. "I'll get to the point—please hold your questions until the end because there's a lot to cover and the circumstances are pretty strange.

"Yesterday morning at the DUSEL facility in South Dakota, one of the researchers discovered a new life-form that appears to be aggressively dangerous—so much so, that a team of researchers were attacked unprovoked. There is a silver lining in that the victims' injuries, though quite painful, do not appear life threatening.

"But because of the increasing risks and our need to seek rapid solutions, we thought it would be helpful to examine the creatures—yes, there were a number of them captured—here, in a controlled environment. We want to thank the military for their joint efforts in securing and transporting the subjects to the University in such quick order."

"If these things aren't life threatening, why be concerned? Why not just avoid them, why the need for a response?" I didn't expect that the rules for holding questions until the end would be honored, and sure enough, the Secretary of State plays the rebel.

"I believe that question and many others will be answered quite effectively with this exercise—so with no further delay, let's get started. My wife has volunteered to work with me at this lab station—we will first dissect one of the creatures that had been destroyed in the attack. Then we'll do a real-time observation of a live captured specimen. We have lots of cameras in the room so we'll try to give you a view from many different perspectives as we proceed. I do want to warn any of you who may be squeamish at the sight of a dissection—you may want to let others do your observing for you."

Misty, because of her biology background, has stepped right up to the plate. She has no reservations about handling, examining, or cutting up creepy crawlers—hence she's really the one in charge of this show. I'm playing the trusty side-kick and video director.

As I position two cameras and a light kit for the best visuals, Misty opens the lid of a Lucite box in which rests the deceased creature that Cindy Albertson had managed with a panicked kick, to destroy in the mineshaft elevator. Even at that, the thing is hardly damaged and I half expect it to jump up and start attacking us at any moment. Misty uses forceps to manipulate the wings and turn the monster on its back. It is most definitely dead—thank God—and does not resist.

"Gross!" Everyone looks up to the plasma screen in reaction to the voice. Our images are not up there—only that of the proceedings. But I know the voice to be that of my son Jake. "Sorry," his voice apologizes, but no one reprimands him probably because everyone agrees with his assessment.

Misty speaks forensically but tries not to go into "lab" mode. "The subject is three point one inches in length and weighs…is that scale accurate? weighs nearly one and a half pounds! That explains another aspect—the wings." Misty takes two pairs of tweezers and spreads the wings apart. "They are nine point eight inches—from tip to tip, almost three times the length of the body in proportion. Actually, that's not enough. This thing should not be able to fly—it has the same problem as the bumble bee."

I'm sure some of our audience won't get that reference so I chime in. "The bumble bee is too heavy in proportion to its wings and according to the laws of known physics, should not be capable of flight."

"Examining the body now, it seems to have teeth—not mandibles or pincers as normal insects." Misty is all business, leading us from head to toe over the corpse. "They appear to be made of bone or calcium…" A large tremor shakes the room while she is probing the maw of the creature and Misty's finger catches on one of the bug's teeth..

"Ouch, wow. They are most certainly razor sharp—no apparent secretion glands…uh such as would be necessary for a poisonous injection. From our analysis, it's their saliva, combined with the bite that inflicts the pain. This thing would hurt you if it got a hold of you, but the bite would not appear to be fatal…unless there were enough of them.

"The exoskeleton on this beast is almost metal-like—I've never seen any natural body armor on any creature that would be its equal. But it's the tail that you'd want to watch out for." At this, she takes one pair of tweezers and carefully holds up the tail to reveal through the camera's eye, the wicked pointed barbs at the end. "There are multiple thorny protrusions—looks like some are missing, I'm guessing when it attacks, it lashes out with this thing and leaves a present behind. Maybe the swelling wounds on the victims came from this. Now I'm going to see if I can cut through the skin—if I can find an unarmored section—yes, here between the tail and the midsection. If you don't handle entrails well, you might want to step away for a bit."

As she works surgically to exhume clues from the inert body of the mini-monster, I catch myself in a surge of pride watching her work. My mind strays to our conversation from the night before…

…We had miraculously gotten the kids settled down early allowing us a very rare moment of personal private time together. Strangely, I had been holding back from telling my life-partner everything about things otherworldly that had been occurring in my life.

We had never really delved deeply as a couple into the spiritual aspect of our relationship—not even involving the kids in any church program or searching out our common references—it had just seemed unimportant before. But now…it was the only thing I wanted to share with her and inwardly, I prayed for a way to explain it that would make some sense to her.

I had poured out every aspect from my dialogue with my dad, the dragon dreams, my conversations with Fiz, Moses and Brandon, even my strange out of body experiences. After dumping all of this on her, Misty remained silent for long time,

Then she did something remarkable—the most remarkable thing I've ever seen her do—she moved from her own chair and took a kneeling position before me. Misty Adamson took my hands in hers and kissed them. I stared helplessly as she wept at my feet and then responded in the soft loving tone I had remembered longing to hear when trapped in the bowels of Mammoth Cave. "I've waited so long, so patiently for this moment, Lord. Thank you for answering my prayers and for delivering my beautiful husband into spiritual completion.

"I'm sorry that I've felt a need to keep my love for God a secret from him, but You, Creator of The Universe, know how insecure I felt in broaching the subject. Yet, You in Your wisdom heard my prayers and opened a spiritual portal into my Danny's heart—I am so thankful and now I too can be honest, open to sharing together what You, dear God, have set in motion.

"Let us stand faithfully together, no matter what happens, confessing Jesus as our Lord, who died for our sins and was resurrected in victory over darkness. Teach us not to fear what is happening around us, but to see it for what it is—Your plan unfolding on earth as it does in heaven. In Jesus' name..."

By now I was on the floor with her crying uncontrollably—totally forfeiting my 'man-card', holding her in my arms, praying my own prayer of thanksgiving which concluded at the same time as hers. So, we shared the final word in closing together "Amen!"

...I smile now as I continue filming Misty finishing up the forensic procedure. I cherish last night's memory as a great leap for our family. How could we not have shared our spiritual faith and doubt more deeply before? My reverie is interrupted by the voice of the Rabbi.

"I would like to offer a suggestion to everyone," Reb. Folzman requests.

The Secretary of State's image, whose hopeful look is enhanced by digital technology, speaks animatedly. "Oh good, so you think you have an idea of how to remedy the problem?"

Moses gives us his most serious look, "Quite the contrary, Mister Secretary. I believe it is time that we start preparing for a much worse set of circumstances. It is time we begin speaking about and preparing for what is known in my profession as an End Times scenario."

Entry Eighteen

"All theories, like universal phenomena, eventually collide with Ockham's Razor."

—*Fitzgerald E. Hindeland, Ph.D.*

AUSTIN, TEXAS—UNIVERSITY OF TEXAS COMPLEX, QUANTUM SYSTEMS DEPARTMENT

Moses Folzman has just dropped a bombshell. On the plasma screen, the President and the participating members of his Cabinet all look like still-life pictures, completely shocked into frozen-faced caricatures of themselves. Only Fiz seems unaffected at the suggestion of an impending *End Times* episode. He continues to play with Jake and Sylvia whom I suddenly want to cradle in my arms. I can only imagine how my own face must appear. Finally, an unfamiliar Cabinet Member finds his voice.

"Rabbi, or Doctor, or whoever you are. We are trying to seek solutions here, not create panic and it would be appreciated if you would…"

"Mr. President, I mean no disrespect," The Rabbi addresses, speaking over top of the dignitary who is offended back into silence. "But the evidence is indisputable and there are very specific realities we must prepare for, including some events that are predicted to occur soon."

"What events? Predicted by whom?" The President is standing now as he speaks, pacing in and out of camera view.

"God, of course," It's Fiz who answers as he carefully takes Sylvia off his lap and sets her beside him, giving both children smiles and using a hand motion to instruct them to stay put while he faces the camera and continues. "Mr. President…Greg, please excuse me, but it's time we drop the formalities and protocols here—there is simply no time left. I want to speak to you as one believer to another. There are remarkable things going on around us and to be blind to them is insanity.

"I apologize to those of you who do not share my acknowledgment of Jesus Christ as the true king of this planet—I will be glad to have that discussion with any of you individually after we are done here—but even you should find a copy of the Bible and pull it out immediately: Read Matthew, chapter twenty-four and the book of Revelation beginning in chapter five through to the end. The language and the imagery appear strange, I admit, but look past that at the physical and spiritual activities taking place."

"Fiz," The President is sitting back down again and has his hands clasped in front of him. He is wearing a very sad smile. When I saw the same smile on his face years ago during a campaign speech, it caused me to believe everything he was saying and eventually to vote for him. "We can't shape policy or general action based on religious convictions and you know it…"

"…I know nothing of the sort, we are beyond policy here," Fiz interrupts—not about to be trapped into a political discussion. "We just received a report that the Pacific Rim, where eighty percent of the world's volcanoes exist, has just come alive with activity. Not just isolated eruptions, but everywhere. Besides the immediate threat to lives, the dust and debris from this activity will soon cover the planet causing a diminished ability for crop production, even inhibiting the ability for natural plant life to produce oxygen. Animal and insect populations are being adversely affected as well and there is increasing human panic across the globe.

"Any one of these signs would be a concern, but all of them together affirm undeniably the predictions of the Bible—dire images of worse things to come. This is not something we can stop, but it is something we **must** prepare for."

"All of those things can be explained by the laws of nature," corrects the Secretary of State. "What possible evidence can you present which alludes to a Godly influence in all of this?

"Excuse me," It's my wife of all people, speaking out. Every eye on the screen seems to follow her as she walks over to a metal box the size of a refrigerator. She flips a switch next to the box and the metal cover lifts off to reveal a thermoplastic container holding the still living bugs that were captured at the Homestake Mine. With the metal lid removed, not only can these nasty critters be seen, but also heard. The noise of their vibrating wings is piercing and I'm tempted to hold my hands to my ears. Several Cabinet members and the President himself do exactly that. Misty is merciful however, lowering the soundproof cover back over the box. "These specimens would seem a pretty good indicator that there are greater influences at work here. They are not, by any stretch of the imagination, normal creatures."

Moses resumes his role as The Crazy Prophet. "…Which means we must now recognize that Biblical events are already starting to play out. And my conclusion is that they will begin to increase at a rapid rate.

"Are you out of your mind?" It's the offended Cabinet member again. "Are you suggesting some kind of Twilight Zone moment where the mother ship comes to take us away? What in the world would you suggest we do?"

Fiz answers the question. "Professor Folzman is correct in suggesting Biblical study at this point. Though many of us have forgotten, the scribes of those times were in many cases the brightest minds, schooled as they were not only in spiritual studies and religion, but also astronomy, anatomy—in fact, all the sciences. These were not simple country folk and as we do today, they tended to tone down their message in order to have it better understood by the general public.

"So when Paul of Tarsus, a brilliant legal research mind of his time, wrote in his first letter to the Thessalonians, predicting those asleep and alive would be gathered up and very specifically separating this moment from that of the 'last days'—we might want to give his writings at least as much if not more credence as we would say Plato, Michelangelo or Darwin."

"Thanks for the historical lesson, but I haven't heard you say exactly how many people you think will be involved in this 'gathering up' moment?" The Secretary of State is not above sarcasm.

Fiz looks suddenly very tired. "We simply don't know—that part of the message is kept a mystery from us. It would be as difficult as determining how many people cheat on their taxes or how many have been unfaithful to their spouses. The only certainty is that the real number of those taken will include a great many strong community members and leaders whose loss will be significantly felt by those who are left."

The lights suddenly go out at our location. The backup generators kick in, but the emergency lighting makes Fiz appear as dim as his prediction.

Strangely, in the lab site where Misty and I are stationed, even though the light kit I have set up for our bug camera shoot has flickered out—the illumination variance is not apparent at all. The battery pack on the video camera is still running strong, so I take the focus off of Misty, panning around the room, trying to determine where the source of light is coming from.

"Danny." It's Misty trying to get my attention. I signal with my free hand, holding up my index finger asking for her to wait one minute as I continue to swivel the camera on the tripod in search of the answer. "Danny!" She now walks over to me and gently places her hands on my shoulders to move me away from the tripod. Then she herself takes hold of the video camera and swivels the lens to focus on me. I'm now on the monitor, lit up like a 'blue-light special' at a grand opening sale.

Moses finds this amusing—he is now chuckling. "Behold, ladies and gentleman, another Biblical sign of the times. Professor Adamson is demonstrating how we must be a light to the world!"

GENEVA, SWITZERLAND – WORLD TRADE ORGANIZATION

I can sense more than see the frustration of Darius Mede—*How is that possible? Lord, what is happening inside of me that is allowing this kind of ninja observation even to the emotions and physical actions of others?*

The Chairman of the World Trade Organization is Internet browsing and has happened upon an Associated Press story about Professor Fitzgerald Hindeland and Daniel Adamson who had been interviewed by video phone. The article mentions the loss of their close working companion Brandon Lader and notes that they continue on with their efforts, bravely seeking to identify causes and solutions to the worldwide chaos in spite of their grief. Mede shivers at the reading and jots a note on a piece of paper that reads, *MAKE SURE THEY ARE HANDLED.* After a pause, he quickly texts a note on his cell phone to another of his resources and then goes back to the task at hand.

A *Breaking News* piece comes onto his screen. It speaks of simultaneous riots outside the Parliament Houses in both London and Paris, the Bundestag in Berlin, and the National Building in Belgium. Mede clicks on other sites and notices an increase in demonstrations throughout India, the Middle East, Asia, and the Russian Republic. "Excellent," he says out loud to no one. The smile on his face confirms that Darius is grateful for the public outcry.

"Now we'll see who will benefit." Mede pushes away from his desk and, as he stands, is violently rocked to the floor by a strong earthquake and is brought painfully to his knees. He can hear screams outside as parts of buildings fall on panicked pedestrians, fifteen stories below. Darius manages to crawl to the balcony window as the room around him continues to sway. The sky is darkening and a whitish grey dust begins to fall from the sky. As suddenly as the quake began, it ends, yet the mayhem and eerie ashen snow continue. Darius Mede looks down just in time to see emergency crews rushing to help the injured and, without testing, steps onto the balcony. His weight causes the left side of the structure to shudder—there's a snapping sound as the left side of the balcony drops two feet—then sways—kept tenuously from complete structural failure by two steel rebars somehow still secured to the side of the building. The drop however is enough to cause Mede to be thrown off balance and to tumble face first toward a break in the wrought iron railing surrounding the balcony. At the last moment he grabs for a hold of the railing and manages to halt the motion of his sliding body, saving him from becoming one of the casualties below him. Darius summons all his strength and pulls himself up to his feet and away from

the broken platform, back-stepping into his office just as the entire balcony then breaks off and cascades end over end onto the crowd below.

As he surveys the carnage, a guttural gasp is at first all he can manage. Then a strange gurgling laugh begins at the back of his throat and rises up into a hysterical cackling that echoes over the crowd. Darius lifts his head to the sky and screams out his

hysteria, "You can't get rid of me that easily! You know you can't!" Then he looks down again at the disaster and shouts to the crowd. "I will save you! Just a little while more and this will be over. I will save you!"

Only a few react to his cry by looking up. The falling ash has coated everyone and they appear exactly alike—grey, ghostly—their eyes peering stunned and emotionless up to the berserk and macabre figure screaming down at them. Most ignore the madman, grimly attending to those still trapped and wounded by the rubble. The rain of warm volcanic soot increases, dampening all sound into a deathly hush—all except for the lunatic sitting on his office floor with his legs hanging out the balcony window fifteen stories above. He just continues to giggle shrilly and occasionally shouts out into the void, "You can't get rid of me that easily!"

Entry Nineteen

"In short then, a singularity represents a gate to infinity and we generally don't think nature is infinite."

—Brent Nelson, M.A. Physics,
Ph.D. Student, UC Berkeley

AUSTIN, TEXAS – UNIVERSITY OF TEXAS COMPLEX, QUANTUM SYSTEMS DEPARTMENT

The video conference is finally ended, the President having given various directives to a very anxious and confused staff that are as ill-prepared for the coming events as the rest of mankind.

"I don't understand." I'm speaking to Fiz and Moses who have asked me to keep our end of the conference running for a bit. Misty is keeping herself busy storing equipment and making sure the bugs are secured. The lights have still not come back on and I'm still glowing like Blue Rudolph—only my nose is not the source of my illumination. "If we can't do anything to change the course of events, what are we bothering with?" I'm sensing great anxiety and a need within myself to draw my family and friends close to me to pray and wait for…I don't even know a proper name for what I'm waiting for.

The Rabbi nods and is silent for a moment, and then he asks, "Daniel, have you not wondered at your reappearing vision of the dragon? Why does it keep revealing itself to you?"

"Yes! I just hadn't bothered to ask you yet. It doesn't seem Biblical at all. I did research and there is definitely an evil dragon mentioned in a number of places, particularly Revelation. But my dragon…" *It is mine,*

how do I know that it's meant for me—to protect or warn or help me somehow?
"...is not bad. Just the opposite, I know in my heart it's good...VERY good!
But it doesn't fit what I've been taught."

"You've probably started to recognize something about the nature of
evil," Moses explains. "Satan tries to present himself as a god—there is an
antichrist trying to imitate Jesus. So it can be assumed that the red dragon
of Revelation would also have a righteous counterpart."

"Then why isn't it mentioned in Scripture?" Her work completed;
Misty has come to stand at my side—together we face the camera. She has
asked this question while reaching over to clasp my hand in hers."

"To be revealed to all, Biblical content needs to carry the message of
Christ to all. It would seem that your Silver Dragon is the harbinger of a
message for you alone, Daniel Adamson."

"Okay, but what's the message?"

Moses shakes his head and replies, "God wants to have a conversation
with each individual—at least one chance to offer a light to guide them back
home. He cannot visit personally—holiness cannot mingle with unholiness
just as matter cannot touch antimatter without disastrous results. But
He can send messengers to lead the individual, hopefully toward a right
decision. For you it is a dragon; for you Misty, and for the rest of us,
something, or someone different. Each in his or her heart knows they have
been approached. Each for their own reason may or may not respond."

"So are you saying that we all need to look for some signal from God
that the elevator is going up?" Misty is full of great questions.

"I'm saying that God wants to love each one and to be loved by each one.
Moses smiles at us both as he continues to illuminate. "He will wait until His
chosen moment before closing the door to that love permanently. What I'm
saying specifically to you, Daniel, is that just because you have responded to
your messenger does not mean God is through sending messengers. Which
leads me to the most ironic question of all: Have you considered that you
may be someone else's—perhaps many others'—silver dragon?"

Before I have a chance to consider the complexity of the Rabbi's
question; Fiz signals us from his office, his face on the screen showing
concern. Danny, "I think you and Misty should come up here immediately.
Moses, you and I need to have a conversation later, but something pressing
is occurring in our area."

With a quick goodbye, Moses signs off and we head out of the biology lab to meet Fiz in his office.

SOMEWHERE INSIDE DANNY

It's happening.

"Dad is that you? I don't quite recognize your voice."

It will be different for you than it was for me. All transitions are unique.

"What transition is it you're referring to?"

You need to warn the others.

"Warn who? Who are the others? Warn them of what? What transition is it you're talking about?" Are you telling me that this is the end?"

If this were the end, I would not be speaking to you. If this were the end, there would be time. There is no...

"...time. Yeah I got that. But you know what I mean. I can't warn about what I don't know is about to happen, can I?"

Your knowledge will become unimportant. Your faith is what you must hold on to.

"What happens after all this?"

Some will experience beauty beyond belief; others will see darkness without hope of light. Not all will die, but all will be changed—in a moment, in the blinking of an eye, at the sound of the first trumpet.

"Changed? How changed?"

...In all ways. Physically, mentally, spiritually—nothing will be as it was. Those who are gathered will become new. Those who remain will be altered. Those remaining will fear the darkness. They will have another chance to understand, but it will be more difficult for them. They will need help.

"How can I help before that happens?"

Tell them what is happening to you. Tell them what you have seen. Seek its purpose and share it with them.

"Dad, I've got to work through all this, it's very...foreign. But I do want to know one other thing. If you've seen that all of this is going to happen, why did you wait? Why...didn't you tell me before?"

Why hadn't you asked me before?

AUSTIN, TEXAS – UNIVERSITY OF TEXAS COMPLEX, QUANTUM SYSTEMS DEPARTMENT

"Who are they?" Misty asks with more than a little concern in her voice. We stand in Fiz's office at the window, staring out at a crowd that has converged on the campus.

"At least two- but I'd say more like three-thousand of them," murmurs Fiz, not responding exactly to her question. He is punching buttons on his cell phone as he surveys the scene below, slaps the phone shut and walks over to his desk and out of a drawer pulls a small pair of binoculars which he brings back to the window and uses to investigate the content of the crowd. "…The audacity of that Mede!"

Fiz hands me the binoculars as he opens his phone again and punches more buttons—probably texting whatever security forces, if any, that may still exist on campus. I peer through the lenses to try and make sense of it all. The crowd is made up mostly of young men and women—certainly by their dress and the disorganized way they are moving, I'm guessing they are college students and possibly staff. There are signs and placards carried amongst them displaying pithy slogans such as 'Let The Planet Heal', 'Mother Earth Is Fighting Back—Get Out Of The Way' and 'Shut Down The Power'.

Apparently Fiz believes that Darius Mede has orchestrated the demonstration. I can make out baseball bats, shovels and other menacing garden implements, hammers, rocks in hands and, being Texas, a gun or two. The sea of the throng is also distinguished by dots of yellow which turn out to be hard hats worn by the majority. This group is here to work and their business appears to be with the College of Physical Sciences, for they are all headed our direction.

"I've sent a text message to…" Fiz's words are interrupted by a jolt, and I mean a real jolt. This is no tremor that has thrown all of us to the floor—it's a bonafide full scale earthquake. I manage to slither/crawl over and place my body over Misty's as books, chairs, laptops and Fiz are tossed like salad about the room. We too are sliding and bouncing with no control of direction. Miraculously, the window does not burst into a thousand shards of doom, but the rest of the room is most definitely in motion. This quake is slow to subside, but finally the room stands still.

I'd like to get up off of Misty who is pushing on me so she won't suffocate, but there is something on top of both of us. I hear Fiz say, "On the count of three, roll to your left: One, two, three!" There is a grunt and then the creaking and groaning of wood, then the weight is off me and I roll. Misty rolls in concert—her arms around my waist—toward the center of the room. I look back to our former location to see Fiz, let go of the massive bookcase that had fallen on us (*how did that not crush us?*) and see it crash onto the books and debris strewn over the floor.

"The kids!" are the first words out of my mouth. Misty—now on top of me—jumps into action. She is out the doorway before we can stop her and I try to get up to follow her.

Fiz puts a hand on my chest, keeping me from getting up. "Hold on," he says gently and looks around the room finally locating a burnt orange University of Texas Longhorn tee-shirt which he manages to tear into strips of cloth. He comes to me and ties one—bandana style—around my head and the other around my right forearm. It's only as he does this that I realize I'm bleeding from both locations.

"You should be dead, not wounded," Fiz states matter-of-factly, then pushes me toward the doorway and follows behind me in pursuit of Misty. My mother had come out of seclusion after the teleconference and had taken Jake and Sylvia, at Fiz's suggestion, to the cafeteria in the building to find drinks before we had come up to his office. I get into the hallway, picking my way through the rubble and hear footsteps. Jake, Sylvia, Misty, and my mom round the corner—they all look thankfully unscathed.

"Daddy! Uncle Fiz! Are you OK?" the kids shout in unison as they run, eagerly piling into my arms.

Misty comes to me and tenderly touches the bloodstained bandana on my head. "How did you..." She can't finish the sentence and simply hugs me with her head in my chest. I can feel the shudders of her sobs which she is trying to hide from the others.

Fiz answers for me. "You have to get used to the fact that you are now married to God's version of a superhero. Pretty soon he may even be able to leap tall buildings in a single bound."

Misty can't help but laugh in spite of her tears, but it's my mom who brings us back to the seriousness of the moment. "We need to start cleaning up. What happened anyway?"

Fiz takes the lead again, "A massive earthquake to be certain—my guess would be at least seven or above on the Richter scale—but I think we need to attend to the crowd that was outside before we worry about this mess."

My mom is ever the delegator and family politician, the perfect balance to Fiz's 'just fix it' personality. "You three go out there—my grandchildren need to take care of an old lady."

But when we get outside, there is no crowd—just a few injured from the quake who are wandering around, obviously in shock. We go to each with the first-aid kits we found inside and minister to their needs. The work is quick, as most of the injuries are cuts and bruises. We set up a makeshift triage center—the people we bandage and sew up explain what happened as the shock factor wears off.

"We were planning on completely surrounding the physics building," says one campus Humanities professor whom Fiz recognizes. She has a gaping wound on her forehead which Misty expertly stitches and wraps with gauze. "The idea was to see how many people would show up after reading the manifesto. If enough had come, we were going to break into the building and try to scare you into leaving. We were just all waiting… for…I don't know what. That's when the earthquake hit."

"What manifesto?" Fiz is trying to quickly get to the heart of the issue.

"Haven't you been tracking the Save Earth blog?" another injured asks as if assuming everyone in the world was glued to that particular website on their computers. "The Green Order Coalition has called for the people to confront those who are against reducing mankind's planetary and social abuse." This guy who has just spoken is probably a student. He's of Asian descent and is dressed in purposely torn designer blue jeans and a *Whales Have Rights Too* tee-shirt. He notices our blank expressions and questions,

"Don't tell me you've not heard of Darius Mede? He is bringing us all together with amazing solutions. He even…"

Fiz knows where this is going and is impatient for immediate facts. "Where did everyone go?" He waves his hand from left to right indicating he wants more information about the crowd and where they have dispersed to.

'Humanities Professor' answers his question. "Well, that's the strange thing. After the stupid brick that hit my head—I don't know, everyone was just wandering around. Then I heard a scream. Maybe I was hallucinating—I looked over in the direction of the noise and saw someone swatting at the air as if there were insects around them."

Another student-looking person, that Misty is now bandaging, nods her head and speaks. "Yeah that's what I saw too, only…they weren't just swatting, they were backing away and twirling around…like there were bees or something coming at them. Then everyone just started running and yelling."

Fiz, Misty and I all exchange glances. Misty then hands me the iodine and sanitary swabs. "Finish this," she says simply, gets up and runs full speed toward the building. I finish up cleaning the wounds of Designer-jeans-boy and start looking for anyone else who needs attention. Across the concrete mall, sitting on a brick pathway, sits a lone figure—staring out to the east towards the Biology building. I walk his direction and notice as I draw nearer that he is not moving. As I approach, he seems unaware of me and continues his wide-eye gaze into somewhere or maybe nowhere, far away.

I decide to walk casually in a wide circle around him, my internal radar warning me that something is very wrong here. Giving him a wide berth, my scientific nature kicks in and I begin to make visual observations while walking a perimeter around my subject. He seems frozen in time—I can't even detect breathing. He wears a full beard and glasses so it's difficult to perceive his age. Peering at him from the backside, I notice something strange on his neck, now I have to make another decision—a closer examination or keep my distance? Curiosity killed the cat…I come closer, letting him know I'm doing so by leaning forward, so that he can see me. I take one extra precaution as to not startle him. "Hi there—I'm just going to have a look at you to make sure you weren't injured during the quake. Okay?"

No response—whatever has his attention in the netherworld, has it completely. I carefully reach out and touch the collar of his shirt—no response. I pull the collar down and simultaneously, with my other hand, lift up the hair on the back of his neck for a better look. There is an angry red boil that is swollen and raised up several inches from the skin. Puss leaks from the wound and I have to believe it is painful, yet 'Statue Guy' remains inert. He continues to stare. *Is that fear in his eyes?* As I begin to carefully raise up the bottom of the loose-fitting shirt to inspect his back, I hear a breathy whispered voice. "Please don't."

He speaks! I decide to encourage him and slowly walk around to kneel down and face him. "I just want to check you out for…"

"Please don't." The whisper is a little louder and insistent. Statue Guy's focus remains fixed on a galaxy far, far away—a scary galaxy to be sure. I notice dried tear tracks running down his face.

Suddenly, movement down around his forward midsection, underneath his shirt: "No!" His whispered voice is anxious and pleading at the same time. Something— not a part of him—is under the shirt exploring more personally than I am. I begin to slowly stand up and back away with my palms raised toward him. "Fine, don't worry, I won't hurt you…"

In that same moment, Statue Guy stands straight up—rigid—and screams at the top of his lungs. "No! Please, no!"

I hear running footsteps behind me and from that direction a familiar voice, "Danny, out of the way!" I don't know which way is *out of the way but* choose *left* and I dive to the ground—looking up as I fall to watch Misty leap at Statue Guy, knocking him over on his back and to the ground. In her hand is an electric stun pistol, which she shoves into his stomach and triggers. A hideous raspy screech pierces my ears and I watch Statue Guy start to do a jerky dance on the ground beneath Misty—then he goes completely limp. Misty waits breathlessly, still poised on top of him for at least ten seconds. She stands up, backs away and comes over to me.

"Are you alright?" She reaches down and helps pull me up into her hugging, tremulous arms.

Am I all right? I've just watched my wife perform an athletic maneuver I'd never have imagined her capable of. Then I saw her wrestle a crazy guy to the ground and shock him into a stupor for no explainable reason. Am I all right?

Misty releases me. She turns and bends over the unconscious body of Statue Guy, raises up the front portion of his shirt and delicately lifts from his terribly welted stomach, one of the nasty South Dakota winged wraiths. Fiz and the others who have remained in the mall area approach as Misty proclaims, "The bugs have escaped. The earthquake knocked over the containment box. One of them was still in the lab when I came in—it didn't attack me for some reason, but I wasn't going to let it get out...the children..."

Misty involuntarily shudders—I know she's imagining what would have happened if one of the bugs latched onto Jake or Sylvia. She regains her composure and continues to explain, "I saw the stun pistol in a holder on the wall, grabbed it and cornered the bug. It still wouldn't attack me and I was able to shock it pretty easily and find a more secure container for it."

I watch as Fiz walks to Misty and takes the incapacitated bug from her hands. He surveys it by holding it up to his face and orders, "Let's get this one inside and freeze it before it comes to. All of us should get into the building—the remaining bugs could return and besides, I don't like the look of the sky."

I hadn't been paying attention, but now I look up to see thickening clouds, with lightning evident in the distance to the West. Strange—they don't appear to be rain clouds, just a dark ashen shroud. The air is electric and smells of burnt rubber. Whatever is happening is causing the sky to quickly darken as in some foreboding horror film—Fiz is right, time to move indoors. The other people around—who we treated for their wounds—are scattering as well. The good news is that no one besides Statue Guy is immobile and they all seem to have places they want to go to in a hurry.

I bend down and lift Statue Guy over my shoulder to carry him in with us. Misty looks at me, as does everyone else and she asks, "Are you sure he's safe to bring in? He was acting pretty strange."

"I can't leave him out here," I reply.

As we walk back toward the Physics building, there is a rumbling in the ground that causes us to quicken our pace, fearing another quake. Several of the protestors follow behind us, apparently having no other place to hurry to. One of our new tagalongs is the Humanities Professor who looks to the West and then calls out, "What the...?"

I turn to follow her line of sight in time to see the Colorado River off in the distance beginning to rise dramatically, then to change direction, literally aiming toward us.

"Everybody—quickly!" Fiz commands and we all charge for the doors of the building. We get in and climb the foyer stairs to the second level just as the water pummels and shatters the glass on the first level, surrounding us quickly with a moat of swirling foam. Fiz surveys the rising waters and makes a command decision. "…To the fourth level." And with that he starts climbing stairs to set the example. No one objects and the group heads single file up to the higher floors. I hold the rear position, still carrying Statue Guy over my left shoulder and taking a mental count of our new community members.

Besides me, Misty and Fiz, there is the Humanities Professor, Designer-jeans-boy, and another female student type—and of course, the limp body I am now porting up the stairway. Earlier this week, Fiz had suggested that the rest of the faculty, staff, and any remaining student population of the Physics building, go home to be with their families until he had a better idea of how or if they could help. So that meant, with my mom and the kids, we now have a group of ten. My thoughts go to the concern of how we can feed such a crowd—the cafeteria in the building is not an impressive storehouse. We also have no idea who our new guests are—they could all be serial killers or bi-polar Green Order Coalition activists. *Listen, learn, love*, a voice inside me counsels.

We all follow Fiz to the fourth floor—his domain—and he leads us into the lounge area that overlooks the campus to the southwest. Or did—now what we see is a great lake with tops of buildings sticking out like man-made icebergs. Fiz quickly locates a Lucite container with a secure top—he deposits the stunned bug into it and re-secures the lid. Then he turns to help me as I carefully flip Statue Guy off my shoulder and onto one of the couches where Misty immediately starts applying some antiseptic cream to the boils on his neck and chest.

"One of the dams, either at Lake Travis or Lake L.B.J., must have burst," someone guesses.

"That much water? I'd say both." It's Designer-jeans-boy who is looking out the window as he responds—I think he must be from the Ecology department. "But even that wouldn't be enough water to drive the current to this height—we're pretty far up on the bluff. Something must be happening with the Edwards Aquifer."

Another of the protesters—she looks about eighteen to twenty with long brown hair and sports a well-worn backpack which she carries with one strap over her shoulder—raises her hand to ask a question: The action of hand-raising pigeon-holes her as a freshman. Fiz, being ever the educator, nods his head to her, granting permission to speak.

"Can someone please tell me what the Edward's Quack Fur is?" It's an innocent question that causes everyone else to chuckle—the first time in a long time I've heard a collective sense of humor displayed here. It's like a breath of fresh air on a cool morning, but Freshman-girl, who has bright red hair and three nose rings, acts embarrassed. She's wearing a tank top and shorts that reveal arms and legs full of tattoos suggesting she would like some attention. She starts crying. Strangely, I see her subtly glancing around to see if we are watching her performance. She lays back on the vinyl covered couch, her left forearm raised up to cover her eyes.

Misty walks over, sits next to her and gently lifts her to a sitting position. "Don't mind us," she says with a smile. "Those of us who've lived around here for a while get to be a little presumptuous about our understanding of Texas geology. She puts her arm around the girl's shoulders and holds her there as the student continues her good cry to release her tensions. "You're not from around here then: What's your name?" Misty falls naturally into *Mom*-mode with her new charge.

"…Roxanne," I'm from Charleston, Freshman-girl offers in an exaggerated Southern drawl as she sniffles. "Sorry, I'm just a little frightened by all of this."

At this moment I sense no fear in Roxanne's demeanor.

"Fair enough, based on what's happening, I think we all have a right to be a little jittery," Misty offers, and everyone including Fiz, nods in agreement. "To answer your question, the Edwards Aquifer…Danny, why don't you explain it."

Misty, with this simple gesture, has managed to subtly begin introductions and to appoint authority within the room. Everyone turns toward me expectantly. *Okay, now everyone knows I'm Danny.* "Uh, an aquifer is basically a naturally occurring underground storage system, usually carved out of limestone or other kinds of porous rock, which replenishes itself from the runoff of rainwater."

I'm wondering why I'm the one doing this presentation—I'm sure Designer-jeans-boy can spout this stuff off just as easily. Still, I prattle on. "But the Edwards Aquifer is the grand-pappy of them all, occupying portions of Mexico, Texas, Oklahoma and Arkansas making it one of the greatest natural resources on the planet. Even in the driest conditions, we can survive here because the E.A., as it's fondly called, is so huge."

I could have gone on for much longer talking about the ecosystem of the aquifer or the biology including many rare and endangered species that hide within, but I gauge that a surface explanation is all that's necessary. Roxanne's attention already seems to be on other matters.

"You look awfully familiar, were you ever on TV?" She has put away her tears and throws a most charming smile my way. Misty also changes— Super Mom is gone, replaced by Wary Wife who immediately charges into action, standing up and attaching herself to my right arm.

"You're right. This is a good time for us to get to know each other. I'm Misty Adamson and this is my husband Danny. He is on staff at the University and also the Science Editor for N.H.Q. Broadcasting Services." I feel well introduced and <u>very</u> protected. Misty glances toward Fiz and continues. "The gentleman over there is Professor Fitzgerald Hindeland, Chairman of the College of Physics for U.T. So who is everyone else?"

Designer-jeans-boy steps right up to the plate. "I'm Travis, Travis Chang—I'm a teaching associate with the Ecology, Evolution and Behavior Center," *Bingo!* I knew he was an Eco-con, "You're the ones we were protesting about outside, aren't you?" Before anyone can respond, Travis looks around and says, "I want to apologize—you came out to help us and even brought us here when the water came. I had the idea you were all some kind of evil planet killers intent on snuffing us out. You don't seem like bad people at all."

"Thank you," Fiz responds. "We're just as concerned for the planet as you are. Perhaps we can work together now." Travis smiles and shakes Fiz's hand.

"I'm Tonda Peterson," says the Humanities Professor. "I'm an adjunct professor with the College of Humanities." The warm smile on this slightly rotund black woman, who stands in at no more than five feet tall, tells me she's the type that would be able to patiently clear the confusion in any room without talking down to the occupants or making them feel foolish.

Roxanne continues to lay very suggestively on one of the couches and says to the air, as if no one else is present. "All right, I suppose I'll play along too." She stands and places her right palm over her ample chest. By her fluid motion and extravagantly over-emphasized vocal tones, I suspect her to be a performing arts student. "I'm Roxanne Temure and I'm in my freshman year of Drama and Media Production." She states this as if it's very important.

That leaves Statue Guy, who is still unconscious. Everyone looks toward him now and no one offers to identify him. He is a stranger in a strange land. Suddenly, Roxanne realizes she has lost her audience and again raises her hand, shouting out at the same time. "Oh, and I do have one other question." She looks straight at me with a slanted, quirky grin. "Why are you glowing?"

Before I can come up with an explanation, another small tremor unsettles everyone in the room and Statue Guy begins to stir on the other couch. Eerily, at the same moment, the bug-in-the-box also starts to revive. Misty walks over to the captured critter and carefully picks up the box. "I'll take this down to the lab and make sure it's secured so we don't have any more escapes. Then I'll check on the children and your mother." She comes over and plants a very visible kiss on my lips directly in line-sight of Roxanne and says, "Be careful until I get back." She walks out the door—box in hand—without another word.

"You glow <u>and</u> you have kids?" Roxanne exhorts. "Damn."

Entry Twenty

<hr>

Hindeland's First Principle – You cannot prove or disprove a theory by presenting another theory.
Hindeland's Law –Theories die when laws are born.
Hindeland's Corollary – Einstein died. So will we all:
Thus we are theory. The question is; what is born when we die?

—Fitzgerald E. Hindeland, Ph.D.

V4641 SOL PLUS ONE-C – REGION OF THE MAGELLANIC GAS CLOUDS

My dreams are beyond the universe—*my visions are eternal. Peer into the very idea of creation if you dare—you will not escape. Its beauty is where beauty originated—its power is the immensity of the unknown.*

All will appreciate what is about to happen because they cannot escape its happening. How will you know the moment? How will you not? If you do not believe now, you will pray for belief then. Pray that I hear you.

I have given you a glance at what is to be. It is written. Have you read?

Have you tasted its nectar or do the words reek of acid in your soul? This is what is and what is to come. Taste and see...

AUSTIN, TEXAS – UNIVERSITY OF TEXAS COMPLEX, QUANTUM SYSTEMS DEPARTMENT

His name is Mustif, pronounced "moo-steef." We know no last name—we know no history—just Mustif…Mustif Statue Guy. He came to in the lounge and has since melded well into our new clan. I like Mustif, I'm not sure why, other than he's inquisitive like me, he's diligent like Misty, he's observant like Fiz and he's adaptable like Brandon…was. The dark skinned, heavily bearded nature of this man hides a myriad of mysteries. Where is he from? "It's a long story, perhaps another time," has been his repeated response. What does he do? "It's difficult to explain, I will try later," is his continued claim.

Misty places his accent as Middle Eastern, I hear a deeper African tone, Fiz insists there is an Eastern Indian lilt to his voice…and Mustif simply won't say.

But looking past his secretive nature, he has proven to be a great asset, helping with further study on the bug in the lab with Misty, running analysis on the earthquake with Travis, and trying to figure out how it affected the water table. He has helped Fiz and me with calculations, proving to have a natural ability of spotting errors in equations.

Tonda has also chipped in, trying to account for students, friends, and family members to make sure they were not swept away by the flood waters, and it was Mustif who put together a successful Facebook query to help with the effort. Mustif the Dark, as I have come to think of our guest, has even proven a favorable audience for Roxanne, remaining attentive and seemingly concerned for her needs when she is demanding attention.

We have been trapped here by the water for two days, though the mood has been actually upbeat. The power grid has miraculously held up and we've learned from texting, internet inquiries, along with local radio and TV reports, that we are not the only area affected. San Antonio, Laredo, and many smaller towns have been swamped. Austin is unusual, as it has literally been surrounded by water making it a virtual island accessible only by boat or by vertical flight aircraft.

We've surveyed the surroundings from the roof of the Physics building and have surmised that we are most probably the only remaining people on campus—the others long since abandoning ship when the administration officials pronounced the University closed for the duration.

When the serious quakes and weather started happening a week ago, a security team visited the Physics building and ordered us out. It literally took a cell phone call from Fiz to one of the Board of Regents to get approval for us to remain.

The other downtown buildings are also surrounded by the risen waters and are inaccessible to us at the moment. We even experimented with the idea of swimming over to other structures but observed that the current running between them is extraordinarily strong—who knows what undercurrents exist. Without a boat or other means of transport, we are marooned.

Speaking of cell phone availability—that in itself is a miracle along with the continuation of internet service—we can only assume that there is some serious work going on across the country and the world to keep that infrastructure functioning.

Several years back, the powers-that-be who think of such things at U.T. decided that every major department building needed back-up chemical toilets—thanks be to God! We aren't in jeopardy in that area—at least for a while—and the school's recyclable water system also seems to be operating efficiently. My mom, though, remains cautious and has taken to boiling water for cooking and drinking.

ON THE THIRD DAY

The power throughout campus has finally crashed, but the backup generators and solar panels are doing an adequate job of supporting our energy needs. Hopefully, we won't be here too long without relief.

Per our request, the Governor of Texas—yet another strong contact of Fiz's—has promised additional food, medical and other necessary supplies dropped into our location. The need is so great throughout the State, however, that they have not yet shown up.

Looking out the windows of the fourth-floor lounge late at night, I can see isolated buildings in the distance that also appear to have independent power sources. I'm a little surprised that our little island oasis has not been visited or attacked by others who might be jealous of our good fortune. Maybe other survivors are just too busy trying to figure out their own circumstances. Whatever the reason, I continue to pray for our safety and theirs. *If we have visitors, please let them be friendly and have extra room in their boat!*

That's all the good news.

The bad news involves the federal government. According to the President and other contacts in Washington, assets are stretched far beyond their ability to provide—having even taken the drastic step of borrowing heavily from the nation's gold reserve assets—both at Fort Knox and from the Federal Reserve in New York.

Political maneuvering has turned into actual State separation. Texas, Louisiana, Arkansas, and a number of other Southern States are more than threatening secession—claiming they have the natural, industrial, and economic resources necessary to cope with the crisis. So far they have been very careful not to put the name Confederacy into play.

Closer to home, I've learned one other interesting aspect about all our new clan. Fiz and I took the time to indiscreetly interview each of them individually, and then as a group, about what happened on the Mall between the time of the quake and our arrival. We were particularly curious regarding the events surrounding the bug attack and why none but Mustif were attacked. There is an amazing connection that all of them share—when these people experienced the big quake and panic of the crowd around them—every one of them, regardless of their past beliefs and religious positions, had begun a serious dialogue with the Almighty. They had each prayed for escape!

Speaking of, I have caught sight of Mustif in times of prayer—at least that's what appears to be going on—off in a corner of the lounge area intently focused on a dialogue with someone or something not present. Why he had been abused by the bugs is one more question to be answered.

I'm pondering all of these things as Travis and I are huddled with Fiz in his lab, listening with one ear to the news reports broadcasting increases of unusual geological and physiological occurrences around the globe. We are trying to focus on the peculiar abilities and behavior of V4641.

And it hits me, "Why not?"

"Why not what?" Travis snaps. The pressure is affecting us all.

"Why does the universe have to be ordered according to location? Who said so? What if…a particular mass could be in one place one moment and at another location the next…or even…in the same moment? What if distance, motion and time are not associated the way we think they are?"

"Hey, you guys stop your bickering and get to the lounge on the double—the chow line is already forming!" My mom, the drill sergeant is standing at the door—hands on hips—expecting immediate obedience. She has become the designated cafeteria organizer and has harnessed the kids' energy and curiosity, delegating them to finding food sources to keep us alive. They explored and identified the contents of each refrigerator and cupboard in the cafeteria kitchen and Sergeant Mom then devised a strict rationing plan in case we are sequestered here for a long time. So far we've eaten well and no one is complaining about not getting enough— nothing fancy mind you. Ordinarily we have been eating in small groups or individually grabbing food according to personal habits. But today mom has pronounced that we have been together long enough to be considered 'family', so for the evening meal we will gather as a family—tonight's fare? Hotdogs with pork and beans.

Behind my mother I catch a glimpse of Mustif, standing in the hallway. For some strange reason I have the idea that he has been out in the hallway for a while—listening into our cosmic conversation. He has a contemplative look on his face and as we all file out of Fiz's lab, he falls into the ranks alongside Fiz who gives him an encouraging smile and puts his hand on Mustif's shoulder in a friendly way…*curious*.

I continue the conversation with Travis as we walk down the hallway and into the lounge where everyone else is gathered for the feast to come. "I'm suggesting that we should be thinking more abstractly about what is happening instead of defending our absolutes," I spout a little too dramatically with Roxanne-like effect.

Everyone looks up as we enter. No—everyone looks at <u>me</u>. Is it the excitement in my voice for what I'm trying to convey to Travis? Is it the Shimmer Glimmer as Tonda has kiddingly now defined my unusually pronounced aura? Interesting—I have started associating these people's character traits and nuances with my own and I realize—they are becoming *kin*.

It's Fiz who pulls me out of my reverie. "Danny, would you lead us in a prayer of thanksgiving?"

Oh, now this has definitely gotten everyone's attention. I give Fiz my best sideways glance and mouth the words *thanks a lot* in his direction.

"Hey folks, I appreciate the invitation, but I'm just not into this Kum-ba-ya stuff." Roxanne has spoken her mind. "If you don't mind, I'd…"

"I've gone to the trouble of making this meal for everyone and I expect it to be blessed," my mother breaks in. "Please, any of you who don't want to participate, feel free to shut your ears and do whatever else you need or want to do, but respect my wishes."

Wow, where did that come from, I wonder? Our family has not until recently been prone to communal prayer or outward sharing of personal faith. Since our captivity in the building, Misty and I came to a decision to have nightly Bible studies with the kids and we invited my mom and Fiz, who both gladly accepted. He particularly has proven to be a wealth of scriptural insight—connecting chapters, books, and rabbit trails from both Old and New Testaments in order to help us discover the rich continuity of the message. Why does Fiz want me to lead the prayer? I'm not nearly as articulate as he is at these kinds of things.

Speak from your heart. This is a new voice in my head that I've been hearing lately—I can't identify it as mine or any of the other ghosts from my past. Every time I hear it though, I know to trust it.

"I know everyone's hungry and I don't want my mom's hard work ending up as a dish served up cold, so I'll try to make this short."

"Please!" Roxanne encourages. Misty gives her a glaring look.

"Some of you know this, others of you suspect I'm sure, that recently, God has been reminding me that we have a relationship which He very much wants renewed. To that point I've come to believe He's the one responsible for what is happening with the mini-quasar V4641 and its effect…on us all.

"To me that's the most important discovery ever made because it says there's a Being so powerful that He can create and manipulate matter in any way He wants—even ignoring or altering the laws of physics towards His purpose. And that same incredibly powerful Entity also says that, if He can break those laws, why not break the one that says there is to be a separation between God and man? Why not create the opportunity to reconnect the two—intertwine them and make them…one?

"I believe that God has had a plan for this to happen all along—a very strange plan that challenges every scientific fundamental and even some of the social laws I've depended on for a long time. I believe He offered a part of himself at one time in the form of a Savior who became a physical man to show us how to draw near to The Eternal. I believe this Savior Jesus, willingly died at the hands of other men, becoming the scapegoat for our selfish behavior so that anyone who surrenders their will to him as Lord of their life will become a new kind of creation.

"It may sound like spiritual voodoo to some of you—it sounded that way to me for a long time and there's much more I want to share—but my stomach and some of the expressions on your faces tell me I need to wrap this up. So…let's get praying!

"Father in heaven, thank You for being…bigger than us: Thanks even in the midst of all the chaos and strangeness going on around us for showing us a way—Your solution in the form of faith. Help us make sense of what Your plan is leading us to. Thanks also for Your love, protection and for providing us with good food and good company. Show us how to share that kind of love so that the world we live in can see You at work in our actions. I pray this in Jesus' name. Amen."

There. It's done—I've just unloaded my soul. We've dropped hands in the circle of people and everyone waits for someone else to make a move for the food. I suddenly feel peaceful, relaxed—full of…life! I close my eyes for one more moment and pray silently. *This is good!* And my nose picks up a new smell in the room. *What is that?* I open my eyes to see my mom, all four foot nine inches of her standing proudly before me, holding a cafeteria tray. On it rests a cheeseburger with bacon. "It's the last one," she announces. "I know it's your favorite and you've been working so hard—I assumed kitchen privileges and cooked it for you just the way you like it—rare with pickles only."

"Thanks mom." I'm getting a little teary as I receive the tray from her hands.

Not one to prolong an emotional event, she quickly changes the mood of the room by stating, "Okay everyone, quit lollygagging. The food's ready and I need volunteers for clean-up duty!"

GENEVA, SWITZERLAND – WORLD TRADE ORGANIZATION

"Are you certain?" Darius Mede is now fully attentive. I again, in *Morph Mode,* am seeing and hearing things I shouldn't be able to. Mede's unwavering eyes are focused dead center on the view screen image of Winston Torin. Winston and another un-introduced guy in a lab coat, complete with a pocket protector full of pencils, sit at a table, presumably at their M.I.T. laboratory. "If what you've discovered is accurate…"

"I assure you Mr. Chairman, the data is conclusive and the equipment has already been tested. We can have the ship launched to target within a day or two. All we need is to be given the word."

Mede nods, wearing a sober smile. He is apparently very pleased with his new power and tests on his tongue, the name of the institution providing that authority. "I, the Chairman of the Green Order Government, grant you permission for launch."

But Winston is not quite sold. "Don't we need to run this by the Council Membership for a vote of confidence…"

"Do not question my provision!" Mede shouts as he slams the palm of his hand on his desk causing pens, other articles and even Winston Torin to jump. "I have been granted full and complete ruling authority in this matter—your duty is to take the action I have approved. Is that clear?"

Winston responds, "Perfectly clear sir, I'll give the order for immediate countdown towards launch."

"Very good. Jonathan, are you there?" Another image pops up beside Winston's on the screen. It's none other than Jonathan Trimble, my boss, and CEO of N.H.Q. Broadcast Corp.

"I'm here, Mr. Chairman, but I just received your request to be on this Web Conference so I'm afraid I caught only the tail end of the conversation."

"I certainly understand," Mede responds magnanimously. "As Council Chairman representing the new Media Affiliation for the Green Order Government—M.A.G.O.G. for short—I need you to clearly understand what is about to take place based on a strategy begun several weeks ago at the outset of all our problems. Dr. Torin, please summarize your findings"

Winston is caught off guard, not having readied himself to reiterate the circumstances to a layman. I can almost see the thoughts tumbling around in the M.I.T. Director's head: *Trimble is nothing more than a glorified news hack who has bragged about building his fortune on a high school degree and fifty dollars.*

"Any time, Professor." Mede sounds impatient.

"Of course: Er uh...Prior to the V4641 anomaly, we had been doing some testing of a new propulsion system that operates using a non-traditional fuel source. There's a long name for it—Recombinant Aprotonic Plasma, but you might recognize it by its more trendy title..."

"...Antimatter, right? But isn't it known more familiarly as R.A.P.?" Trimble interrupts smugly.

Winston Torin quickly swallows his shock at Jonathan Trimble having this information at hand. He maintains his mask of professionalism and continues. "I'm impressed, but let's make sure the information you've been fed is accurate. R.A.P.—*antimatter*—was accidentally discovered during the Chernobyl Meltdown and has been kept a secret under Soviet/ Russian care until recently. It is highly unstable but has qualities, which if properly controlled, make it a perfect fuel. I won't bore you with the details other than to say that temperature, radioactive structure, conductivity and particle bonding all play major parts in its creation."

"So far you haven't told me anything that I don't know," Trimble claims casually and appears distracted by other objects on his desk.

"Well perhaps then you can tell me the characteristic that distinguishes Recombinant Aprotonic Plasma from any other compound?" Winston is not casual—he sounds more incensed at having his secret bag of tricks so easily accessed.

"You mean the property of Ambient Coexistence—something that exists in several places at one time?" Jonathan Trimble is filing his fingernails as he speaks to the camera.

"Yes...but we are not speaking of places—we have proven that R.A.P. exists interdimensionally!" Winston, the professor, will not be outdone by Trimble, the student. "This property will actually allow us to control space travel from starting point to destination without concern for time or distance. We can send a rocket from location A and have it arrive at location B nearly instantaneously! Do you realize the ramifications of this?

"Teleportation—you've proven this?" This is the first time that Trimble looks interested in the conversation.

"Hypothetically, yes," Torin says less confidently. "The only complication is in actually understanding exactly where we are going. It is one thing to look at a star or a nebula many light-years away—what we are seeing through even the best telescope is an image thousands of years old—it's another to know a cosmic object's actual location in real time."

"How have you solved that problem?" Trimble has set his nail file aside and has a notepad before him.

"We didn't—you did. Or rather your little schoolboy Danny Adamson did with his Evolutional Echo Tracing program." Winston Torin's punitive tone suggests he believes he now has the upper hand in dealing with this ingrate. "Adamson's formula now allows us to see space as it looks without the clutter of reoccurring echoes. It has, in a sense, un-curved the cosmos."

Trimble questions skeptically, "If you can do this in space, why not do it on earth? Why not teleport from home base?"

"I already mentioned the instable nature of R.A.P., and because we are not sure of the side-effects of a successful transport, we've decided that an off-planet demonstration is more practical," Winston states with a condescending tone.

The head of N.H.Q. Broadcast glances at his watch and seems to realize he's heard enough and is ready to conclude. "And when's the launch?"

"Immediately," announces Torin. "As soon as we conclude this conversation, I will give the command."

Jonathan Trimble scribbles on his pad, sets his pen down and puts out one last query. "So please explain why we're going to this much effort. How on Earth—excuse the word-play—will this technology help us with the current situation?"

Winston smiles with eyes closed—he must realize with great satisfaction that he knows something Trimble doesn't. "That would have to do with another unique property of Recombinant Aprotonic Plasma—the destructive nature of the component if allowed to interact with normal high energy matter."

"High energy matter such as?" Trimble asks."

"Such as within the bowels of the mini-quasar V4641," Winston proudly announces.

AUSTIN, TEXAS – UNIVERSITY OF TEXAS COMPLEX, QUANTUM SYSTEMS DEPARTMENT

"What's going to happen now?" Roxanne stands at the back of our group meeting with her arms crossed and foot tapping, expecting someone to fix her world. She's been informed by Travis that the water doesn't seem to be receding and that we may be here a while, unless the State of Texas or the U.S. Military can get their acts together and send a spare helicopter or boat to pick us up. That hardly seems likely as the entire governmental structure seems to be in temporary shambles.

Our drama queen is the only one who seems anxious about our current conditions. Everyone else has chipped in to help on projects and the atmosphere has pretty much been one of a family working together, but Roxanne remains aloof and non-participatory in most things such as the Bible study I've offered up to everyone. Travis and Tonda have sat in on occasion over the last week and I've spotted Mustif outside the door of our sessions, but he will not enter in. He has been, however, a contributor in other activities and is a willing, if quietly effective, lab assistant. Surprisingly, it's he who now responds to Roxanne.

"Sometimes one has to accept their conditions without understanding— your fate and mine are not in our hands at this moment. I hope that is not too unsettling for you," he says in a peacefully even tone.

"Fine, I'm going to go wash my hair," Roxanne makes a flamboyant show of exiting, stage left.

It reminds me as she leaves the room of how strangely selective my new powers are. It seems I'm able to break into the thoughts and parley of people thousands of miles away more easily than I can those within these walls. It appears I'm only able to catch conversations and see images—how else can it be described—of which a Higher Power wants me to be privy.

I've shared the full extent of my out of body moments only with Misty, Fiz and Moses, relaying the most recent dialogue between Mede, Torin and Trimble. We were all concerned enough to try to make contact with the President, who will not respond. We have no idea if he is involved or just incognito for the moment, which means there is no way of politically influencing the situation. We even tried to reach Mede to implore him to reconsider his course, but he is also unresponsive.

"How am I doing this?" I asked Fiz and Moses in a private meeting. "The images seem to be getting stronger and when it's happening, I seem to be more there than…here."

"Daniel," the Rabbi explained, "the best I can do is give you some Biblical examples that seem to parallel your condition. "Moses glowed after experiencing the Shekinah Glory…the immediate presence of God. Ezekiel, Daniel, John, and others had dream state premonitions or prophesies implying they were transported spiritually to another location a higher level of existence…for temporary periods. Jesus even passed through hostile crowds untouched, suggesting that he could transcend from a physical to a spiritual state and back again."

"But I'm not Jesus! What's going on?"

"So many questions when faith is the greatest need." The Rabbi sighed. "Daniel, your point is a valid, if not totally accurate statement: Remember what Paul said, 'We are the body of Messiah.' He is contained within those who acknowledge him as Savior. If you take that notion seriously and examine it scientifically, you are, in part, Jesus. And you have specific power bestowed on you as part of his body."

The master can see that the student isn't focused on the right question so the Rabbi poses a brain smoking question. "Daniel, you are so good at thinking differently—consider the following: What if the matter within matter is not matter at all? What if the very thing that holds us together is a different kind of element altogether—perhaps even dimensionally removed from that with which we are familiar. What if the medium of our composition is invisible to us because it is not physical in nature at all, but spiritual?"

What? We are held together by God? "I…no, that can't be. Fiz, you, Pastor Fa…uh, other people…have pointed out to me that we are born spiritually dead. If our atoms and the atoms of all other things…" I couldn't finish the argument—it was too crazy, using theology to explain physiology—so far out of the box that I had no reference points to lean on. Fiz jumped in, seeing that I was floundering.

"Child, think it through. Death in spirit does not imply non-existence of spiritual matter. When your physical body dies, does it disappear? Certainly it breaks down, but the physical stuff of it still exists. If we had no spiritual material to work with, God would not be able to commune with the world or to offer redemption."

My head was exploding. If one believes that God is The Spiritual Being, and if The Spiritual Being created all that is, He would have had to have started with something—a metaphorical Petri-dish in which to culture His creation. At that point, as far as we know, the only thing that existed was…spiritual matter. My God, that's the answer—the substance that holds us together microscopically is the same substance that connects things macrocosmically—the mystery of gravity, the origin of positive and negative energy—all answered. Quantum and molecular vacuums aren't the answers "It's all about spirit—Light Matter, not Dark Matter!" I had shouted this answer out loud causing Fiz and Moses to laugh together. They knew I had jumped a threshold.

"So what will you do with your new-found discovery?" Fiz asked almost innocently.

Time…_and_ space have become little more than curiosities replaced in significance by a whole new set of parameters to explore. No more time? Big deal. The real question has become: how do we prepare for what now seems, the inevitable—the beginning of the end of time?

V4641 SOL PLUS ONE-C – REGION OF THE MAGELLANIC GAS CLOUDS

So predictable—they need so much love.

AUSTIN, TEXAS – UNIVERSITY OF TEXAS COMPLEX, QUANTUM SYSTEMS DEPARTMENT

"Pardon me, Professor Adamson, may I come in?" It's Mustif who I've not yet heard call any of us by our given name. I'm in one of the lab rooms reading my Bible—a new habit for me that requires concentration and no interruptions. We've been here a full five days and I'm finding the time alone to have remarkable consequences. They include some interesting conversations ensuing with *the voices* as well as some scriptural discoveries which seem to significantly tie in with our predicament. The others seem to sense how much I cherish this time so the interruption by Mustif is a little surprising and a bit annoying. Still, any time he voluntarily begins a conversation is a truly rare event, so I can't deny him the time.

"I'm very curious about something," he continues as I wave him into the room and clear off another chair for him piled with books and research papers. This quiet young man instead remains standing in front of me with hands folded—fingers interlaced. He peers almost bashfully at the floor between us. "Can you tell me how your God is different?"

How my God is different? Different from what? On an impulse I ask Mustif to hold on for a minute. I close my eyes and search for the right words. And then they come, *Lord, please help me to understand Your purpose at this moment—give me the right way to help Mustif know You.* Then I open my eyes to see him observing me quizzically. "Mustif, I don't know how God differs from what you know or perceive about Him because frankly, I don't know your experience or history concerning spiritual relationships. Can you help me out with a point of reference?"

"I'm sorry, I…it would be inappropriate for me to share that with you at this moment. I was hoping though, that you could tell me at least why I see such a difference in you, your family and Professor Hindeland when I compare you to the others or in fact to most others with whom I have had relationships."

I feel like we are circling in preparation to dance—eyeing each other with curiosity—is this someone I want to get to know better? What good or bad could come out of this encounter? What kind of emotional investment do I need to contribute?

I realize how selfishly protective my thoughts are. *Take the gamble,* someone whispers inside me. "Mustif, I'll do my best to explain what I think you're noticing. You are welcomed to ask as many questions as you want when I'm done."

He nods and now sits in the offered chair. I guess I've passed whatever pretest was given, so now I get to move on to the full exam.

"What I think you may be recognizing in us is a quality that is often very misunderstood and misinterpreted in our culture—probably in most cultures. Some people try to build it by connecting similarities between themselves in ideology, history, and beliefs. Some pursue it based on physical attraction and even sexual desire. Others challenge it and see it as a conquest to be had, winning over the hearts and minds of others.

"And then there are those who recognize it as a spiritual spark, something inspired from a…Greater Source that changes us inside. It causes our focus to change from selfish attention into a consuming desire to please and honor the One providing the inspiration."

Mustif appears to be considering my words and asks, "How does one get this spark?"

"It's not something you get, but it's given…freely, as a gift and that's the way we're taught to offer it to others."

"What do you call this gift?" Mustif asks softly.

"The ancients had a specific word for it—*Agape*. We have poorly translated and generalized the use of the word to mean something else. We typically call it *Love* and that's the confusion. There are so many… lesser ways we define love and Agape Love should not be a category, but rather the standard by which all love should be measured." I realize this is starting to sound like a sermon and so I again pray inwardly, *Lord, what is Your desire here. Help me out—give me the right words!*

"Mustif, there is something you have to do in order to receive the gift. You have to"…*Don't preach, share your heart!*…"To be able to love in this deeper way, I had to recognize the legitimate originator and giver of Agape."

Go ahead, ask me what… Who it was that changed me—ask me about my Savior! I try sending a secret coded message from me to Mustif, imploring him to ask me about Jesus. It should be his inquiry, not my promotion. *Spirit, speak to him and let him know You!*

Mustif sits silently for several moments and then nods his head as if to say he has drawn some unspoken conclusion. He stands again and speaks politely acknowledging me with a half bow—no handshake. "Thank you Professor, you have shared a very personal thing with me and I appreciate your time more than you can know. I will let you get back to your studies."

With that he exits the room as quietly as he entered. *Lord, what in the world was that about? Did I mess up?*

GENEVA, SWITZERLAND – WORLD TRADE ORGANIZATION

It's an incredible thing to behold: From this vantage point, an average looking launch vehicle of composite steel, titanium alloys and carbon fiber, all blended somehow into this elegant fuselage, not much bigger than two semi-truck trailers set on its end. But this Space Truck carries a very different kind of payload.

I watch with my *out-of-body eyes* and observe Darius Mede smile as he observes from his opulent and very protective underground bunker, located beneath his now demolished headquarters, ravaged by repeated earthquakes and windstorms. He must be appreciating the genius of what is now about to happen.

The design of the rocket is itself an amazing accomplishment— reducing solar system travel from months and years down to hours and days, using a very compact power source known as the Deep Region Recombinant Aneutronic Gas Engine, which he has fondly dubbed the DRRAGEN-One

"—Aneutronic fusion is very clean and stable," Winston Torin had bragged to Darius when demonstrating the concept.

N.A.S.A. had been very helpful in the process. They had already produced and tested a working prototype of the unit and voluntarily offered to launch the vehicle if the new Green Order Government would foot the bill.

But then there was the discovery of Recombinant Aprotonic Plasma that Winston Torin had introduced to Mede earlier. R.A.P. was being heralded as the perfect solution to efficient travel beyond the solar system. Darius had patiently explained to the world's scientists and leaders how the two mechanisms would work together to save mankind.

"Once DRRAGEN-One's Aneutronic engine has taken the rocket safely away from earth, the Aprotonic Reaction will be initiated in a separate section of the rocket. The navigation information provided by means of Evolutional Echo Tracing, will instantaneously teleport the entire unit to the target which is at the mouth of V4641. The singularity will absorb the delivered package which will already be creating both an Aprotonic reaction in one chamber and an Aneutronic reaction in the other. The intense gravitational forces within the singularity will then crush the chambers together causing a colliding mix of matter and antimatter. This reaction will destroy the mini-quasar from the inside out, ending whatever geo-cosmic relationship exists between it and Earth and thus ending the mayhem we now experience."

"What if it fails to kill the quasar?" a non-prominent official asked.

"Kill?" What an interesting choice of metaphors to describe this process," Mede had reacted offhandedly, buying time so that he could think through his response carefully. "This project has been thoroughly tested and we trust it will not fail," he responded using the confidence of his voice and the charisma of his position to sweep aside any pervading doubt among the internet audience.

"What if it does work and we are wrong in assuming V4641 to be an enemy?" An all too familiar voice tags in.

"Is that you Moses? I don't recall seeing your name listed on the security list for this web-conference." Mede was visibly perturbed at Moses Folzman's intrusion. "How could we possibly be wrong in that assumption?"

"Just because there is a relationship that radically alters the behavior of one of the involved parties does not mean that the interaction is harmful," Folzman replies. "Indeed, geological history would suggest that this planet has gone through several such changes and that these have resulted in improved conditions after the period of adjustment."

Darius was ready to do battle. "How would you comfort the Earth's population concerning the massive tectonic upheaval, floods, famine, overall economic and societal chaos which now exists? Are these also benefits we should embrace?"

But Moses Folzman, distinguished rabbinical scholar and noted microphysicist, was not apologetic, nor was he finished. "Ladies and Gentleman, honored colleagues and distinguished leaders, whether we are right or wrong in our abilities does not make our attempted action the correct action. Reconsider this course you are taking and the potential consequences. Perhaps even ask the question within your hearts—not just try to manufacture an untested solution with your proud minds. What question is it to which I'm referring?

What is the intention of The Eternal, and how should we best obey His desires?"

Power was in danger of shifting. Darius was losing control of his support and responded with the most familiar weapons available to him in his arsenal—the emotions of fear, doubt, and worry. "Indeed, these would be wonderful questions to contemplate, sipping brandy in a warm and cozy room filled with books and cozy fire. But those rooms are crumbling, as is the rest of our infrastructure. Our families are suffering, even dying. We who are responsible have countries and populations pleading with us for remedy and you offer nothing more than speculation about the existence of some well-meaning master-mind who set this all, in motion."

Mede held more sway with the audience than the Rabbi and was encouraged to move forward by the governments of the world. Of course, he would have acted anyway, but having the support gave him blank-check authority to proceed with impunity, the results of which he is witnessing on the view screen in real-time…

—It will be a night launch and the spotlights illuminating the DRRAGEN-One emblazoned on its fuselage, along with the vibrant Forest Green flag of the Green Order Government, reveals to Mede the beautiful creation of which man is capable. There's steam venting from some source on the rocket, obviously a normal condition—a blue streamer at the bottom of the screen scrolls the words, ALL SYTEMS GO, WEATHER CONDITIONS ACCEPTABLE. Mede mouths the words, "Please don't let an earthquake occur before lift-off," and he watches as the gantry is cleared of all equipment and personnel prior to the final countdown.

I wonder as I peek into this private moment, *to whom is he mouthing those words: Himself?* Is he imploring some other unintroduced individual or entity? Could he be recognizing and praying to the entity whose existence this all-powerful world leader has often disclaimed? I'm amazed at the natural tendency, even of those who espouse to deny God's existence, to fall back to dependency on prayer in times of great need and uncertainty.

As he watches the last minutes tick down on the screen's virtual clock, Darius picks up the telephone and sends a text message. To whom? Darius offers no clue as he gives a simple command to the receiving party. "Proceed."

Turning off his phone, he relaxes into the leather couch he sits in and lets the moment unfold, turning up the volume on the television just in time to hear: "Five, Four, Three, Two, One; we have ignition…" and there is a different sound, not like a typical solid fuel booster—it sounds more like a turbine engine winding up. Then follows an explosive roar accompanied by a brilliant crimson cloud of smoke. The rocket emerges out of the top of the cloud and quickly rises—the video cameras capture its image—an immense ball of red flame shooting toward the heavens.

Mede holds a congratulatory glass of champagne he has poured for himself into the air as he renames the rocket on the spot. "Red DRRAGEN." He downs the drink and a smile of satisfaction warms his face. "Adamson, Folzman, Hindeland, you are all so right—there is no time for you. Your time is up!" He laughs richly and stares dreamily at the picture of the rocket fading away into space. "And my time is just begun!"

Entry Twenty-One

"Theorists have tried repeatedly to construct a sub-atomic extension of gravity—prove the existence of gravity at microscopic distances—while still respecting the rules of quantum mechanics. Many suggestions have been made for such a theory, but not one has gained universal acceptance. All encounter difficulties and it's easy to see why. Marrying quantum mechanics with Einstein's gravity theory requires space itself to fluctuate—a mind-boggling concept. If there are a variety of spaces, which one do we live in? There must be one answer that ties the quantum and sub-atomic worlds together, but it is yet to be discovered. And so, the construction of a quantum theory of gravity is one of the greatest unsolved problems of theoretical physics."

—Reb. Moses Folzman, Ph.D.

SOMEWHERE INSIDE DANNY

Danny.

"I hear you Dad."

It is The Time.

"Wait…what?"

It is The Moment; you must be ready.

"I'm…confused…all you've been telling me and all I've been telling everybody else is that there <u>is no time</u>! Suddenly there is <u>time</u>? A Moment in time? What exactly am I supposed to do, what is or isn't time? I…"

A wind or a breath of wind washes over my face. *Danny. Be at peace.* And I am.

Man is so naïve and at the same time so self-important. He thinks that because he observes something and names it that somehow he has defined its cause—that he has created its origin; that he owns its destiny. There is and always has been only One Moment. My Moment—My Time. Have you not been listening to your own words? In a moment, the cosmos was created—in one moment all that is, became and exists now. Before that moment, I saw what would be and spoke it into existence. I was, I am and I will be when all else is finished.

Everything inside me trembles. I figure this is a very good time to drop to my knees and do so. It doesn't seem enough and I fall completely prostrate with my hands stretched in front of me and my forehead fixed firmly to the cold floor. "You…aren't my father, are you?"

I Am.

"I mean, you're not my…natural father who…"

"I AM! I speak to you in a voice you recognize. I know your father and your father's father—all before you and all to come. I give you comfort. I provide you forgiveness and love and redemption. I AM that I AM!

I am, on the other hand, he who is frightened and I think I've wet myself. I'm suddenly very aware of and absolutely ashamed of who I am and how poorly I've presented myself to whom it is now speaking to me. "Why do you…why would you love me?"

You are my beloved son in whom I am well pleased.

"I am so sorry. You've…made a mis…You have mistaken me for…"

Jesus the Messiah dwells within you just as he dwells within your father. You have claimed My Son as your redeemer and so you are redeemed. It is not you I see, but My Son that you have become. And now it is The Time. Go. Prepare everyone.

"I don't know what to do. How do I…how do we prepare?"

My breath is now in you. Go and it will be done.

AUSTIN, TEXAS – UNIVERSITY OF TEXAS COMPLEX, QUANTUM SYSTEMS DEPARTMENT

Misty and I watch as Fiz sips on his club soda and works out some calculations on a pad of paper, then glances over at a book he has opened on his desk and makes another note. He has asked us to his office for a private conversation and, as usual, has not stated the purpose of the meeting.

"That's why we're not referred to as instructors or teachers. *We're Professors. We Profess!*" Fiz had once touted when I had, long ago, impatiently asked him to please get to the point. I've learned over time that a visit with my mentor is always revealing and to be patient in waiting for him to illuminate his topic du jour.

And in this present moment, his topic is powerful. "To the best of my calculations, we have about twelve hours," he suddenly expresses.

"Twelve hours until?" Misty has an interesting way of asking a question that requires at least one word from the part of the queried party in order to complete the phrase. I now recognize it as a skill she uses to shape the response in a way that helps her to learn. And I had not picked up on this characteristic of hers before because?

"…Until Mede's rocket is ready to shift from transport mechanism to weapon." Fiz looks back down at his notes, then back up again. "After that, I believe the world will be a very changed place. We must prepare."

It's now that I notice the book he has opened is a Bible. From my vantage point, I can see that it is one of those study versions with notes in the margins. I can't see which particular book or chapter he's resourcing, but I can see the meticulous notes in the margins and the verses marked in yellow and green highlighter ink, suggesting this particular section of the book is one with which he is very familiar. Now he points his pen at a verse already highlighted and underlines it for further emphasis. "The door of heaven is about to be opened," Fiz announces.

"…And?" Again, Misty throws in a fill-in-the-blank question.

Fiz smiles grimly and elaborates, "Depending on who is interpreting the passages, Revelation plus several other books and passages in the Bible suggest that there will be a time when we are all gathered up into a heavenly realm just prior to or right after the beginning of a time of unparalleled chaos on earth."

"Danny, do you interpret it that way—that God is going to radically change the things on Earth?" Misty is looking like I imagine I did as a child when I was told by my mother that my father was dying. I had desperately wanted my mother to assure me that the doctors would fix my dad and that his condition was greatly exaggerated. I didn't care then if it would be a lie—I wanted to hear comfort, not truth. My wife's eyes now say, *lie to me.* I want to tell her *everything will be normal soon, it's really just a theory, no one buys the concept,* but recent events and my own studies cause me to answer in a totally different way. Instead, I offer something that I haven't shared often enough with her in our relationship—the truth.

"I do believe that way, yes. And if accurate, it means that something very frightening and at the same time wonderful is about to happen." I pause because I think I might be scaring my wife—*Lord, give me the wisdom and the right words, to explain this.* "Misty, God is about to complete His work and He needs helpers, He's going to ask us to be those helpers and we need to be ready. If Fiz is correct, very soon we'll all be going on a little…trip."

"Where are we going…Danny!" A virtual light bulb of awareness goes off over her head—awareness and anticipation now shine on her face. "How can we prepare for…how do we get ready?" She has on her *brave-smile* now, the one I see her wearing when I know she's building up her resolve to see something through—I know now she's going to be fine and her strength helps me know that I'm going to be fine too.

"Well first," I smile at her, "I think a real feast is in order. What do you think, Fiz?"

"Child, a feast would be a marvelous idea and that will give us a chance to prepare the others as well."

"The others," I echo. "That reminds me—I need to get something out of the lab—I'll be back in a little bit. Misty, why don't you go get the family, Fiz do you mind telling the others we'll have an announcement and will be eating in a couple of hours? Then if you don't mind, we'd be honored to have you lead our devotion."

"The honor will be mine Child."

ROCHESTER, NEW YORK – THE CHESTER F. CARLSON CENTER FOR IMAGING SCIENCE AT THE ROCHESTER INSTITUTE OF TECHNOLOGY

On the plasma screen, an off-camera newscaster is speaking to Spencer L. Lynd, Ph.D. – Director of the Hubble Telescope Monitoring System. He sits importantly at his station in The Hive with extra equipment placed strategically around him to make the little room seem very *high-tech*.

"We have repositioned the main telescope for a perfect view of the V4641 mini-quasar that now has become our solar system's closest neighbor. We believe we will be able to offer a nearly *real-time* view of what will happen when DRRAGEN-One encounters the singularity."

"Nearly real-time?" The camera pans back to a shot of the commentator who we now discover is none other than Jonathan Trimble, looking very serious while tilting his head to convey his interest. The camera pops back to Spence and he continues to explain.

"Well, V4641 is a number of light-years away. That means that the light we are observing from it still takes time to travel to Earth. In its current location, we are actually seeing the mini-quasar as it was about six to seven years ago. I know that's a hard concept to grasp, but it's the best we can offer at the moment."

"If the pictures are of an object that changed course that many years ago, why are we just feeling the effects now?" Jonathan Trimble acts truly puzzled.

"We don't know that we haven't been affected before this time—we just didn't see what it was that was altering our environment so we didn't know to correlate the occurrences. What we do know is that the activity increased recently and coincidentally, with V4641's change in location."

The camera catches Trimble making a note on his paper pad and then he looks up to ask, "What else can we expect to happen from this point forward?"

"Although the shift in V4641's position has certainly impacted our planet's environment, we believe that everything is now settling down and that soon, things will return to normal."

"In other words, there's nothing to worry about?" Trimble sounds very calm and professional.

"I wouldn't say that, but certainly we are seeing a subsidence of seismic activity and the weather patterns seem to be returning to predictable norms."

"Then why bother to send the DRRAGEN-One on its mission?" Jonathan Trimble asks provocatively.

"Well, we don't want to take any chances, do we? What is the harm in going forward with the venture? If nothing else, think of the scientific information this project will produce—not to mention the great pictures of the event we'll be able to watch on our TVs."

"So over the next few hours," Trimble commentates, "we'll be keeping a close watch on our little neighbor to make sure it doesn't start misbehaving again."

Both men share a professional chuckle and then Trimble puts a hand to his ear, dips his head in concentration and looks back to the audience. "As a matter of fact I'm being told that we now have a live feed to the monitoring system and can show you exactly what Dr. Lynd and his colleagues are watching."

The picture switches and now on the screen appears an enhanced image. We know it's an enhanced image because at the bottom of the screen it says so. What the audience sees is a computer image of V4641. Spence's voice is heard trying to help us understand what we are observing. "Before shifting positions in the Galaxy, V4641 was very easy to monitor because it was sucking the life out of its binary star partner. Now? It's difficult to see because there is no star next to the anomaly. This enhanced image is computer generated and doesn't really show what it's doing. But…" he quickly adds, "…the evidence suggests its effect on us is winding down."

"How did it move from the center of the galaxy and arrive here?" Trimble presses his interviewee.

"We really don't know how—we can only speculate."

"Is there anything we do know?" Jonathan Trimble doesn't want to leave a single morsel on the table.

This time Spence's chuckle is a nervous one, "Yes. It was somewhere else and now, it's here!"

AUSTIN, TEXAS – UNIVERSITY OF TEXAS COMPLEX, QUANTUM SYSTEMS DEPARTMENT

After listening to the interview between Spencer Lynd and Jonathan Trimble, I switch off the TV in the lab and begin my search for a special memento—something I believe will help in our study with the kids and later in our meeting with everyone.

Looking around the lab one more time, I'm reminded of how much this building and the people associated with it, have influenced my life. Fiz, Brandon, the other staff and students all encouraged and enabled my path. I find I'm having trouble letting go—I know I'm supposed to want what is going to happen, but the memories—even the unpleasant ones associated with my leaving the department the first time—are like a cool breeze on a hot day, reminding me that the extremes are what make life both challenging and interesting.

I walk down the aisle between work-tables, unconsciously running my hand along the surfaces, taking in the faint odor of microscope lubricating oil and disinfectant that had defined this room for me for so long. I could easily be blindfolded and know where I am. I close my eyes as if to test my point and my wandering hand happens upon a plastic baggie. Looking down, I see what it was I was looking for—a collection of five popsicle-sticks that I've protected as a keepsake since I was twelve years old. Holding the prize in my hand, my thoughts run back to another encounter with Pastor Fale.

"Danny, why does God exist?" He once asked me.

"Why?" At the tender age of fourteen, I was totally not ready for the question.

"Yes, what is God's purpose?" He reiterated.

"Does God need a purpose? He's God! If He didn't have a purpose, would He disappear?" I was thinking out loud.

"And yet without purpose based in belief and faith, you and I perish. Is that not a defining connection between God and man? Our purpose is His purpose." The man of the cloth actually chuckles, the only memory I have of my old shepherd where I remember him laughing.

"I don't see what's so funny about that. Why would God let mankind be destroyed?"

I'm answering the good Pastor in present tense…because even now I still don't want to draw the conclusion. My mouth feels dry and I turn on the faucet at one of the lab sinks to catch some water in a glass. There is a shudder and a groaning noise as the underused tap struggles to produce a stream. When the liquid finally does come out, it is the color of over brewed tea, but smells more like a leaking sewer drain. "Of course I won't drink it," I find myself speaking again out loud to the uninterested lab equipment.

And then I realize that, in the mouthing of those words, I've been taught a new lesson. If I remain in a dark musty place, unused and motionless—not moving over new ground that cleanses and revitalizes me—then I become foul. It wasn't God who had hidden from me after my father died. It was my behavior which made all-things-spiritual appear to be light-years away, when in reality, my Creator has been beside me—even within me—causing changes, refining me into something He can now use for a new purpose—just as He is doing with the planet.

"Thank you again, Lord," I voice through a smile. "I'm ready now." And as I open my eyes after this brief prayer, I notice Mustif standing at the door across the room. His stare bores a hole in me, and there is a set in his stance which suggests an attack is imminent. The mystery man holds something in his hand and it's not until he begins his charge in my direction that I realize he's holding the live monster bug in his hand. It is also in attack mode, buzzing angrily and wanting very much to do damage to something or someone…me.

I frantically look around for a sharp object, a knife, a stick—anything with which to defend myself—and find nothing, I take my only option as my nemesis lunges at me—I turn and crouch. In the slow-motion of the moment, I'm surprised to catch sight of someone else behind me. It's Roxanne who is wielding something shiny and sharp—a dissection scalpel in fact—and she is aiming it at Mustif in order to defend me…no she has actually plunged it into my chest. Why don't I feel anything? Why is Mustif now flying into Roxanne and tumbling her over? Why is Roxanne now screaming and waving her arms in panic as Mustif rolls past her—his body thudding into the bookshelf at the end of the aisle?

I continue to lie on the floor and have a clear view of the doorway where I can see the feet of other people running into the room. Then I can see slender legs, labeled with tattoos, running past the others. Watching the running tattoos with glazed fascination, I hear fading screams and a diminishing buzzing sound. As I lose consciousness I remember thinking, *Hmm—Doppler Effect: The noise of an object heading away from me becomes lower in pitch because the associated sound waves are elongated and...*

V4641 SOL PLUS ONE-C – REGION OF THE MAGELLANIC GAS CLOUDS

Weep for those of the world where darkness is cherished above light. I am the Light...

GENEVA, SWITZERLAND – WORLD TRADE ORGANIZATION

Darius Mede opens the door of his private study to greet Brenda Anders, "Brenda, what a pleasant surprise." Mede does not sound pleasant, nor surprised, as well he shouldn't: His security detail already informed him that Ms. Anders was in route in her private jet with a flight plan that suggested she was on her way to see him, Mede had told his minions to allow the flight to continue, explaining that she may prove useful in the near future.

Now me, I am definitely surprised. I'm unconscious on a laboratory floor, thousands of miles away, yet watching the encounter. Am I dreaming or is this part of my newfound spiritual telepathy skill? *How surreal! Go with the flow, Danny, go with the flow! This is your new reality.*

Things are in motion that must not be stopped. DRRAGEN-One is drawing ever closer to its destiny; his operative in Texas should have performed her duty by now; and the governments of the world continue to line up in progressive succession to honor Mede as their leader. I'm now even able to hear Darius' thoughts—*I am in control. Do not try to limit me.*

He admits Brenda into the room toward the couch and says pointedly. "Sit." She complies and watches as he walks to his desk, sits down, and begins to open his cell phone as if to make a call, then thinks better of it and places the device in his sweater pocket.

Anders recognizes the mood of her lover, but she apparently did not come here to be dismissed so easily and now speaks out. "You will need a wife."

"What?" Darius' expression says that he is completely caught off guard by the comment.

"The world is watching you. They want to follow you willingly, but they need to know that you are trustworthy and conventional. Taking a wife—a partner—will complete your image.

Entry Twenty-Two

Folzman's Principle — There is only one law and it is not our creation.
Folzman's Corollary — Everything proven in the physical realm
validates mankind's ignorance of the spiritual realm.

AUSTIN, TEXAS – UNIVERSITY
OF TEXAS COMPLEX, QUANTUM
SYSTEMS DEPARTMENT

I walk into the lounge where Jake and Sylvia charge into my arms just as I bend down to hug them.

"Daddy, you're brighter!" Sylvia exclaims as both of them nuzzle their heads into either side of my neck. Everyone in the room laughs.

My mom is next, standing expectantly before me—hands on hips—with a look on her face that says, *What about me?* I whisper to the kids some special instructions and they charge off with secret mission glee. I hug my mother as only a son can—letting her know she is still the most special woman in the world for having given me birth.

"Now will you please explain what happened down there?" She demands, pointing toward the stairway to the lab where I had been attacked.

Misty, Fiz and Mustif are standing behind me and come forward to help in the explanation. Travis and Tonda come from the kitchen area, obviously also wanting to hear all the details.

"Well, I was getting some things together for our gathering when I saw Mustif coming toward me. I didn't even have time to think and he jumped over me in an attempt to stop Roxanne."

"Stop Roxanne—stop her from what? Where is she now?" Travis and Tonda both are firing questions at me in rapid sequence.

Fiz takes over for this part of the story. "Misty and I were in my office and heard a scream. We ran toward the lab where the sound came from and just as we got in the door, Roxanne charged out with something tangled up in her hair."

"It was the monster bug," Misty explains. "I spent a lot of time with that thing. Even though it was under her hair, I'd recognize its motion anywhere. It was after Roxanne in a big way."

Fiz nods and continues. "Misty went over to find Danny and I chose to follow Roxanne to see if I could help her—she was in some obvious pain—but I couldn't catch up with her in time."

"…In time?" My mother is captivated by the unraveling of the soap opera action.

"She ran into a room across the building where she had apparently planned an escape." Fiz explains. "One of the windows had been scored and cut open and she dived through it, into the water. I reached the window just in time to see her take off in a boat with an outboard motor, still screaming and grabbing at her back as she steered the boat away."

"Boat—there was a boat out there and we didn't know about it?" This is Tonda. She seems very frustrated at the news. "But how did she know it was there?"

"She had help." Everyone turns to look at Mustif who has spoken for the first time before the group. His face turns crimson from embarrassment, but he bows his head and continues to explain. "I have been watching. You see, my purpose here is to protect Professor Adamson…it is difficult to explain."

No one says a word, but Tonda comes over and puts a reassuring hand on the quiet man's shoulder. She smiles at him and we all follow suit, waiting for him to reveal the mystery we've all sensed surrounding him.

"Several years back," he begins, "I was a leader of a group that proclaimed another god from the one you recognize. We were convinced that our mission was to make sure everyone believed as we did. Anyone who did not believe as we did was not worthy of existence. We took it upon ourselves to hurry the process of their demise along—we were proud of, and zealous for our cause."

I can see a change in Mustif. As he speaks, he's gaining confidence— his accent smooths out and the flow of his story is less halting.

"Seven months ago, something strange happened. In order to better understand our enemies, I had begun to read their books, including the

Hebrew and Christian Testaments. It was there I started to find another side to the story. Apparently the One you follow—instead of only laying out laws—is seeking a relationship. Instead of demanding obedience, He asks for willingness to obey—leaving the option to the individual, not forcing it upon them by physical threat or demanding through the false authority of others.

"I must admit that I was wary of what I read because, in observing most Yahweh and Christ Followers, their behavior did not always mirror what the scripture portrayed. Still, I read and searched and eventually prayed to Yahweh to be my God."

Mustif hesitates for a moment and then continues. "I am ashamed of my past and will not even speak the name of the one I had followed—it is vile to me now. Unfortunately, there are many others who, if they had known my secret, would have made every attempt possible to take my life. So for a time, I lived two identities. I was known to the others as a great leader of their faith, but within I was a captive of my new Master. It was a great burden.

"One day I heard a voice, a terrible wonderful voice, that said to me, *Choose!* I thought I had chosen, but I then realized I had been hiding from both my old ways and from my new commitment. It was on that day that I announced to my group that I would no longer be in allegiance with a false god that demanded such a price of obedience—the killing of others who did not believe as I did. I then shared my newfound love for a newfound God who loves me. It was on that same day—barely escaping that room with my life—that I came to the University mall area and sat in that very public place. I believe I was thinking it the safest place I could be for the moment—I knew I would soon be dead."

Everyone is enthralled by his story. Mustif looks directly at me. We lock stares as he continues his confession.

"Sitting on the bench on the mall, I heard the voice again. Stronger and more…loving this time, *Pray for the names I am about to give you.* And then I saw specific names in my mind—I could see nothing else:

Travis Chang
Tonda Peterson
Roxanne Temure
Fitzgerald Hindeland
Daniel Adamson and his family

"I did not know what to pray for—I did not even know how I was to pray. So I just repeated the names again and again, asking Yahweh to protect them and to watch over them. It was apparently during this time that the bugs began their tormenting, but I was unaware—I don't know—I was in a kind of trance. All I could see were the names before me."

Now I can see wonder flashing in the eyes of Mustif. He reaches out his hand to me and I hold it in mine. "It was soon after that Professor, that you in turn rescued me. Afterwards, I did not know what to think or how to explain myself—it would have seemed odd…did seem odd and strange to me—how strange would my story have seemed to you?"

He's right! I would have deemed him a lunatic even under the strange circumstances, and I'm suddenly convicted by the thought that this man whom I had once so flippantly referred to as Statue Guy, is a far better servant than I will ever be. It was obviously his prayer action that helped protect us from the bugs and his intercessions had also led us all safely into this building before the flood waters hit.

Misty ventures a question to Mustif. "Why were you attacked by the bugs and why were you supposed to pray for Roxanne?"

He shrugs his shoulders. "Perhaps my character was being…improved. On the other hand, there is a part of the story that, until this time has remained unfinished. You see, I had accepted Yahweh as my God, but it was not until later after seeing what your family demonstrated in your love for Jesus, that I was led to accept him as Savior of my life. It was only then that I recognized the connection of God's love to his people—a love so great that He would sacrifice even a part of Himself in trade for the eternal salvation of believers. I see that love also reflected in your prayers and your daily life and in your love and willing sacrifice toward others. You proved the Bible to me."

Tonda is now openly crying and this triggers tears in most everyone else. I offer a suggestion through my own sniffling. "I think we need to pray for Roxanne. Maybe the reason she was on the no-bug list is because there is still hope for her and until I'm told there's no more hope…"

"Wait just a minute!" This is Misty and I've obviously tripped her trigger. "You want us to pray for the drama queen who tried to plant a butcher's knife in your chest?"

"She didn't try—she actually succeeded. I saw her do it." Everyone looks at Mustif who has just added "eyewitness" to his list of growing credentials. Embarrassed all over again, it takes him a moment to work back into the role of communicator. "I saw her coming at you from behind, Professor. That's why I charged toward you. When you pivoted it allowed her to target your chest which is where I saw her spear you."

"But I didn't feel a thing. For that matter I'm not injured now," I refute.

"No, you are not because I observed a very incredible thing." Mustif closes his eyes now as if to better visualize the memory. "The knife did go into you. When I dove over top of you, I had a perfect view of the act and your response. Your body had become translucent—nearly invisible. As I tackled Ms. Temure and released the bug into her hair, she panicked causing her to release the weapon which dropped to the floor through your body as if the flesh and bone did not exist."

"Spiritual Transfiguration," Fiz offers as explanation. "Your body is becoming less physical in nature and you're developing the ability to shift from one plane to another."

My mother walks directly up to Mustif and starts examining his hands. "I don't understand," she states. "How were you able to grab the bug from the other lab and carry it to Danny's location without it stinging or biting you? You just related that your last encounter with one of those things did not turn out well for you, but I don't see a scratch on you now."

Mustif shakes his head to express his own puzzlement. "All I can tell you is that the same voice I had heard before commanded me to retrieve the bug and to bring it to the lab." Now he flashes a rare smile and laughs quietly. "You can be assured that I was in no way looking forward to following through on that request. When I did extract the beast from its container, it simply crawled into my hand and rested. It was not until I released it onto Ms. Temure that it began its assault."

"So many *bads* goin' down," Tonda says in a convincing ghetto drawl and then reverts to her natural dialect. "We still don't know who enticed Roxanne to come after you. We don't know why this is all happening and we are just sitting ducks here waiting for something else to happen."

"I'm relatively positive I know who motivated Roxanne," Fiz announces. The whole Green Order Protest event you were involved with was orchestrated, I'm sure, by Darius Mede and his lackeys—it would not be a stretch to imagine he could have had a contingency plan in place."

"But why me—what have I done to merit all this attention?" I'm having trouble wrapping my arms around the idea that I am of some greater universal significance.

"Child," my mentor chides, "not only does your ability to eloquently dismantle faulty science put you in direct confrontation with world powers right now, but also you—more than anyone—are a representation of things to come from God. Do not attempt to be self-deprecating where the plans of your Maker are concerned. You are wondrously and marvelously made!"

"Plans of the Maker—what plans? Is there something you haven't shared with us yet?" Travis asks nervously…

NAVEH SHAANAN, ISRAEL – THE TECHNION-ISRAEL INSTITUTE OF TECHNOLOGY

Moses Folzman is in Semicha Rabbi mode, sporting the traditional black garb of the trade—made of a single woven cloth and a black wide brimmed hat worn over a Yarmulka that fails to cover his massive head of hair. He kisses the fringe on his prayer shawl—a well-cared-for Tallit handed down through countless generations of Folzmans—and walks up to one side of the ancient altar table that we had once sat at together in communion and discussion.

Now however, the table is broken in two: Damaged by numerous quakes that have recently ravaged Naveh Shaanan. It stands outside under a canopy of clouded sky, not because it has been moved, but because the room itself—the cozy little dining study we enjoyed—is now also in ruins, burned to the ground during the terrorist attack which took Brandon's life. The surrounding buildings of the campus all show signs of damage, but also of intent to repair. Scaffolding and construction equipment dot the area, reminding anyone who might question their resolve, that the residents of this establishment will not be chased away. Smoke from dwindling fires in the distance suggest there is much more in need of repair—much more to be done by those who honor this land.

Speaking of the populace, there is a large crowd of them standing in attendance waiting for their Rabbi to address them. They are the surviving students and faculty of the Technion—their faces as grim as the landscape surrounding them. Reb. Folzman looks them over with a smile and begins the message he has prepared for them to receive.

"Once long ago, a large group of people were convinced that there were lots of gods. Others thought that spirituality was an invention of man. Those even tried to control people by inventing new gods who supposedly wanted people to follow the rules made up by the crafty kings. Soon it became very difficult for people to know what was the will of The One True Eternal, or even if there was a Supreme Being at all.

"But The One above all had foreseen what was happening to the character of mankind. He gave one man in particular, power even over natural elements. This man could cause droughts and torrential rain upon command.

"The righteous man and his simple message became so popular with the people that he was able to speak out and remain protected against attack from the kings who wanted him eradicated. What was his message? That there is only one Ruler of the Universe and He will one day establish an eternal kingdom on earth, offered as a holy domain for those who are worthy to worship the King.

"Would our lives not look different if we truly believed and anticipated these things to come? How many of you have lived completely within the Torah, the living law of the Eternal? I confess before you that I am incapable of such a claim and yet you know me to be a righteous man. So how am I or any of you to hope to dwell in this new place in the presence of a perfect, holy God?"

There is a murmuring among the crowd. They have come, as they always do when this mighty man speaks, to a point of uncomfortable understanding.

"Of course, we are unworthy, of course this is known by all of us," he smiles again, warmly reassuring them. "Are we even alert to His design? What if…what if He has already, in the past, offered a perfect *fix* and we have missed or dismissed the holiness of it because it does not appear to match up with our perception of how we want The Eternal to work on our behalf?"

Now the crowd starts talking amongst themselves. It's a typical sign that Moses is stirring the pot with the intent of challenging their preconceived theology. Their Rabbi has always presented them with great inspiration and so they anticipate—as one—some powerful message of hope about to be unveiled.

"I tell you now that it is not possible! We will all perish, but for one." Moses Folzman looks solemnly over the crowd of astonished faces and begins to turn and walk away from the cleaved altar. Then as if in afterthought, he turns back and strokes the broken stone. He closes his eyes and what appears to be a silently whispered prayer can be seen moving on his lips. He opens his eyes to the masses and speaks again, a whimsical smile now on his face.

"Oh my—did I forget to mention that many years after the prophet Elijah, another great man walked the earth? He too was considered a prophet and far more. He too spoke of a new kingdom. This man claimed a unique relationship with the Eternal—even referring to him as Father— upon some occasions even daring to use the familiar term *Abba*—meaning 'daddy' or 'papa'—to address Him who's name we revere above all names. This man claimed that he would die and rise again and that his death would negate the spiritual death of anyone who would claim him Lord over their life."

The crowd is deathly still, hanging on the words and Moses bends down this time to examine the break in the altar. "On the day, this man died there was another altar much like this one in a place near to here. At the cry of his death the earth trembled, the holy veil that separated that altar from the worshipers of the time was torn and the altar itself—the most holy of altars on earth at the time—was broken in two. It would seem its heart and that of the Eternal's was rift in empathy at the sacrifice of Jesus Messiah."

Still looking down to examine the broken altar, Folzman continues to speak in his booming baritone. "I had tried earlier to tell you all, but we were interrupted by the earth moving."

Murmurs of disbelief and questioning ripple through the masses—they apparently do not willingly receive the Rabbi connecting the name of Jesus to that of Messiah, *The Redeemer Promised of God.* Smiling reflectively, Moses comes up from his crouching position to stand at his full height to face the crowd. The eyes he can see in the congregation are wide with expectation. He is literally on shaky ground and his next words to this group of Jewish worshipers will be crucial.

"I am a faithful follower of The Eternal. Of that there is no argument just as you are faithful followers. But our altar is broken. We are unsure by what means that we can enter the presence of our Maker. I say unsure because certainly there are means. It rests in the death and return to life and ultimate heavenly ascension of the son of God, the Messiah of Israel and of the world—Yeshua of Nazareth whom I have embraced as my Lord and Savior. I would like very much to share with you—each of you, if you will allow it—how I was made aware of this conclusion and how the God of Abraham who is our Father in Heaven had planned our means to redemption from the beginning."

There is no turning back. The Crazy Prophet has committed himself. A small stone strikes him in the forehead. A larger one bounces off his chest. These are a warning. Once his friends, students, and colleagues—the sea of faces in front of him now have a stormy look. Larger rocks—ready to be punished on Moses—can be seen in their hands, made conveniently available by the rubble strewn at their feet. Their response to his testimony is easy to discern—recant or retreat but do so quickly.

"Blasphemer," a cry goes out. Others join in chorus and the sky grows darker still to match the mood. A raindrop, then another and soon the mob is pelted with a healthy downpour—their reproach literally awash.

Concurrently something else begins to happen. A smaller group begins to separate themselves from the larger. They move toward the broken altar table and momentarily appear as if they mean to take physical action against Folzman. But instead, they assemble in front of the slab, forming a human curtain between Moses and the others.

So he does have friends and allies! Even as the clouds continue to thicken, Moses Folzman is refreshed. He begins to hum and then to sing the tune of a familiar Jewish folk hymn:

Hava nagila	(Let's rejoice)
Hava nagila	(Let's rejoice)
Hava nagila v'nismecha	(Let's rejoice and be happy)
Hava neranenah	(Let's sing)
Hava neranenah\	(Let's sing)
Hava neranenah v'nismecha	(Let's sing and be happy)
Uru, uru achim!	(Awake, awake, brothers!)
Uru achim b'lev sameach	(Awake brothers with a happy heart)
Uru achim, uru achim!	(Awake, brothers, awake, brothers!)
B'lev sameach	(With a happy heart)

One by one, his supporters begin to join in the song and eventually the rest of the masses pick up the tune as well—it is just too strong an urge for the faithful worshipers. Reb. Folzman, now in full voice, will not take the chance of another mood change. He begins slowly to walk away from the site, his entourage following behind him. Amazingly the remainder do not pursue but continue to sing as the rain cleanses the refuse. Finally, as the deluge increases, their song-spirit wanes, and the crowd dissolves into individual people intent on seeking a dryer habitat.

Moses has led his followers to his private quarters where they begin to towel off and warm themselves against the bitter thought of separation from this wonderful place. Discussions grow into strategies, strategies into plans—they all realize by their admission to being Christ Followers, that they have sacrificed their educational and spiritual sanctuary. Now the question is—where to go from here?

But Moses has known his destination long before this part of the journey began. He speaks among the group—they pray, they cry and even laugh together and unity is achieved. After packing whatever possessions, they can quickly squeeze into their various cars, trucks, and other forms of transportation, they will all travel caravan style to their new home. Moses has many connections there and he is confident he can find at least temporary food and shelter for them. "It will be sufficient for our purpose," he assures them. They all agree and so he moves them forward with a charge, "Onward then, to Jerusalem!"

And I, Daniel Adamson with my strange new gift of transformative vision, have the privilege of watching this all unfold. I wish I could actually be there with them in body as well as spirit to help cheer them on their new Exodus.

AUSTIN, TEXAS – UNIVERSITY OF TEXAS COMPLEX, QUANTUM SYSTEMS DEPARTMENT

…Fiz responds to Travis' question about whether or not we have been keeping information from them. "You all deserve whatever information we have, but first I need a moment with my student."

Fiz motions me outside of the room for a private conversation. "These people have a right to know our suspicions and also, there are some things I think you and I can do to help our cause beyond these walls." He explains what he has in mind and I concur with the strategy, even if I question our ability to pull it all off. We re-enter the room and my mentor takes temporary lead of the discussion. "I think it would be a favorable time to explain to this new family how our lives may be about to change. Why doesn't everyone sit down?"

Each person finds a seat or claims a comfortable place on the carpet and Fiz continues. "We have just learned that the world's governments have cooperatively launched a new kind of weapon directly toward V4641. You may be considering in your mind, *is that not a good thing?* The capabilities of this technology suggest that it may indeed influence the anomaly, but may also profoundly, perhaps even adversely change the conditions of our planet."

Everyone looks to one another in nervous anticipation as Fiz continues. "Now you may not agree with my or Danny's positions on scientific matters, but I think we are all closely aligned on Whom it is that has set these forces in motion. How He is going to react to the V4641 provocation is of paramount importance."

"What are you telling us?" Travis intervenes. "Is this going to be the end of the world or something like that?"

"It may appear so to many, but my heart tells me that for all in this room, this will be an incredible new beginning. I and Danny will be glad to explain to each of you individually in more detail, but for now please trust me when I say that we have only a little time left. So little in fact, that I encourage you to get on your cell phones or use the internet to contact your friends and family to alert them as well. If we can do anything to assist you via microwave transmission, satellite, or cable enhancement so that you can reach your loved ones, let us know. The University communications center is still operable.

"What do we tell them if we do reach them?" inquires Tonda.

Fiz looks to me, indicating it's my turn to unravel the unknown.

"There's a lot of natural evidence," I begin clumsily, "and corroborating language in the Bible that suggests a large-scale *event* is about to take place. The weapon that is being sent toward V4641 will most likely trigger that event. I say *most likely* because nothing like this has ever taken place before. We are in uncharted waters, having to speculate the outcome."

"Can't anyone stop these lunacies?" Tonda is visibly agitated.

"We've tried." Fiz answers. "I even received a very unusual text from the President of the United States—a personal friend—indicating that he is impotent to stop the proceedings. For him to openly admit this means that our government is basically at the mercy of others who do not share our interests. He also urged us to do whatever we can to prepare for the inevitable."

This news has a chilling effect on everyone including me. I can see that the group, as a whole, has gotten the message: *We are on our own.* Fiz continues to move the discussion forward. "Danny and I have a plan and we need to make several phone calls as well before we will be ready to implement our idea. Meanwhile, I suggest you begin communications immediately. The Adamson family has agreed to cook up another great feast for us and so I suggest we all meet back here in three hours."

Everyone looks at their watches or phones to mark the time. Tonda and Travis excuse themselves and then Fiz turns back to address me. "Our work is cut out for us, Child. You contact Moses and then, based on his input, make your other call.

ROCHESTER, NEW YORK – THE CHESTER F. CARLSON CENTER FOR IMAGING SCIENCE AT THE ROCHESTER INSTITUTE OF TECHNOLOGY

Spencer Lynd, Ph.D. is still sitting in his command center chair within The Hive. He's very busy recalibrating the great telescope known as Hubble for the upcoming extravaganza, wanting to be sure that the eye of the scope captures, in concert with the DRRAGEN-One, every possible detail of the reactions about to take place. He has ramped up the activity level in The Hive to a fevered pitch and is extremely annoyed when his assistant runs up to him holding a cell phone towards his face.

"I'm too busy for whoever it is," exclaims Spence.

"You'll want to make time for this one," his protégé insists while continuing to hold the phone in his direction. The Director of the R.I.T. Color Imaging Center of the Hubble Telescope Monitoring System reluctantly takes the device and examines the name listed on the screen. Immediately he snaps the phone to his ear, shooing away his assistant without even a "thank you."

"Fitzgerald, what a surprise," he greets the head of the U.T. Physics Department over the static filled line.

"Spence, thanks for taking the call. I know you're running full speed ahead so I'll make this quick—what I have to share will be of great advantage to you."

Spencer Lynd is all ears. "Fitzgerald, I owe you a lifetime of favors— you got me this position in the first place—I wouldn't deny you a thing."

"My request is a simple one," Fiz moves on, uncomfortable with accolades, "I know you have a unique screening interface there at your center which allows you to view three different events at once and that's why the governments have asked you to be the data feed source for DRRAGEN-One."

Spence is not sure how Fiz knows all of this, but everything his benefactor has said is spot on. So he acknowledges tentatively, "Yes?"

"I would like to offer you live video feed of two other locations on this planet that we believe will be directly affected upon the interaction of DRRAGEN-One with V4641. We'll send you the links at the appropriate time. All you need to agree to do is keep your three feeds opened and visible to the public during the live broadcast—no matter what. Will you do that?"

Spence sounds puzzled and reluctant in his response, "Fitzgerald… Fiz…this isn't some kind of prank or diversion…"

"No, Spence." Fiz interrupts, bent on making the deal, "this is absolutely legitimate and you'll have to trust me—I would do nothing to interfere with this project or harm your reputation."

"I've always relied on your integrity, but this…this is a very strange request at a very strange time."

Fiz is losing patience. "Will you or won't you, Spence. I need to know whether I need to take this request up the chain."

Silence is Spencer Lynd's response. He's weighing the risks and quickly decides they are minimal. "I'll do it for you, of course. Let me know the video codes to enter for up-linking into the Trinity System."

Fiz complies and step one of our secret mission is complete.

AUSTIN, TEXAS – UNIVERSITY OF TEXAS COMPLEX, QUANTUM SYSTEMS DEPARTMENT

"Are you sure about this?" Spencer Lynd is not the only one with doubts. I have just heard an incredible prediction from Reb. Moses Folzman, A.K.A., The Crazy Prophet. Fiz and his teacher had spoken earlier, but my mentor wanted me to contact Moses in order to coordinate our plans.

"Daniel," his voice assures even over a ragged cell connection, "I have never been more certain. I will have the video camera set up in the appropriate location—please do what you need to let the world see the Truth as it is revealed."

If he believes it, then I believe it, I say to myself. "I'll make the call right now," I assure him. As poor as the audio quality is, I can still hear him sipping from a drink—the scent of honey and lemon mixed in tea invade my memory. It reminds me of this great man's recent and profound influence on my life and I suddenly miss him terribly. "…Rabbi?" I add quickly, not knowing exactly how to convey the emotions stirring inside me.

"…Daniel. Let me say it for you…for both of us. It is an honor to know you and to share this moment together. Shalom my friend," and the line goes dead.

ATLANTA, GEORGIA – NETWORK HEADQUARTERS BROADCAST CORPORATION

I never make the next call. I don't have to—my resource seeks me out: Just as I'm about to punch his number into my cell phone, Jonathan Trimble's identity card flashes on the screen. Right at this moment, I can both hear him on the phone and strangely, see him at his backup offices in Atlanta. The odd thing about it is—I don't have a video phone, yet his image is clear as day in my mind as he speaks. "Danny!" He greets me cheerily as he pours himself a fresh glass of ice water. "It has been too long since I've heard from you. I hope you haven't forgotten our agreement?"

You work in wonderful ways, Lord. "How could I possibly forget, sir? As a matter of fact, I have some incredible information to share with you that will change the way we're looking at the relationship between V4641 and Earth."

No words are emitted from the other side of the phone, but I can see Jonathan Trimble set down his water glass and stare blankly at the speaker box. I now pray for his curiosity to get the better of him and I'm quickly rewarded. "What kind of information?"

"Before I get your hopes up too high, I'll need your help in validating my sources."

"Of course, anything you need!" Now Trimble is fully engaged. I know his reporter's intuition has kicked in—when someone wants to validate a source prior to release of information, it typically means they have a monster story by the tail.

"I know we don't have very much time so here's what I want to do." I explain quickly how we believe we have found several *sympathetic sites* which seem to be reacting more to V4641 than any others. I tell him we have worked out a cooperative agreement with R.I.T. (hoping Fiz has already struck the deal) to have camera feeds all linked so that we can show both sites in concert with the images of the DRRAGEN-One entering V4641. "If we're right, when the weapon is released into the mini-quasar, these sites will immediately react."

"How will they react?" In typical Trimble fashion, Jonathan traces a picture of a rocket with his finger using the condensation of the ice-water pitcher on his desk for his medium.

"The best way I can explain it is that we believe it will be as nothing else observed in our lifetime—let's just say it will be the best show you've ever produced. I'd go into more detail, but again for time sake, I ask for your trust on this."

"And if they don't react?" Trimble is not one to give his trust easily.

"…And if they don't react, the camera shots can just be explained as *Areas of Interest*. The audience's attention will most likely be so glued to the images of the DRRAGEN-One zooming into its target seven light-years away, that if what we expect doesn't happen, they won't even notice. But if these sites are sympathetic and we are the ones capturing a live feed—you'll have the greatest story in the history of digital video."

"Which sites—what are they?" His story-senses are all alive, but he has been warned by Mede to treat me cautiously, so his guard is still up.

"Sir, at the risk of sounding protective, the people in and around both locations are willing to cooperate in our capturing this footage, but they've asked that all the up-front preparation be low key and anonymous. I'm going to have to respect their wishes and safe-harbor the information for the time being—at least until the moment of the event—if you want the story. If you still have doubts, I understand and am willing to scrub the project on your word." Now I hold my breath and wait.

"Of course you have my permission." Trimble seems actually comforted by my asking for my source's protection.

"There is one more thing I need to ask."

"…Of course," Trimble's catch phrase. "Name it."

"The live video feed of the locations is probably going to look very boring and innocent right up to the point of reaction—kind of like watching an egg before it begins to hatch. As a matter of fact, I suspect that because of the very nature of a singularity—which permits no light to escape—the images from DRRAGEN-One just prior to reaction will be equally mundane.

"Will you please speak personally with the producer at the studio to make sure they stay with the program and aren't tempted to get creative; you know: switching over to shots of a commentator or some specialist or run some side interest story? I know it's a risk, but this is all new territory— we don't have any re-tries on this and it would be terrible if the viewers missed anything happening on the live feed cameras. The greater reward will be in capturing what should be a spectacular event."

"I must say Danny, you have my curiosity peaked. Yes, you have my word…and Danny?"

"Yes sir?"

"Thank you. I admit that over the last several months, I've had my doubts about you, but it sounds like you will be providing us with a very worthy Theme indeed!"

"I'm praying for it, Sir."

Entry Twenty-Three

"Knowing is not enough. We must apply."

—Leonardo da Vinci.

GENEVA, SWITZERLAND – WORLD TRADE ORGANIZATION GARDENS

"Thank you for coming out here with me, Brenda," Darius Mede concedes. "We still have time before the event and I know you're uncomfortable with the darkness of early morning before the sunrise, but I was feeling a bit claustrophobic in my office and needed some fresh air." The two walk without a word for a few paces and then Darius admits the other purpose for his request of a walk in the gardens at such a strange hour. "I've been considering your proposal regarding our…union. I see its merit and will agree as long as certain conditions are met…"

"—Conditions?" Brenda Anders stops the walk.

"Nothing of consequence—I expect only that this will be a business partnership primarily. At times, if we both consent we can share our bed but I am not one to be limited to any long-term monogamous agreement."

"Business partnership, non-monogamous…that would make me no better than your personal whore!" Brenda expresses her disappointment in the arrangement openly—hinting that she desires something much more intimate and traditional in nature.

"Don't be ridiculous," Darius defends practically. "In this day and age, relationships of convenience are readily accepted by all. We certainly need each other, but I am not of the marrying kind. The media will make sure the world perceives us as wed, thus your reputation will be unspoiled. Plus, your power and influence, under supervision of my own of course, will be far greater than what you enjoy now. Besides my dear, as much as I…cherish your skills you must admit that you have your difficulties relating to men or for that matter, most individuals. You should be grateful that I'm even considering…"

—I confess that I receive at least a little pleasure at watching from afar as all six foot, five inches of Brenda Anders' power is focused in the punch that hits Darius squarely in the nose. He is on the ground before he knows what has happened. I suddenly feel grateful that Misty only slapped me that fateful day seven weeks ago. Mede looks up to the figure of Brenda looming over him. He can now feel the blood streaming down his chin onto his freshly starched shirt.

"How dare you!" The blood that remains in him is now at a boil. "I offer you the world and you return the favor in this way?" He rises to his feet again, reaching into his pants pocket for a handkerchief to stem the flow still pouring out of his nose. The nasal quality of his voice is now even more pronounced. "I should…"

"—You should be grateful that I didn't follow through with a healthy kick to other parts of your body," Brenda fills in, pointing a finger at Mede's chest. "Just remember, Mr. High and Mighty, it has been my assets and my people around the globe who have helped put you into power—don't ever forget that. As for your offer…I accept with a few of my own conditions: One; forget the bed part—your words have now officially committed us to a chaste relationship and two; I expect you to personally announce our faux matrimony in a very public way on a worldwide broadcast. You will state your love and devotion to me in no uncertain terms or I will make sure my people take your kingdom apart piece by piece." She smiles through gritted teeth and then challenges Darius. "Do we have ourselves an agreement my beloved?" The last word Brenda has spoken does not come out as an endearment.

"We do." Mede glares at her. "Until death do us part!"

It's at this moment that Darius' cell phone signals he has a text message. Without taking his seething eyes off of Brenda he brings the device up to read the content:

ATTEMPT TO ELIMINATE AUSTIN THREAT FAILED. STRANGE CIRCUMSTANCES, BADLY INJURED IN ATTEMPT, ATTACKED BY BUG! BARLEY ESCAPED WITH LIFE. EXPLAIN LATER, MY LOVE. ROXANNE.

A guttural moan begins in Darius' throat. His body trembles and the sound rises; escaping as a raging animal scream aimed upward toward the predawn sky. New blood flies with the outcry, then Mede throws the phone full force at a tree. The phone loses the encounter, shattering into multiple pieces. Without a word to Brenda—whose own anger is dwarfed by this display—he storms back to his sanctuary, alone.

AUSTIN, TEXAS – UNIVERSITY OF TEXAS COMPLEX, QUANTUM SYSTEMS DEPARTMENT

We're all back from our calls and emails. Misty and I spoke together with her parents, then with Brandon's folks, and I even had a chance to contact a few of my aunts, uncles, cousins, and friends, urging them to prepare with faith for a life changing event. I shared my new awareness and recognition of Jesus as my Lord and asked if they would mind praying with me. In several cases, I was received with love and appreciation. In others, the reaction was one of polite dismissal. Still, seeds had been sewn. Greater things have grown out of beginnings smaller than these.

The Physics facility seems slightly dimmer now. It may be my imagination, but I know that, even with our conservation efforts, we'll soon run out of operating fuel. The surrounding water is also taking its toll—there's a subtle new scent of stagnancy in certain parts of the building.

The aroma floating from the kitchen however is heavenly—or seemingly so. My mom is outdoing herself with the remaining vestiges of meat, poultry, frozen vegetables, and fruit. She is convinced this is to be our Last Supper in this place, so there are no thoughts of holding back in content or calorie count.

Everyone grabs hungrily at roast beef basted in onion broth, baked chicken smothered in cream of mushroom soup, green beans mixed with bacon, corn and, of course, our old family standard—mashed potatoes and brown gravy. Warm dinner rolls are ready to be buttered, chilled apples and grapes are set out in bowls and cheese is sliced to complement crackers on small plates around the table. A variety of drinks, from soda and water to milk, iced tea and coffee are placed on a separate table. There will be no growling of stomachs this night.

Crayon colored name tags have been placed around the large rectangular table where we gather. The names on the notes are funny: Travioli and Tondue, Fizzy Water…my children have been busy and creative too. My moniker is obvious to all—Blue Boy—and is set at the head of the table. This makes me a bit uncomfortable because I don't consider myself head of this family. The honor should go to Fiz, but he and all the others encourage me to take the place quickly and to bless the meal before it grows cold.

I stand at the table looking first out at everyone and I feel tears in my eyes. These little routines we so look forward to—the gatherings and traditions of loved ones around the seasons—are about to be replaced by something new. I feel as I did when I left home for college, knowing only what I was leaving and not what I was heading for.

"It's a great and hopeful, but also a sad table we sit around," I begin. "So many things we've shared together, so many things to come that we can't understand. There are things we wish to continue but must forfeit in trade for things more wonderful. Someone recently reminded me, *Life is a tricky thing.*

I open the paper bag I've brought to the table and pull out my five popsicle-sticks, already assembled into the configuration I had played with so long ago. "I brought something to share at this table one last time. Something that has special meaning to me and which I hope will mean something to you." Words came to my mind. Not my own, nor those of any of my visitor voices. These came from the conversation I had had with Jonathan Trimble at the lunch table in Atlanta years ago and I'm surprised, after all that has happened, that they are fresh in my memory:

> *People do give a damn; they just don't give it in the same way you do. And to get them to share a little more about what their giving a damn is—you have to shock them out of their past diet, feed them a tiny delicacy for the present and then offer them a feast beyond what they could ever have expected for the future.*

"This little contraption helped me work through my father's death, got me a scholarship to this institution, has been used for a job interview and now is going to serve as an example as to what can happen without the right nucleus as a foundation in our lives." I signal to Jake and Sylvia who readily charge up to be at my side. I hand the assembled sticks to Jake and give him the go ahead. "Fire away." As practiced, he turns and throws the device through the air against the wall. The sticks explode with a loud snap as they strike the surface and the pieces fly away to the floor.

"Now you see what I originally intended my adolescent science project to be—a tool of destruction, aiming all my anger and frustration out at a God that seemed bent on taking away the things and people most important to me. It wasn't until later in life that I realized I was blaming the wrong person and that really, blaming anyone was pointless. There are reasons things happen and it's how we react that is important. I had to learn that, even in tragedy and destruction, there is a plan for healing."

I nod to Sylvia who runs over and picks up the scattered popsicle-sticks. With great ceremony, she brings them back over to the table and climbs into my lap. Jake gives me his best puppy-dog look and so I invite him onto my other knee and both children work together to reassemble the sticks into their original configuration. They look so focused, Sylvia even biting the tip of her tongue in concentrated effort and Jake helping by trying to carefully and patiently explain how each piece fits to the other.

Jake now nods his head in sage approval at his sister's completed work. They both smell like…crayon—I guess from their name card art project earlier. *I wish you were here to share this Unky Brandon*, I smile to myself. Sylvia also smiles, but she aims hers at her brother in gratefulness for his help and now it hits me. They're ready. They're not afraid of anything that's going on around them. I feel my love for them so deeply in my heart now that, for a moment, I just hold them tightly in my arms—a moment may be all we have. I don't want to let go of them…ever.

"Dad, people are watching!" Jake says in low tones. He tries to tickle me under my arm—my weak spot as he knows—and I respond by tickling him and his sister in their spots. We're all laughing and crying now—our very public display of affection not hindering the emotion of the moment. Misty too comes up and we all embrace—silently, gently, praying for more future together.

Then one by one, each of the others comes up, kneels, or stands around us to join the group hug. The declining temperature of the food suddenly seems so trivial—the time together is an increasing warmth inside us that stimulates our true hunger for each other's love. *Now*, my father's voice prods kindly.

Finish gracefully.

I ask someone on the outside of our human cocoon to reach on the table and carefully hand to me the reassembled popsicle-sticks. "The one other thing I want to show you about this contraption is that it is not only a deceptively powerful weapon, but also a study on the Love of God—Agape Love as the Greeks termed it." I hold the pieces up and explain. "Notice how each stick is strategically necessary to the unity of the whole. Also note that there is only one way these five sticks can be wedged together, each dependent on the proper placement of the other.

"But what is most crucial are the center sticks. They are the part that holds the secret to the others. It is this part that must be first for everything else to hold tight. It is an unequal yet complementary relationship—the outside not being capable of proper function without connection to the inner. The inner being fully perfect in construction yet not completed without connection to the outer."

As I talk, I've carefully taken the outside pieces apart. People move from in front of the table, allowing me to lay the sticks out and then to place the center section in the middle. The graphic is telling.

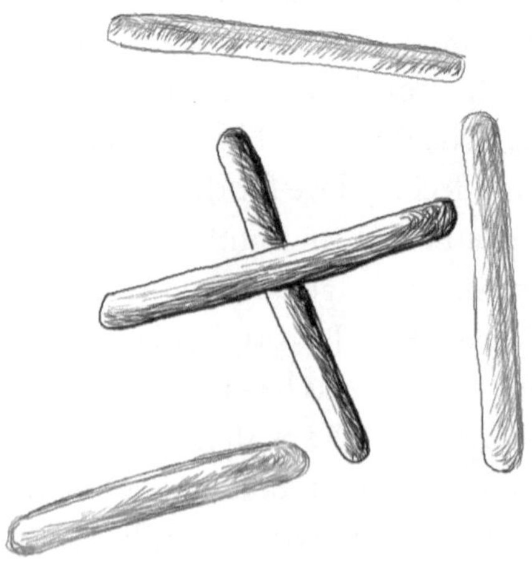

"My mentor, friend and adopted father figure, Fitzgerald Hindeland and another great mind, Moses Folzman once described V4641's behavior as integrating with that of our planet. I like that terminology and think it even describes what is happening with this group of people and their God.

"The desire of our hearts has been changed to reflect that of the One at the center. We're being bonded to Him and to one another, by an action played out thousands of years ago on a cross—the most despicable act of <u>destruction</u> ever turned into holy <u>construction</u> - the most wonderful and beautiful construction ever. And soon, by God's plan, another act of destruction will be turned to great construction.

So, if you don't mind, I'd like to ask you to pray with me now, in thankfulness for this meal, and for the greater feast to come—the long-anticipated wedding celebration of believers married to their Savior.

"AMEN!" Jake and Sylvia shout together before we even have a chance to start.

"AMEN!" Everyone else echoes with laughter. We bow our heads and share each other's open conversations with our Maker.

GENEVA, SWITZERLAND – WORLD TRADE ORGANIZATION

Darius Mede is alone again. Brenda Anders has found other quarters in the building and is apparently content to watch the events unfolding on television in her seclusion. From my spiritually acute vantage point, I see him turn on the television to watch the N.H.Q.'s broadcast. The DRRAGEN-One will soon create an antimatter reaction within the mini-quasar that has been both a provider of opportunity and an aggravation to the Chairman of the Green Order Government. The end to this annoyance is at hand.

Darius shifts the ice bag covering his nose and left eye to help minimize the consonant pain created by Brenda's blow. A scowl crosses his face. "What is that?" He actually speaks the words out loud and turns up the volume to hear the commentator's explanation of why there are three pictures on the screen.

The center image reveals only a dark void—a caption in red below the image simply says, DRRAGEN-One. The left-hand picture is the unmistakable image of *al-Haram ash Sharif,* the site of the Muslim holy temple in Jerusalem also claimed to be the former location of the old Jewish Temple. The caption below it reads, THE DOME OF THE ROCK. The picture to the right of center is of a group of people in a room—it looks like a dinner setting and the caption mysteriously describes it as, AREA OF SYMPATHETIC POTENTIAL.

The voice of the unseen commentator is marginally informational with his limited understanding. "As far as we've been told, the two locations to either side of the DRRAGEN-One are areas that scientists believe may be unusually affected by the infusion of antimatter into V4641. We have not been told why or how these conclusions have been reached, but that the reactions may be somehow as spectacular as that within V4641."
"Turn them off." Darius Mede is talking to the TV and entering a number on his landline phone at the same time. My *tuning in*to his quarters is so acute that I can actually hear the busy signal he receives. "Turn Them OFF!" He slams down the phone, reaches in his pocket for his cell phone and remembers that he used it earlier to attack a tree. He picks up the desk phone to redial again; the same busy signal taunts him. "TURN THEM OFF, TURN THEM OFF, T U R N T H E M O F F!"

The unseen commentator is helpful with this also, "By the way, we have been told that there is unusual and unexpected telephone usage across the globe as people seem to want to talk about and text about this historic event. It is causing many carrier services to overload, so if you're having problems, please just be patient…"

Darius is not patient. He goes to his laptop computer and types a message directly to Jonathan Trimble. Trimble though appears to be unresponsive at the moment. Mede retypes the message and repeatedly presses the Send button with no results from the receiver.

"You can't do this!" It's unclear exactly who the leader of the G.O.G. is speaking to, but he is very upset. "You can't, you cannot!" Apparently he thinks yelling phrases in repetition will help matters. To this strategy he adds sweeping his collection of pictures and awards off his desk with his arms. He switches to taking books out of their cases and throwing them against the wall, even using one to crush his laptop to a pulp. As a last resort, he grasps the heavy crystal lamp on the table by the couch and hurls it at the heavy oak door, breaking the energy saving light bulb within, and significantly darkening the mood of the room.

But none of Darius' efforts change the picture on the screen—now the only illumination available. His attention is drawn to the picture on the right. "I know that room." He must be speaking to himself. "I…" Now he goes up to the screen to examine the people at the table. It's a wide angle shot so he has to concentrate with his one good eye and mutters as he stares…"Hindeland. Adamson! How did you…?" His emotions erupt—en masse—as he begins bellowing. "I forbid this! I will not let you! Do you hear me?"

Only I hear him and I can't help myself—I turn my face directly at the camera, a look of sad concern on my face and mouth the words, *I'll pray for you, Darius*. Mede reads my lips, screams, and begins his rampage anew.

AUSTIN, TEXAS – UNIVERSITY OF TEXAS COMPLEX, QUANTUM SYSTEMS DEPARTMENT

I've shared some fine and interesting meals over the last two months—at the altar table of the Technion, deep in the earth at Mammoth cave with Brandon, on the Pacific Ocean prior to a seven-mile-deep plunge and right here in Austin—but this supper has trumped them all. It's not just the great food and the company that shares it; there's something else—a sense of anticipation felt by everyone. They've all mentioned it and keep looking to Fiz and me for explanations.

Finally, my mentor stands, drawing everyone's attention to him. The din of table talk subsides as he eyes each of the gathered. "I was going to suggest Danny present more information to you about what is expected soon, but I fear he may pull out his sticks again and begin some new object-lesson."

Everyone laughs including me—*fine, maybe I went a little overboard with the allegory.*

Fiz moves on. "You have all been indiscreetly trying to pull information out of me as to what will be happening soon. I can tell you only a few certainties, the rest you will have to experience, just as I will, in faith.

"Biblical passages in the Old Testament talk about God calling or, more precisely, gathering His people to Him. There are many *pictures of this picture* throughout scripture for us to practice. The New Testament goes so far as to describe a day when believers—followers of Jesus—will be called up to the clouds by a trumpet, both *those sleeping in the ground* and *those still alive*. I believe that day is now."

My mom and Tonda whisper to one another; Misty, Travis and Mustif share looks between them—this is new food for some of them to be digesting. Fiz continues, "Some of you may disagree with, or doubt the timing I am suggesting—it doesn't matter. If I'm incorrect, let this be a good practice session and we can then enjoy more of Ms. Adamson's fine culinary skills in the future."

Clapping begins, Fiz bows to my mother and she blushes at the attention. "But if I'm correct, this is to be our last moment together on this planet as it exists now." No one whispers or responds—my mentor walks over and stands behind my chair, putting his hands on my shoulders.

"You may notice something odd about this particular Child. He is surely the brightest among us." More laughter—I've never recognized Fiz's qualities as a stand-up comedian before. "I speculate that Danny has been changed in this way for several purposes. The most important of these is that he serves as a testimony. What was the word I used earlier—to reveal a *picture of a picture* of what each believer will experience at the moment of transfiguration. Granted, he <u>is</u> demonstrating this in a very colorful fashion..."

Laughter bursts out again—even the quiet Mustif can't help himself and Misty blows me a kiss. I look up and over my shoulder at Fiz and I see his expression turn instantly from whimsical to very serious. "...but I tell you now, Danny Adamson's contribution to the world and his service to his God will be soon a song sung in heaven—a great and honorable ballad of a man who loved and was loved beyond the capabilities of human experience. For he is God's work and I have been privileged to know him—I shall miss you, Child...and all of you who share that same love... when you are taken up."

...When we are taken up? What about Fiz puts his hand out—palm open to the group, reassuring us that he will explain. He walks over to where Jake and Sylvia sit; bends over and whispers something to them conspiratorially. They both nod and stand, allowing him to sit in their place and then they climb up on his lap. Fiz looks at both of them, moisture forming in his eyes as he continues.

"Jake, you are nearly too old to be on my lap and I know part of you fights to be even older—you want to be like your father and I don't blame you. Yet you cling to your childhood, savoring the innocence and appreciating a family that lavishes attention on you without high expectations in return."

He hugs my son and looks over to Sylvia. "Such a beauty, Sylvia daughter of God—you will be a joyful spirit in the next kingdom—so willing to please, so appreciative of what you receive." Now Fiz looks down at the table space in front of him and mutters, "I'll miss these two most of all. They have reminded me of the transformations we all have experienced even early in life."

There's an uncomfortable gap in the conversation. I perceive that everyone is looking for me to ask the question so I open my mouth to speak, but Fiz shakes his head at me and cuts back in. "Don't worry, Child. I know your question—it's the one on everyone's mind in this room.

Then Fiz drops his bombshell. "I will not be privileged to be a part of the gathering up." I start to object, as does the rest of our clan and he once again has to raise his hands in a motion of protest. "Hear me out, please. Hear me out."

My mentor helps my children off his lap, stands and turns to look at me with a smile. "You are not the only one who has been hearing messages from other places, Child. How do you think I have come upon some of the premonitory knowledge that has put us all in this room tonight?"

Jake and Sylvia are clinging to his legs as if their efforts will keep him with us despite his prediction. He bends down to administer another hug to Sylvia and a very manly handshake to Jake. He pulls them close once more and whispers some secret to them. They both nod with brave but reluctant smiles and release him at the same time and he continues to enlighten. "I have been given a very specific, a very wonderful mission that I wholeheartedly want to carry out. It requires me to remain here for a while longer.

Now Fiz makes a peculiar move. He goes to where my mother is seated, takes her hand in his and kisses it. "Mrs. Adamson, may I call you Mary?" She nods, blushing a hundred hues of crimson. "I want to thank you for sharing your special abilities, your hospitality and your sense of humor. You have turned this building into a home for us and I can tell that there is not a one in this place who you have not made to feel a genuine part of your family." I have not often seen my mom caught speechless—I wish I had a camera.

Again smiling, Fiz moves over to Misty and kisses her gently on the cheek. "I can tell the care and the patience that you have put into your relationship with Danny and am so very grateful. He is a far better man because of you, Misty. And your reward, daughter of The Beloved, will be in heaven."

Fiz moves to Tonda and peers deeply into her eyes. "Great pain—I regret not having learned more of what wounded you in your history, but now it matters little. Actually, I'd like to offer you a gift!" Tonda smiles sadly, I'm not sure she believes Fiz has anything to offer. He touches her ebony cheek with his hand and says, "In just a short while, your past suffering will be as a wisp of wind that has brushed against your skin. You will remember that it happened but won't be able to recall its effect on you." Tonda closes her eyes and sighs a *thank you.*

"Travis, you are such a dedicated steward of the earth." Fiz looks over to him. "You will carry that passion to your next destination." He says nothing more to our ecologist, but the words seem to be enough. The two men clasp hands, Travis rises from his seat and they embrace. Fiz smiles warmly at the young man and then turns to Mustif.

"Something amazing has happened by God's efforts through you here on Earth Mustif. And more amazing things will be done in the next kingdom because of your protection of Danny. Thank you for being faithful even when you haven't understood the purpose. Thank you for enduring hardship and still believing—you are an inspiration to us all." Mustif the Dark simply bows and tilts his head in acknowledgment and looks toward me. Everyone actually looks toward me…because Fiz has made the full circuit and is once more standing next to my seat.

He signals me with a subtle hand gesture to stand up—I don't want this. I'd rather he share a thousand days of silence with me than speak a single word of parting. He reassures me with his eyes and then says softly. "Daniel Adamson, Child of the Almighty, you have been my most wonderful student, a dedicated friend and…sometimes an absolute pain in the backside." Now he has us both—has everyone in the room in fact—crying and laughing at the same time. "Of course, I mean that in the warmest way.

"You once accused me of being as a father to you and I confess that you are as a son to me. But our adventures in relationship have been far beyond that of parent and child. I am honored now to tell others of your drive, your compassion, your insatiable curiosity, and your unique ability of communicating a new perspective to the world. I am in awe of what The Eternal has done through you and I know greater things await us."

He looks me over, head to toe, as if assessing some scientific experiment to evaluate its properties and then he states simply. You are released of your duties as Keeper."

"What?" I hear myself say in almost a defensive tone. "But why now? There isn't much point in keeping that…information from anyone anyway."

"Precisely," again, Fiz is economical with his words.

I find myself strangely frustrated. "So, why even bother? What's the point?

"Danny, my secret was not meant to be kept from others, but to be kept for you. To be held and treasured so that one day, you would come to realize it's significance and its true meaning. You were not ready to understand then. This is that moment."

But I don't underst…and suddenly, I do. Like the gears of a clock all coming together, each meant to meet at a certain point, matching up to signal a specific moment, I get who my mentor truly is, who he has always been—though I was stupidly blind to it—and what his significance and purpose must be for staying behind. I look at him through new eyes, nodding my recognition and we embrace, clinging to each other as one, neither wanting to release. "I don't think I'm able to leave without you," I sob. I'm not being a very brave example to the others.

"You are able and you will, Child." Fiz finally breaks the hug and says to my mother. "Ms. Adamson, is there any dessert to be had around here?"

GENEVA, SWITZERLAND – WORLD TRADE ORGANIZATION

Darius Mede is much more composed than he was the last time I dropped in to observe him. He's again propped on the couch, holding an ice bag to his wounds with one hand and surfing channels with the other. All the stations apparently think N.H.Q. Broadcasting has some kind of exclusive story they are keeping secret, so all 200 stations have tied into the same signal—all except for the Home Shopping Network which apparently is running a special Doomsday Paraphernalia sale—at least <u>they</u> are calling a spade a spade!

Three picture inserts on every channel haunt the good eye of Mede: Left insert—THE DOME OF THE ROCK—same footage, nothing happening there; Middle insert—DRRAGEN-One—just the continual boring color variations depicting a computer's idea of what deep space should look like; Right insert—AREA OF SYMPATHETIC POTENTIAL—Ozzie and Harriet meet Andy of Mayberry. The group continues to eat and talk and hug each other as if these are important things at this critical moment.

Now his attention peaks as the center image flickers and different colors begin to appear: Red, blue and yellow variances dance in the distance and Darius turns up the volume to hear the commentator's explanation. "We have just been told the power-up sequence for the Aprotonic device on board DRRAGEN-One is about to be activated. As we've explained, the Aneutronic drive of the ship will transport the DRRAGEN-One into the heart of V4641 and, at that same moment, a matter/antimatter reaction will commence, hopefully destroying the mini-quasar."

Darius argues out loud with the TV voice over. "It will <u>definitely</u> blow that thing to hell!"

The commentator continues his droning. "Again, what you are now seeing on the center screen are incredible live images from beyond our solar system, sent to us by a special camera on the DRRAGEN-One. It should be noted that, even though these images are real-time in nature, they are being sent from millions of miles away so there will be a slight delay from the time the image is captured to the time we receive the signal. We estimate that delay to be fifteen minutes, possibly more. That means that whatever effect DRRAGEN-One has on V4641 will be experienced fifteen minutes prior to our seeing it on camera."

Mede flips the channel again, bored with that particular speaker: The next channel—same pictures, different voice. "The images are computer enhanced—the colors we see are depictions of the energy patterns emitted by objects many light-years away from us. Our target, in fact, is still seven light-years away." This guy is more interesting, he makes it sound like he's actually on the rocket. "We still have a long trip ahead—however the advanced technology of this ship will make our journey seem just like a walk to the next-door neighbor's house."

"Excuse me," New Commentator must be receiving fresh information from somewhere. He twists his head stage right, listens, nods, then turns back to the camera. "Ladies and gentlemen, fasten your seatbelts. The DRRAGEN-One Aprotonic device will be engaged in T-minus one minute and counting!"

AUSTIN, TEXAS – UNIVERSITY OF TEXAS COMPLEX, QUANTUM SYSTEMS DEPARTMENT

There's supposedly a full moon outside, but the heavy ashen cloud cover keeps the midnight pitch black. We've been spending time with each other as a group and individually. Besides watching deep space and Earthly events through the eyes of Darius Mede, most of my attention has been centered on Misty, the kids, and my mom. I'm not sure what the upcoming change will mean and I confess that I'm feeling possessive, not wanting to lose what we have now. I have to consciously push my selfishness away.

"What about you, Danny? Anything you wish you could do or say before we go?"

Tonda has been asking the group if they had regrets or things they wanted to accomplish but hadn't. I've never thought it right to express remorse or longing for things I know for a fact are out of my control and am about to share this when another thought hits me. *I might have had a chance to keep this from happening.* The Rabbi once recently reminded me to reflect on where my actions and beliefs have led me. So, I decide to be honest—once and for the remainder of time.

"As proud as I am of the Evolutional Echo Tracing formula and process I developed, truthfully I wish I had never conceived it."

Even Fiz is caught off guard by this statement. "Why would you say that?" he inquires, peering over his glasses.

"Only because it has allowed Mede and his government to aim their rocket accurately at V4641; I feel like the Jewish scientist who created a cheap method of making nitrogen fertilizer only to see it used to exterminate millions of his own people in the gas chambers of Nazi Germany."

Fiz studies me hard for a moment and then replies. "We could all look at things we have accomplished in our lives and see how others have warped good intentions into evil or misguided purposes. But your discovery also allowed us to trace the very origins of our galaxy and to redefine our understanding of the universe. Without your efforts, we would likely not have made the connection of V4641 and the changes we are experiencing here on Earth. These are no small matters that God has put in motion and it is by His design, not yours; that they have unfolded."

I understand what he's saying, but I'm thinking it would have been a lot easier if God had just waved His hand and changed the world without us having to go through all the tragedy. Fiz reads the doubt and insecurity on my face. "Danny, don't you find it a bit ironic that the use of your concept may be the very instrument that will initiate God's plan to gather believers to Him?"

I hadn't thought of it that way. "But why would God use a scientific formula and for that matter, a rocket equipped with an antimatter device to move His plan forward?"

"*For those who love God, all things work together for good, for those who are called to His purpose.* Paul of Tarsus reminded us of this long ago. Why shouldn't The Almighty Creator of the universe use the tools of science and technology for His purpose?" Fiz is figuratively back in the classroom challenging me. "Trust in your faith and let your faith give your plans flight! Just because some wind comes along to challenge you, doesn't mean you should stop flapping your wings!

Jake looks at me and says, "Dad, are you getting brighter?"

I look around and then go over to him. "It's not just me now," I reply, pulling him and his sister close to me. "It's you too—all of you." That's not exactly true because Fiz is not registering on the Glow Meter at all.

"The moment has come," he says simply, looking at me more somber than excited. "Anyone care to lead us in a new song?"

GENEVA, SWITZERLAND– WORLD TRADE ORGANIZATION

Darius Mede watches the virtual clock tick down on the television. Five, four, three, two, one There is no change on the screen—the center camera still displays the computer rendition of the colors of the cosmos—but he knows that right now, the Aprotonic device has been initiated. Barring any breakdown in the systems, the DRRAGEN-One should now be on its way into the mini-quasar V4641: Molecules should be stressing and colliding, trying to fly apart and snap together in the same motion— tearing apart matter and fusing it simultaneously. It will be impossible for even a singularity to contain the astronomically devastating effects of such a reaction.

Unfortunately, he will have to wait patiently for the camera eye so many miles distant to depict what has already taken place—the destruction of the enemy! He decides to pour a drink in celebration and speaks again to the empty room, "Brenda, you have missed a great opportunity!"

Just as he touches the bottle to the champagne flute, a low rumbling begins under Darius' feet. He seems unconcerned because the rocket is safely away and doing its work. "Go ahead," he spouts. "Let's see you try to stop this with another earthquake!" His laughter is cut off however because the reverberation of the quake grows in volume and intensity. He looks around, aware that something is very different about these oscillations. It no longer appears to be only coming from below him, but from all around him.

Then he listens. The noise is not that of a rumbling tectonic rupture, but more like a single reverberant note, as if played on a musical instrument.

The note literally vibrates everything—his body, his bones—everything is resonating! The sonic wave continues to amplify and the champagne flute in his hand shatters. He looks up at the TV and still, nothing appears to have changed on the center view…but the right-hand view has changed. In Austin, there is a new intensity about the scene—the lighting seems all wrong and…it's the people. They are the source of lighting at the location. The images—all but one of them—are blurry. Mede can still make out faces and motions—they all seem to have joined hands and are…singing?

"What are you doing, Hindeland?" Mede now covers his ears as the timber of the tone changes to a piercing squeal. His good eye catches motion on the television monitor and he watches as *al-Haram ash Sharif*, The Dome of the Rock, begins to distort oddly and then in one instant crumble and collapse. The screech tortures his ear drums and now there is a sharp cracking sound. The glass front of the television monitor cracks diagonally through the center picture as DRRAGEN-One's camera now captures the image of a blinding white light. The TV has had enough of this abuse—its wall mount breaks away from its location, causing the whole unit to crash and explode into shards on the polished wooden floor.

Darius has trouble paying attention to the mayhem—the sound in his head tears at him like the claw of a wild beast. "What is that wretched smell?" He screams…

AUSTIN, TEXAS – UNIVERSITY OF TEXAS COMPLEX, QUANTUM SYSTEMS DEPARTMENT

…Cinnamon; a rose garden, bubble gum, fresh rain, mountain air—everyone is describing it differently—to each, this moment is an intensely individual encounter. We're singing; have been singing since before the music started. What is to Darius Mede, a shrill screeching rake across a chalkboard, is to us a chorus of perfectly tuned horns and other unknown instruments of indescribable beauty. It plays along as we continue to lend our voices—we change to another tune and the music changes with us. Starting out with *How Great Thou Art*, we've now switched to a contemporary version of an old Psalm verse: *Better Is One Day In Your Courts.*

I look over and notice that Fiz is difficult to see. I want to reach over and touch his hand one more time, but something else catches my attention over our heads. There is an even brighter light above us—I can look right into it and don't have to squint or blink. I have a hard time in fact taking my eyes away, but I want to say a final farewell to…he's gone. Fiz has disappeared from my vision. *Holy, Holy, Holy,* we sing as I look back into the light and am transported with the others to its source.

I'm finally alive, as if all parts of me—my body, my behavior, and my spirit—are now perfectly tuned as one. In a strange way, I don't need to sing any longer. I'm part of the song—a note of many, sung in honor of a perfect being so lovely, that I've become lost in the crescendo of his symphony. He has me in His arms and He too is singing. I cry and laugh with Him as we look at the others. Somehow He's holding them too, along with countless people from countless times and places. The part of me that had at one time wanted to know how such a thing could happen—is no longer: We are the finely polished tones of one instrument now—a horn I think. I've heard something like it in a past life—they called it a *shofar*—an ancient trumpet made from a ram's horn. And then in the distance floats a familiar image—long, sleek, very large and many colors…iridescent, yet brilliantly white with a silver sheen—ever changing, ever the same. Pure… and…I'm spoken to…

…*Danny, what are you doing? We've got to go right now.*

As I'm embraced and lifted up, a hazy lone harmony note echoes. I trace it back and listen with new clarity to its hope—Fiz calls to me from beyond—faintly, warmly. *I will be with you again*—and our notes all resonate their joy.

Epilogue

Fitzgerald E. Hindeland stands in solitude. He looks skyward, but now sees only ceiling tiles where just a minute ago, a brilliant awning of illumination bathed him. He turns toward the camera and speaks.

"To you who have eyes and ears, open them—watch and listen. What you have just observed is not some visual trick or computer enhanced fantasy. Nor are the changes that our planet is experiencing—the chaos and turmoil you are going through—an accident of nature. These actions and events are intentional: Anyone who recognizes them as being a part of the plan established long ago by The Eternal God of the Universe; any of you who can look past your own futile efforts—seeing a greater work in progress; you have a chance of survival.

"Science, technology, politics have all become historical relics—be prepared for things of a spiritual nature to now dominate your attention and life. For those of you who seek Truth, I refer you to the books of John and of Revelation—while you are at it, you might want to become familiar with the entire works of the Bible. I would point you toward those who believe these words as Gospel, but at the moment, there are few of us available. If you look around, you will understand—those you considered Christ Followers have been gathered to another place—if you have considered yourself one of these and remain, you should reflect on your beliefs: Maybe you remain for a mission—there are those of us who have chosen this path; maybe your allegiance is not an honest one—you must examine your heart more closely.

"And I too will be honest. If now you are convicted to believe and receive Jesus Christ as your Lord and Savior, your life will not be much easier, in fact surrounding conditions will worsen. But your rewards will be far greater than even that of your departed loved ones. Prepare and don't lose heart. He who has come will return again to dwell with you."

The physicist-turned-prophet now walks over to shut off the camera—causing the third screen on the worldwide broadcast to turn to static. Suddenly there is a buzzing sound. Hindeland is annoyed but looks down and searches with one hand to find his phone in his pants pocket. He stares out the window into a coming dawn, answering the phone without looking at the screen name. "Hello?"

"Fitzgerald Elijah Hindeland, my Talmid! This is Moses. Are they well?

"It is completed. They've departed.

"Here as well. Praise the Eternal! It is now up to us, my good friend. Hurry and make your way over here. There is much to do. The rebuilding of the temple must begin. Shalom!"]

"Moses, there is something else that has happened—it is profound. Somehow, I possess Danny's memories—all intact—the memoires he had written down, his last experiences, and more. In my mind I know what we need to do next. I can actually see it."

"Then you must not delay writing down the remainder of his work—completing all if it, Talmid. And then come quickly, there is much to do. The rebuilding of the temple must begin. Shalom!"

The landscape is changing, but the universe remains constant. New questions, new realities, new ways that people must consider. Until now I haven't explained these things to you completely.

You are a part of an invisible history that was kept from you: Nothing that we thought was firm footing; is any longer. What is reality—my words on this page, my voice in your head? I may speak to you from a cell phone or the whisper of the wind or I may join in a song with you. Who am I? Listen carefully—you may hear me as a father or a mother or some long forgotten friend. I may appear in a dream or simply as a sudden thought that inspires you or convicts you in ways you never imagined before. To some my name includes 'Danny'. To others I have names that mean infinite things. I have gathered many names to me—they are all mine.

I am still The Keeper, and as Keeper, names are extremely important to me. Are they important to you?

Does Elijah hold any special, deeper meaning to you? It does to me, as does the Rabbi's name—Moses. Then again, if you are reading this, your name may not yet be mine to keep. Consider this new reality and ask, "What should I do? Should I just keep on living out the existence I always have and hope all will be well?" The fact that you're asking such a question means all is <u>not</u> well. Look deeper, listen to me.

I am coming back and when I return, my questions to you will shape your continued existence—they will determine how and where your new existence will unfold. Chase my questions with everything you are—have them answered in your heart before my return:

Who is at the center of the universe?
And
Do you choose to honor Him?
I AM forever. But prepare without delay, because for you…

…THERE IS NO TIME.

Is a trumpet blown in a city and the people are not afraid?
Does disaster come to a city, unless the LORD has done it?
For the Lord GOD does nothing without revealing His secret
to his servants, the prophets. The lion has roared; who will
not fear? The Lord GOD has spoken; who can but prophesy?

—Amos 3:6-8, The Bible

AUTHOR

MARK A. CORNELIUS

Mark A. Cornelius has authored numerous books, video productions, a journal ministry, musicals, and several podcast series.

His works include *RUT Management—Discovering Adventure in the Routine of Life, Believement—Breaking Through the Belief Barrier, Welfare Christianity, Thunder Buffalo Goes Home, Tomorrow's Bread, Marginalized, UnMeasuring—What if we are ALL Wrong?* and the popular fiction series *The Ruach Saga* (including *The Singularity, The Book of Seconds, Bronzeman, and War of the Lost Song*).

His books can be purchased at https://quantumdiscovery.net/shop/, and at www.RUTmanagement.com.

Amos 3:6-8, The Bible

Mark has authored other insights and blogs, all of which can be obtained on his website. You can experience Mark's passion for writing at **www.MarkCornelius.me.**

Catch Mark's podcasts at:
Watchmen podcast:
https://www.youtube.com/channel/UC3fA03AhXRh RZNhNyrEhgA

Mark My Words (Critical Thinking) podcast:
https://www.youtube.com/channel/UCR8Csunh9mJMOZHjT97NUZg

Travel with Mark at his blog: **www.DeepEndFaith.blogspot.com**, and dive into discussion on **E-mail: Markcwrites@gmail.com**, or Facebook: **https://www.facebook.com/Mark-My-Words-103741988034911.**

Join Mark in asking his ongoing journey question…

"What If?"

Looking forward to our journey together!

ILLUSTRATOR - SHAY CAVENDER was born in Nashville, Tennessee. She began her drawing career at a young age doodling and writing short comic strips. Her unique style specializes in animals both real and fantastical. Currently she is a student at the University of Tennessee at Martin as a Graphic Design major. She plays Trombone in the UTM Marching Skyhawk Band and aims to continue playing her instrument later in life despite her art-oriented career direction. Drawing and illustrating are her passions along with her love of animals including dogs and reindeer. In the future, Shay hopes to secure a profession that will utilize her distinctive talents.

www.ingramcontent.com/pod-product-compliance
Lightning Source LLC
Chambersburg PA
CBHW051130190726
48290CB00006B/1784